Blythe Wood

Blythe Wood

Fern J Franks

First paperback edition 2022

Book design by Publishing Push

ISBN 978-1-80227-484-4 (paperback)
ISBN 978-1-80227-485-1 (ebook)

Typeset using Atomik ePublisher from Easypress Technologies

Preface

Having read about the evacuation of children during the Second World War, I was deeply moved by all their stories. Some of them were lucky enough to be placed with good families, others were not so lucky. I began to wonder what it must have been like for childless couples suddenly faced with caring for children, then becoming so fond of them that they didn't want to hand them back. I wanted to write a story depicting this.

The story centres around the kitchen table, where the family congregates for their meals, enjoying all the gossip from around the village over cups of tea and striving to keep body and soul together during very trying times.

Blythe Wood was the name of the house my grandfather lived in. I was taken there a lot as a child and have many happy memories of playing in the large rambling garden with my cousin. I particularly remember a large kitchen with a black leaded range, where my grandmother fed us on bowls of tapioca pudding. There were grandfather clocks in nearly every room, which chimed on the hour. The house was eventually demolished and in its place stands a row of very smart townhouses, but I still, to this day, stroll down the street to stand and stare at the corner on which Blythe Wood stood and the happy memories come flooding back.

This story was written with love and I hope you enjoy reading it as much as I enjoyed writing it.

Chapter One

Dorothea adjusted the blackout blinds and made her way into the library. It had been a long night on fire watch duty and she was cold and tired. She sank into her favourite chair with the high back and kicked off her shoes. She would manage to get a couple of hours sleep before the children got up.

Closing her eyes, she suddenly wondered if she'd ever see Raif again. His parting words to her were, "War or no war, I'm not coming back." Before she knew it, he had picked up his kit bag and then he was gone. He joined the Royal Air Force and he looked so smart in his uniform. They'd had rows before, of course, but not like this one. He accused her of being totally selfish and not considering the feelings of others. How those words had haunted her these past three years. She'd written him long letters telling him how sorry she was and promising to become a better person. She also told him about the four evacuee children she'd taken in and how lovely they all were. After nine years of marriage, they'd given up the hope of ever having children of their own. It just hadn't happened for them.

Raif hadn't answered any of her letters. Three years had gone by and still no word from him. He hadn't sent her any money either and she had ploughed through all of her savings. She was virtually penniless. Rumour had it the war was coming to an end. She couldn't imagine life without Raif. It was unthinkable and the very thought of losing the children now was unbearable. They were such lovely children and she loved them dearly. The thought of them returning to their own families filled her with an overwhelming sadness. She knew she would have to break it to Grace about the money. She wasn't sure if she'd stay if she wasn't being paid any wages and she'd probably take Daisy and the baby with her. Once again, she'd be all alone rattling around in this big house. She closed her eyes and let the tears flow.

Daisy glanced at the clock on her bedside table. It was six o'clock. She decided to have ten minutes extra before getting up to start the breakfast. She glanced across to where little Jenny was sleeping in her cot, her mop of red hair just showing above the covers. She counted her blessings every day that things had turned out so well. It could all have been so very different. She'd fallen in love with this beautiful house the minute she set eyes on it, with the luxurious carpets and window drapes, highly polished antique furniture and beautiful paintings on the walls. She never wanted to leave it.

She washed and dressed as quietly as she could, so as not to wake Jenny, and crept downstairs. The kitchen was empty which was strange as Dorothea was normally bustling about making the porridge. She filled the kettle and got out the teapot.

Tiptoeing into Grace's room, she placed a mug of tea on the bedside table.

"What time is it?" asked Grace, somewhat alarmed.

"It's all right, Grace. It's only half past six so there's bags of time. Dorothea's asleep in the library, so I didn't disturb her. I've left her a cup of tea on the side, in case she wakes up."

"Right, good girl. I'll be up in a few minutes as soon as I've drunk this."

As Grace sipped her tea, she too was counting her blessings. Her house in Munsell Street had been bombed. Luckily, she was out visiting friends two streets away when the bomb fell. Her husband George wasn't so lucky. He'd been in the pub at the end of the street. By the time Grace had arrived home, there was virtually nothing left. The whole street had been reduced to a pile of rubble.

The scene that greeted her was all too common in London during the raids. Firemen, policemen, ambulances, people screaming and running all over the place. Those images would haunt her for the rest of her days. All she possessed were the clothes she stood up in. Everything else she'd worked for over the years was all gone in an instant.

She had made her way into the church hall along with the others. Someone gave her a blanket and a cup of tea with a biscuit resting on the saucer. That's where she'd met Daisy. A sixteen-year-old slip of a lass who was far too thin in Grace's opinion. All her family were gone. She was shaking and shell-shocked. Grace had put her arms around her and they huddled up together on one of the pews. Daisy explained she'd been to a dance with some friends. She was only a ten-minute walk away from home when the bomb fell. She wanted to tell Grace what else had happened to her on that walk home, but thought better of it. Now wasn't the time or the place. It could wait.

Chapter Two

It was the second of December, a Thursday, at The Embassy Rooms ballroom on Sackville Street. The date was forever etched in Meg's memory, for it was the night she had met Eddie. He was Canadian, charming, funny and handsome. She'd fallen in love with him from their first meeting.

He was with a fellow officer from his regiment, Bradley. Meg was with a girl friend from the factory, Josie. They'd worked together for eight years and were best friends. As was usually the case, Josie soon found a man to dance with and Meg knew she'd be lucky to see her again that night. Likewise, Bradley was enjoying the company of several ladies in a group on the dance floor. Thus, Meg and Eddie found themselves propping up the bar. They got chatting and were soon laughing and enjoying themselves. She'd never felt this comfortable in the company of a man before. She wanted to be with him forever. They saw each other every night they could after that. Then, all too soon, it was over. His regiment disappeared over night. Eddie and Bradley were gone. No one saw them leave or knew where they were posted to. Megan was bereft.

Three months later, she collapsed on the factory floor in the middle of her shift. She wasn't the first girl for this to happen to and she wouldn't be the last, this being a regular occurrence during the war. Luckily, the managing director Mr Apse was out of his office that day and the foreman Joe was very nice to her. He promised not to say anything but Meg knew if Mr Apse got to hear about it, she would be dismissed on the spot.

Three weeks later, she was summoned to his office. Blushing to the roots of her hair, she made her way tentatively across the factory floor. All eyes were upon her. She'd never felt so embarrassed in all her life. Somehow word must have circulated amongst the girls about her condition. She hadn't yet worked out what to do, not that she could have hidden it forever, but a little more time would have helped to get herself organised. She made her way up the steps to the office with her heart pounding. Maggie, his secretary, was waiting for her.

"Go straight in, Meg. He's free to see you now."

She saw her cards laid out on his desk in front of him, even before she sat down. Her fate was sealed.

"I suppose you know why I've asked you to come and see me, Megan?"

"Yes, sir. I can only apologise, sir. You've been a very nice boss and I'd like to thank you for employing me. I've enjoyed every minute of my time here. I'm only sorry that it had to end this way. I'll clear out my locker and hand in my overalls to Margaret on my way out."

As she left the office, Maggie gave her a hug and told her to take care of herself. She didn't have time to speak to her best friend Josie before she left as she wasn't at her work station when she exited the building.

It was pouring with rain outside, but she hardly noticed, so absorbed was she in her thoughts. What on earth had made her say all that to Mr Apse about him being a nice boss and enjoying the work? She hated the place with a passion and she'd never met such a bad-tempered man in all her days.

She was drenched through to the skin by the time she arrived at the flat. Her landlady was surprised to see her and wanted to know what she was doing home at such an early hour. She made some excuse about not feeling well and hot-footed it up to her room before any more explaining could be done. She knew it wouldn't be long before she was thrown out onto the streets.

Chapter Three

Grace sipped her tea and reflected on how different things might have been, had that bomb not dropped on the whole street. George had died doing what he enjoyed the most, with a pint in his hand. It was where he'd spent most of his free time throughout the whole of their marriage. No matter what financial straits they were in, he always found the money for his pint. Still, he didn't deserve to die the way he did and she missed him terribly.

She'd never forget that fateful night. Seeing all the mayhem going on around her, people shouting and screaming and running in all directions. A fire warden directed her towards the church and told her to shelter there. It was where she met Daisy. Her house had gone too and her mum with it. Daisy had told her time and time again to get to the Anderson shelter at the bottom of the garden when the siren sounded but she flatly refused, preferring to remain in the house.

Daisy had looked so pale and weak, Grace thought she was about to faint. They had shared the blanket between them and eventually the lass stopped shaking. Grace knew she wouldn't get any sleep that night but was glad she'd met Daisy. She seemed such a nice natural girl. What on earth would they do now? Daisy had told her she had no other living relatives she knew of. Grace had a sister, Bunty, who lived with her husband, Malcolm, in Sussex. Even as children they never got on particularly well and now they were adults, even less so. She couldn't imagine turning up on her doorstep, cap in hand, begging for shelter. They hadn't spoken for over fourteen years.

She wished with all her heart she hadn't been so hasty and resigned from her job with Dorothea. She was a very exacting woman, rather sharp in manner and didn't suffer fools gladly. It was such a silly row they'd had. All her friends called her Dotty and thought the world of her. The night of the row, she had invited some special guests to dinner and wanted something exotic to give them. Grace promised to do her best but knew she wouldn't be able to cope with anything too elaborate. When Dorothea examined the menu, she had become very cross.

"This won't do, Grace. I want something special," she barked.

Grace had thrown a tin of chickpeas into the stew and added some spices, then renamed it Moroccan tagine, working on the assumption nobody would know what a tagine was but not wanting to appear ignorant of fine dining, they'd all say it was marvellous. Dorothea, of course, was not fooled.

"Grace, it was terrible. What on earth were you thinking?"

Looking back now, she should have just laughed it off but she'd had a row with George about his drinking before she left the house and was nursing a glorious headache. It all got too much and she threw down her apron and walked out. She regretted it the minute she arrived home but pride wouldn't let her go begging for her old job back.

They'd been in the church hall all night and were queuing for a mug of tea when Dorothea appeared at her side.

"Grace, thank goodness, you're all right. I was so worried. I need to talk to you. I'm locking up the townhouse and going down to Blythe Wood in Somerset. It'll hopefully be a bit safer there. I want you to come with me."

Grace was so shocked she couldn't speak for a few minutes. Then she remembered Daisy and quickly introduced them.

Dorothea smiled at Daisy and said, "Hello, I'm Dorothea."

"Pleased to meet you, miss," said Daisy.

"You sit down and drink your tea," said Grace, "Whilst I have a quick chat with Dorothea."

When Daisy settled herself onto a pew, Grace turned to Dorothea and explained about Daisy being homeless and not wanting to abandon her.

"I can't leave her now, Dotty. She's got no one."

"No matter, Gracie. She can come too. Drink your tea and I'll come back for you in an hour."

They were both waiting in the doorway when Dorothea swung the old jeep into the church courtyard. They settled themselves into the back seat and covered themselves with a warm rug.

"It shouldn't take more than a couple of hours. That's providing we don't get hit by any flying shrapnel," Dorothea said. "Have a nap and I'll wake you up when we arrive."

Daisy was so excited she couldn't sleep, not being able to believe her good fortune. Only an hour ago, she was homeless and bereft, now here she was on her way to a new life. The horror of what had happened yesterday would stay with her forever, she knew without a doubt. She hoped that, in time, the memory would fade.

Chapter Four

There was no clock in the library so Dorothea had no idea what time it was when she opened her eyes. The house seemed deathly quiet, so she assumed the children weren't up yet. Samuel and Joshua were usually the first up, followed by Howard and then Beth.

She thought back to the day when the school teacher, Mrs Bray, had turned up on her doorstep with them all. It was nearly five o'clock in the afternoon and they all looked so careworn. Mrs Bray was on the verge of getting very cross as the two older boys refused to be separated. The younger boy Howard was proving difficult to place with a family due to his unkempt appearance. The girl was being a "little madam" and was refusing to do as she was told.

They had tramped around the whole village and watched as, one by one, the children were placed. Most of the families would only take one child. Dorothea hadn't the heart to turn them away as the house was huge and she had plenty of room. She welcomed them all inside with open arms, much to the delight of Mrs Bray, whose manner changed immediately and she scooted off post-haste before Dorothea could change her mind. They were herded into the kitchen where Grace and Daisy were preparing the evening meal. The look of shock on Grace's face was quickly appeased by Dorothea.

"I'll get them organised, Grace," she whispered. "Routine is key. Don't worry."

Joshua seemed to settle in without any problems. He was a very chatty boy with an open and friendly nature. He had befriended Samuel when he arrived at his old school in London, having lived in

Sri Lanka since he was born. Dorothea could imagine Josh going out of his way to make sure Sam was all right. He was that sort of boy.

Samuel was by far the brightest academically. He'd obviously had a good education in Sri Lanka and he spoke excellent English. He explained that his father was a doctor and he had one sister called Selina. When the children were being evacuated, his mother had taken Selina with her to live with relatives somewhere in Essex. His father had offered his medical services in the field hospitals. That was all he knew.

Howard was initially very withdrawn and hardly spoke, but Dorothea spent a lot of time with him, helping him with his home-work. She discovered he was a very intelligent boy with a caring and curious nature. She'd seen a big change in him over the three years he'd been with her. The teacher at the village school, Mrs Bray, commented to Dorothea how confident Howard had become in recent weeks and that his school work had improved considerably.

Beth, the youngest of the children, proved to be the most trouble-some. There were a few anxious moments when she first arrived but things changed slowly but surely over the weeks. Dorothea turned out one of the spare bedrooms and, with Sam's help, they decorated it and made it pretty. When she moved Beth in, there were genuine tears in her eyes. She now had her own room complete with a ward-robe and dressing table. She loved the little pull-out drawer that had compartments which Dorothea had filled with bracelets and beads. All her clothes had been washed and ironed and hung in the wardrobe. Even her shoes had been polished to a high shine. Nobody had ever done anything like this for her before and it made her feel very special. From that day forward, her attitude began to change.

Dorothea smiled to herself whenever she thought of her "new family" as she liked to think of them. She got up out of the chair and went over to the window. It was daylight. She must have overslept. After drawing back the blackout blinds, she had to flop back into the chair. She realised something was not quite right. She just didn't feel right today. Suddenly, everything went black.

* * *

Grace made her way downstairs after waking the children. Daisy had set the table and was stood at the stove stirring the porridge.

"I'll finish that, Daisy. You go on up and see to Jenny."

"Oh, thank you, Gracie. Is Meg up yet?"

"Yes, she's helping Beth. She'll be down in a minute. Off you go."

Grace refilled the kettle and emptied the teapot. It was strange for Dorothea to sleep on. *She must be tired*, she thought. She was a stickler for routine and punctuality, especially where the children were concerned.

They only went to school in the mornings and came home for their lunch. The village school was only small and couldn't accommodate all the extra children so it was decided by the headmaster and teachers to divide the day up. Some children attended in the mornings and some attended in the afternoons. They were given a fair amount of homework too, which Dorothea insisted they do in the afternoons before anything else. She didn't stand any nonsense and made sure they all did as they were told.

Grace had to admire Dorothea for the way in which she handled everything. Once the homework was completed and put away, the evenings were spent in the library. She tried to make it interesting for them, teaching them about kings and queens, rivers and mountains, and used maps to show them different countries. They discussed flags and currencies and all manner of different things. Sometimes they all sat around the wireless listening to music or they played board games or did jigsaws. Daisy and Grace were encouraged to join in. It helped with the bonding process and it proved to be great fun. They really did feel like a proper family now.

Grace thought back to the day Dorothea decided to turn the back garden into an allotment. With the children's help, she planted just about every vegetable they could think of. They now had fruit trees and a herb garden too. When the children had gone to bed, Dorothea had continued planting all through the night with the help of a Davy lamp. Then she volunteered for the neighbourhood watch duty. She said Raif was doing his bit for his country and she must do hers. Grace admired her spirit but thought she was taking on too much.

The boys came clattering down the stairs and burst into the kitchen just as Grace was dishing out the porridge.

"Come on. Quickly, you lot, otherwise you'll be late. Where's Beth?"

"I'm here," said Beth, diving into her seat. "Where's Aunty Dot?"

"She's still asleep in the library. I'll not wake her yet. She needs her rest," said Grace, sitting down next to Megan, who was helping Daisy to get Jenny settled on her cushion.

Half an hour later, the children were marching down the drive, laughing and joking in their usual way. They all liked the little village school but always looked forward to coming home at lunchtime.

Meg and Daisy had just finished clearing away the dishes when Grace appeared in the doorway. Her face was pale and she was breathless.

"What on earth's the matter, Grace?" Meg asked.

"It's Dotty. She's collapsed onto the floor. Daisy, run across the road and fetch Doctor Mattison before he starts his surgery, you might just catch him."

Meg and Grace ran back into the library where Dorothea was sprawled out on the carpet.

Meg felt for her pulse. "She's breathing."

"Oh, thank goodness," said Grace, putting her hand to Dorothea's forehead. "She feels very hot. I hope it's nothing serious. Do you think we should attempt to move her?"

"Best not," said Meg. "We'll wait for the doctor."

Chapter Five

Dorothea opened her eyes to see a nurse standing at the foot of her bed, studying her notes. She had been on an antibiotic drip for three days and was starting to feel a little better. She was diagnosed with pleurisy and remembered very little about how she came to be in the hospital bed.

"Keep this up and you could be on your way home soon," said the nurse.

Dorothea smiled and closed her eyes. She wanted to be alone with her thoughts so she could work out what she was going to do. She realised she'd have to break it to Daisy and Grace about the money. *If they decide to leave, then so be it*, she thought. *I'll get well and strong again, then find work somehow and try to earn some money. I'll explain everything to them as soon as I get home.*

She immediately felt brighter in spirit now she'd decided on a plan of action. Wartime wasn't the time to be dithering about, she would just have to get on with it. *I'll survive somehow.* These thoughts got her thinking about her sister Megan who had a ghostly, haunted look about her. Dorothea could see it in her eyes and felt disappointed she hadn't confided in her. They were sisters after all.

She must have dozed off for a while because, when she next opened her eyes, Meg was sitting at her bedside.

"You're looking a bit better, Dotty," she said.

"Yes, I think I've finally turned a corner. The nurse said I could be on my way home soon, all being well."

Meg gave her a hug and poured her some water.

"Is everything all right at home?" Dorothea asked.

"Oh yes. The children are a little subdued, especially Beth. We haven't told them about the pleurisy, just that you're feeling a little unwell. We didn't want them to worry too much."

Dorothea smiled, then decided to broach the subject of the money, or the lack of it. "Meg, I need to talk to you when I get home."

She saw a brief look of horror cross Meg's face, as though she awaited bad news.

"It's just that… well, Raif hasn't sent me any money since he left and… well, I'm afraid I've waded through all my savings. There's no money left."

A feeling of great relief flooded through Meg. She smiled and took hold of Dorothea's hand. "That makes three of us," she said.

"Three?"

"Yes, Iris arrived last night. She's been thrown out of her digs. The man she worked for decided to close the shop and she got behind with the rent. The good news is that she arrived with a suitcase full of sausages, much to the delight of the children."

"Oh, poor Iris. It was a very high-class butcher that she worked for. One of the best in the area."

"Yes, and the most expensive."

"When I'm fit enough, I'll look for work. It will be all right."

"All three of us will." There was a long pause before Meg added, "Dotty, I've never told you this but something happened that I'm not proud of."

"We all make mistakes," Dorothea said.

Meg took off her coat and hung it on the back of her chair, then proceeded to tell Dorothea all about meeting Eddie and how she'd been sacked from her job due to her condition.

"I managed to hide it from my landlady for about six weeks. I continued to go out at the same time every morning so that she wouldn't become suspicious. I sat in the park and walked around until it was home time. Then, one day something terrible happened. I set out at my usual time and after half an hour, it started to rain.

So I dived into a little cafe for a cup of tea. Next thing I knew, there was blood trickling down my legs."

"Oh Meg, I'm so sorry."

"The manager of the cafe was so nice to me. He bundled me into a taxi and told the driver to take me to the infirmary. By the time we arrived, there was blood everywhere."

Dorothea squeezed her hand, not knowing what to say that would make her sister feel any better.

"I know it was wrong, but I really wanted that baby. I loved Eddie. He was quite simply the nicest man I'd ever known…" And then Meg started to weep. Dorothea threw her arms around her and the two sisters remained like that for several minutes.

"Where is that boy? He should have been home an hour ago," said Grace.

They were all sat around the kitchen table awaiting their meal.

"It's probably my fault," Beth said. "I told Josh I didn't like any of the books he got me last week and that I wanted a story about horses."

"He's such a chatty boy," added Daisy, looking through the window. "Oh, I can see him. He's coming now."

"Josh, where on earth have you been all this time?" Grace said.

"Sorry, everyone. There was a bit of an incident at the library."

"An incident? What kind of incident?" asked Daisy who was bending down to retrieve the plates out of the oven.

"Well, I cut across the grass and entered the library through the doors at the side and there was a man sat reading a newspaper."

"Well, what's wrong with that?" Grace asked.

"He didn't have any clothes on. He was stark naked. Anyway, I ran into the reception area and told the lady behind the desk. It was that French lady, Mrs Kloot. When I told her, she threatened to box my ears and throw me out. I told her to see for herself and when she saw him, she nearly had a fainting fit. 'Mon dieu, mon dieu,' she cried." Josh put the back of his hand to his forehead in a mock faint.

"She ran and fetched the manager. Anyway, it turns out it was a gentleman called Mr Glass. One of the locals, known to everyone in the village by all accounts. He said he had a bath then threw on his dressing gown and nipped out for a newspaper but the shop was closed, so he nipped into the library as he knew they'd have a copy. He got very hot and as there was nobody around, he threw off his dressing gown. He did apologise. I sat talking to him for a while afterwards and he seemed a very nice gentleman actually. I must say I agreed with him about the heat as it was very hot in there. The manager went to turn down the thermostat a notch or two."

Iris burst out laughing. "He sounds quite a character."

Grace and Daisy both said he was all right really but you just had to keep an eye on him as he was prone to eccentric behaviour. He always managed to come up with a logical explanation for his actions. He'd had a few run-ins with the local bobby, Stuart, on numerous occasions.

"Does he live alone?" asked Iris.

"He has a daughter, Kathleen. She works at the factory on Foundry Lane," said Grace. "Strange that the newsagent was closed. Ken's usually open until late. I wonder if he's had another one of his angina attacks."

Iris had just finished the washing up when Meg walked in.

"Sit yourself down, Meg," said Iris, "I'll fetch your dinner, it's in the oven. How was Dotty?"

"Thanks, Iris. She's improved a bit. I think she may be home soon but don't mention it to the children yet as there's nothing definite. She mentioned something else whilst I was there."

Iris poured out the tea. "I'm all ears. Shoot."

Meg lowered her voice to a whisper. "We're broke. There's no money left."

Iris' eyes sparkled as her face broke into a wide grin. "Is that all? I thought it was going to be something exciting. Me and Bob have been broke for years. We're both as bad as each other. I must say I'm a bit surprised though. I thought Dotty and Raif had got plenty. I mean, look at the size of this place for a start. It's like a mansion."

"Well, that's just the problem. She hasn't heard from Raif since he left. Not one letter."

"What, none at all?"

"Not a one."

"My Bob's not a great letter writer either. The scribbled notes I've had from him were hardly legible. He's in the Navy, so I suppose it's difficult."

"He hasn't sent her any money so she's been using her own savings and it's all gone. So it'll be vegetable casseroles for every meal from now on, salad for lunch with fruit and porridge for breakfast."

"I can live with that," said Iris. "I wonder if there's any jobs going at the factory. The one where Kathleen works?"

"Maybe, but there is a war on so there's not much around, especially in a small village like this. We wouldn't want to step on the toes of the locals. It might lead to mutiny."

"That would liven things up a little," Iris said, laughing. "Is there anything here that we could sell to raise some cash? There's some good artwork on the walls."

"This house belongs to Raif, not Dotty," said Meg, "It belonged to his grandparents and he inherited it when they died. They own the townhouse in London jointly. They bought that when they got married. I think Dotty's worried Grace might not stay if she can't pay her any wages and she might take Daisy and little Jenny with her."

"Oh, surely not. Where would they go?"

"I don't know, but don't say anything yet."

"What are you two plotting?" asked Grace who arrived with more dirty pots, which she dumped in the sink. She sat herself down at the table, ready to enjoy the gossip, followed closely by Daisy.

Meg looked a bit sheepishly at Grace and knew she would have to be told sooner or later. It wasn't fair to keep secrets in a house like this, so she decided to take a chance.

"Sit down, both of you."

"Oh, this sounds serious," said Grace who was always glad of a chance to sit down for a few minutes to take the weight off her aching feet.

When Daisy and Grace were settled, Iris poured them both a cup of tea. Daisy's face paled in anticipation of what was to come.

"It's nothing serious. But we've run out of money. We're broke. Dotty was going to speak to you both when she got home from the hospital. She hasn't got any money left to pay your wages, I'm afraid. She hasn't heard from Raif and he hasn't sent her any money either, so she's been using her own savings and… well, there's none left."

"Well, I'm not going anywhere," Daisy blurted out. "Miss Dorothea's been so good to me and Jenny. I never want to leave this house. I love it here and so does Jenny. Just bed and board will do us." There were tears in her eyes as she said this.

"That goes for me too," said Grace. "I don't need wages. There's nothing to spend it on anyway. I've got everything I need here. When our house was bombed, I lost everything. And I mean everything. All I possessed were the clothes I stood up in. When you've been through something like that, it makes you see things differently. Material possessions don't matter. Dorothea's been kindness itself to me and Daisy since that day. We look upon this as our home now. It's our family, our life."

The four girls threw their arms around each other and hugged.

"We'll survive, don't you worry," Grace said. "We've got the allotment so we'll not starve. That Hitler might have taken my George, but he's not having me as well."

"That's the ticket, Grace," said Iris. "Now, let's get these pots cleared otherwise we'll be here until midnight."

Chapter Six

It was a different nurse that bustled about the ward after Meg had left. Dorothea hadn't seen her before. She said her name was Norma. She had hazel eyes and a lovely smile. Dorothea noticed a few wisps of red hair escaping from under her cap. The drinks trolley was doing the rounds.

"Tea or Ovaltine, Mrs Swift?"

"A cup of tea would be lovely, thank you." She smiled at the nurse.

As she sat sipping her tea, she thought back to the day Grace came to speak to her about Daisy. There had been a knock on the library door and a very tentative Grace had entered.

"Yes, what is it, Grace?"

"Could I have a word, Dorothea? It concerns Daisy."

"Daisy? Yes, of course. What's happened?"

"She's with child. She's expecting a baby."

The look of surprise on Dorothea's face had sent shockwaves through Grace.

"Gracious. Are you sure? She's so young."

"Sixteen."

"Sit yourself down a minute." Dorothea moved a pile of books off of a chair and turned the radio off. "Does she know who the father is?" she asked, once Grace had settled herself in the chair.

"Yes. It's that Iain Boothroyd. He forced himself on her by all accounts. She said she'd just left the dance hall and said goodbye to her friends when she heard footsteps behind her. He must have waited for her. She refused to dance with him earlier and he got annoyed. He dragged her into a back entry. She tried to fight him off but he was too strong for her. It was the night the bomb landed on our street."

Dorothea was too stunned to speak for a few minutes. "And do you believe her story? Is it true, do you think?"

"Oh yes. Daisy's a very honest girl, that I do know. I know that Iain Boothroyd too. He's always had an air of arrogance about him, just like his mother. I used to see her every Sunday at church. She looked down her nose at everyone, just because she had money. I had one or two run-ins with her over the years. We used to do tea and biscuits for the old folk on Saturday mornings and honestly, the way she used to speak to people."

Dorothea bit her bottom lip and seemed lost in thought for a few minutes before declaring, "Well, poor girl. She can't be held responsible for what happened. She must stay here, Grace, with us. We'll manage. As long as she does her work, it'll be all right. When the baby arrives, we'll have to manage between us. I can take charge when I get home from fire watch duty whilst she gets on with her duties. We can work the feeds and nappy changing between us."

She had patted Grace's hand and smiled. The thought of having to cope without Grace and Daisy was more than she could bear, for surely if she dismissed Daisy, Grace would go too and then how would she manage with the four children? No, she couldn't even contemplate it.

"Thank you, Dorothea. I'll go and tell her. Put her mind at rest."

When Grace had entered the kitchen a few minutes later, it was to see Daisy sat at the table with her hat and coat on, crying fit to burst.

"You can take that hat and coat off, lass. You're staying," said Grace, her voice taking on an air of authority.

"I can stay?" gasped Daisy between sobs. She'd been determined to walk to the bridge and throw herself into the river. There was nothing else left for her to do.

"She said it's all right as long as you get on with your work. Once the baby arrives, we'll manage between us. Don't you go letting me down now, do you hear me?"

"Oh Grace, I'm so relieved. I will work, I promise. I won't get another chance. A minute ago, I thought my life was over. You must have put in a good word for me. Thank you."

"Nay, lass. It was Dorothea. In any case, I would have come with you if she'd dismissed you and she knows that. All the same, I think a word of thanks is in order. Now go and wash your face and tidy yourself up a bit. I'll brew a fresh pot of tea and you can take it in to her."

From that day onwards, Daisy had worked her socks off. Grace had to admire her for that. Even more surprising was the calm way in which she coped with the birth itself. There was no hysterical screaming or carrying on, just resolve and fortitude. Luckily, there were no complications and everything went smoothly. If she bore any resentment towards the child because of the way in which it was conceived, she certainly didn't show it. Little Jenny was loved and adored by everyone in the household. She had a mop of red hair and big blue eyes. The resemblance to the Boothroyds was unmistakable.

Chapter Seven

Maggie filled the kettle and rinsed the cups. Mr Apse was in a very bad mood this morning and she could feel her headache getting progressively worse. She hoped a nice cup of tea would revive her. Mr Apse was arguing with someone over the telephone and she heard him bang down the receiver. She knew she would just have to keep out of his way until he calmed down.

There was a knock at the door and the shop floor manager, Joe, popped his head in.

"Excuse me, Maggie. There's a gentleman here, wants to speak to you."

"To Mr Apse?"

"No, it's you he's asking for." Joe winked, a big grin spreading across his face.

"Show him in then."

"This way, sir. This is Margaret, secretary to Mr Apse, the manager. Margaret, this is Mr Edward Kennedy." With the introductions done, Joe hot-footed it back down the stairs, no doubt to enjoy the gossip that would prevail throughout the factory.

A tall, well-built gentleman entered. He was wearing a very smart uniform. She recognised it as American or something of that ilk. *Certainly not one of ours*, she thought.

"Very sorry to bother you, ma'am," he said, extending his hand.

Maggie shook hands and gestured for him to sit down. "I'm just making a cup of tea, would you like one? I'm afraid we don't have any coffee. Mr Apse doesn't drink it."

"Tea will be fine, thanks." He smiled at her and placed his cap on the desk.

"You're American, are you?"

"Canadian, actually. I was born in Vancouver, but the family moved to Quebec when I was five years old."

"I have an aunt and uncle in Ottawa, not that I've ever visited them, but we get letters from them occasionally. My uncle Walter has a good job out there, something to do with engineering. Anyway, what brings you to this neck of the woods, Mr Kennedy?"

"I'm trying to trace a nice young lady that I met about three years ago. She seems to have vanished without a trace. Her name is Megan Andrews. I called at her lodgings but the landlady said she left quite some time ago and she didn't know her whereabouts."

"Oh yes, I remember Meg. She was a good worker. She no longer works for us, I'm afraid."

"She's moved on then?"

"Yes." Maggie wasn't sure how much to reveal about Meg's situation as it wasn't really her story to tell. She had felt so sorry for the girl the day she was sent packing.

"Any idea where she went?" asked Eddie.

"No, it was a bit… well, to be honest, she was dismissed."

"Dismissed? You mean she was given notice? Sacked?"

"Yes. She was expecting a baby. Mr Apse is very strict about that sort of thing, especially for the unmarrieds."

Eddie's face fell. A baby? He knew at once the baby must be his. He also knew she'd probably been thrown out of her lodgings. No wonder the landlady had sent him away with a flea in his ear. He had to find her. He stood up and, placing his cap on his head, he thanked Maggie for her time and was about to leave when she spoke again.

"It was very unfortunate the way things turned out. She had a friend here. Josie. They went everywhere together. They were very close. That's the bit I find hard to stomach."

"I met Josie a couple of times. She was with Meg the night we met," said Eddie, turning back into the room.

"You see, it was Josie that betrayed her in the end. She told Mr Apse."

"Why on earth would she do that?"

"She was after a promotion. She wanted to be a supervisor and she thought she could earn some brownie points, but it worked against her. Everyone knew what she'd done, you see, and nobody would speak to her. She left after three months. She couldn't stand it any longer. Prior to that, Joe the foreman was the only one that knew and he kept his mouth shut. The people here might be lowly but they've got hearts of gold and they stick together when the chips are down."

Eddie smiled. "I'm very pleased to hear that. Goodbye, Maggie. And thank you."

When he'd gone, Maggie noticed his tea cup was empty. *He must have liked my tea*, she mused. He seemed such a nice man and she hoped he would find Meg, wherever she was.

Beth was thoroughly enjoying her new role of helping to get Jenny washed and dressed in the mornings. Jenny was only two years old. Well, two and a half, as she liked to remind everyone. Things had changed a little bit in the household of late. This was due to Iris and Megan getting up early as they had jobs to go to.

Samuel was the first one to get a job, helping out in the library three afternoons a week from two o'clock until five o'clock. He was paid a small wage for this, which he insisted on putting into the tin on the kitchen table. Iris was the next one to find work after having befriended Kathleen who worked in the factory.

It was Joshua who had brought Kathleen home with him one day, accompanied by Mr Glass. He had found them in the town centre sat on a bench. He was en route to the post office to get some postage stamps when he spotted them. Kathleen was weeping and appeared to be very upset about something. Mr Glass explained there had been an "upset" at the factory. Seeing the sorry state she was in, Josh invited them back to the house for tea and sympathy.

Iris greeted them in the kitchen and got busy making the tea. Kathleen had explained that one of her friends at the factory had been having an affair with the manager, who was married. His wife got to hear about it and caused a scene. Consequently, he ended the affair and her friend took an overdose. She was taken to the infirmary and had her stomach pumped. Fortunately, she had survived the ordeal and was now on her way to her brother's in Cornwall.

Iris, Meg and Grace sat around the big oak kitchen table all afternoon with Kathleen trying to reassure her that at least she was still alive and she would be able to write to her. Grace enjoyed all the village gossip and was always up for a chance of a sit down with a cup of tea. Mr Glass was in the lounge with the children, regaling them with tales of his duties in the Home Guard.

Megan was the next one to get a job, working in the local corner shop in the village, which doubled as a grocers, newsagents and post office all in one. Kenneth, the manager, suffered from heart problems and had taken to his bed after an angina attack. Megan offered to help out and discovered she rather enjoyed it. The only thing she didn't like was the fact she was on her feet all day, which took some getting used to.

All the money she and Iris earnt went into the tin on the kitchen table. Every penny.

Beth went into Jenny's bedroom and found her up and about sorting through her clothes.

"Come on, honey-bun, let's get you washed," said Beth.

"Not wearing that," Jenny cried, tossing a cardigan to one side.

"No, you tipped soup all over it yesterday. We'll have to soak it. Come on, bathroom." Beth chased her along the corridor, both of them laughing.

Daisy had volunteered to get up early to make sure Iris and Meg had some breakfast before they left for work. It was the least she could do, she told them. When she had asked Beth if she could help to get Jenny up and dressed, she was only too pleased to be of service. It made her feel important to be earning her place in the household.

Jenny was a very likeable child, if a little feisty when she couldn't get her own way, but upsets were usually quickly forgotten by distracting her with other things. So, it was a very changed household which greeted Dorothea when she was finally discharged from the hospital.

Chapter Eight

Today was Saturday and Dorothea knew there would be a full house. She had been home a week now and was still confined to her bed on Dr Mattison's instructions. Although glad to be in her own bed after the noise of the hospital ward, she couldn't understand why she didn't feel any better in herself. The terrible pains in her chest kept her awake at night and she was very low in spirits and missing Raif. If only he would write. Just to know he was all right would be enough. The thought of him never returning was too much to bear.

Propping herself up on her pillows, she could hear the laughter and chatter of the children. How empty the house would seem once they all went back to their own families. She couldn't bear to think about that either. It was too painful but hopefully she'd still have little Jenny. She smiled to herself and closed her eyes.

She must have fallen asleep, for when she next opened her eyes the house was deathly quiet and she had no idea what time it was. Getting out of bed, she put on her dressing gown and very tentatively made her way downstairs to the kitchen. Daisy and Jenny were rolling out pastry.

"Oh, Miss Dorothea. You shouldn't be out of bed. Doctor's orders," said Daisy.

"Oh, never mind all that, where is everyone?" Dorothea parked herself at the table. She watched Jenny as she worked her little fingers around the rolling pin, backwards and forwards. "That's very nice, Jenny. What are you making?"

"Pasty."

"Cornish pasties, hopefully," said Daisy. "I'll put the kettle on, miss."

"Thank you, Daisy. That would be lovely."

"Do you want something to eat? The others won't be back until lunchtime. They've all gone up to the farm to help with the new lambs. Iris is having lunch with Kathleen today and won't be back until later. Meg's gone to make lunch for Kenneth. He's still not feeling too good and his wife's in bed with a cold, so she offered."

"That's kind of her. Where's Grace?"

"She's having lunch with the Women's Institute today. There's a meeting in the church hall, so it's just us and the children for lunch."

"I'd like to join that Women's Institute when I'm eventually allowed out."

"Don't rush things, miss. You're not strong enough yet."

"You're right. I don't feel quite right yet. Were there any letters for me in the post this morning?"

"We've not had the post yet. The boys will collect it this afternoon when they change the library books."

"I'd forgotten. We collect it now from the post office, don't we? Peter joined the army. There's been nobody to take over after he left."

Dorothea watched as Daisy cut the pastry into rounds and put a spoonful of filling in each one. Jenny brushed the edges with milk and watched as Daisy folded them over and sealed them up.

"Now, brush the tops with the milk, like I showed you," Daisy said to Jenny.

They were loaded onto a baking tray and placed in the oven. Daisy washed the dishes and wiped the counter top before joining Dorothea at the table.

"Are Meg and Iris enjoying their jobs?" Dorothea asked, sipping her tea.

"Meg's loving hers, although she said her legs ache from all the standing and it's quite busy so she's very tired when she gets home. She's got to know quite a few people in the village now and Ken and his wife are very good to her."

"That's good. Will they keep her on once Ken's fully recovered, do you think?"

"She's not sure about that but she doesn't seem overly concerned."

"And how is Iris liking it at the factory?"

"She's not keen. The boss is very strict and there's to be no talking whilst they're working. You know Iris, she likes to chat."

"Yes." Dorothea smiled to herself, then added, "But I can see the sense in that really. If you're packing parachutes, you have to concentrate. If you don't get it right, there are consequences. If it failed to open, the poor man would fall to his death."

"I can't see her lasting there. She's already talking about finding something more suitable. I'm sure she'll get something eventually. You know what she's like. She talks to everyone. Once word gets around, someone will offer her something. I'm certain. She's such a jolly girl. She's fitted in here straight away and seems happy to muck in with anything."

"Just as well, Daisy. I've a feeling the next few months are going to be grim. I think I'll go back up to bed. Call me when lunch is ready."

"You stay put, miss. I'll bring yours up to your room."

The church hall was full by the time Grace arrived for the Women's Institute meeting. Fortunately, her friend Ivy had saved her a seat at the back.

"We've got the new regional manager here today," said Ivy. "She's doing a talk, of sorts. Celia Boothroyd."

"Celia Boothroyd?" Grace said, eyes going as wide as saucers. She couldn't believe it. It couldn't be the same woman whose son had attacked Daisy, surely?

"Shush, it's starting," hissed Ivy.

Grace shuffled uncomfortably in her seat, straining her neck to see the stage. It was definitely her. Although she looked a lot thinner than when she'd last seen her, but she supposed most people did these days due to all the food rationing.

When Celia Boothroyd stood up to speak, Grace noticed she

didn't look at all her usual self. Her hair was scraped back into a bun and she was wearing an old pleated tweed skirt and flat brown boots. Not at all her usual coiffure, pristine self. She always wore tailored suits and lots of jewellery and full make-up. She wasn't wearing any make-up or jewellery today, Grace observed. In fact, she looked a bit crumpled.

The talk went on for nearly three hours by the time they'd run through everything the WI had achieved so far and was continuing to do for the war effort, alongside new projects which everyone was expected to participate in with enthusiasm. Being sat at the back had its advantages as Grace and Ivy were the first in the queue for the tea, sandwiches and cakes.

Chapter Nine

Eddie eventually managed to find his way to the ARP office after several wrong turns. He still hadn't managed to find his way around the London streets as they all looked the same to him. He pushed open the door, which had seen better days. The brown paint was peeling and the letter box was loose. There was no bell or knocker so he made his way along the small corridor. The walls were covered in fire notices and various other paraphernalia. He heard voices coming from an open doorway and made his way in. There was a gentleman and a lady in uniform studying a street map.

"Good morning," he said cheerfully.

The man looked up. "Yes, sir, what can we do for you?"

"Sorry to distract you. Can I trouble you for a moment? I'm trying to trace a lady who was an ARP warden."

The lady now looked up and came towards him, smiling. "What was her name?"

"Dorothea. I'm afraid I don't remember her surname."

"Dorothea? Why yes, Dotty we called her. She was with us for quite some time. She's gone to live in Somerset. Her husband has a property there."

"You wouldn't happen to know the address, would you?"

"No, I'm sorry. I know it was in or near Minehead."

Eddie took out his notebook and scribbled in it. "She has a sister. Iris? Worked in a butcher's shop."

"That's right."

"Do you know what street it was on?" said Eddie desperately.

The two wardens looked at each other, shaking their heads.

"Well, never mind. It was worth a try. Thank you." He made his way back along the corridor and out onto the street.

32

Chapter Ten

It was eleven o'clock in the morning when Grace heard a light tapping noise at the kitchen door. Daisy had taken Jenny into the village and Dorothea was still confined to her bed, so she was all alone.

Wiping her hands on her apron, Grace opened the door to find Celia Boothroyd standing on the porch.

"Hello Grace. I just wanted a quick word, if you're not too busy," she said. "I followed you here from the WI meeting yesterday, but as it was late…" She faltered.

Grace's startled expression must have shown on her face. She was just about to ask how she knew where to find her. She wasn't sure she wanted anything to do with the woman and she wasn't in the mood for her high-handed attitude.

"You'd better come in. Have you walked from the village?" Grace asked, forcing herself to be civil.

"Yes. I'm going back on the train this afternoon but I wanted to speak to you first."

"I'm listening."

"I wanted to ask you about… about the young girl you took with you when you left London. Daisy. She was well-known in our street and it didn't take me long to discover that she'd left with you."

There was a long pause, followed by a long intake of breath as though she was struggling to breathe.

"Iain came home with scratches all over his face and neck. When I questioned him about it, he became rude and aggressive but I wasn't going to let it drop. It turned into a full scale row and I eventually got it out of him. The awful thing is… his father thought it was a huge joke and laughed it off. He said 'boys will be boys' and there was a war on. I nearly blew a fuse. I can't remember ever being so annoyed with him. This 'all boys together' attitude doesn't wash with me. I've put up with a lot from my husband over the years but I couldn't accept this attitude. It was callous, to say the least. I packed my bags and left. I haven't been back since. He's making a terrible nuisance of himself, threatening me that I'll live to regret it."

"So, where are you living now?" asked Grace, who was beginning to enjoy herself. There was a god after all. Sweet revenge indeed.

"I rent rooms. Well, one room to be exact. It's all I can afford. I've had to sell all my jewellery and my lovely clothes, just to make ends meet. It's on the other side of London. I tried to get as far away from Tom as possible but he keeps turning up and threatening me. I'm not going to give in. I'm enjoying my freedom too much. Fortunately, I've got some friends in the WI who've been my saviours."

"Yes, they're a lovely crowd," said Grace, filling the kettle. She made the tea and placed a cup in front of Celia. She noticed how pale she was. She didn't look at all well and she was trembling.

"Are you all right, Celia?"

"Yes. Yes, I'm all right," she said, dabbing her forehead with a handkerchief. "I wanted to say how very sorry I am for what happened to Daisy. I don't know why Iain's turned out the way he has. I refuse to take all the blame. We've both overindulged him. I told Tom that, but he wouldn't listen. She's such a nice girl too. She didn't deserve that. No girl does. I know there's a war on but that's no excuse for attacking young girls just because they said no. No means no. I tried to talk to Iain but he said nobody refuses him and gets away with it. I'm appalled, Grace. What an attitude. I know I've been arrogant in the past and I'm sorry for it. I can see that now." Then she started to weep just as Dorothea appeared in the doorway, tying her dressing gown around herself.

Chapter Eleven

Howard was proud of his job helping out at the post office delivering the mail. He got the job through Meg who recommended him to Kenneth. It took him a while to find his way around the town, but he was getting more used to it every day. He didn't get paid for doing it but he was pleased to be doing his bit for the war effort.

Ken and his wife, Evelyn, often gave him food from the store to take home, which delighted Grace and Daisy. It gave him a chance to gather his thoughts whilst he was out and about.

His mother was at the centre of these thoughts and the kind of life they had lived in London. She wasn't a bad woman but she was an alcoholic. His father died when he was seven years old, so it had been just the two of them. He'd often arrive home from school to find her flaked out on the settee, no sign of any meal on the stove and he was lucky if he found any food in the larder to feed himself with. Going to bed hungry was an everyday occurrence for him and strangely, he was now eating better than he ever did before the war, even with all the food rationing.

The teacher in his class at school in London had taken him to one side and asked him if his mother laundered his school uniform. He had hung his head in shame and was acutely aware of the other children in his class not wanting to sit near him. The water was heated via a meter under the stairs which required coins. His mother never had any spare so there was rarely any hot water.

The drinking started after his father's death. As the years went by, she relied on it more and more. Howard knew she was sick. He'd decided a long time ago that alcoholism was an illness. It wouldn't have been so bad if she knew when to stop but she just couldn't help herself and drank until she passed out unconscious.

The day Aunty Dot took him in was the turning point in his life and he was determined to make the most of it. The first thing she did for him was to take him into town for a haircut and then she purchased him some new spectacles as his old ones were held together with sticky tape. The very next day, they were all bundled into the jeep and taken to a warehouse where they were all kitted out with waterproof clothing and sturdy walking boots. Daisy and Grace were included in this as they were expected to join in the country walks Aunty Dot insisted on taking every Sunday afternoon. On Sunday mornings, they all went to church, after which they would come home for their lunch.

Howard was determined not to return to his old life. Much as he loved and missed his mum, he knew if he was going to make anything of himself and build a life worth living, he had to grab this opportunity, the likes of which he'd never get again. He made up his mind to speak to Uncle Raif when he came home after the war was over. He would ask if he could stay, providing he could find work and pay rent. It made him think of Uncle Raif and he wondered what kind of man he was. *I'll ask Grace tonight when she makes the cocoa,* he thought. Aunty Dot once said there was no guarantee Raif would return at all. Well, he would pray to God every night and ask him to be spared and send him home safe. Yes, that's what he would do.

Thanks to Mr Glass, Joshua ended up with two jobs, helping out at the Women's Voluntary Service and running errands for the ARP. He was loving every minute of it and had become quite popular with all the locals. His gregarious nature endeared him to them and he often came home with little gifts which they insisted on giving him. Sometimes it was a bit of chocolate or some biscuits, which he always shared with the family.

He'd taken to calling on Mr Glass almost every day. He enjoyed his company and they had become great friends. He loved hearing all about his duties in the Home Guard. Although the war was a serious business, they always found something to laugh about.

His first duty had been to stamp a huge pile of leaflets for the ARP, then he had to hand deliver them to every household in the village. His next task had been for the WVS sorting clothing into piles. They were running a clothing exchange scheme which was proving very popular. He was only sorry he wasn't able to contribute to the household expenses. To be able to put money in the tin on the kitchen table each week, like Meg, Iris and Sam, would be wonderful, but he wasn't paid for his duties, so it wasn't possible. He looked forward to the day he would be able to do so, as he very much wanted to stay.

The thought of returning home to London filled him with horror. His mother had died when he was six years old and his father had taken a new wife. She hadn't taken kindly to having to look after Josh but she knew it was part of the deal, so she went along with it – just. She hadn't gone out of her way to bond with him and showed little or no interest in him. He began to feel as though he was in the way. His father seemed oblivious to any of it. He had obtained what he wanted: someone to cook and clean for him and to deal with his child. Josh missed his mother terribly but Aunty Dot was proving to be a wonderful substitute. She was kind and generous and went out of her way to see they were all happy. He loved being with Sam, Howard and Beth. He couldn't imagine life without them now. Where would he go once the war was over? The thought of going back to London didn't bear thinking about.

Beth was feeling as though she'd been cut adrift. Howard, Sam and Josh all had jobs to go to and she felt left out. They were all doing their bit for the war. Even Aunty Dot had now gone back to her fire watch duties, much to the discernment of Grace and Daisy who didn't think she was quite recovered from her illness.

Meg and Iris left early in the mornings and only returned at tea time. Grace and Daisy were knitting for the soldiers. The WI sent them in batches once a month after their meetings. Aunty Dot spent a lot of time teaching them all the basic stitches and they unravelled some of Raif's old jumpers. The wool was then washed in the kitchen sink and wound around the grill pan to straighten out the crinkles. Beth and Jenny had enjoyed doing this. Their evenings were spent knitting and listening to the radio. Meg and Iris were good knitters and soon taught the boys. The more experienced knitters were tackling balaclavas and socks. The others were doing scarves and blanket squares. It was Beth's favourite part of the day when they could all be together in the library, laughing and joking.

It was Jenny's birthday tomorrow and Grace wanted to bake a cake but she had no butter or eggs. She could use the powdered egg but a fresh egg would be better. She called Beth into the kitchen and asked her if she'd run up to the farm and ask Alf if he could spare a fresh egg and a little butter.

Glad to be of service and doing something useful, Beth skipped along the lane with a smile on her face. She'd put on her wellingtons as the lane was muddy and she stopped to admire the new lambs which were frolicking in the field. The little black ones were her favourites.

After knocking on the farmhouse door and wiping her feet on the mat, she greeted Alf who was hand-feeding one of the baby goats.

"Hello Uncle Alf. Can Grace please have an egg and a little butter? It's for Jenny's birthday cake."

"Hello young lady. Come in. Sit yourself down on this stool here and give this little fella his breakfast whilst I go and see what I can find," he said with a chuckle, handing her a bottle of milk with a teat on the end.

Half an hour later, Beth was walking back up the lane clutching a bag. She'd enjoyed an ice cream which Ivy had given her. Ivy had wanted to know all about Beth's family and asked about her parents.

"My brother Alan has joined the sea cadets so he stayed in London. He's older than me, sixteen. Dad's a fireman and Mum's a school teacher," Beth had told her, not wanting to dwell too much on the thought of going back home, for the very thought of it depressed her. The truth of it was simply that she'd fallen head over heels in love with her new life here in Somerset. There was something very special about the big house.

It was called Blythe Wood and the style was Georgian. It had ten bedrooms and years and years ago, it used to be an hotel. There was something quite magical about it for Beth. It seemed to wrap itself around her, drawing her in and casting its spell. The thought of leaving filled her with dread.

Thursday nights were spent in the company of Mrs Kloot who gave them all French lessons. Dorothea, Meg and Iris could all speak French a little and they relished the chance to put in a little practice and even Grace and Daisy joined in. They could all say their names, their ages, where they lived and who their brothers and sisters were. Mrs Kloot, whose name was Rosine, enjoyed talking to them about the French culture, the food and the markets, places of interest and local customs.

They spent hours poring over maps and practised asking for directions, ordering train tickets and they even had a good laugh pretending to order food and drinks. Beth enjoyed these evenings more and more as time went on. There was a whole world out there she never knew existed and promised herself she would visit France one day.

Chapter Twelve

It was five o'clock in the afternoon by the time Mrs Bray got back to the staffroom. The afternoon maths lesson hadn't gone down well with the little ones. They were fidgety and restless. The air raid siren had sounded in the middle of the class, which hadn't helped. She herded them into the shelter where they remained for over an hour before the all clear sounded.

"Ah, Elsie," the headmaster, Lionel Waters, greeted her as soon as she opened the door. "There's a Mr Ansard here, enquiring about his son."

A smartly dressed gentleman smiled at her and extended his hand. She shook his hand.

"It's Samuel," said Lionel, "I said you'd be the best person to help as you were instrumental in placing the children with families throughout the village."

"Yes, of course. I'll drop you off, it's on my way. If you just give me a minute to get my things together," she said.

It took her a good five minutes to get the old Hillman fired up and running before they set off.

"Have you travelled far then, Mr Ansard?"

"I've come from London. It's taken me a long time to squeeze in a few spare hours to myself in order to find my family but I was determined to do it."

Elsie glanced sideways at him and saw the look of concern on his face. He explained about being a doctor and had lost touch with his wife and children.

"You needn't worry about Samuel. I placed him with a very good family and he's settled in very well," she reassured him.

"My wife doesn't speak English very well and when the children were being evacuated, she panicked and fled to her sister's house, taking our daughter Selina with her. I'm not even sure where they are. She's not handled this at all well."

She pulled up outside the big house and told him to contact her at the school if he needed anything further. Normally, she would have escorted him to the door to make the introduction but she didn't want to risk shutting down the engine as she wasn't at all sure she'd be able to get the car going again.

Bhutan Ansard eyed the big house and took in its grandeur before venturing up the driveway. *It's certainly a very fine house indeed,* he thought.

It was Dorothea who opened the door to see a smartly dressed gentleman of foreign extraction standing on the step.

"Good evening, my good lady. I'm sorry to trouble you but I've come to see my son, Samuel," he said, eyeing the ARP uniformed lady that stood before him.

Dorothea smiled broadly. "Gracious. You're Sam's father?" she gasped.

"I am indeed," he replied, extending his hand.

Dorothea shook his hand firmly and ushered him into the kitchen where all the family were gathered for their evening meal.

"Sam, you have a visitor," she said.

Sam's eyes went as big as saucers when he saw who it was. "Father!" He got up from the table and the two of them threw their arms around each other.

"Hello son." His face broke into a big grin on seeing his boy. Introductions were made and a seat was found for him at the table so he could join in the meal.

"Well, this is a nice surprise, Sam," said Dorothea. "Have you travelled from London?" she asked, then continued without waiting for an answer, "You must stay with us whilst you're here. Are you in a hurry to dash back?"

A sudden thought came to her that perhaps he'd come to take Sam back with him and her heart plummeted to her boots. Her fears were allayed on hearing he'd like to stay the night with Sam, then be on his way tomorrow as he only had a few days of leave before returning to his duties and he was yet to locate the whereabouts of his wife and daughter.

At seven o'clock, Dorothea left for her fire watch duties. The family were all gathered in the library and she wished with all her heart she could stay and join them. Sam's father seemed a very jolly gentleman and there was much laughter as she left the house. Grace would give her all the details of their evening over breakfast tomorrow morning and she looked forward to that.

On arriving at the ARP office, there appeared to be a panic on. A piece of shrapnel or something had landed on the farm and set the barn alight. The fire brigade had been called and they were all running over there to help.

Dorothea couldn't run as fast as the others as she was still not fully recovered from her illness but shouted that she'd follow them. She walked as quickly as she could without getting out of breath and hoped Alf and Ivy were all right. They were good friends now and she thought of them as her extended family, as indeed a lot of the residents in the village had become over the years.

She turned up the lane to see Mr Glass wielding two buckets.

"Earnest," she shouted. "Is everyone all right?"

"Hello Dotty. Yes, they're all right. We're trying to get all the lambs into the field. Take one of these buckets. The lads are all here. They're doing a grand job."

She followed him up the lane to see an orderly queue of people passing buckets of water along the line. All the ARP wardens and the Home Guard were there, alongside half the village. It took them nearly five hours to get the fire under control. Fortunately, none of the animals were hurt but there was considerable damage to the barn.

Most of the villagers went home to their beds but Dorothea stayed with Ivy who was very distressed. They sat in the kitchen drinking mugs of tea and warming themselves on the stove which Alf had lit to help keep them warm.

"We're getting too old, Alf and me, to be doing all this. Farming's a hard life," said Ivy.

"Yes, I'm sure it must be," Dorothea said.

"But it's been a good life," said Alf. "I wouldn't have wanted to do anything else."

It was then that Dorothea started to cough.

"That smoke's not done your chest any good, Dotty. I suggest you go home to bed," Alf advised, feeling guilty they'd been the cause of it.

"I'm all right, really," she said. There were a few moments of quiet contemplation where she seemed lost in thought. "But you're right. I think I will go home to my bed."

She made her way back to the office where the night watchman was just making a brew. He wanted to escort her home but she wouldn't hear of it.

On reaching the house, she let herself in via the back door very quietly and crept into the library. She kicked off her shoes and curled up in her favourite chair. She wondered where Raif was and sent a silent prayer to the universe to keep him safe and bring him home. She wondered if there were any letters at the townhouse in London. Having left in such a hurry, it didn't occur to her to get her mail redirected.

Once again, she suddenly felt overwhelmingly sad and started to weep silently into the night.

Chapter Thirteen

Eddie made his way to the ARP office in London once again, hoping to see the lady he'd spoken to on his first visit. He'd been called back to his duties, so he only had about an hour to spare.

He knocked on the door and was pleased to see the gentleman who had greeted him on his first visit, although there was no sign of the lady.

"Hello again," said Eddie cheerfully.

"I know you, don't I?" said the warden.

"We spoke a little while ago. I'm trying to trace a lady whose sister used to work here. Dorothea. I've written her a note and wondered if you could get that nice lady who was here last time to post it for me. I've put the postage stamp on. Would she know the address, do you think?" He knew he was clutching at straws, but it was worth a try.

The warden scratched his head. "She might do, which lady was it?"

"I didn't get her name but she had very blonde hair tied back in a bun. She wore a signet ring on her little finger."

"Ah yes, I know. Carole. I'll give it to her. Can't promise anything, mind."

Eddie hot-footed it back out onto the street with a spring in his step. All he had to do now was wait.

Today was Saturday and Iris was glad she didn't have to go to the factory. She only worked Monday to Friday as different staff came in at the weekend. They earned extra money for working Saturdays and Sundays but Iris didn't mind as she wasn't really enjoying it at all. She knew she was lucky to be earning a wage of sorts and she was grateful.

When she went into the kitchen, the children had already had their breakfast and were on their way to the farm to help out. Meg had gone to the shop for provisions and Dorothea was on her way out of the door with her coat on.

"Where are you off to, Dotty?" she asked.

"I'm going to London. I've a few things to sort out and I want to check if there's any mail at the townhouse. I forgot to get it redirected. I've also written to the bank to find out what's happened to Raif's money. If he's moved it to another account, I'd rather know."

"Could I come with you?" asked Iris earnestly. She would do anything to relieve the boredom and inertia she was feeling of late.

"Yes, if you like, but you'll have to hurry as I want to get going."

Iris dashed to the hallway to fetch her coat and handbag and was greeted at the back door by Grace who'd wrapped her some biscuits as she'd had no breakfast.

The hammering at the door was getting louder and louder. Any minute now her landlady would be making an appearance, demanding to know what was going on. Celia knew who it was, of course. Tom hadn't left her alone since the day she'd left him and was making her life an absolute misery. His pursuit of her was relentless, like a person possessed.

Switching off all the lights, she locked herself in the bathroom and crouched down by the side of the bath. She didn't know how much more of it she could take. Trying to think clearly, she knew she would have to leave here and go somewhere where he couldn't find her. But where to go? Having very little money and not knowing anyone outside of London, the prospect of moving looked bleak.

Curling up on the bath mat, she willed herself to fall asleep. With her fingers in her ears, the banging grew fainter. Eventually, it stopped altogether and she heard footsteps on the stairs, followed by a car engine starting up. Good. He was gone. But for how long?

She thought back to the day of the Women's Institute annual general meeting in Somerset when she visited Grace. The day was etched into her memory. When she had left the hotel and walked to the bus stop at the top of the road, she had spotted Daisy with a little girl in a trolley. The child bore a striking resemblance to her own son Iain when he was a baby. There was no mistaking it. She knew instantly Iain was the father. Such a pretty child. She wondered why Grace hadn't mentioned it. Why would she not have, when she'd had every opportunity? Her heart ached at the thought of having a grandchild and never being part of their life.

Letting herself out of the bathroom, she made her way into the lounge and got out her writing pad. She scribbled a note for her landlady, explaining she'd had to vacate the premises due to sudden unforeseen circumstances. She decided it was now or never. It wouldn't go down well, but needs must and packing what little possessions she had wouldn't take long.

Chapter Fourteen

It was one o'clock in the afternoon when Dorothea and Iris arrived at the townhouse and after checking the mailbox, which was full, she quickly bundled the whole lot into a bag and headed up the driveway. Her heart missed a beat at the hope of there being a letter from Raif and she could feel her mood brightening at the prospect.

The blackout curtains twitched at the window of the house next door and no sooner had they unlocked the door and entered the hallway, there was a knock at the back door.

"Hello John, come in," said Dorothea smiling. It was good to see a familiar face from her old life.

"Hello Dotty. It's good to see you. How have you been?"

"Oh, you know, surviving. How are things here? It was quite grim when I left, with bombs dropping all over the place."

"Yes, it's been very grim, Dotty, but we're still here. We're not beaten yet."

"Oh, I'm so sorry, John. This is my sister Iris. Iris, this is John."

Iris stepped forward and they shook hands. "Nice to meet you, John. Actually, I know you. I worked at Monks, the butchers."

"Goodness me, yes. I thought your face seemed familiar. It's been closed a good while now. I walked all the way up there one day only to find it all boarded up. Can't say I was surprised though."

"We've just come to collect a few things then we're going," said Dorothea. "We've got a few errands to complete. I must say I'm so glad the house is still standing. When I turned the corner, I didn't know what to expect."

"You'll pop next door for a cup of tea before you go, won't you?" insisted John. "My daughter left me a fruit cake when she called yesterday."

"That would be lovely. How is your daughter?"

"She's coping very well. I'll tell you all about it when you pop over. I'll go and put the kettle on."

"I just need to nip upstairs for something, Iris. Do you need the bathroom or anything?" Dorothea shouted over her shoulder as she made her way upstairs.

Opening the wardrobe door, she retrieved a jewellery box which was buried under some spare blankets. Taking out the small black box containing the ring Raif had given her on their first wedding anniversary, she opened the lid and stared at the huge stone. Then she saw the necklace she'd never liked and knew she would never wear. It had belonged to Raif's grandmother. The woman never had a good word to say about Dorothea. In her opinion, she wasn't good enough for Raif. She wasn't of the right calibre. Parting with it wouldn't be too painful. She could save the pawn ticket for Raif. He could retrieve it if he wanted to.

A sudden thought crossed her mind as to how Raif would react, knowing she had parted with a family heirloom. She sank down on the bed, suddenly feeling defeated. Raif hadn't written and there was no guarantee she would ever see him again. Furthermore, she told herself, there was a war on and she had four evacuee children to support with no money in the bank.

"You must realise that the stones aren't worth very much. It's the gold that holds the value." He peered at her over the rim of his half-moon spectacles.

He's used to people like me turning up, thought Celia. Not that she had expected any special treatment but she had nothing else left to sell. It was her last-ditch attempt at raising enough money to buy a train ticket out of London. She started to feel very hot and her heart was pounding. Getting cross wasn't going to help on this occasion, she knew that.

Resigned to her fate, she said, "Very well."

He wrote out the ticket and handed it to her. As she stood up and retrieved her bag which was under her seat, she heard the doorbell ping. It was Dorothea and Iris.

It was eight o'clock in the evening by the time Dorothea and Iris arrived back in Somerset. When they entered the hallway, they could hear laughter coming from the library. They went in and found all the family sat around the big table. Mr Glass and Kathleen were also present and appeared to be enjoying themselves. Grace immediately jumped up from her chair and made her way towards them.

"Oh, thank goodness, you're home safe. I was starting to get worried. I've saved you some supper."

"Thank you, Grace," said Dorothea. "We've had nothing since lunchtime."

Iris went over to Kathleen and gave her a hug. Dorothea dashed upstairs to her room and locked the mail bag in the wardrobe. She would sort through it later. She made her way back down to the kitchen and was joined by Iris. They were both cold and hungry. Grace placed a plate of stew in front of each of them and filled the kettle to make the tea.

"I'll see if the others want a drink as it's too early for the cocoa." Grace disappeared momentarily and the two sisters sat in silence whilst they ate.

Iris mulled over what Dorothea had said to her in the car coming home from their trip to London. It had been a lovely day and she'd enjoyed it but she was shocked at the scenes of devastation which greeted them. Whole streets seemed to have disappeared with houses and buildings torn apart and reduced to piles of rubble. It was heartbreaking to see and she wondered how on earth everyone was going to be rehoused.

Dorothea commented that she wasn't at all sure she would ever see Raif again. They had discussed the possibility that he may decide to start a new life elsewhere once the war was over. They had heard of cases like that, where men who were unhappy with their former lives decided not to go home. Was Raif unhappy? Iris didn't think so but one never knew the truth about what went on inside a marriage.

Once the war was over, any men not returning home to their wives and families would be presumed missing or dead. She wondered if she'd ever see her husband Bob again. There had been no letters from him since she had come to live in Somerset with Dorothea despite the fact she'd written to him three times telling him where she was. *What on earth will become of us all?* she wondered. How long would it be before the cinemas, theatres and dance halls reopened? Would life ever be the same again once the war was over?

Chapter Fifteen

Dorothea finally got into bed around midnight. After running Earnest and Kathleen home, she had helped Grace to wash the mugs and tidy up the library. Too tired to even think about opening the mail bag, she closed her eyes and was asleep in seconds.

Daisy roused her the following morning with a cup of tea.

"The children are just washing and dressing. Will we be going to church as usual?" Daisy asked.

"Yes, of course. I'll drink this and be down as soon as I can. Thank you, Daisy."

It was Sunday. Their usual routine was to go to church after breakfast then home for a quick lunch after which they would put on their walking gear and take off for a long walk. Weather permitting and providing there were no air raids. They would all take their gas masks, just in case.

It was Dorothea's favourite day of the week as all the family could be together. She smiled as she remembered the little walking boots she'd bought for Jenny on her third birthday. Grace had made a lovely cake with three candles and everyone managed to produce a small gift from somewhere.

Howard wrote her a story about kittens and drew pictures, fastening the pages together to make a book. He sat and read the story to her, which she loved. Meg managed to get a bag of sweets from the shop and Iris knitted her some mittens. Grace knitted her a scarf and Daisy knitted her a monkey, which she named Coco. Josh and Beth made a rag doll, with the help of the WI ladies. Josh got all the materials and instructions and they sewed it together between them. The result was beautiful.

They arrived back at the house late in the afternoon. Dorothea went straight up to her room with the intention of sorting through the mail bag. Retrieving it from the wardrobe, she tipped the contents out onto the bed. There was the usual stack of bills which she placed to one side with the intention of dealing with them later. There were just two letters addressed to her, in handwriting she didn't recognise. Her heart missed a couple of beats on realising there was nothing with Raif's handwriting on it. It would seem all hope was now gone and she burst into tears, curling up into a ball on the bed. She lost all track of time and eventually fell asleep.

A knock at the door woke her and Daisy appeared with a mug of tea and some biscuits.

"We've put the stew in the oven. Have this for now. Are you all right, miss?"

"Oh yes. Yes, I'm all right, Daisy. I was just opening the post from London and came across a stack of bills. Got myself a bit worked up. I'm over it now," she lied, quickly wiping her tear-stained face on a handkerchief, which she'd hastily pulled out from the sleeve of her jumper. "Thank you. I'll be down when I've had a quick wash and change."

Downing the tea in one go, Dorothea stripped off her clothes and ran herself a hot bath. Wallowing in the hot soapy bubbles, she reflected on the reality of events that were unfolding around her. How was she ever going to find paid work if she didn't get herself out into the community? A bit of networking was required and she was determined to put word about that she was looking for work. What's more, she also decided that if Raif no longer wanted her then she would jolly well find a man that did. She wasn't going to spend the rest of her life living alone.

After dressing and sweeping her hair up into a chignon, she was about to make her way downstairs when she noticed the two letters on the bed. Ripping open the first letter with more enthusiasm than she felt, she turned to the back page to see who it was from. It was from her friend Carole at the ARP office:

Dearest Dotty,

I hope this letter finds you as I don't know your Somerset address. Oh, how we all miss you here at the ARP base. The laughs we had, the cups of tea at all hours of the night, moaning about our aching feet. A gentleman in uniform called into our office on two occasions asking for you. He was trying to find the whereabouts of your sister Megan. I think he was American or Canadian but certainly not one of ours judging by his uniform. He left this letter for her. I will leave the decision up to you as to whether you give it to her or not. She might not want to continue the friendship. Please write back and let me know that you are safe and well. More news next time.

Carole

At least someone was missing her, she thought. Putting the letter in her bedside drawer, she looked at the envelope addressed to Meg. Whoever it was had very neat handwriting. The second letter was from her bank in London asking her to contact them at her earliest convenience. No other information was given.

After a show of hands, it was decided the evening's entertainment would be a game of cards. A tiring afternoon marching around all the local green areas had put a stop to anything more strenuous especially for the older members of the household.

Meg fingered the envelope in her apron pocket which Dotty had handed to her in the kitchen, quickly explaining where it had come from. She knew, or rather hoped beyond hope, that it was from Eddie. Would it be good news or bad? She dared not hope it was the latter. Preferring to wait until she was alone to read it in private, she struggled to concentrate on anything that was going on around her.

The air raid siren sounded just after seven thirty. They all scrambled into the Anderson shelter at the bottom of the garden.

"God, this is all we need," said Grace. "It's so damp in there."

They huddled together and spent the next hour singing songs. As it grew colder, they wrapped themselves up in blankets and waited for the rumble of enemy aircraft overhead.

Meg wondered where Eddie was right at this minute and if he was safe. She closed her eyes and sent a silent prayer into the universe to keep him safe. The all clear sounded just before midnight.

"Must have been a false alarm," said Daisy, lifting the sleeping Jenny into her arms.

"Come on, let's get back into the house quickly. The sooner we get into our beds the better," said Grace.

Dorothea picked up the torch, water bottle and first aid box. "It's raining," she whispered to the others.

"Last one in the house is a sissy," shouted Josh, making a mad dash across the lawn with Beth, Howard and Sam. They entered the house through the kitchen.

"Shall I make the cocoa, miss?" asked Daisy.

"No, it's late. Let's get into our beds before we all freeze to death," said Dorothea.

Meg waited until Iris was in bed and dozing off to sleep before opening her letter.

Dear Meg,

I've been trying to find you for quite some time now, without success. If you receive this letter, please write to me at the address below. It's our military base in Wilmington in Devon. There hasn't been a single day gone by that I haven't thought about you. We were called away suddenly by our command, so there wasn't time to contact you. I hope and pray that you are safe and well. The same thing is happening again now as I have so very little time to make any sort of arrangements. Such is life!

Much love,
Eddie

Chapter Sixteen

Howard had been instructed to look out for envelopes containing the OHMS insignia. These were telegrams informing loved ones of anyone missing or dead. He'd been given strict instructions to hand the letter only to the person they were addressed to and nobody else. He hadn't had any up until now, but today he had one.

It was addressed to Mrs Kloot who worked in the library. Her husband was in the Air Force in the same battalion as Uncle Raif who was a flight lieutenant in the intelligence branch. He hoped nothing bad had happened to them.

Making his way up to the reception desk, he handed over the envelope, not waiting around for a minute longer than he needed to. Sam was stacking books onto the shelves and Howard waved to him on his way out, mouthing the words, "see you later".

Once back out onto the streets, his next delivery was for the factory where Iris and Kathleen worked, which was over the bridge at the far end of the village. As he walked, he reflected on the things he had learnt since living with Aunty Dot. He knew the names of all the rivers and mountains, not only in England but in other countries in Europe and beyond. He also knew the kings and queens of England, how to wire a plug and change light bulbs, how to make pastry and cakes, how to make bread and stews and casseroles. He was also learning French and was now good at art.

Aunty Dot was a good artist and instructed them all in the use of watercolours and oils and the use of different canvases. She also taught them a little about all the great artists of the world and the works they were famous for. He could also knit and sew a little bit. He would never have thought to hear himself say it, but he had enjoyed it all. Dorothea made learning such fun and it gave them all something to do in the evenings which were always spent in the library. Even Grace, Daisy, Iris and Megan joined in.

The first few months were challenging, to say the least, as Aunty Dot was very strict and a stickler for routine. They all had their chores to do and woe betide anyone trying to duck out of them. The one he liked the most was on a Monday afternoon. After school in the morning, Dorothea insisted one of the children help Daisy with the laundry as all the beds were stripped in the morning. By lunchtime, the sheets were washed and just needed feeding through the mangle and hanging outside on the washing line. He loved spending time with Daisy as she was such a pleasant girl.

Arriving at the factory, he handed over the mail bag to the foreman and immediately remembered the letter he'd given Mrs Kloot. He knew her name was Rosine as that was the name on the envelope but Norman, the library manager, called her Rose. He'd ask Sam tonight if he knew what was in the letter.

The cafe was only half full and Celia managed to get a table in the far corner where it was a bit quieter. She had arranged to meet her husband's elder brother, Angus, for coffee at ten thirty. She glanced at her watch nervously and hoped there wasn't going to be a scene.

Angus arrived five minutes later and ordered coffee for them both at the counter before sitting down opposite her.

"It's nice to see you, Angus. Thank you for coming," said Celia.

"My pleasure, Celia. How are you keeping?" He placed his hat on the table and unbuttoned his coat.

Celia kept hers buttoned up as she didn't want him to see how shabbily dressed she was these days.

Angus noticed the difference in her appearance and was a little shocked. There was no comparison to the Celia he knew. He also knew about all of Tom's affairs that had gone on over the years and didn't blame Celia if she'd finally had enough. *Tom's had it coming to him for years*, he thought.

Celia waited until the waitress had placed their coffee cups on the table and was out of earshot before speaking. "Look, Angus, I really need you to speak to Tom. You're the only one he'll listen to."

She hesitated before continuing, not sure how to phrase things. Would he believe her? Would he be sympathetic? Would he understand? She wasn't sure about anything anymore. It was like being stuck in shifting sand.

"Ours wasn't a marriage in the… well, in the normal way of things," she said, stirring her coffee. "In the traditional sense. We had a sort of… arrangement."

"What kind of arrangement?" asked Angus, a look of surprise flooding his face.

She suddenly noticed how much better looking he was than Tom and wondered why she'd never seen it before. He was slimmer and smartly dressed too. Tom was overweight and always wore his hair a bit too long for Celia's liking and he tended to wear slacks and jumpers most of the time rather than suits. He very rarely wore a shirt and tie.

"As you know, I worked for him as his secretary for years before we married. As the chairman, he was expected to do a fair bit of entertaining of important clients and potential customers. Most of these functions were of a formal nature and it was expected that he'd attend with a partner. I accompanied him on a lot of these. Then as the company grew and the client base expanded, he had to start travelling abroad. Some of these countries weren't as liberal as ours and it was discussed between us that it would be better if we were married. He wanted to continue living like a single man and made it clear that he would still be free to live his life as he saw fit. In return, I would accompany him on these trips and cook and keep house for him. I was in a very precarious position, you see. I was already pregnant with Iain and my parents had thrown me out. They said I'd disgraced them.

"So, you see I had no choice really. In exchange for his freedom, I didn't have to perform wifely duties of a physical nature, if you get my meaning. It worked very well, most of the time. Of course, I knew about all his affairs but that was the deal, you see. I had a comfortable home and Iain was well provided for and… well, it wasn't too bad, really. I mean he wasn't violent or anything. Argumentative, yes, but never violent."

She looked up at Angus and saw his eyes had taken on a wide glassy look.

He didn't speak for a few minutes, then he blurted out, "Good grief, Cella, I'm appalled. How could he do such a thing? Pardon me for asking this, but is Iain—"

"Tom's child? Yes, he is. That was a mistake too. It was at one of the functions. He'd booked a hotel room for us. We'd both had a lot to drink. It should never have happened really."

Angus' face turned puce and his fists were balled up, she noticed.

"So, you see, Angus, I'd like you to speak to him. He's got to let me go. This war has changed all of us. I want to be free too. I want to live my own life, before it's too late. Please speak to him. I've been to a solicitor. I want a divorce."

They lingered in silence over their coffees a little longer, neither of them speaking.

Finally, Angus buttoned up his coat and retrieved his hat. A few minutes later, he was gone. *Well, that was a waste of time*, she thought.

Outside in the street, Angus strode purposely towards his car, his anger mounting with every step. He would have a few things to say to Tom all right. How could he do such a thing? The selfishness. The arrogance. To seduce a woman then treat her like that. He knew Tom had his faults but he didn't think him capable of this.

Chapter Seventeen

Howard waited until lights out before broaching the subject of Mrs Kloot's letter. They were all clambering into their beds when Howard whispered, "Sam, what was in Mrs Kloot's letter? Did you find out?"

"She turned very pale when she read it. Norman took her into the office and gave her a cup of tea," he whispered back.

Josh sat up in his bed. "Did you ask Norman about it?"

"He just said 'missing' and then he sent her home early," said Sam.

"I'll speak to Mr Glass tomorrow. He gets to know everything," Josh added.

"Missing doesn't mean dead though, does it?" said Howard hopefully.

"Depends on the circumstances, I would imagine," said Sam.

Howard sat up in his bed and whispered, "Josh, do you think Mr Glass could find out what's happened to Uncle Raif? Aunty Dot's had no letters from him and there's no money left in the bank. Daisy said that when she took Aunty Dot's tea up yesterday, she'd been crying. There were bills from the house in London piled up on the bed and she was distraught."

"Golly, I didn't know it was as bad as all that," gushed Sam.

"I'll ask him," said Josh. "He'll want to help. I know he will. If anyone can find out, Mr Glass will."

It was Grace's afternoon off and she'd gone to the church hall for the WI meeting with Ivy. She asked Dorothea if she wanted to come but she declined, stating it was good for Grace to spend some time away from the household on her own.

As she walked up the lane to the farm to call for Ivy, she thought back to the time Dorothea was in the hospital. The household had quickly descended into near chaos. It was Dorothea that kept all the children in line. She ruled with an iron fist and didn't stand for any nonsense from them. Being firm but kind, the children seemed to love her all the more for it. They thought the world of her and were very subdued as the days went on and only bucked up when they knew she was coming home. Grace smiled to herself as neither she nor Daisy had the same influence with the children.

Ivy was waiting for her in the kitchen when she knocked at the back door.

"I want to have a word with the vicar if he's around when we get to the church," said Grace.

"Oh? What about? Not getting married again, are you?" joked Ivy.

"As if. What social life do I get these days? Especially with this war going on. No, it's this." She handed a sheet of paper to her.

Ivy read aloud, "'Ballroom dancing lessons, four-week course. Week one: cha-cha. Week two: waltz. Week three: slow foxtrot. Week four: jive. All ages welcome, children included. One hour six 'til seven followed by a Christmas Eve dance seven thirty to nine. Includes glass of beer or lemonade.' Wow, I fancy this, Grace. Count me in. Who's doing the tuition? You?"

"No. Dorothea. She found some old 78 records up in the loft, together with an old gramophone. She thought it would be good to get all the village together to boost morale."

"She's not asked the vicar yet then?"

"I think she did mention it to him. Do you think he'll be up for it?"

"Leave it to me. I'll talk to him. We need this."

"Haven't you two gone yet?" chipped in Alf as he washed his hands in the sink.

"Don't you be falling asleep in the chair whilst I'm gone," Ivy said. "Get the vegetables peeled. Make yourself useful."

Alf gave her a mock salute. "Yes, m'lady."

Meg heard the door ping as she was stacking the newspapers onto the shelf and looked up to see Dorothea approach Evelyn who was manning the post office. She asked for some coins then disappeared into the telephone booth.

Dorothea unfolded the letter from the bank and gave the number to the operator.

"Good morning. This is Mrs Swift, could I speak to Mr Manns please?" she said tentatively, fearing what she was about to hear.

"I'm sorry, Mrs Swift, but he's not in today but he has drafted you a letter explaining the situation regarding your account. He's been called up to head office on a matter of a rather serious nature. I'll leave him a note to say that you called."

"I would appreciate that. Thank you." She replaced the receiver and walked over to Meg and whispered in her ear. "See you at tea time."

Meg had a good idea who Dorothea was trying to contact and hoped it wasn't bad news. She hadn't been on the telephone for very long, she observed. Only a matter of seconds. She thought that to be a bit odd.

Dorothea wondered what the "seriousness" of Mr Manns' visit was. He'd been called to head office, wherever that was. She told herself it couldn't possibly be in connection with her and Raif's account. Could it?

Walking back up to the house, she suddenly remembered something Raif had told her years ago and wondered if it had any significance. When she first met Raif, he was engaged to be married to a girl who worked at the bank in the London branch. Her name was Juliet Baines. She made a dreadful scene when Raif called off the engagement and she threatened him with all sorts. Raif reckoned she'd secretly been seeing someone else, which she flatly denied. The truth of the matter was he'd seen her having dinner in a restaurant on the night she'd told him she was going to the pictures with a friend. Raif had been suspicious for quite some time and on the night in question, decided to follow her. What made matters worse was they'd chosen a table directly next to the window. They were all over each other. When he confronted her, she blew a fuse.

Dorothea never liked her. In fact, she couldn't see what Raif ever saw in her but they were both very young. She thought they'd rushed into the engagement a bit too soon. Juliet's mother was the pushy type who would no doubt have been instrumental in smelling Raif's money and would have made sure her daughter got her claws into him before anyone else did.

Chapter Eighteen

The dance classes at the church hall were proving to be a great success. By week four, practically everyone in the village was attending. Dorothea was very popular and threw in a couple of extra lessons in preparation for the dance on Christmas Eve.

Stuart partnered up with Iris. Although dancing wasn't something he would normally consider during his leisure hours, due to all the walking about he did during his beat, he was loving every minute of his time spent in Iris' company. She was clever, witty and jolly good company.

Grace danced with Mr Glass, and Daisy danced with Howard. Dorothea took charge of Jenny, who took to it like a duck to water. Samuel danced with Beth and Joshua danced with a girl from his class at school. Megan danced with Kathleen, due to the lack of male partners. Mrs Bray danced with Lionel and encouraged all the school children to take part, even paying the entry fee for those families who couldn't afford it. Mrs Kloot danced with Norman but she didn't seem her usual self due to the sad news she'd received about her husband being reported missing. A month had passed and she'd had no further news from the war office regarding his whereabouts.

Stuart ironed his clean shirt in preparation for the dance tonight. It was Christmas Eve and everyone in the village was attending. He just hoped there wouldn't be an air raid to spoil it. He'd seen too many deaths over the last three years and he began to wonder if the war would ever come to an end. There was every chance of him being promoted to sergeant next year so that was something to look forward to, although he knew he would miss being on the beat and mixing with all the locals.

He put his uniform away in the wardrobe and took out his grey slacks and black shoes, which he had polished to a shine. Not that it mattered what he wore because Dorothea had emphasised the fact it was an informal evening and advised everyone to dress casually. It was a chance to show off their skills and enjoy themselves, she had said.

Stuart still felt as though he had two left feet but Iris didn't seem to mind. He had practised every day to improve his technique but he just felt so awkward. He hummed to himself as he sauntered up the road towards the church.

Thanks to the dance classes, they had managed to put a Christmas dinner on the table – of sorts. Dorothea asked the children what they wanted instead of turkey, which was out of the question due to the rationing. They all voted for sausages and mash with gravy, followed by apple crumble and custard. So that's what they had. Grace managed to get milk, butter and eggs from Ivy and Alf, plus a small fruit cake, although there wasn't much fruit in it. Each member of the household got one present, all homemade. It was the best Dorothea could do.

They all gathered around the table in the library and spent the afternoon doing jigsaws and listening to music on the wireless. Grace made the cocoa and cut up the fruit cake. By ten o'clock they were all tucked up in their beds. Dorothea lay awake for quite some time before falling asleep. She dreamt of the townhouse in London, and of Raif.

"I wonder what sort of Christmas Raif and Bob had," said Daisy, handing Grace her tea.

Grace sat down at the kitchen table. The children were due home from school any minute and the lunch was almost ready.

"Iris seemed to get on well with Stuart at the dance, didn't she?"

"I think he likes her, Daisy. Although to be fair, he did dance with Meg and Kath as well."

"There weren't enough men to go around," laughed Daisy. "I can't believe the number of people that turned up. I heard one or two people asking when the next dance would be and if the classes would be continuing."

"The vicar didn't charge her for the use of the hall, you know," said Grace.

"That was kind of him."

"She made a generous donation to the church fund by way of a thank you and I think he appreciated it."

"I've notice that there are more people attending the Sunday morning service now. That's got to be down to the dance."

"Yes, I noticed that too. Dorothea and I had to sit on the back row last week. There was a terrible draught from somewhere. I must remember to take my cardigan next week."

"The children are here, Grace. I'll get the bowls out." Daisy opened the back door and shouted out to Dorothea and Jenny who were weeding in the back garden.

"Where's Josh?" asked Daisy.

"He's having afternoon tea with Mr Glass. It's his birthday and Kathleen's treating him and Josh, together with Alf," said Sam. "They're going to the cafe."

"He did mention it. I'd forgotten." Grace ladled out the soup and buttered some bread. They all washed their hands in the sink and sat down.

"Are you all right, miss? You look a bit pale," said Daisy on seeing Dorothea's face which had a slightly greenish tint to it.

"Yes, you do look all in," admitted Grace. "Get into bed and I'll fetch you a cup of tea and some aspirin. That's an order."

Seeing the look on Grace's face, Dorothea decided not to fight it. "Yes, I think I will have a lie down. It's nothing, just a bad headache."

When she'd gone, Jenny was all concern. "Was it my fault, Mummy? Did I do something wrong?"

"Goodness me. No, darling," said Daisy. "Aunt Dotty suffers from migraines. She's not had one for quite a while. It's probably the heat. It's very humid." Daisy hugged her daughter. "Now eat up, there's a good girl."

"She's asleep. The rest will do her good. Of course, we all know why she's unwell," said Grace, making her way over to the sink to start the dishes.

"I'm sure it would help if she received a letter from Raif. Three years and not a word," Daisy said. "Something's not right there. What do you think has happened, Grace?"

"I don't know, but I agree, something's not right. Josh said he'd speak to Earnest to see what he can find out. I mentioned it to him at the dance as well. Iris also asked Stuart to see if he can find out anything. The war office would have informed her if he was injured or missing. So, I suppose no news is good news."

"Iris hasn't had any news from Bob since she's been here with us either. She's getting anxious too. Let's hope there's some post for them soon."

The children were doing their homework in the library and Jenny was having a nap. Daisy got out the dusters and polish and put on her overalls.

"Oh, leave that. It can wait for once. Let's have a cup of tea," ordered Grace. "We've done enough for today."

Stuart arrived at the station early and immediately rang his friend at the London branch.

"Good morning, Graham. How's life treating you?"

"Stuart? Well, well. The honeypot man. How's things in Somerset? Keeping you busy, are they?" The Honeypot was the name of the cottage Stuart lived in. He smiled to himself. Fancy Graham remembering that. It must have been five years since he'd left London.

"Oh, you know how it is with this war. Not as bad as for you lot, but bad enough. Look, I'm after a favour. Can you do a bit of digging around and report back to me?"

"Fire away. I'll help if I can. Got to be worth a couple of beers at least."

Stuart laughed and got out his notes from the conversation he'd had with Iris.

"So, how was the tea, Josh?" asked Beth. She would secretly have loved to have been invited too as the idea of afternoon tea seemed very glamorous.

"All right. We got chapter and verse on his bowel habits. He wouldn't eat the scones which Kathleen had ordered. He said they didn't agree with him."

"Didn't agree with him?" said Grace. "You wouldn't see me refusing a scone."

"He said they turned his stools into hard rubbery pellets," Josh said. "He was talking in such a loud voice, I'm sure half the cafe heard him. Kath had to tell him to keep his voice down and change the subject."

"I should think so. Coming out with all that at the table whilst people are eating," Grace said, tutting.

Iris started laughing. "It's probably the way they're made. There is a war on after all. They're probably full of baking powder or something."

"He's been on to the war office about Uncle Raif. They're going to look into it and report back to him. He should have some news by next week." Josh looked at Aunty Dot and saw the look of concern on her face. He made up his mind to keep on at Mr Glass to get information.

Chapter Nineteen

The Monday morning post brought a letter for Dorothea, postmarked London. It was a large brown envelope containing two letters. One was from Celia and the other one was from the bank manager. She read Celia's letter first:

Dear Dorothea,

I cannot thank you enough for letting me rent your house. You are my saviour. I keep the blackout blinds drawn at the front of the house and only open the back ones when it's daylight. I've given all the rooms a good clean so everything is sparkling. I've managed to find a new job, which is good news. I only leave the house on the four days that I go to work and I exit via the back gate and turn into Fog Lane. As you know I decided to leave my old job in order to get away from Tom. I'm earning less money but I will be all right. I now work in a book publishers and the work is mainly cataloguing but as I say, all fine.

John next door has been a great help to me in tidying up the garden. We tackled it between us and it's now looking back to normal. We pool all our food rations and eat our evening meal together. He's very good company and I'm starting to feel more like my old self again. It's all down to you, Dorothea. I am so very grateful. I haven't felt this good about myself in years. It has put quite a spring in my step.

When I visited you last, the day after the WI meeting, I spotted Daisy pushing a trolley with a young child. She looked so like Iain, I was sure that she is my granddaughter. Please correct me if I'm wrong but I would so like to be part of the child's life. May I send a small gift for Easter? It would probably only be something homemade. The ladies from the WI will help me out, I'm sure, as I'm not a great craftswoman really.

I hope you are all managing to survive and stay fit and well. How very busy you must be with all the children. I will send you the mail in weekly batches, if that is all right with you.

Much love,
Celia

"Grace, you'd better read this letter. It's from Celia." Dorothea handed it over and opened the letter from the bank. They were sat at the kitchen table having their mid-morning tea break. Monday was wash day and they both pitched in, helping Daisy to get everything washed.

Dear Mrs Swift,

In response to your enquiry, I refer to the matter of your joint account. It would appear that an irregularity has taken place and the matter is now under investigation. Please accept our sincere apologies. I should know more in a few days' time when further details become available. I cannot say too much at this stage due to the seriousness of the situation but rest assured we will do all we can to resolve the matter.

Yours faithfully,
Mr C. Manns, Branch Manager

The front door bell rang, breaking into Dorothea's thoughts. "I'll get it, Grace."

She found Stuart, the local policeman, standing on the step.

"Hello Stuart, come in. If it's Iris you're after, she's at work," said Dorothea.

"No, actually it's you that I wanted to speak to. Just a quick word if I may."

"Come through into the library. I'll get us some tea. You make yourself comfortable." Dorothea ran through to the kitchen to put the kettle on. "It's Stuart. He wants a quick word."

"I'll make the tea, Dotty, and bring it in," said Grace. "Find out what he wants."

Grace filled the kettle and got out the cups, wondering what on earth Stuart could want with Dorothea. She hoped it wasn't anything serious.

"We're investigating Juliet Barnes. I presume you've heard of her?" Stuart asked.

"Yes. She was engaged to Raif. It was before he met me. She didn't take it well at the time when he broke off the engagement."

"So I gather. Do you know anything about the boyfriend? The one she was seeing whilst engaged to Raif. Martin Blackwood?"

"No, I've never heard of him. Sorry."

"It would seem they have been working together, emptying people's bank accounts. She's been forging cheques and he's been intercepting people's mail, namely Raif's. We searched their premises and found enough evidence to convict them. They're both under arrest."

"Does Raif know about any of this?" Dorothea asked, not knowing whether to be shocked or relieved that it wasn't down to her husband that the account was now empty.

"We've not managed to trace him yet. Mr Manns has written to him explaining briefly, but I suppose he's got more important things going on at the moment."

"Yes, I know. I haven't heard from him myself. It's getting on nearly four years now." Dorothea felt her face reddening and was relieved when Grace appeared with the tea.

"We're looking into that as well. We'll find out what we can, so don't worry too much. Mr Manns has assured us that all will be resolved regarding your account, so don't go worrying yourself unduly on that score either. If you're short of money, you would be quite within your rights to ask for a loan, temporarily, to tide you over. It is the bank's fault after all. Mr Manns had to report to the head office as they're not sure at this stage exactly how long this little scenario has been going on. Juliet has been in their employment for quite some years it would seem."

"That's right. Raif and I have been married for fourteen years this year. She worked at the bank well before that. Were they living together? Juliet and this Martin?"

"Oh yes. Nice little set up according to my mate Graham in London. A mews property in Kensington. Beautifully fitted out inside."

"How did you know this Martin was intercepting Raif's mail?" asked Dorothea.

"He was followed. Caught in the act. He waited until the mail was placed in the mailbox at the end of the driveway, then he hung around until the postman disappeared. He then helped himself to the mail and stuffed the letters into his pocket. He denied it all, of course, when questioned. Reckoned it was all Juliet's doing. She did the same when we arrested her. She blamed everything on him."

"They sound as bad as each other."

"Her mother came down to the station and made quite a scene, protesting her daughter's innocence. She said she was under Martin's influence. She was so abusive that they had to caution her. I can see where the daughter gets it from."

"So, what happens now?"

"They'll be charged. Could be looking at a custodial sentence for her, due to the length of time this has been going on. Not sure about him though. Forgery is a very serious offence. I can't see any judge being lenient just because there's a war on. I'll keep you updated with developments. Thanks for the tea." Stuart stood up to leave, wondering whether to ask about the dance classes, but he thought better of it. Now wasn't the right time. He would give anything to be able to dance with Iris again.

"Thank you, Stuart, I'd appreciate that."

A series of air raids disrupted their sleep five nights in a row. Dorothea found some books of plays by various authors. She sifted through them and marked the ones she deemed suitable for children. They spent their evenings in the Anderson shelter reading these plays aloud. Everyone played a part, putting on accents which the children found hilarious. Dorothea would hang up the Davy lamp so they could see in the dark. She though it would be good for them to develop their reading skills and it proved to be successful. It helped to pass the time and kept them all amused, as sleep was impossible.

They were packed in like sardines with their knees touching and wrapped themselves in blankets to keep warm. They drank tea from the three flasks Grace had filled. They whiled away the hours like this until the all clear sounded and they could escape back into the house.

Mr Glass received news from the war office that Raif's aircraft had taken a hit and come down into the sea. No more had been heard from them. His co-pilot was Mrs Kloot's husband, Charles. Dorothea was distraught.

A few days after receiving this news, Iris received a letter from her husband, Bob, who was in the Royal Navy. The good news was Raif and Charles had been picked up by Bob's ship. They'd both been in the water for several hours by this time but Raif, being a strong swimmer, managed to keep them both afloat. Charles had swallowed a lot of sea water and was sick and struggling to breathe. He had been airlifted off the ship by helicopter and taken to the nearest infirmary.

Chapter Twenty

The house was unusually quiet as everyone was out. The children were at school and Daisy had taken Jenny to the village for the weekly shop. Dorothea had gone to see the vicar regarding using the church hall for more dance classes.

Grace made herself a cup of tea and carried it up to her room. She decided to have a lie down whilst it was quiet. As she lay on her bed sipping her tea, she reflected on how things had developed over the four years since the children arrived. It hadn't been easy in the beginning but Dorothea's strictness soon licked them into shape. There had been some difficult and awkward moments to begin with but Dorothea's ideas regarding keeping them active and interested seemed to have worked wonderfully well. They were all teenagers now and were developing into well-rounded individuals. She instilled into them the importance of learning and opening their minds to new activities and events.

"The learning process goes on until the day you die," she had told them.

More importantly, she insisted on them being well spoken, well-mannered and respectful of other people at all times. Grace would never have thought it possible initially, but things had turned out rather well. The fact the children adored Dotty went without saying. She just hoped they had a space in their hearts for herself and Daisy too, for they were a family in the true sense of the word. Little Jenny thought of them as her brothers and sister, for she didn't know any different. She wondered how she would react when they all went back to their families at the end of the war, but she preferred not to think about that. She said a silent prayer to keep them all safe.

Dorothea received a letter from the war office confirming what Earnest had told her regarding Raif. Meanwhile, she managed to get herself a job with the local bus company. It was five mornings a week, Monday to Friday from eight in the morning until noon covering a circuitous route of five or six miles around the neighbouring towns. The route was easy for her as she knew the roads. It gave her a small income which was greatly needed as Celia's rent money was going to Grace and Daisy. Expecting them to work for nothing ate away at her conscience and she was glad to be in a position to give them a little something. It meant giving up her fire watch and ARP duties but she was feeling better in herself as she was now getting a proper night's sleep – air raids permitting. Most days, she arrived home at the same time as the children, just in time for lunch.

Making her way around the side of the house, she could hear the children chatting in the kitchen. They were all seated at the table when she entered.

"Hello Aunty Dot. We're just about to start," said Beth.

"You carry on. I'll just go upstairs and change." Dorothea cast off her uniform and laid it on the bed. Tonight was the fourth week of the new dance classes. They'd learnt the quickstep, the rumba and the tango so far. She was undecided about tonight's lesson. It would have to be the samba or the two-step. The dance was to be the following Saturday.

"I've dug some material out of the loft," said Dorothea on seating herself at the table. "I'll make us something to wear for the dance next week. Beth, you can help me. I'll show you how to cut out the patterns and sew the seams together on the old treadle sewing machine. We'll make some shirts for the boys too."

Beth's eyes sparkled like diamonds. A new dress. She hadn't had any new clothes for a long time. "I shall enjoy that, Aunt Dot. Thank you."

The boys, not wanting to miss out on a new skill, all chimed in. "We'll help too."

"Good," said Dorothea. "We'll make a start tomorrow. It's going to be wet so we won't be going walking and the garden will be sodden. It will give us something to focus our minds on."

"What are you doing with these?" asked Earnest.

His daughter Kathleen was spreading out an old pair of curtains on the floor.

"They're from the back bedroom," she said. "I thought I'd try to make something to wear for the dance on Saturday."

"Good luck with that. I'm off to Alf's. We're going for a pint in the village."

"Don't be too late, Dad."

"I can look after myself, you know. I'm not a teenager."

"I know, but I worry when you're out."

He kissed the top of her head and left via the back door. Their dog, Raffles, made an attempt to follow him, hoping for another walk.

"You've had your walk today, Raffles," said Kath, ruffling his ears. "We'll stroll around the garden later."

He was rescued from a house fire a year ago and Earnest had brought him home. He was only a puppy then and they had to bathe him in the tin bath in the yard as he was full of soot.

She rooted out an old dress pattern and decided to omit the sleeves. She couldn't do sleeves and anyway, there wasn't much time. The next hour was spent cutting and snipping until she had finally achieved the right fit. She pinned the pieces together and got out her sewing box.

Thinking about the dance last Christmas Eve brought back happy memories for her. The highlight of the evening was the dance she'd had with Stuart. She was hoping he would ask her out on a date but he only seemed to have eyes for Iris who was better looking and more vivacious. Stuart wasn't the only man giving Iris the eye, she observed. The manager from the library, Norman Potts, for one and the school headmaster, Lionel Waters, was seen chatting to her at the drinks counter for quite some time. She wished she could be more like Iris. *But such is life, those of us not blessed with good looks just have to make the most of it,* she told herself.

Earnest came home just after ten thirty carrying a bundle.

"What have you got there, Dad?" Kath had walked Raffles around the garden for half an hour then got ready for bed. She greeted her dad in the hallway, tying the belt of her dressing gown tightly around her. It had seen better days and was practically in holes.

"Edna's cat had a litter. She was giving them away."

"Dad, we can't have a cat with Raffles. They won't get on."

"How do you know that?" He handed over the little kitten which had dark fur and a white bib. Its two front paws had white tips and it had big blue eyes which seemed too big for its face.

"I'll ask Iris at work on Monday. They might take it. I know it's Beth's birthday soon. It would make a nice present. Do you want some cocoa?"

"Aye, go on then. It's a bit parky out."

They sat in the kitchen as it was warmer.

"What was the name of that ship Iris' husband was on?" asked Earnest out of the blue.

"I don't know, Dad. Why do you ask?"

"Oh, it doesn't matter. We'd best get into our beds. Good night, lass."

It was Sunday morning and the rain was batting against the window panes in great torrents.

The dance had been an even bigger success than the last one with more people attending from neighbouring villages. Dorothea threw open the doors so people could dance out in the courtyard as the hall was so packed. Joshua danced with his classmate Rebecca, who was becoming a very good friend. The more he got to know her, the more he liked her. Her father had joined the army along with her elder brother who was eighteen, so there was only her mother and their dog for company.

It was seven thirty and nobody was awake yet, so Josh quickly dressed and made his way down into the kitchen to forage for something to eat. He poured himself a glass of milk and buttered a slice of bread. The windows were taped up behind the blackout blinds but he could just see the rain beginning to ease off.

He quickly scribbled a note for the family telling them he was going to see Mr Glass before church at ten thirty. He checked himself in the mirror which hung in the hallway to see if he was respectable before creeping out of the back door. He ran along the lane at quite a speed. He couldn't stand having nothing to do and just wanted to be out and about.

Kathleen was at the stove stirring the porridge when he knocked.

"Hello Josh. You're up and about early this morning. There's nothing wrong, is there?"

"No, the others aren't up yet and I was bored. Is Mr Glass up yet?"

"Yes, he's just polishing his shoes. Do you want some of this porridge? There's plenty."

"Yes please, Aunty Kath."

Josh popped his head into the dining room to see Mr Glass putting his cleaning kit away. His face lit up when he saw Josh. He didn't get many visitors these days and he was always glad to see the lad as he was a delight and took an interest in everything that was going on around him. He was becoming quite fond of him.

"Breakfast is served," shouted Kath, placing the bowls on the table. "Dad, you know when you asked me the other night what the name of Bob's ship was? Well, I've just remembered, it's HMS Swift. The same as Dorothea's surname. That's how I remembered it."

"Yes, that's right," said Josh, who was now all ears. "Why? What have you heard, Mr Glass?"

"It was just something Alf said in the pub the other night whilst we were having a drink. He keeps up to date on all the ships, being an ex-Navy man. The papers are full of news about the Normandy landings at the moment. I'm sure Alf said the HMS Swift was sunk by a mine near Sword Beach. There were a good number of casualties by all accounts, although numbers haven't been confirmed yet."

"Oh, Dad!"

"Don't say anything to Iris yet. Let's just wait and see. We don't want to upset the lass. He might have… actually, I've just thought of something else…"

"So have I," said Josh. "Uncle Raif was also on that ship."

"Good grief. Is there any way we can find out for sure?" said Kath.

"Alf doesn't normally go to church as there's too much to do on the farm but Ivy's usually there. We'll talk to her." Earnest picked up his mug of tea then added, "Now remember, mum's the word, Josh, until we know for certain."

Chapter Twenty-One

The evening meal was almost ready and Grace put the plates on top of the range to warm. She looked forward to all the family gathering around the table and to hearing all their news, especially Josh. Being a very sociable boy, he always had amusing tales to tell and Grace loved hearing them. It gave her a picture of what village life was all about.

Smiling to herself, she recalled some of the incidents Josh had encountered on his rounds. Mr Glass was often at the centre of these skirmishes. Last week, he had a run-in with the butcher about his sausages being full of sawdust. Ivy had a set-to with Edna, who knitted a cardigan for the church fund-raising day. She'd sewn odd buttons down the front as she couldn't find any that matched. Ivy said she wouldn't insult anyone with it, which resulted in a heated exchange which was intercepted by the vicar, who reminded them they were in God's home and could they please tone it down. Alf was driving the hay rick when a bale of hay flew off the top and knocked Stuart off his bicycle. Josh said it was the funniest thing he'd seen. He was outside the school gates talking to Rebecca when it happened. They ran across to help Stuart. He was unhurt but annoyed with Alf for not securing the bales properly. Josh and Rebecca dragged the hay bale up the lane to the farm and got a free ice cream from Ivy. Alf got his ears bent by Stuart, then he immediately got out the whisky to smooth things over.

Daisy came in from the garden carrying a small bunch of herbs. "Will these do, Grace?"

"Champion. I'll just chop them and add them to the casserole. Did you have a chance to read Celia's letter?"

"I did. I'm not sure about this, Grace. I can't forget what her son did but I know it would be unfair to Jenny. She is her grandmother when all is said and done. Who am I to deny her that privilege? What do you think?"

"I agree. It's not as though she's going to be nipping down here to see the lass every week."

"I'll tell Dotty to mention it in her next letter. I'll have to be careful what I tell Jenny when the gift arrives though. She's asked me where her daddy is a couple of times. She wanted to know if he was fighting in the war like Uncle Raif. I tried to explain that we weren't together and lived separately, but she's too young to understand. I don't ever want her to know the truth. It would be too awful for her."

Grace smiled and thought what a lucky girl Jenny was to have a mother like Daisy.

Saturday morning brought a visit from Mr Glass and Kathleen. Earnest had a rolled-up newspaper under his arm. He silently unravelled it and laid it open at the appropriate page to read: HMS Swift sunk by a mine off the coast of Normandy, close to Sword Beach. Iris read it with care, then turned very pale and handed the page to Dorothea, who read it aloud so they could hear.

"I'll make us some tea," said Daisy.

"Were there any survivors, do we know?" asked Samuel.

"I don't suppose they'll know for certain just yet," said Earnest. "We'll have to wait and see. We can only hope."

"What a thing to happen," said Grace. "Raif surviving an attack and then after spending what must have been hours in the water, being picked up by the ship, only for it to be destroyed like that."

"Raif's a very strong swimmer. Maybe he managed to get ashore," Josh offered hopefully.

There was a long silence before Beth spoke. "Let's pray and hope for a miracle. I've got a feeling they're both still alive. Don't ask me why, but I just feel it."

Dorothea put her arm around her shoulders, "Let's hope you're right." She went over to Iris and hugged her. "I can tell you something, Iris. If Raif did get off that ship and swim to the shore, I'm damn sure he'd have taken Bob with him. He'd make it his business to see him right. They didn't make him flight lieutenant for nothing." She knew she was talking nonsense but she had to say something to reassure Iris. "Let's not give up hope yet until we've had it confirmed. They may have survived. Stranger things have happened throughout this war."

Chapter Twenty-Two

Inspired by one of the plays the family had spent hours reading, Howard wrote a children's book based on eccentric characters. It was centred around a wealthy family who had a butler called Cedric. The lady of the house kept taking in stray animals until they ended up with three dogs, three cats and two rabbits. The animals slowly take over, much to the annoyance of Cedric. Samuel read it and was so impressed he showed it to Dorothea.

"Do you think Celia could show it to her employers and get it published?" he asked.

Dorothea read it and had to agree that it was humorous and well written. "I'll write to her. There's no harm in asking. I'll make a copy and send it."

Howard was in the library working on his follow-up book when Dorothea came in with the letter. It was from Celia advising that after some persuasion from herself and her boss' wife, they'd decided to publish the book. Howard had never been so shocked in his life. The letter asked him to call into their offices at his earliest convenience to discuss illustrations.

"We'll go next week," said Dorothea. "I'll write back straight away."

The children were very excited. A published author? Who would have thought it?

They had just settled around the table in the library when there was a knock at the door. It was Stuart.

"Sorry to disturb you, Daisy. I need a word with Dorothea, if possible." He took off his helmet and stepped into the kitchen.

He looks very serious, thought Daisy as she went into the library to fetch Dotty.

He was seated at the table when Dorothea entered the kitchen.

"Hello Stuart." She saw the look of concern on his face and knew instantly that whatever he had to say, it wasn't going to be good news.

"I'm afraid I've got some very sad news, Mrs Swift." Dorothea's heart missed a beat. She felt sure it had something to do with Raif or Bob.

"We've had a report regarding the death of a Mrs Lockwood. Young Howard's mother."

"Oh no," exclaimed Dorothea. "What's happened?"

"It would appear that she drank herself to death. She was an alcoholic according to all that knew her."

"Gracious heavens. Are you sure? I can't believe it."

"According to her neighbour, a lady of a similar age to herself who'd known her for a number of years, she'd had a problem with alcohol ever since she lost her husband. She went to pieces. Strangely, three months before her death, she had decided to straighten herself out. She was missing Howard and realised the poor lad deserved better. Eaten up with guilt about the neglect, she hadn't touched a drop for weeks when an unfortunate incident took place and it tipped her over the edge.

"Two weeks ago, she remarried. Unfortunately, he was also an alcoholic. He was someone she'd met in the pub and he'd had his eye on her for some time. He filled her head with all sorts of nonsense about how she would be a kept woman and could give up work and hold her head up high in society. I think she saw it as a fresh start in life. A chance to turn her life around. He saw things very differently. She handed in her notice at the factory where she worked and married him. The marriage only lasted about a week when he upped sticks and left. Just took off into the night and she never saw him again. He left a note to say that she was stifling the life out of him. It seems he didn't like this new sober version of her. It wasn't what he'd signed up for when he married her, preferring the fun-loving, jovial woman he'd met in the pub. No doubt he saw their future together whiling the hours away in drunken bliss. At the same time, he'd got someone to cook all his meals for him, keep house and generally look after him.

"Of course, she then had to go back to the factory, cap in hand begging for her job back. The women on the factory floor gave her a hard time. She'd 'given herself airs and graces way above her station in life,' they said. Telling everyone she'd no need to work anymore and was going to be a kept woman. The post mortem showed that she had downed a full bottle of aspirin with about two bottles of gin."

"Poor woman. What a rake he must have been to just take off like that. He might at least have sat down and discussed things with her before taking off into the night like that. What a coward."

"Yes, I agree, but he wasn't that sort of bloke. He only saw life through the bottom of a beer glass."

Chapter Twenty-Three

October 1944

"Dolly's got herself a gentleman friend," said Josh. "An admirer. Edna's livid."

"Why?" said Grace.

"I don't really know but Sam and I heard them arguing in the library and Norman had to have a word with them to keep their voices down."

They were all around the table in the library having just finished their evening meal.

"I think Edna's concerned about being left on her own. She and Dolly have lived together since they were girls," said Sam.

"Where did she meet him and who is he?" asked Iris.

"His name's Aubrey," said Josh.

"He's a gardener," added Sam. "He was recommended by a lady from the WI. They're finding their garden a bit too much to tackle themselves these days."

"Yes, well, it is a large garden and there are a lot of trees and bushes," said Dorothea. "But why were they arguing? Surely if Dolly's managed to find a companion, Edna should be pleased for her."

"I think Edna had designs on him for herself, judging by the conversation they were having. She accused Dolly of 'muscling in'. Is that what they say?" said Sam.

Grace was loving this conversation. She'd never had much time for Edna as she was apt to be rather bossy and domineering. *Poor*

Dolly's had to put up with it all these years. If she's found an escape route with this Aubrey, then good for her, she thought.

"According to Edna, he's got quite a few women on the go," Sam continued.

"How does she know?" asked Meg. "It sounds like jealousy to me."

"We must try to find someone for Edna, then she won't feel left out," offered Beth. "I know what it's like to feel lonely, having an elder brother who never had time for me. Dad only ever wanted boys, so all his attention went on Alan. I often felt left out, so I know how Edna feels."

Dorothea put her arms around Beth and gave her a hug. "Well, not anymore."

Howard immediately thought of his own childhood and how isolated he felt most of the time. "Beth's right, perhaps we can let her know that she would be welcome to come here if and when she feels lonely?" He looked across at Dorothea for approval.

"She knows lots of ladies at the WI. I can't see that she's ever going to be that lonely. She's one of the organisers. She's been doing it for years," said Dorothea. "Perhaps you can have a word with her, Grace, at the next meeting?"

"I'll see what I can find out," said Grace, not really intending to do any such thing. The thought of having Edna in her kitchen criticising everything would be a bitter pill to swallow and one she could well do without.

Josh started to think about his own childhood, especially the years following the death of his mother and knew the feeling of isolation all too well.

"I'll keep an eye on her and pop in from time to time on my rounds," Josh said. "If I think there's anything amiss, I'll let you all know. It's the least we can do."

"Good lad," said Grace.

"Howard took it rather well, didn't he? His mother's death, I mean," whispered Daisy. They were lying in their beds drinking the cocoa.

"Yes, poor lad. He said he'd been expecting it to happen a lot sooner, but he didn't know about the marriage. She never told him," said Grace. "The good thing is, he wrote to her a few weeks before she died, telling her how happy and settled he was here in Somerset and not to worry about him at all."

"It's almost as though he had a premonition that something was going to happen."

"He never doubted her love for him, just that she was sick. Alcoholism is an illness. She couldn't cope after her husband died, poor woman."

"What did his father die of?"

"Pneumonia. He went to see the doctor feeling unwell and a week later, he was dead."

The meeting with the book publisher had to be postponed for two weeks whilst they made the funeral arrangements. Dorothea was surprised to see quite a few local families attending the funeral. It would seem Mrs Lockwood was well liked despite her fondness for the drink.

When the service was over, they were just about to get back into the jeep when Dorothea felt a tap on the shoulder. It was Irene, the next-door neighbour.

"We've had a little collection in the road for young Howard," she whispered in her ear. "We thought it would be more useful to him than a wreath of flowers. It's not much, but it's something."

"Oh, how very kind. Thank you, Irene. I'll see that he gets it." She quickly put the envelope into her handbag and gave her a kiss and a hug.

"I've boxed up all her things. They're in the spare room. If Howard wants any of it, then he can take it back with him. Otherwise, I'll dispose of what's left. Not that she had much mind you. Towards the end, I think she'd pawned most of her possessions."

They went back to Irene's house where they were treated to tea and cake. Howard didn't want anything except a few photographs. Three, to be precise. One of his mum and dad on their wedding day, one of Howard's christening, and one of the three of them on the sands at Brighton during the summer when he was four years old, just before he started school.

The meeting with the publisher went wonderfully well. Celia helped out with some illustrations of various cats, dogs and rabbits. A young illustrator, straight out of art college, had been engaged to carry out her first professional assignment. The prints were humorous and appealing. Celia's boss had asked the young illustrator, whose name was Belinda, to do some more sketches of the other members of the household too, as he thought it would help to sell the book. They finished the meeting with tea and biscuits in Celia's office.

That evening, they all ate together at John's house. He proved himself to be a very good cook.

"We've probably eaten the whole of your meat rations for the next month," laughed Dorothea.

"No, we've been saving them up," said Celia. "It is a special occasion after all."

They stayed overnight at the townhouse and then made their way back to Somerset the next morning. Howard was very subdued for a few days and Dorothea kept him off school for a week. She told him he must now consider Somerset as his permanent home, after which he seemed to buck up and was soon back to his old self.

"Hurry up, Mummy. Mrs Kloot will be here soon," said Jenny.

"I'm nearly done. You go in, darling. I'll be along in a minute." Daisy cleared away the last of the dinner plates before wiping down the range. She was tired and not really in the mood for a French lesson tonight. It had been a long day and she felt as though there was a head cold trying to break out. She answered the knock at the back door to find Rosine waving a letter in her hand.

"Hello Rosie, come in. What have you got there?"

"It's a letter from Charles. It came this afternoon. I've brought it so you can all read it," she gushed. Her eyes were wide with excitement. *It must be good news*, thought Daisy, *otherwise she would be weeping.*

Rosine waited until they were all seated at the table before opening the letter. "It's dated six months ago. Goodness knows where it has been but it only arrived today."

There was a stunned silence around the room as she read out the contents of the letter. It was all in French, so she had to translate it into English.

Charles and Raif had been flying near the Normandy coast when there had been an almighty bang and their plane caught fire. They lost height rapidly and before they knew it, they hit the water.

Fortunately, the plane was sideways on when it landed and Raif managed to get the door open and pull them both free. Charles had already swallowed a lot of sea water by this time and was only kept afloat by Raif. They were in the water for what seemed like hours before being spotted by a ship, which they managed to get aboard.

Charles had been struggling to breathe so they bundled him into the helicopter and took him to the infirmary. He spent the next three days wired up to a drip and an oxygen mask before being able to breathe normally.

He finished the letter by saying he was all right and not to worry about him, hailing Raif as a hero, without whose help he wouldn't be alive to tell the tale. He hoped she was well and safe and he was counting the days until they could be together again.

"So, if that was six months ago, where is he now?" asked Josh.

"I don't know. Maybe he was declared fit to recommence his duties, perhaps?"

"Let's hope so," said Dorothea who was concerned for Raif and Bob. She hadn't had a single night's sleep since hearing about the ship being sunk and knew Iris hadn't either. She glanced across at Iris who was looking down at her hands resting in her lap.

Rosine must have sensed their mood for she added, "I know this is hard for you both." She looked across at Iris and then at Dorothea. "Let us hope there is more good news soon."

"Is there such a thing as good news in any of this?" sighed Dorothea. "I'll be so relieved when this is all over and we can get back to living a normal life again. Whatever that is."

Chapter Twenty-Four

Beth crept into the boys' bedroom just as they were all scrambling into bed. Hearing them whispering, she wanted to join in the conversation.

"You're lucky, Howard, being able to stay. I don't want to leave this house, ever," she said, parking herself on the end of his bed.

"I'll have to find work and pay rent," he whispered. "I can't expect to live here free of charge. Not long term anyway. Of course, all that is dependent on Uncle Raif being agreeable to the idea. He might not like it. I have to consider that."

"That's if he comes back," said Josh. "Aunty Dot and Iris haven't heard anything since the ship went down. We don't know if Uncle Raif and Bob are even alive."

"I've got a feeling they are both still alive," reassured Beth. "I think they'll both come home too. Don't ask me how I know, I just feel it."

"I hope you prove to be correct, Beth," said Sam. "Otherwise things could get difficult for all of us. I don't want to leave this house either. I like being here with you lot and Jenny too. I can't imagine… well, I'm not going to even think about it. Not yet anyway."

"Me too," said Josh. "I'm hoping Uncle Raif will let me stay. What about you, Beth?"

"I'm not leaving. I'm staying here. Wild horses couldn't drag me out."

"Your parents might insist on you going back," said Sam.

"Then I'll just have to find a good reason to stay. We'll make a pact to all stay together. Uncle Raif will know what to do, I'm sure."

"Agreed," they all chorused.

"Come on, you lot, get those lights out. It's ten o'clock," said Grace. "Beth, why aren't you in bed?"

"We were just chatting about Uncle Raif and Bob. We're all worried."

"I know, sweetheart, but let's sleep on it. All we can do for now is to get on with living."

There was much excitement in the village as there was to be a wedding at the church. It was early November and the weather was icy cold. Aubrey and Dolly were to be married at two o'clock. Aubrey, lothario or not, said he'd found the woman of his dreams and was in love. He proposed and Dolly accepted. Edna told her she was mad at her age to even consider it. Dorothea, with Beth's help, made Dolly a new suit in cream silk. It fitted her like a glove.

It was decided they would live at Aubrey's house and there was to be no honeymoon as they deemed it unsafe to travel anywhere. Dorothea also made a new outfit for Edna out of some nice blue material she had left over from the dancing outfits they'd made earlier in the year. Grace thought she looked crestfallen during the ceremony and actually started to feel sorry for her.

They held a simple reception in the church hall with pots of tea and a two-tier cake which one of the WI ladies had made. The butcher donated some sausage meat so they could make sausage rolls, which the children devoured together with fruit jellies.

"Are you all right, Edna?" asked Grace, sitting down beside her.

Edna seemed not to have heard at first, then turned to face her and there were tears in her eyes. She just nodded and Grace knew she was too choked to speak.

"She's not going far, only a couple of streets away," said Grace. "You'll still see each other, you know. It will be strange at first, no doubt, but you'll get used to it. Then there's the WI. You've lots of friends, dear. Don't despair."

Edna fumbled in her handbag for a handkerchief and the next minute she was sobbing.

"Would you like to go home?" asked Grace.

Edna nodded and stood up to leave.

Stuart stepped in and offered to escort her. "Don't worry, Grace, I'll see that she's all right."

"There's a leaflet here from Edna. The WI are organising a fund-raising day. It's for the 'war on want' or something, for the families who've been bombed and lost their homes. She came into the shop with it this afternoon and asked if we could consider making a contribution," said Meg. "There's various categories. Cake baking, picture painting, dress making, flower arranging, best homemade biscuit…"

"Presumably we've to find our own materials and ingredients?" asked Iris.

"Well, yes, I think that's the general idea."

"Josh and I could make something for the dress making section. Have we any material left, Aunty Dot?" Beth asked.

"I'm not sure what's left, I'll have to check what's up in the loft."

"I'll have a go at the cake and Daisy could bake some biscuits." Grace looked at Daisy for approval.

"I'll do a painting," offered Sam.

"So, that leaves the three of us," said Meg, looking at Dorothea and Iris.

"What's left?" asked Iris. "I don't fancy flower arranging. Where would we get the flowers in November?"

"You're right. We haven't got any. Our garden, what's left of it, is full of weeds. We need the allotment otherwise we'd all starve." Dorothea couldn't drum up any enthusiasm for this project. "We've done enough knitting. I'm not doing any more. We've no more wool left anyway. I've used all Raif's old jumpers. I vote we all do a painting with Sam. Jenny can do one too. So that's one cake, one batch of biscuits, one dress and four paintings. That should keep Edna quiet. How did she seem when she came into the shop, Meg?"

"She's still a little quiet. Ever since Dolly left for wedded bliss, she's lost that fiery spark."

"Fiery spark? That's not what I'd have called it. It'll do her good. She was far too bossy by my reckoning," barked Grace. "It's about the only thing she didn't get her own way on. Poor Dolly. What she put up with all those years… the woman's a saint."

"I'm inclined to agree," Dorothea chipped in. "What about you, Howard? What do you fancy doing?"

"It says here," he said, studying the flyer, "Best children's toy. I can have a go at making something for that. Can I have a root in the loft with you, Aunty Dot, to see what I can salvage?"

"I can't bring the chest down. It's too heavy. So, we'll go up there tomorrow before tea."

"Who's doing the judging?" Iris asked.

"I dread to think." Grace pulled a face. "Hopefully it won't be Edna."

They all laughed and got out the jigsaw they'd started two nights ago.

It was Saturday evening and there hadn't been any air raids for over a week. Iris did the shopping as Daisy was fretting over Jenny, who had a bad cold. She managed to get meat from the butcher which went into the hotpot.

"Wash your hands, you lot," Grace shouted. "Meg will be home soon. Then we can all eat."

They were just getting sat down around the table when Meg appeared.

"I'll just nip upstairs and change, Grace," she said kicking off her shoes and hanging up her coat in the hallway.

"She looks tired," Grace said to anyone that was listening. "She's on her feet all day in that shop. It's all right for Evelyn. She's sat down behind the post office counter."

"There's a fair amount of lifting too, moving all the boxes of stock about. Ken can't do it with his weak heart," said Iris.

Meg took off her overalls and pulled on a wool skirt and jumper. She hadn't received any letter from Eddie and she wondered if he'd received hers telling him where she was now living. She was tempted to write another letter but decided against it. He'd obviously forgotten all about her and who could blame him? After the war, he would probably go home to Canada and get on with his life. She felt the tears welling up in her eyes but quickly pulled herself together.

"So, what's new everyone?" Iris asked, hoping for some light entertainment.

Meg started to laugh and replied, "You'll never guess. Edna came into the shop today asking us to put a postcard in the window. She's hoping to let out Dolly's old room and take in a lodger."

"Good for her. I suppose the extra money will help."

"They'll need a strong constitution, whoever takes it," mused Grace.

"Yes. Good luck to them," agreed Dorothea. "I couldn't live with her."

"Me neither."

They all laughed.

Grace was just finishing the washing up when Meg whispered in her ear, "Grace, Dotty was in the phone booth again this morning. I'm sure she was on to the bank. Do you know if she's heard anything yet, regarding that scenario with her account?"

"No, she hasn't said anything to me, but I know she went to the police station to speak to Stuart again."

"Did she mention what…?"

"No, unfortunately, and I'm a bit wary of asking her for fear of upsetting her."

"Right," said Meg. "I'll speak to her. Perhaps we can all have a word later when the children are in bed?"

"I wouldn't want her to think she's carrying this problem alone. We're family now."

Meg gave Grace a hug and fetched the tea cloth to start drying the dishes.

* * *

"So, what did you find out from Stuart?" asked Meg after broaching the subject of the missing money.

"It seems the manager, Mr Manns, has disappeared," said Dorothea.

"Disappeared?"

"Yes. They don't know where he is. They gave him a hard time when he went to head office. They wanted to know how on earth this situation had gone on for over three years without anyone noticing anything irregular. He had no answers for them and left in a bit of a temper. He hasn't been into the bank since and he's left his lodgings."

"Charming. So, we're back to square one?" said Grace.

"Well, the deputy bank manager is taking over the handling of it, Mr Lawrence Mehan. He's promised to get things moving for me. Stuart's in regular contact with his friend at the London police station." Dorothea sighed and rubbed her temples. "Oh, I do wish Raif was here to sort this out."

Iris put her arm around her shoulders and said, "Never mind, Dotty, we've got the allotment so we'll not starve. Just think how healthy we'll be when the war's over. I've never eaten so much fruit and vegetables. And Grace's salads are to die for."

"Thanks," said Grace and Daisy, pleased to know their efforts were appreciated.

"I'd never tasted herbs before," added Meg. "I quite like them. They can really lift a dish or a salad. I love cinnamon and nutmeg too. What I really miss is sherry trifle."

"My mother used to make a lovely sherry trifle," said Daisy. It was the first time she'd mentioned her mother since the bombing.

Grace made a mental note to ask Earnest if he could find out anything more from the war office regarding Raif and Bob. She wondered if there were any survivors. Josh had said there were fifty-three casualties, according to Mr Glass.

Dorothea was just walking back to the house after her shift, having parked the bus in the depot, when she heard someone calling her name. She turned around to see Stuart cycling towards her.

"Stuart." She smiled at him, hoping for some good news.

"I just wanted a quick word, Dorothea. I won't keep you as I know you'll be tired and wanting your lunch. It was just to let you know that Graham rang me this morning to advise us that they've managed to locate the bank manager, Mr Manns. He had some sort of a breakdown. His mother died very suddenly. Natural causes from what Graham tells me. She was eighty-nine. He went to pieces and fled to her house where he's been ever since. His elder brother answered the door when the local bobby called. They were making the funeral arrangements. The post mortem delayed things and they had to wait for it to be completed before they'd release the body. The funeral's fixed for next week but his brother told us that he's not sure if Mr Manns will be going back to work at the bank any time soon as he wasn't in a fit state. He was very close to his mother and although she was eighty-nine, her death shook him up. He didn't see it coming as she hadn't been ill or anything."

"I suppose when you get to that age anything can happen. I don't mean that in a nasty way. I witnessed it with my own parents. Here one minute, gone the next. Thanks, Stuart. I appreciate your efforts. Would you like to come back to the house now and have a spot of lunch with us?"

"No, I'll not inconvenience you. I've got quite a bit of paperwork to catch up on before I finish my shift today."

"Well, feel free to call in any time for a cup of tea whenever you're passing. You'll be most welcome."

"I will. Take care."

She stood watching him as he cycled back up the road towards the station.

When she arrived at the house, there appeared to be a bit of a panic on. Daisy and Grace were flapping about like mother hens.

"Oh, miss. Thank goodness, you're home. There's been an accident. Beth's been taken to the infirmary."

"What's happened? Is it serious?" Dorothea's heart went into overdrive, suddenly realising the responsibility of taking care of other people's children. If anything happened to them whilst they were in her care, she knew she'd never forgive herself.

"It's not serious according to Doctor Mattison. Beth and Jenny were helping out at the farm when Beth got butted by one of the sheep and she fell against the wall, banging her head in the process. She lost consciousness and was feeling sick when she came round. Doctor Mattison said he thought it was concussion but sent for an ambulance to get her properly checked out," said Grace, fighting for her breath with every sentence.

"Oh dear, Grace. We'd better get to the hospital straight away. Is anyone with her?"

"Yes, Ivy is. She's beside herself with worry."

"Daisy, will you be all right here until we get back?"

"Yes, of course, miss," she said, herding the children back to the dinner table.

It was late afternoon when they all got back to the house. Daisy was all alone as the children had all gone about their various duties. Iris and Meg hadn't arrived home from work yet and she was relieved to see Dorothea in the jeep. The ambulance swung into the driveway behind the jeep and Grace climbed out, followed by Beth in a wheelchair.

"Is everything all right, miss?" asked Daisy, hugging Jenny who was anxious.

"Yes, Daisy. She's got concussion. She's to stay in bed for a couple of days. Doctor Mattison will call tomorrow to check on her."

"That's a relief. I must admit that I was a little worried. The stew's in the oven. I'll put the kettle on for a cup of tea."

Daisy made a cup of cocoa for Beth and they tucked her up in bed. She fell asleep almost immediately after her head hit the pillow.

"I won't sleep tonight," said Dorothea. "Not until I know she's out of danger. You never know with head injuries."

The grazing on her forehead was worse than she'd expected but Dr Mattison assured her the wounds were superficial and would soon heal, leaving no scars.

"Poor Sam seemed very concerned when he heard what had happened," said Daisy. "They all ate their lunch in silence, which isn't like them."

Howard was out and about on his rounds delivering the mail when the accident occurred. He had a large brown envelope for Edna, which was too wide to fit through the letterbox so he had to fold it in half. He was struggling to get it through the slot so he knelt down in order to hold the flap open.

That's when he noticed the body lying on the floor at the foot of the stairs. It was Edna and she didn't appear to be moving. He shouted as loud as he could through the slot but he couldn't make her hear him so he rang the bell. There was no response. He ran around the side of the house to try the back door but found it was locked.

For a minute or two, he couldn't think what to do but then he suddenly remembered seeing Stuart's bicycle propped up against the wall outside the newsagents. He ran as fast as he could, arriving just in time to see Stuart getting on his bike.

"Stuart," he yelled.

"Hello young Howard. What's to do?"

"It's Edna. She's lying on the floor at the bottom of the stairs. I rang the bell and there was no reply. The back door's locked so I can't get in. I think she must have fallen." His words were coming out in odd bursts as he was so out of breath he could hardly breathe.

"Right. I'll get straight over there." He shot off with Howard trailing behind.

By the time Howard arrived at the house, Stuart had broken his way in and was checking Edna's pulse.

"She's still alive. I'll need to call an ambulance. You stay here while I get things organised." Stuart disappeared into the kitchen and Howard heard him talking on his radio.

By the time the ambulance arrived, Edna had regained consciousness but couldn't move. She said she tripped on some torn stair carpet and lost her footing.

"My back hurts," she groaned.

"Don't try to move, you could be doing more damage. We'll get you to the hospital and they can check you over," said Stuart who was already on the radio organising a locksmith to come and secure the door with a new lock.

Howard fetched a cushion from the lounge and wedged it under her head. This would make for some lively conversation around the dinner table tonight.

It was Friday evening and Dorothea was the last one home. The family were all seated around the kitchen table awaiting their meal when she came in the back door.

"You're late, Aunty Dot," said Beth.

"Yes, sorry, everyone. I've been to see the vicar about doing a dance on the twenty-third of December. We can't do Christmas Eve because that's the day of the fund-raising event Edna was organising. Anyway, we've got the hall until eight thirty." She hung her coat up in the hall and washed her hands in the sink.

"Are we doing any classes beforehand?" asked Daisy. "I think I've forgotten some of the steps."

"Yes, just one refresher class the week before. We'll do a two-hour class covering all the dances. I'll run off a leaflet for you to pin up in the shop window, Meg." Dorothea thought Meg looked a bit downbeat and made a mental note to speak to her later when the children were all in bed.

Meg sat down at the table and threw her handbag under the seat, kicking off her shoes like she always did.

Sam must have noticed the look on Meg's face too when he asked, "Are you all right, Aunty Meg?"

Meg sighed before speaking. "Ken's had another angina attack. A bad one this time. They've carted him off to the infirmary. He didn't look good, to be honest. Evelyn's fretting. She said they might have to give up the shop as she doesn't think he's up to it anymore."

"Dear, oh dear," said Grace. "What would happen to the shop then?"

"It's part of a large group or chain or whatever they call it, so they could send a manager from another branch to run it, according to Evelyn."

"The joys of getting old," said Grace. "Ivy was saying exactly the same thing last week that Alf and herself were getting too old to manage the farm. I asked her where they would go if they were to give up the farm. It's a bone of contention between them as they can't agree on where to settle. Alf has a sister in Plymouth and Ivy has relatives in Ireland. He won't settle in Ireland and she doesn't want to go to Plymouth as she's not keen on his sister. Not that they don't get on or anything but she's just not her type."

"Ivy would make a good market gardener," said Beth. "She knows an awful lot about trees, bushes, plants and flowers. She was telling me one day that, when she was a little girl in Ireland, they had a huge allotment and their Uncle Patrick used to sell all the vegetables and plants to the local tradesmen. They made a good living out of it for years, according to Ivy. They won a competition one year at a trade show for the best marrow. She told me how big it was and what it weighed."

"It would suit Ivy that," agreed Grace. "It's still hard work, mind."

"We'll just have to see what tomorrow brings," said Iris, wondering whether to go down into the cellar for a bottle of wine. They could all do with a drink to cheer themselves up.

Saturday morning brought news that Kenneth had passed away during the night. He'd had a heart attack as they wheeled him into the ward and they weren't able to save him. The news spread like wildfire throughout the village. Evelyn was numb with shock. There was a new manager arriving in a week's time and he was to lodge with Edna in Dolly's old room.

Dorothea cancelled the dance as a gesture of respect to Evelyn. Kathleen invited Evelyn to Christmas dinner along with Stuart. She wanted to get in first before Edna commandeered her, for which

Evelyn was grateful as Edna wasn't known for her gastronomy. Edna was invited to have Christmas dinner with Dolly and Aubrey and the invitation included the new lodger. The hospital had given Edna strong painkillers and she was hobbling about on sticks but seemed quite cheerful despite the discomfort.

It was Christmas Eve and after lunch, everyone made their way over to the church hall for the fund-raising day. The WI ladies had arranged for some local dignitary and his wife to do the judging. The mayor and mayoress of somewhere or other. Meg wasn't really listening when Edna told her as she was trying to keep the shop going and look after Evelyn at the same time. The funeral for Kenneth was arranged for the day after Boxing Day. Meg's heart wasn't really in anything at the moment as she was still thinking about Eddie.

They were all greeted at the door by the WI ladies who told them where to deposit their exhibits. Grace and Daisy put theirs on the food table and Beth made her way to the garment table. Howard had made a Spitfire plane out of the wood from an old clock and hand painted it. The effect was impressive and as he made his way through the crowd to the toys' table, he received compliments galore. The others stood their paintings on easels at the back of the hall. There were over sixty entries in total as most of the WI ladies had also chosen to do paintings rather than handicrafts.

"Right, come on, everyone. Let's get some refreshments before they all go," said Dorothea, rounding everyone up.

Threading their way through to the side door which led into the kitchen where drinks were being served, they all had tea and cake which they ate sat huddled together in a corner.

"Huddling together for warmth?" said Edna, who was gadding about on her sticks. Bad back or not, she wasn't going to miss out on anything.

"I'm glad I put my cardigan on," Grace said.

"Yes, well, the heating's not working at the moment. It's been on the blink for years but I don't suppose there's any money for a new boiler," Edna said, planting herself down beside them.

"How is Dolly enjoying married life?" asked Iris.

"Iris!" laughed Meg.

"I'm only asking."

"No idea," said Edna. "They seem happy enough. His garden is beautiful, as you'd expect, him being a gardener by trade. I was a bit jealous when I saw it, I'll admit."

"Your garden is nice enough, Edna," said Iris.

At three o'clock on the dot, the mayor arrived and after refreshments, the judging started. The vicar was keen to "push things along" as the hall was needed for the evening service.

The first task was to judge the artwork and after deliberating for a good twenty minutes they selected a scene of wild flowers. It was Dorothea's. The second prize was awarded to a portrait of a war veteran which was done by a Mrs June Blomfield from the WI. The third prize was a seascape painted by Samuel. They all had their photographs taken for the local rag.

The next section was the children's toys. Howard's Spitfire won first prize. The mayor thought it was a true work of art and the attention to detail didn't go unnoticed. The second prize went to Kathleen who had made a Welsh doll dressed in national costume. The mayoress just happened to be Welsh, which helped. She said it reminded her of home and bought it herself to take home as a souvenir. The third prize went to another lady from the WI who made a jack-in-the-box.

Grace's cake won second prize and Daisy's biscuits won third prize. The judging went on for another hour before they got to the garments table. Josh and Beth jostled to the front. They had made a gentleman's dinner jacket lined with silk. The mayor tried it on and it fitted him perfectly. Everyone clapped and cheered when he announced, "I'm having this for myself."

Needless to say, it won first prize. Edna had resubmitted her cardigan after Ivy changed all the buttons to a matching set and it won third prize. Ironically, nobody bought it and she ended up taking it back home with her, no doubt it would turn up at the next fund-raising event.

The vicar seemed in good spirits as the money was collected and counted by the WI ladies. There were more photographs before everyone finally drifted off home.

Dorothea placed a cake on the kitchen table. It was the one Grace had made.

"Who bought that?" asked Grace in surprise.

"I did," laughed Dorothea. "There's good fruit in that. I'm not wasting it." She had also bought quite a few things she deemed suitable for birthday presents, which she hid in the bottom of her wardrobe.

Chapter Twenty-Five

"Hurry up, everyone. She'll be here in a minute," said Sam.

It was Thursday evening and they were settling themselves in the library for their French lesson with Mrs Kloot.

"She had another letter from Charles," Sam continued. "It came this morning and she's bringing it for us to read."

Dorothea and Iris looked at each other but said nothing, which Grace and Meg observed. Dorothea was still having chest pain which Dr Mattison said was anxiety. It felt like chronic indigestion that never went away.

Rosine seated herself at the table and after being prompted by Josh, proceeded to read the letter. "I won't bore you with the translation as it will take too long but he was released from the hospital and placed on light duties so they've given him an office job, which he hates. He's still having trouble with his chest and has to take medication."

"Any news of Bob and Uncle Raif?" asked Josh trying not to let his irritation show.

All eyes were on her when she added, "I'm so sorry. There is more. I was so excited when I got his letter. So, they weren't on the boat when it sank." She paused, looking at all the startled faces which were fixed upon her. She was struggling to find the right words as her English became muddled when she was excited or stressed.

"How do you know they weren't on it?" asked Dorothea, who was also starting to feel more than a little irritated herself.

"So sorry. When the helicopter came to take Charles to hospital, they took Raif and Bob too. Raif had a leg injury which was bleeding badly so they applied a tourniquet. They were not able to stop the flow of blood so they put him in the helicopter too with Charles. Someone had to accompany them due to the seriousness of the injuries and as Bob was related to Raif, they asked him to go."

The silence permeating the room lasted a couple of minutes before Grace broke it by asking, "So, where are they now, Rose?"

"Raif is still in hospital after Charles was discharged. He had an operation on his leg which went well. I think Charles said he was walking with the help of a frame. Bob was sent back to his base to await instructions. I will write a letter tomorrow asking for more information for you." She looked around the room at all the eager faces hanging onto every word. "It's good news, no?" she said as her cheeks started to colour pink.

"Well, thank the Lord," cried Daisy. "They're all still alive. This calls for a celebration. I'll make a pot of tea."

Stuff the tea, thought Iris. "I'll go down to the cellar for a bottle of wine."

Chapter Twenty-Six

Photographs of the church fund-raising event were splashed all over the centre pages of the local rag which Meg had fetched from the shop. The family were studying them in the library after their evening meal.

"Mr Glass bought your Spitfire, Howard," said Josh. "He said it was worth every penny."

Howard was secretly pleased his work of art had gone to a good home but made no comment.

"Edna bought your biscuits, Daisy," said Meg.

Daisy smiled and said, "I saw a lady from the WI looking at Edna's cardigan but she didn't buy it. Aubrey bought your painting, Dotty, for his dining room wall and a lady from the WVS bought Sam's. She said it reminded her of holidays in Brighton when she was a child. I was behind them all in the queue. I bought Jenny's painting of the sunflower for my room."

"Oh, thank you, Mummy," squealed Jenny delightedly.

"Did you buy anything, Aunty Meg?" asked Beth.

"No, I'm afraid not. I was a bit distracted, with Ken's funeral and everything."

"It was a good turnout for the service, wasn't it?" said Grace. "I think most of the village turned out to pay their respects. How is Evelyn?"

"She's still a bit shell-shocked, to be honest. The post office counter is always busy and I think she's struggling a bit."

"How is the new manager settling in?" asked Iris.

"He certainly knows the business. His wife died last year in a bomb raid. He thought it would be a fresh start coming here."

"Where did he live before?" asked Dorothea.

"Somewhere in Kent, Maidstone. He has one son who's married and lives in Norfolk. That's as much as I know."

"Is he getting along with Edna?"

"I've not asked him but he seems happy enough. His name's Douglas but Edna calls him Douggie."

"Not 'my Douggie'?" laughed Iris.

"Not yet, Iris. Just Douggie."

A knock at the back door interrupted their laughter.

"I'll get that," said Daisy, jumping up from her seat.

A gentleman in uniform stood before her when she opened the door.

"Hello, can I help you?" she asked.

"I hope so, ma'am. I don't even know if I've got the right address. I'm looking for Megan. Megan Andrews?"

"She does live here, yes. Do come in."

He took off his hat and twirled it nervously around in his fingers.

Daisy smiled at him and thought he was quite handsome. "We're all in the library. It's where we spend most of our evenings. Meg, you have a visitor."

The laughter stopped immediately as all eyes were upon the guest.

"Eddie!" screamed Meg. She shot off her chair and ran straight into his arms, not caring that everyone was watching her make a fool of herself for this was the moment she'd dreamt about since the day they parted. "Everyone, this is Eddie. Eddie, this is my family." There was nothing to cloud her joy now.

Once all the introductions were out of the way, Dorothea ushered them in to the parlour so they could talk in private. "I'll bring some drinks in. It's so nice to meet you at last, Eddie." She hoped for Meg's sake he hadn't come to deliver bad news and that he was returning to his wife and family.

"I'll give you a hand, Dotty," said Iris who was grinning from ear to ear.

"No, let me do that," insisted Grace.

"No, Grace. You and Daisy have done enough for today. Sit down and relax whilst you can," said Dorothea.

"Well, this is a turn up for the books and no mistake," said Iris. "He's finally arrived. Who would have thought it?"

"Don't get too excited, Iris. We don't know what he's come to say yet. He might be married and be about to go home to his family."

"Yes, I did think of that too. But surely he wouldn't have come all this way just to tell her that. He would have written a letter, wouldn't he?"

"He does seem a decent sort and I pride myself in being a good judge of character but you know he might have wanted to do the decent thing and tell her to her face. I'm only guessing, mind. He might genuinely be fond of her."

"From all that she told me, I think he is definitely very fond of her."

The children were full of questions about the mysterious Eddie. They wanted to know how and where Meg had met him and would he be staying with them. Jenny secretly wondered if her own daddy would suddenly appear at the door like that and looked forward to that day when it came.

After about an hour, they heard the front door being opened. They all raced to the window to see Meg following Eddie out to his car. He handed her a carrier bag then gave her a kiss on the cheek. Jumping into the driver's seat, he waved and took off at some speed. Meg explained he'd borrowed his boss' car and had to be back at the Wilmington military base before he noticed it was missing.

"He's sorry he didn't have much time to chat to you all. He borrowed the car without his boss' permission, you see. So, he had to get back. Otherwise he would have come in to say goodbye to you all. He's pleased to have finally met you all and he's left us this bag of goodies." She dumped the carrier bag on the table for the children to delve through the contents.

* * *

Three days later, Jenny scooped up a pile of letters from the mat at the front door and placed them on the table next to Dorothea. The family were just finishing their lunch and the children were about to start their homework. There were three letters for Dorothea, one for Iris, one for Meg, one for Sam, one for Grace and one for Beth.

"Goodness, they must have been saving these up," said Dorothea.

"They were probably posted months ago," said Grace, opening hers straight away. "Oh, it's from Lilian, one of my friends from the WI in London. I'll read it later with a cup of tea. It'll be news of the flying bombs no doubt."

"They had it really bad in London last year. How they're ever going to get everyone rehoused is beyond me," said Dorothea with a sigh.

"Mine is from my brother Alan. What can he have to say?" frowned Beth, then proceeded to read through the letter which was several pages long.

Sam's letter was from his father advising him he was now in the field hospital in Normandy and hadn't yet managed to locate his wife and daughter. When he got back to London after visiting Sam last year, he telephoned Magda's sister who informed him Magda and Selina never arrived there, which greatly worried him as that was where she was heading. He hoped that wherever they were, they were safe and well.

Meg's letter was from Eddie. A note scribbled quickly as he was reporting for duty any minute.

Iris' letter was from Bob, letting her know he'd joined another ship in Normandy and asked her to write to him, for that was the only thing that was keeping his spirits up. No other details in the letter about what happened previously or indeed what the conditions were like on the new ship. She supposed he'd done it on purpose to save her from the worry. *Typical Bob*, she thought smiling to herself.

Dorothea's first letter was from Celia. Enclosed were more bills that had arrived at the town house.

Dear Dotty,

We've had the most horrendous six months here with the flying bombs. I think half of London has now been demolished!

On a more personal note, I decided to give up my post with the WI. Tom was waiting for me in the car park every month after each meeting. I made my way to a friend's house (by prior arrangement) as I knew he would follow me home. I became afraid of him. I've got an address book full of names from the WI ladies, who I hope will remain friends. Tom doesn't know where I'm living now, so that's good. I've no idea where Iain is. I'd like to think he's doing his bit for the war effort somewhere but as he takes after his father, probably not.

Howard's book is due to be published at Easter. Belinda (the young illustrator) has been interviewed for a programme on the local radio and she mentioned the book. The ladies at the WI know all about it too, so fingers crossed! I'm quite excited and hope the second book will be ready soon.

John and I spend all our evenings together. His daughter comes with the children every Thursday. She's very easy to get along with.

I hope things aren't too bad for you in Somerset. I was surprised to hear that you're driving the local bus now! The buses here aren't allowed to put their headlamps on. I don't know how you manage!

Much love,
Celia

Her second letter was from her friend Carole at the ARP office. It was a newsy letter about all the people she knew. Some people had lost their homes, some had lost their wives, husbands or sons. Some women were having "flings" with American soldiers whilst their husbands were away. Food was in short supply and there were a lot of homeless people. Despite all that, Carole's sense of humour shone through, which made Dorothea laugh.

The third letter was from Lawrence at the bank informing her the situation regarding her account had now been rectified and they were just waiting for someone from head office to approve it and the money would be in her account. They were going to send her a statement in the post. As there was still no letter from Raif, Dorothea was convinced he had no intention of rekindling their marriage. If what Rosine had said was true and he was lying in a hospital bed somewhere in France, then surely he would have had all the time in the world to pen a letter to her. Just a short note would suffice. She was going to have to come to terms with the fact she may never see him again.

Chapter Twenty-Seven

The portrait of Raif's grandmother hung on the wall above the fireplace in the lounge and was worked in oils by a local artist to commemorate her sixtieth birthday. Beth sat staring at it. It was her favourite place in the house and she'd taken to sitting quietly in front of it with Smoky the cat sat on her knee for company.

Smoky was a beautiful Persian Blue with clear sparkling grey eyes given to her for her twelfth birthday. Beth liked to talk to the lady in the painting, thanking her for letting her stay in this magnificent house, which she now considered to be her home. There were other paintings adorning the walls all around the room but she liked this one the best.

She wondered how someone acquired such wealth as to be able to afford all these beautiful things. Glancing momentarily around the room, her eyes focused on the antique clocks, gilt-edged mirrors, colourful wool rugs, beautiful ornaments in glass and china. A mahogany writing bureau graced the back wall and was polished to a high shine. She never tired of looking at them and felt so different when she sat in this room. It had a calming effect on her. No matter what was going on in the world outside, the moment she sat in this room, she felt different. It was like an internal flame, glowing brightly within her. Aunty Dot said material things didn't matter and it was people that mattered. Aunty Grace agreed with her.

"Oh, here you are, Beth. We've been looking everywhere for you. Breakfast is ready. What are you doing in here?" asked Sam.

"Talking to Raif's grandmother."

"The lady in the painting? Dorothea didn't get on with her at all from what I gather. What were you saying to her?" He was intrigued now.

"I was thanking her for letting me stay here in her beautiful home."

"Yes, it is a lovely house. You love this room, don't you?"

"Very much."

"Come on, or Grace will be cross."

Megan let herself into the back of the shop with her key. She hung up her coat on the peg in the back kitchen and looked into the stock room to see if Douglas was around but there was no sign of him this morning, which was unusual. Wondering if he was ill or indisposed in some way, she wandered into the shop and switched on one small light nearest to the door.

The morning papers were in bundles on the pavement outside. It was starting to rain so she opened the door quickly and hauled them all inside. Glancing at the clock above the post office counter, it told her it was six thirty, plenty of time to get them all sorted out and onto the stand.

Cutting the string with scissors, she'd just opened the first batch when she heard strange noises coming from upstairs. Her first thought was that Evelyn must be ill. Switching on the light in the corridor, she crept upstairs to investigate. Encroaching on some-body's private quarters wasn't something she would normally do but if Evelyn was sick and needed help, she would never forgive herself for not helping.

When she reached the top of the stairs, she heard laughter and a man's voice. The bedroom door was open so she popped her head around to investigate. The sight that greeted her shocked her to the core. It was Douglas! They were stark naked on the bed and clearly having a good time. Not wanting to be seen, she crept back downstairs again. Kenneth was hardly cold in his grave. How could Evelyn do this? Some women couldn't live without a man and she supposed Evelyn was jumping in quick before anyone else could get their hands on him. It would certainly make life easier and more convenient for her having a man around the place.

Meg was appalled and could feel her face burning with indignation. All the roots of her hair were tingling. She supposed Evelyn was "getting her feet under the table" and wondered what Edna's reaction would be when she found out, which she inevitably would sooner or later.

"Right, everyone. There's money in the bank at last, so after breakfast tomorrow we'll all go to the warehouse for some much-needed items. I'll make a list. Don't make any plans," said Dorothea. The bank statement in the morning post, together with a covering letter advising her of an added bonus by way of compensation, was just the tonic she needed as things were getting desperate. "We'll use Raif's car as well as the jeep. Iris, can you drive the jeep? I'll take the car. It's not far, only a couple of miles away."

"I'd be nervous in Raif's car," Iris said. "I'll be fine in the jeep." The prospect of some new clothing to keep them warm in the winter filled her with joy.

"I'll prepare the casserole for our evening meal before we set off so that it can go straight into the oven when we get back," said Grace.

They had a very enjoyable day choosing waterproof coats, walking boots and warm underwear. After lunch in Minehead town centre, followed by a stroll along the beach, they arrived home exhausted.

"Aunty Dot, is it all right if Rebecca comes on Wednesday after school? We can do our homework in the library. Her mum goes out with Douglas as it's his half-day off from the shop," asked Josh.

"Of course, it is. Bring her. She can have some lunch here with us."

"Thank you. She would be in the house on her own otherwise."

"How long has her mum been seeing Douglas?" asked Iris.

"Three weeks. Rebecca doesn't like being in the house on her own, even though they've got a dog."

Megan decided to keep quiet. If she valued her job, it wouldn't do to start spreading rumours about Douglas. Iris also decided to say nothing, as Douglas had approached her for a date on two occasions when she went into the shop. She politely reminded him she was happily married and not looking for anything more. There had been rumours circulating at the factory that one of the girls had been dating Douglas on a regular basis and not just for tea and cake either.

"Mr Glass said he sees Edna in the pub with Douglas every Friday night. I wonder if she knows about Rebecca's mum?" said Josh, innocently.

"Take my advice, Josh. Don't get involved. Where relationships are concerned things can be very complex. Stay out of it and be very careful what you say and who you speak to. Just pretend you know nothing about it," advised Dorothea.

"Wise words indeed," agreed Grace, who had already made a mental note to speak to Ivy at the next WI meeting, for she knew without a doubt nothing got past Ivy in this village.

"Tea's on the table, Dad," shouted Kathleen.

Earnest was in the back yard cleaning his old bike which he'd unearthed from amongst all the junk in the shed.

"You've made a good job of that, Dad. It's shining like a new pin."

"I just need to oil the chain and pump up the tyres a bit." He washed his hands in the sink and sat down at the table.

"You know when you said that you saw Edna with Douglas in the pub on Friday, how did they seem together?" asked Kathleen, helping herself to a hunk of bread.

"How do you mean?"

"Well, did they seem all lovey-dovey like?"

"Not really, no. They were just sat talking from what I saw. Why?"

"Don't say anything but one of the girls at the factory is seeing Douglas on a regular basis. She's not bothering to hide the fact that she's having a good time."

"Well, more fool her, that's all I can say. Take my advice, Kath. Don't have anything to do with him. He's not for the likes of you. You're much too good for him."

"Thanks, Dad. Chance would be a fine thing. He's not even looked in my direction."

"You just watch yourself and be on your guard."

Grace was just putting the soup on the stove for lunch when Meg appeared at the back door. She looked deathly pale.

"Hello Meg. What's wrong? Are you unwell?"

"No, Grace. I got the sack," said Meg, flopping down onto one of the chairs without even taking off her coat.

"The sack? Why?" asked Grace.

"Had a bit of a set-to with Evelyn. She accused me of spreading rumours about her and Douglas. I tried to tell her that if there were any rumours doing the rounds, they certainly hadn't come from me, but she wouldn't listen."

"Heavens, it's all over the village. She must know that, surely?" said Grace, sitting down at the table opposite her.

"She asked me to leave. As I went to get my coat from the back, Douglas was in the stock room. I told him that I hadn't said a word about him and Evelyn but I'm not sure he believed me either."

"The silly cow," muttered Grace. "She'll regret getting rid of you, mark my words."

"He's moving into the flat with Evelyn."

"Is he indeed? Does Edna know?"

"I don't know, Grace, but I wouldn't like to be around when he breaks the news to her."

They both laughed as Grace filled the kettle to make the "cure all" cup of tea.

Chapter Twenty-Eight

Holding up the jacket for them all to see, Beth asked, "What do you think?"

With Josh's help, they had made a blazer just like the one the mayor bought at the fund-raising day. Josh wanted a nice present for Mr Glass' birthday.

"It's perfect," said Dorothea, examining the seams, lining and cuffs. "It's beautifully finished. Well done."

Grace had offered to prepare a special supper for him and Kathleen but he declined, saying he was going to the pub with Alf. Dorothea said it was no slur on her cooking skills but he just probably preferred male company and the pub was more to his liking.

Beth had practised her hand sewing under Dorothea's instruction and it had to be perfect to meet her standards. She now knew without a doubt that it was what she wanted to do for a living and Dorothea had promised to get her a place at college when she was old enough. Josh also expressed an interest in becoming a master tailor and Beth secretly hoped they could study together.

"There's a letter for you, Iris," said Daisy, handing her the envelope.

Iris knew by the handwriting it was from her husband. "It's from Bob. About time too."

Iris tore open the envelope and unfolded a single sheet of paper with just a few lines on it. She smiled to herself as she scanned the contents. The others all waited in silence for snippets of information regarding Uncle Raif, but not daring to ask.

At last, she put the letter down on the table and said resignedly,

"Typical Bob. He says nothing of the new ship, just that it's bigger and the food's marginally better."

"Does he say where he is?" asked Josh.

"I don't think they're allowed to say," said Sam. "They would have censored it in case it fell into enemy hands."

"That's right, Sam," said Dorothea who was secretly disappointed that once again there was no news of Raif and she immediately felt her spirits plummeting.

"No, but I know that he's in France. He said he thinks Charles and Raif have both been put on light duties in the offices. Charles is still on medication for his chest and Raif isn't yet fully mobile due to his leg injury. He made it his business to find out as he knew we'd be worried." Iris hugged Dorothea and knew she welcomed the good news.

Later, when the children were in bed, Dorothea said, "I'm not sure if Raif will come back to me, you know. It's a feeling I've got."

"This war's a bad business," said Grace, not knowing what else to say to comfort Dorothea. "It changes people. I wouldn't give up hope yet though. Wait and see."

"It's all any of us can do," agreed Iris. "Is there any more wine in the cellar?"

"There's lots," Dorothea laughed. "Why? Do you fancy a drop?"

"Yes, I need a drink. Come on, help me choose a bottle."

Meg opened her eyes the following morning to find Jenny sat at the side of her bed dabbing her face with a damp flannel.

"I'll look after you, Aunty Meg," she whispered. Her big blue eyes sparkled like diamonds and her red hair fell in soft curls, framing her rosy cheeks.

Meg smiled at her. "I'm not ill, darling, just a little tired."

"Aunty Dot says you need to rest as you've been working very hard in the shop. You've missed breakfast but Aunty Grace has saved you some porridge."

"Tell her I'll be down in a few minutes." Knowing the importance of finding another job to help out with the family finances, Meg had decided to take a trip into town to see what she could find. She hoped there might just be a cafe or such like that needed an extra pair of hands.

Reflecting on the events of the last twenty-four hours, she was disappointed at the way Evelyn had spoken to her as they had worked together for quite some time and she began to consider her a friend. It wasn't so much what she had said but the manner in which she had said it. Her spirit was broken and she hadn't slept at all well.

Grace was at the stove when she entered the kitchen.

"Oh Meg, you needn't have rushed to get up. Dorothea said to let you lie in."

"I'm going into town. I've got to find work."

"Don't feel unduly pressed. Dorothea said you need a good rest. It's been hard work in that shop. Evelyn put on you a bit."

"Yes, I think she did but I began to think of her as a friend."

"Don't waste any time on regrets. Concentrate on the here and now. You've got us. We're a family. Don't ever forget that."

"Thank you, Grace. It means a lot to me."

"Now eat up and I'll put the kettle on for tea."

"We've got two more orders for the blazers, Beth," said Josh.

Beth's eyes went as big as saucers. "Really? Who for?"

"Alf and Aubrey. We'll ask Aunty Dot if we can rummage through the trunk in the loft later after supper."

Beth felt the excitement fizz through her. Any practice she could put in before she went to college, the better prepared she would feel.

Aubrey, Alf and Earnest were all members of an ex-servicemen's club and word had spread like wildfire at the last meeting with everyone admiring the blazer with the silk lining. The three of them got on famously and had taken to meeting in the pub every Friday evening, leaving the wives and Kathleen on their own to amuse themselves. Kathleen was fearful of the air raid siren sounding as she hated the Anderson shelter, which was cold, dark and damp.

* * *

Meg jumped off the bus at the depot and started off down the lane when she spotted Iris. The two of them walked home together.

"Where have you been today?" asked Iris.

"I went into town to see if I could find some work."

"Any luck?"

"No, I'm afraid not."

Iris thought her sister looked pale and weary. "I wouldn't rush, Meg. Have a rest first. You deserve it."

"I need to pay my way. It's not fair on Dotty. She's got enough on her plate with the children. What's news at the factory?"

"Well, don't say anything but there's a girl in the accounts office that's seeing Douglas. She's expecting a baby. Her husband's a sergeant major in the army. He's been gone for over four years."

"Oh dear. What will she do?"

"No idea, Meg." They linked arms as they sauntered up the lane towards the house.

"Douglas has done a runner," Howard announced.

They all looked at him in amazement.

"How do you know, Howard? He's not been with us more than five minutes," said Dorothea.

"Edna told me. He's upped sticks and gone. Disappeared. Evelyn went round to Edna's last night asking if he'd moved back in with her. All his things were gone out of the wardrobe." Nobody spoke, so he continued, "I asked Edna if she'd be taking another lodger and she said not. 'I'm happier on my own,' she said."

"Good for her. She's talking some sense for once," said Dorothea.

"Well, well, well," whispered Iris, to nobody in particular. She looked across the table at Meg and the two of them were both thinking of the pregnant girl at the factory and wondered if he'd taken her with him.

"What is it with these men that think it's all right to just take off into the night like that?" protested Dorothea. "But to be fair, Mr

Manns at the bank had just lost his poor mother and he was in a bit of a state."

"Rebecca's mum won't be too pleased either. According to Rebecca, it was all her mother talked about. Doug this and Doug that," said Josh.

Sam entered via the back door as they were all talking. "High jinks at the shop," he announced.

They all waited for him to sit down at the table and give them chapter and verse on the events.

"I was just passing the shop on my way home when I heard raised voices. Well, shouting to be exact. There were three ladies all shouting at Evelyn. They were demanding to know where Douglas was. It turned into a bit of a fracas. Stuart had to wade in and break it up."

"Who were the three ladies?" asked Grace, trying to sound nonchalant but secretly enjoying the gossip.

"One was Rebecca's mum. I didn't recognise the other two."

"Was Edna there?" asked Josh.

"No, it was a lady with an Irish accent and a tall slim lady with short dark hair. I heard some unsavoury language going on. The Irish lady called Evelyn a trollop."

There was a stony silence permeating the room before Grace jumped up and announced, "I'll put the dinner out."

Daisy followed her to the kitchen. "Grace, do you know who the tall slim lady could be?" she whispered.

"I think Ivy might know. I'll ask her at the next WI meeting." Grace knew full well who it was but decided that enough had been said on the subject.

Chapter Twenty-Nine

Dorothea entered the church via the main entrance and made her way down the centre aisle, her heels clip-clopping on the stone floor.

"Morning Cyril," she said gaily.

"Hello Dorothea. I'm just about to have my morning cup of tea. Come through to the vestry and you can join me."

"That sounds grand. Thank you kindly." She followed him into the small galley kitchen and fished in her handbag for the notice she'd penned whilst he filled the kettle.

"I've no milk, I'm afraid."

"It's all right, Cyril. I've not had milk in my tea for over three years now," she laughed.

"Biscuits we do have." He put a small tin on the table along with two mugs.

"I was thinking of this." She smiled at him and handed over the flyer for him to read.

"Mary would enjoy this. She used to paint a lot before we were married. We'll both come. Multimedia? Is that watercolours or oils?"

"Anything you like. Oils, watercolour, charcoal, acrylics, pastels, pencil. I'd like the children to come along too. It will be good for them," she said, bubbling with enthusiasm. "I'll try to dig out as much gear as I can. We can always double up and share. I'll ask Grace and Ivy to mention it at the WI meeting this week. Perhaps they can come up with a trestle table."

There was something very comforting about sitting in the vestry drinking tea with the local vicar. Dorothea felt the pains in her chest beginning to ease slightly. Cyril's voice had a certain resonance to it which had a calming influence. His sermons had the same effect upon her.

"I'll get Mrs Bray to pin a note up on the school notice board and Mrs Kloot can have one for the library. I'd normally get Evelyn to put one in the shop window, but I'm not sure she'd oblige. She sacked Meg, you know."

"Yes, I heard about that. It was most unkind and inappropriate. I had a word with her about it. Megan's the last person to spread gossip in this village. Mr Glass and Mr Thompson told her the same thing. I hear Douglas has gone?"

"Yes, so it seems," she said, taking a second biscuit from the tin.

"She'll be needing help now, no doubt. Are they sending someone else to replace him? It's a busy shop and she can't manage it single-handed."

"I've no idea. I don't go in anymore, I'm sad to say."

"There was a bit of a to-do there yesterday. Stuart ended up with a black eye."

"Really?"

"Yes. One of the ladies at the factory got into an argument with Evelyn and when he tried to caution her, she clouted him with her handbag."

"Is he going to charge her for assault?"

"I'm not sure, but she became extremely abusive and he carted her off to the police station. I only know all this because Mary was in the shop at the time buying her weekly magazine."

Dorothea suddenly realised Mary was tall and slim with short dark hair. She felt herself becoming hot and uncomfortable. Surely not? She decided to ask Grace about it later.

Daisy was in the library trying to build up the fire when Dorothea came in.

"I'm trying to get this heat going a bit otherwise we'll all freeze to death," she said.

"It is a bit chilly. Was there any post today?" Dorothea asked hopefully.

"No, but we had a visit from Evelyn. She asked Meg if she wanted her old job back at the shop. Meg refused. Evelyn was surprised and asked her if she was in any fit position to turn it down, seeing as she was out of work and residing free of charge in someone else's house. I must say I was shocked at the off-handed way Evelyn spoke to Meg."

"Did she indeed? I hope Meg didn't change her mind."

"No, she didn't. She just got up and left the room."

"Good," said Dorothea.

Grace appeared, wiping her hands on her apron. "Dinner is nearly ready, girls. Everyone's home, they're just washing their hands. Howard's collected the post. There's a letter for you, Dotty, one for Meg and one for Sam. I've noticed Josh never seems to get any post. Does he write to his dad?"

"I think so. I'll ask him. I hope Meg's letter is from Eddie. She needs cheering up."

"Sam's letter will be from his father. I hope it's good news and he's finally managed to find his wife and daughter," said Daisy.

"It's curious that she never arrived at her sister's, which is where she was meant to be going. With bombs dropping everywhere, anything could have happened to them," Grace added mournfully, thinking of her husband George, who just happened to be in the wrong place when the bomb fell on their street.

Sam's letter was indeed from his father who was now at a hospital in London. He was still active in trying to locate Magda and Selina and had written to all his relatives and friends. He was back off to France the following week and urged Sam not to worry. He promised to visit him as soon as he could get some free time.

Meg's letter was from Eddie, who couldn't say where he was but hoped it wouldn't be too long before they could be together again. She smiled as she read through the letter before tucking it back in her bedside drawer. It was enough to know he was thinking of her and missing her. It lifted her spirits and gave her the confidence to hold her head up and try again to find paid work. Evelyn's visit had shaken her up a bit but she tried not to show it.

Dorothea's letter was from Celia informing her she was now spending most of her free time with John. They spent their evenings listening to plays or music on the wireless. Sunday mornings they completed The Times crossword together over cups of coffee. John liked to cook and was happy to sort out most of the meals. It took Dorothea back to the days when she was first married to Raif. They both loved crosswords and jigsaws and used to spend many a winter evening sat in front of the fire with a glass of wine.

Celia went on to say that John's daughter was moving to Scotland once the war was over. It was something to do with her husband's job. John asked Celia if she would consider going to live there with him, perhaps renting a little cottage somewhere. She finished the letter by saying Howard's book was due to be published at Easter and she promised to send a few free copies in the post. There were two household bills enclosed which Dorothea tossed to one side.

News of the art classes spread like wildfire throughout the village and Dorothea's popularity was evident for all to see. She chose a different theme each week to make it interesting and with the help of all the WI ladies, things soon got organised and under way. They tackled flowers the first week, then landscapes and mountains, then beach scenes and boats. This week, they were doing portraits.

Each week, they chose one picture as "the best in class" which proved very popular. Grace sat next to Ivy so they could gossip. Grace looked forward to these evenings as Ivy made it her business to know everything that was going on in the village.

Mrs Bray encouraged all the children from the school to attend as many sessions as they could and even made sure each child was equipped with an apron to save their clothes. She paid the fee herself for those families that were struggling financially.

Tonight was a particularly good turnout as it was to be the last class before the Easter break. All the paintings and drawings were going on display in the library.

"Has Evelyn got anyone to replace Douglas yet?" asked Grace.

"She's been on to head office," replied Ivy.

"Where is he? Do they know what happened to him?"

"She wouldn't say. She's not likely to tell the likes of us, even if she does know."

"Who's helping her in the shop then?"

"It's closed at the moment. She told them she couldn't run it on her own. I think she said someone's coming next week."

"Good luck to them. Let's hope he lasts longer than the last one. He went through the ladies of this village like a dose of Epsom salts."

"Didn't he just. If you need anything from the post office, just knock on the side door. She let me have some stamps yesterday."

The lady sat on the other side of Grace lay down her brush and rummaged in her handbag for some sweets. She offered one to Grace and Ivy.

"I wish they'd sort the heating out in this place, I'm going stiff," the lady grumbled.

"Yes, I'm cold too," agreed Grace.

The cold didn't bother Ivy as she was used to working outside in all weathers on the farm.

"My name's Ruth, by the way," said the lady with the sweets, who had now extracted a scarf from her bag and was tying it around her neck.

"Oh, are you Doctor Mattison's wife?" asked Grace.

"I am. Roland's working late tonight. No point in sitting in the house on my own. I could murder a cup of tea."

"I've got some whisky," said Ivy, producing a small flask and offering it across.

"That's kind of you, thanks. It's Ivy, isn't it?"

"Yes."

"Your Alf certainly has a good time in the pub with his pals on a Friday night. The three musketeers we call them. They were making so much noise last week the whole pub was looking at them. Whatever it was they were discussing certainly caused hilarity. They were laughing so loud that the landlord shouted for them to pipe down."

"I don't begrudge him his one night off. He works hard on the farm. We both do. I keep telling him that we're getting too old but he loves it and won't give it up. Not yet anyway."

"What would you do if you were to give it up?" asked Grace. "Where would you go?"

"We'd go to his sister's. She has plenty of room. As to how we'd fill our days, I'm not sure. It's so busy on the farm. We'd be like fish out of water. We wouldn't know what to do with ourselves. I can't stand being idle. I like to keep busy."

Grace couldn't think of anything nicer than having no work to do. She would spend her days knitting and gardening. She'd be quite happy.

"That James is coming on Monday to manage the shop. He's been here before," said Ruth.

"What's he like?" asked Grace.

"A right misery guts," laughed Ruth and Ivy together.

Later, in the library, they were sipping their cocoa when Josh said, "There's a man starting on Monday to manage the shop. His name's Jimmy. According to Mr Glass, he's been here before, a few years ago. He wasn't very popular."

"Yes, we heard," said Grace. "I bet Evelyn's not too pleased."

"It will serve her right for dismissing Aunty Meg," said Beth.

"I can't understand the change in Evelyn," said Meg. "When I first started work in the shop, she was so kind to me. It was only after Kenneth died that things started to change."

"Bereavement does strange things to people," said Dorothea. "Her behaviour could have been based on fear. Fear of being left alone in the shop and not being able to cope."

"When Douglas arrived, it must have given her a false sense of security. Then he let her down," said Iris.

"I don't suppose anyone's heard from him?" asked Grace. "I was thinking of your work colleague, Iris."

"As a matter of fact, she has. She had a letter from him."

They all stared at Iris in astonishment. Iris sipped her cocoa without adding anything further.

"And?" they all chorused.

"She wouldn't say but we're working on it. It'll all come out eventually, no doubt."

"How did she seem? Happy? Excited? Sad? Upset?" Daisy asked.

"She seemed all right, actually. Just her normal self. Being Irish, she's a very chatty sociable sort. I try not to judge people. You never know what their circumstances are. We don't know what sort of marriage she has. Perhaps she was unhappy. This war makes you grab your happiness where you can. Let's face it, you might not get another chance with bombs dropping."

"That's very profound, Iris, and true," smiled Dorothea, thinking of Raif.

"Kath and I gave her a hug and told her that we'd always be here for her if she needed us. Her eyes misted over and she thanked us."

Lying in bed later that evening, Josh reflected on how well Aunty Dot seemed to cope with everything. Her general knowledge was certainly greater than anyone else he knew. How on earth one acquired and retained all that knowledge was totally beyond his comprehension. She was certainly a ferocious reader. Right from day one when they first arrived, she took them into the library and showed them all the books lining the shelves.

"You must read," she had said. "Read every day and keep your mind open to new ways and ideas. It's very important."

They had to choose a book and read for one hour before bed every night with special emphasis on familiarising themselves with the great authors and poets of years gone by, often advising them on what they should be reading.

When pressed about the work she did before the war, she said she had studied the sciences at Oxford University and then had taken a job in a laboratory doing research, which is where she met Raif. Josh asked her if she would go back to it once the war was over but she wasn't at all sure about it.

Josh knew in his heart he wasn't a great scholar and never would be, no matter how hard he studied. He just wasn't academic. He loved textiles and fine tailoring. Having made up his mind to follow this line of work if he got the chance, he knew Aunty Dot would help him to achieve his dream of becoming a master tailor. He fell into a blissful slumber dreaming of his own office within a bespoke tailors in Saville Row.

Chapter Thirty

"Hostilities will end at one minute after midnight tonight." Churchill's address to the nation came over the radio as the family were crowded together in the library. It was 3 o'clock on 8th May 1945. The war was over.

Dorothea hoped the speech didn't lull them into a false sense of freedom. Many men were still fighting, lost or missing. Many were dead or seriously wounded. Many were yet to come home. She didn't feel like rejoicing.

"Shall I brew some tea?" offered Daisy.

"Yes, Daisy, thank you," said Dorothea. She was a delightful girl and Dorothea felt very lucky to have her in the household. Knowing it would be a long time before things got back to normal, Dorothea knew the food rationing and the short supply of clothing would be with them for some time yet. Thank goodness they had the allotment. It had proved to be a lifesaver.

The clothing warehouse nearby was run by a close friend of Raif's which was also a lifesaver as they were able to buy clothes at cost price. They all had dressing gowns to keep them warm in the winter months but they had very little else.

She silently reflected on how much longer she would be able to keep the children now the war was officially over. The very thought of parting with them filled her with sorrow. With the exception of Howard, who had nowhere to go, she knew sooner or later their own families would lay claim to them once more and they would be lost to her forever. They weren't hers to keep.

They were only on loan and she had to hand them back to their respective families safe and sound. No, she did not feel like celebrating. Her heart was breaking.

It was October and Grace was putting the finishing touches to the sherry trifle, which was a surprise to celebrate Daisy's twenty-first birthday. A homemade cake graced the centre of the table alongside sausage rolls, pasties and finger sandwiches. Iris and Meg were in the dining room laying the table.

Howard had insisted on taking Daisy out for lunch at the cafe as a special treat out of his royalties from the book sales. He told her it would only be a pot of tea and a toasted teacake but it didn't cloud her joy. He insisted on taking Jenny too. They found a table near the back and settled themselves comfortably on the sofa so the three of them could sit together. He wanted to ask her about Jenny's dad but didn't know how to broach the subject without offending her. Grace failed to enlighten him when he probed her for information. Daisy didn't seem the type of girl to harbour secrets but in his heart he felt something bad must have happened.

Waiting until the waitress placed their order on the table and then disappeared, he took the carefully wrapped parcel out of his pocket and placed it in front of her.

"Happy birthday, Daisy. Jenny helped me to choose it. I hope it's to your liking," he said sheepishly, suddenly feeling a bit awkward.

Daisy felt herself blushing as she opened her present. It was a silver bracelet encrusted with a single diamond.

"Oh Howard, it's beautiful. You shouldn't have spent all your money on me. You may need it one day," she said.

"Put it on, Mummy," said Jenny excitedly.

It fitted perfectly and it was the first piece of jewellery Daisy had ever possessed.

"It's perfect, Howard. Thank you. I shall treasure it forever." She poured the tea and handed the glass of lemonade to her daughter who was beaming.

They spent the afternoon walking around the park, circling twice around the duck pond to keep Jenny amused.

When they arrived back at the house, the table was set and Dorothea was opening a bottle of wine. There were more presents for Daisy to open, one of which was from Celia with a short letter wishing her well.

Daisy made the cocoa and took it into the library. The children were playing a game of snakes and ladders.

"What did Celia have to say?" Grace asked.

"She wasn't at all sure about relocating to Scotland, although she wants to stay with John. She asked if Jenny and I would visit her one day if she did go."

"Would you go?" Iris asked curiously.

"I'm not sure, Iris."

"I know how she feels about the move," said Dorothea. "She wouldn't know anyone in Scotland and if anything happened to John… well, at least she's got all her WI friends in London."

"Have you heard from your son Gordon, Grace?" asked Meg.

"Yes, he's a good lad. He writes every week." Grace set her cup down on the table before continuing. "He's met someone. A lady. Wants to marry her," she chortled. "I never thought I'd see the day. He's forty next year. I thought he was a confirmed bachelor. He wants me to meet her."

"What line of work is he in?"

"He's a fireman like his dad. He wants to retire next year as he and his new lady have got plans of their own. Heaven knows what," she laughed.

"Sounds interesting. Why don't we invite them down here? Perhaps near Christmas or New Year?" Iris looked directly at Dorothea hopefully.

"Yes, Grace. They would be very welcome."

"We'll see. I've not seen him for nearly five years. She's a nurse but he omitted to tell me her name. Typical Gordon. Takes after his dad. Leaves out the finer details."

"Have you just got the one son then, Grace?" asked Dorothea.

"Yes, I had three miscarriages after out Gordon was born. It was a terrible time."

"Oh Grace!" Meg was thinking of her own miscarriage, which was bad enough but three was another matter altogether.

"We gave up after the third one. George put his foot down. 'We're all right as we are, Grace,' he said."

Meg was secretly praying nothing happened to Gordon. It would be terrible to lose him as well.

As if reading her thoughts, Grace added, "I do worry about him though. I won't be sorry if he changes profession. Being a fireman's not without risk."

"Grace, I'll pay your train fare," said Dorothea. "Go and visit him."

"I appreciate the offer, Dotty, but I would rather he came here to me. Don't ask me why. I want to stay in this house."

"There's cake left in the tin. Who wants a piece?" asked Dorothea.

There was a loud shout of "me" from all the children.

"Did you notice how quiet Josh was yesterday?" Earnest was at the sink washing the dinner pots as Kathleen had a bad headache.

"Yes, poor lad," she said. "He's worried that he'll have to go back home now the war's been declared at an end. He wants to stay here."

"He wasn't happy when his father remarried. It often happens. His step-mother wasn't unkind or anything but it was more a case of her not devoting much time to the lad. He felt isolated."

"Then we'll not let him go back. We'll have to think of a way to keep him here," said Kath. "Put your thinking cap on, Dad."

He was silent for a while, until he'd finished the dishes.

"Leave them to drain, Dad, I'll sort them out later. Have you been into the shop since the new manager arrived?"

"Yes, I called in yesterday for my newspaper. He said he's only doing six months then he's retiring. He'll probably be gone by Christmas."

"Oh. Did he say what he was going to do or where he was going?"

"I didn't get the chance to ask him as it got a bit busy."

"Where is he lodging?"

"No idea," said Earnest, "But I'll ask Ivy when I see her. She knows everything."

Dorothea climbed into bed and reflected on how most of her life had so far been spent trying to please other people. As the eldest of three children, she was expected to set a good example by being a model of good behaviour with impeccable manners. She was constantly reminded of how lucky she was to have such a good education and it was expected that she would excel in her exams and proceed to a top university – which she did.

Aside from this, she was expected to help her mother with all the household chores, including the shopping and keeping her younger sisters amused. When she married Raif, she threw herself into her marital duties with the same energy and enthusiasm she'd used all her life to please her parents. The house was kept spotlessly clean and she learnt to cook and prepare nutritious meals whilst not being wasteful with the housekeeping. She took an interest in Raif's work and made time to sit and discuss events surrounding the workplace.

After five years, her parents started asking about grandchildren and when were they going to start a family. Her mother made it clear she was failing in her wifely duties by continuing to pursue a career, which she deemed selfish and inappropriate for someone in her position, the wife of an eminent worthy. Dorothea refused to discuss this matter with her parents. The fact she and Raif had never used any form of contraception since the day they married wasn't something she wanted to discuss with her parents, no matter how well meaning they were but she did feel guilty at letting them down. To be able to provide them with grandchildren would have given her more joy than anything else she had ever achieved in her life. Whether the problem lay with herself or Raif, she did not know as they never had any tests to find out but they did discuss the possibility of adoption on numerous occasions but decided to continue with their careers, which provided them with a good standard of living.

She thought back to the day he had departed for active service with the Royal Air Force and that frightful row they'd had. At first, she couldn't think what on earth it had been about, then she remembered. Casting her mind back to that day, Raif had been approached by a work colleague who was setting up his own business. He wanted Raif to become a sleeping partner which would have required a substantial investment, robbing them of most of their savings. Dorothea didn't like the sound of it and said so, in as diplomatic a fashion as she could muster, pointing out the pitfalls of such a decision, which would leave them with virtually no savings. Of course, there was no guarantee the business would be a success or even get off the ground. There followed a very long heated discussion about how being successful involved taking risks. Nothing ventured, nothing gained. When you analysed millionaires, they all took risks.

In all the years she'd been married, she had never witnessed such fired-up enthusiasm in Raif. He was animated and buzzing with ideas and plans. He really thought this was his big chance in life, the likes of which he may never see again. He reminded her that his grandfather had been a millionaire and did she really think he got there by not taking the odd risk now and again. When she didn't share his vision, he said maybe they were following different paths in life and should think seriously about whether they had a future together. It all now seemed too ridiculous for words.

Despite all this, she instinctively felt her marriage was a good one. One worth fighting for and she wasn't ready to give up on it yet. On reflection, she wondered if selling his grandmother's necklace was disrespectful to Raif as it was a family heirloom and worth a good deal of money. He'd given it to her as a token of his love.

She quickly shot out of bed and rummaged in her dressing table drawer, eventually finding the pawn ticket amongst her underwear. Holding it in her hand seemed to be symbolic. Was she giving up on her marriage? The urgent need to buy the necklace back overwhelmed her.

* * *

The lads at the bus depot were making fun of her for wearing sunglasses when there was no sun but Dorothea hadn't slept well and she was nursing a glorious headache. They were a good crowd and she enjoyed their friendly banter. There were only two other female drivers apart from herself, Norma and Cath. Norma was married to the bus depot manager and Cath's husband was in the army. Neither of them had any children, so she felt as though she had a certain affinity with them.

She strolled up the lane towards the house and looked forward to hearing all the children's news and more importantly, to a bowl of Grace's homemade soup and a chunk of bread. The children were already home, judging by the noise emanating from the kitchen as she entered the back door. They'd just sat down at the table when they heard the letterbox click.

"I'll go, Mummy," said Jenny, who'd taken to retrieving the mail on a daily basis now. She handed the letters to Daisy and sat down again.

"Two for you, Dorothea, and one for Grace," she said handing out the letters. Daisy thought how nice it must be to receive a letter. She'd written to her friends, which were few, but they'd obviously moved on with their lives and forgotten about her long ago, for none of them ever wrote back to her, so she gave up. It didn't seem to bother her as much as it used to because she now spent most of her days off in Howard's company. He insisted on taking her for a walk with Jenny, then to their favourite cafe for a cup of tea and a bun. They got along famously and she secretly looked forward to their outings more and more as the weeks passed.

"Oh Lord," gasped Dorothea.

"Not bad news, is it?" asked Grace.

"It's from Mildred, Raif's sister. His father's passed away."

"Oh dear. How old was he?" asked Daisy.

"He was ninety-four and in a nursing home. The funeral's next Friday."

"You'd better attend, Dotty. It'll look very bad if you don't," Grace advised.

"Yes, you're right. It wouldn't go down well if I didn't make the effort. They'd look upon it as very bad form. Not that any of them ever had a good word for me anyway. Although to be fair, Mildred wasn't as bad as the rest of them."

It will give me a chance to stay overnight in London the day before. I can then retrieve the necklace from the pawnbrokers, she thought.

"I'll stay overnight at the townhouse with Celia. It will give me a chance to catch up with Carole at the ARP offices."

"Do be careful, Dotty, won't you?" said Grace, suddenly concerned for her safety. London was no place for a woman on her own, especially so soon after the war.

The pawnbroker let her have the necklace back and said it was too expensive for most people's pockets and he'd probably never have sold it. She took this to be a good omen regarding her marriage. Maybe things were going to be all right after all.

Carole was nowhere to be seen at the ARP office so she decided to write to her instead.

John was cooking supper for them at the house.

"We're out of wine, I'm afraid, Dorothea. Would a glass of sherry be all right?" Celia offered.

"That will be fine, Celia, thank you." Dorothea loved sherry as it took her back to her younger days when all the family gathered around the fire at Christmas. Her mother and father weren't big drinkers but her mother allowed herself a schooner of sherry on Christmas Day before dinner and another one at New Year.

John was in the kitchen putting the finishing touches to the meal as Celia settled herself on the sofa next to Dorothea. Handing her the sherry and then taking a sip of her own, she put down the glass on the coffee table before whispering, "Tom's being difficult. My solicitor issued him with the divorce papers but he won't sign them. I was hoping Angus would have a word with him but it's obviously not going to happen."

"Who's Angus?" asked Dorothea, sipping her sherry.

"Tom's brother. He knows everything. I had a word with him. He's the only one Tom will listen to."

"Does he know you've been to a solicitor?"

"Yes. I was hoping he'd have a word with Tom on my behalf and talk some sense into him."

"What's the point of hanging on? You're never going to go back to him, are you?"

"Heavens no. He's just being awkward. He's a control freak. Vindictive. Iain takes after him, unfortunately. John says it doesn't matter, especially at our age."

"Well, if you move to Scotland where nobody knows you, just wear your wedding ring. Who's to know?"

"I can't. I pawned it." They both laughed at this. "I'm not at all sure about this move to Scotland. Don't say anything to John though."

"No, of course not. I do understand your concerns, really I do."

"Dinner is served ladies," shouted John from the doorway.

Chapter Thirty-One

"Josh, are you asleep?" whispered Beth, creeping into the boys' bedroom.

Josh groped under the bed for his torch and switched it on. Beth sat on the end of his bed sipping her cocoa.

"Don't forget what we agreed," she said.

"As if I would," whispered Josh.

Sam and Howard sat up in their beds, all ears.

"We all stick together, no matter what. Don't you three dare let me down. I'm relying on you," said Beth. "Agreed?"

"Agreed," they all chorused.

"Don't worry, I'll think of something," said Sam. "I haven't worked out what just yet. We'll ask Uncle Raif when he comes home. He'll be able to advise us." As the eldest of the four of them, Sam felt he should take charge.

"That was strange, wasn't it?" whispered Howard. "When Aunty Dot said Raif's family didn't have a very good opinion of her. I wonder why that is. I think she's absolutely marvellous."

They all agreed.

"She's very popular in the village too," said Josh. "Aunty Meg said everyone that came into the shop mentioned her dance classes or art classes. She certainly livened things up around here. All the ladies at the WVS and the WI think so too. All those people can't be wrong."

"What was wrong with Rebecca yesterday, Josh? She looked a bit sad," asked Sam.

"She had a row with her mother over Douglas. Rebecca said it was unfair to her dad, who was away fighting for his country and here she was going out with another man behind his back."

"What was her excuse?"

"She said she wasn't 'going out' with him as such. He was just a friend and they only had tea and cakes. Rebecca said she wasn't sure her dad would see it that way."

"It's a bit naive to think that he won't find out. It's only a small village and she didn't exactly hide herself away. Word soon gets around."

"Yes, I know. Anyway, her mother hasn't spoken to her for three days now."

"Hopefully it will all blow over eventually."

Megan made her way into Minehead town centre and commenced her usual walk along the main street where all the shops were. As she checked all the shop windows for any signs asking for help, she collided with a gentleman who was loading old books onto a trolley. A good number of them fell onto the floor.

"Oh, I'm terribly sorry," said Meg. "I was distracted and not looking where I was going." She helped him to reload the books, which he then wheeled into a small shop that had the windows blacked out.

"These are for our boys. We post them out to all the troops," he said, heaving books off the trolley onto a desk.

The place was an absolute tip, Meg noticed.

"I'll get organised eventually," he added.

"I could help you put them into some sort of order if you like," Meg offered. "It would be a lot easier for you then."

"That would be most kind. Yes, I could do with some help. I couldn't offer you much in the way of a wage, I'm afraid. Just a few pounds a week."

"That's all right. I can start now if you like. My name's Megan. Call me Meg."

He offered his hand. "Harry Sutton."

She noticed he wasn't young and he seemed to be puffing and sweating profusely. She took off her coat and smiled at him.

"Let me make us a cup of tea. Where's the kitchen?"

Harry explained he collected all the old books every Monday and then spent the rest of the week parcelling them up. He took them to the post office every Friday. He only worked until twelve o'clock as his wife was disabled and he was needed at home.

By lunchtime, they'd sorted all the books into neat piles on the table.

"Right," said Meg, "Tomorrow, we'll sort them into categories and then label the shelves."

As she walked to the bus stop, waving Harry off in his car, she realised she'd thoroughly enjoyed his company and consequently had a very enjoyable morning.

It was seven o'clock in the evening by the time Dorothea arrived back from London. Meg and Iris were in the kitchen making the cocoa when she entered.

"Hello girls," she said, with more enthusiasm than she felt.

"Hello Dotty. Did you want some supper? Grace has prepared you a sandwich as we weren't sure what time you'd be back."

"Super. I'll have some of that cocoa if there's enough." She gave them both a hug.

"How was the funeral?" asked Iris.

"I'll tell you later when the children have gone to bed." She kicked off her shoes and made her way into the library.

Grace was asleep in the chair and the boys were studying a crossword in the newspaper. Beth and Jenny were playing with Smoky who seemed to come alive at night. Daisy was reading a book. Dorothea noticed she was doing a lot of reading lately and she was sure that was down to Howard who was spending a lot of time in her company.

"Aunty Dot!" they all shouted.

Grace opened her eyes. "Oh Dotty, you're back. I'll get your supper. You must be exhausted."

"Yes, I am a little. I'll have an early night."

"Mr Glass found out where James is lodging," said Josh. "Jimmy, or Jim, they call him. He's renting a room at the pub. He joined them for a drink last Friday."

"The landlord's a decent sort," said Dorothea. "He'll not over-charge him."

"It's a good job I went, Grace. There were only five of us there. Mildred and myself, the next-door neighbour, the cleaning lady and an old work colleague. The solicitor's got the will but he's away at the moment visiting his family in East Sussex so Mildred wasn't sure what was in it."

"Will there be a legacy for Raif, do you think?" asked Iris boldly. "He's the only son, after all."

"I know but Mildred never married so he may have been sensitive to that, although she's not without funds by any means."

"What line of work is Mildred in?" Meg asked.

"She's a teacher. She's been at the same school since she qualified. She's on the Board of Governors for the whole area."

"A career woman then?" added Grace.

"Oh yes. Very much the career woman. The school has been her life. We all went across the road to the pub afterwards. Mildred had pre-ordered sandwiches and we all had a beer."

"What did he die of?" asked Daisy.

"Just old age, I think. Although he had been a heavy smoker for most of his life and he developed emphysema."

"Did you get on all right with him?" asked Iris.

"I didn't really know him all that well. I only met him two or three times. His wife saw to that. She never liked me and didn't want me around. I wasn't good enough for her boy."

"It's a common problem with mothers. Nobody is ever good enough for their sons. I shall have to watch myself when Gordon visits," Grace chuckled.

As Dorothea climbed into bed that night, she reflected on whether

Raif wanted a different life to the one he'd been living with her. Mildred hinted it wasn't the path he originally intended to go down but, due to pressure from his father, there was a general expectation of rising right to the very top in whatever industry he chose to be part of. His father constantly reminded him he'd invested everything in his education and he was expected to succeed.

Dorothea knew the feeling well and the war would be the perfect excuse to do something entirely different when things eventually got back to normality. She had no idea herself what she was going to do. A return to the laboratory didn't appeal to her at all and there was every reason to believe Raif felt the same. Oh, how she wished he were here with her now to discuss things. The good news was she'd managed to retrieve the necklace. Placing it back in the box, she'd hidden it in her underwear drawer.

"Mrs Bray's car broke down at the traffic lights," said Josh. "Sam and I had to push her all the way up the hill to the garage."

"I'm surprised it's still going. She always manages to get petrol I notice," said Dorothea.

"She gave Edna a lift home from the WI meeting last week and it took her a good ten minutes to get it going. Edna said it would have been quicker to walk," said Grace laughing.

"Edna's been seen in the pub enjoying the company of Jimmy," added Josh.

"I'm glad she's found some company," said Beth. "Perhaps she won't be so lonely now. Does she see much of her sister Dolly?"

"I'm not sure that she does, since Dolly got married. They don't even seem to sit together at the WI meetings anymore," said Grace, who was thoroughly enjoying the gossip.

"Does Dolly seem happy, Grace? Since she married?"

"I didn't know her all that well but she seems content."

"Aubrey gave me a compass the other day," said Howard, fishing in his pocket. "It's solid silver and it belonged to his father."

"That was kind of him, Howard," smiled Dorothea, secretly

delighted someone thought so much of her boy – which is how she liked to think of Howard now. "It must be worth something. Look, there's an inscription on the back. I can't read it, the print's too small."

"I'll fetch the magnifying glass," Josh offered. "I'll get Mr Glass to look it up. It'll give us something to do next week."

Meg was enjoying her new job at the second-hand book store. Harry was friendly and easy going. They were comfortable in each other's company and there were no awkward moments.

She discovered his wife had lupus and was confined to a wheelchair for most of the time. They had hoped she would make a full recovery after the initial diagnosis but her condition hadn't improved with time. Consequently, most of the household chores fell on him. Despite all this, he was remarkably cheerful and they laughed a lot.

Meg cleaned the whole shop and organised the books into categories and labelled all the shelves. It didn't matter she wasn't earning much money for she was just glad to be doing something to help the troops, although she wasn't sure for how much longer as the war was officially over.

I'd like to keep this shop going, she thought. Knowing people didn't have much money to spare, the idea of a second-hand book shop might appeal to them, especially for those who had no access to a library close by.

As she waved Harry off, she walked to the bus stop. She had ten minutes to wait for the service that took her back home. It suddenly clouded over and she felt a few spots of rain. She rummaged in her bag for an umbrella and then spotted a familiar face across the road. It looked very much like the vicar's wife, Mary. She was linking arms with a man in uniform and they were laughing, probably at some private joke. They stood on the steps of the pub before facing each other for a farewell kiss, then went their separate ways. Meg knew the soldier was definitely not the vicar.

* * *

It was now early December and a lot of the school children were returning home to re-join their families. Beth, Joshua and Samuel were very nervous in anticipation of being summoned back to London.

Raif still hadn't put in an appearance and there had been no letter from him, Bob or Eddie. Dorothea asked the children to write home but Beth never posted her letter. She had no intention of returning to her parents and tore the letter up into tiny pieces, then dropped it all down the nearest drain.

Joshua told Dorothea he'd done his letter and posted it but he hadn't bothered. It was the only time he'd ever lied to Aunty Dot, who'd been so kind to him and he felt guilty about deceiving her.

Samuel drafted a letter to his father but when he came to address the envelope, he realised he didn't know where to send it. His father was away working in the field hospitals somewhere in France. The house in London, which the family called home, was only rented and he wasn't sure it was even still standing. He contemplated for a long time whether to send it anyway, in the hope it would somehow reach his father but in reality, he felt sure the house would have some new family living there. The letter went into his bedside drawer and was forgotten about.

Grace dished out the soup and placed the bread on the table. She looked forward to the children arriving home for their lunch and filling the house full of laughter with tales of life in the schoolhouse and around the village.

"Mr Glass has joined a club for ex-servicemen, along with Aubrey, Alf and Jimmy. They asked me if we can make some more of the blazers. The members have all expressed an interest."

"How many members are there in the club?" Beth asked.

"About forty."

"Forty?" she gasped.

"They're talking about getting monogrammed badges to sew on the lapels. I thought it was a nice idea. There are various clubs all over the country, so if we get the contract to make them all, we could be in business. What do you think, Aunty Dot? We'd need material and another sewing machine."

"We'd need to ask the bank manager for a loan of some description. I'm not sure how that would go, but we can only ask. If we get the contract, that will strengthen our case. I'll write a letter. Then we'll see."

"Dorothea's late today," said Daisy. "Shall we start lunch or wait, Grace?"

"We'll start. The children are hungry. She must be delayed at the bus depot for some reason, or she may have gone shopping. I'll put some soup aside for her."

"All this rain has played havoc with the vegetable plots," said Daisy. "The ground's sodden. Howard and I had a job finding some decent veg. Perhaps we need to plant some more. If we run out, we're well and truly up the creek."

"I know. I'll mention it to Dotty when she gets home. She'll know what to do. The potatoes and carrots are all right but the lettuces are no good." Grace was worried that they were facing a very bleak Christmas this year. Their rations didn't seem even remotely adequate. They only ate meat once a week at the weekend and their butter ration only lasted two days. She had no idea what she'd be able to put on the table by way of a Christmas dinner and she'd given no thought as to presents for the children. There never seemed to be any parcels from their parents, which Grace found rather strange. Christmas and birthdays passed unnoticed.

Her own son Gordon was never forgotten but she only had the one child and she supposed it was a case of out of sight, out of mind. She felt sad for them.

They heard footsteps on the driveway and looked through the window to see Meg approaching the house.

"I've just seen Dotty. She's taking a little dog to the vets."

"A dog? Are we getting a dog?" Josh was beside himself with excitement. He'd always wanted a dog.

"A broken leg, she thinks. She was following a car which was hogging the road and all of a sudden, the car door flew open and she saw this dog go flying through the air and disappeared over the fence into a field. Someone had kicked it out. Abandoned it. Poor little thing."

"How cruel," cried Jenny.

"There are some awful people around. I don't know how anyone could be so callous." Meg kicked off her shoes and hung her coat in the hallway.

"Will we be able to keep it?" pleaded Josh. His father would never allow him to have a pet as he said it was an extra mouth to feed and that money didn't grow on trees. Apart from which, they made a lot of mess he said. Josh was sure that wasn't true. Not if you looked after them and trained them properly. He was already imagining brushing it and taking it for walks every day.

"I didn't get the chance to ask her. The poor little thing was in pain and she was practically running up the hill."

"It was very irresponsible just kicking it out of the car window like that," tutted Grace.

It was three o'clock by the time Dorothea arrived home for her lunch, having left the dog at the vets. He'd had an operation on his leg to set the bone and she was to collect him the following day.

She arrived home complete with a dog collar, lead, basket, toys and a feeding bowl, together with a dozen tins of dog food. "Heaven knows we can't afford this, Grace, but what was I to do? I didn't have the heart to leave him in the field like that. He was yelping in pain," she smiled ruefully.

"The children are quite excited," Grace told her as she lit the stove to reheat the soup. "Especially Josh."

"How does Iris seem today?"

"Still a bit subdued. Sam caught her crying again when she discovered there was no letter from Bob. She's starting to panic."

"We can only hope that no news is good news."

"Meg's not heard from Eddie either, although she seems to be bearing it better."

"Oh dear. What's to become of us, Gracie? You're my rock. I couldn't have done any of this without you."

"It's the other way round. You're my rock. You rescued me. I dread to think where I would have ended up—"

"Grace, come quick. Beth's fainted," cried Daisy, all of a dither.

They ran into the library where they were all doing their homework. Sam was lifting Beth off the floor and sitting her on the couch.

"I'm all right," mumbled Beth. "I just came over all dizzy for a second."

"Right, young lady," said Grace, "Let's get you upstairs and into your bed. Sam, give me a hand."

The vet said the dog had been well looked after and was in good health despite his unfortunate accident.

"There is a war on, Mrs Swift," he said. "Although I don't condone the ill treatment of any animal, they are an added expense."

The children loved the dog on sight and named him Max, due to him being small.

"What type of dog is he, Aunty Dot?" Jenny asked, as Howard had shown her pictures of dogs but she had never seen one quite like this.

"He's a pug."

"I thought pugs were a sort of beige colour. I've never seen a black one before. He's so cute."

Max was drowsy after his operation and slept for the first day but after that he seemed to come alive, limping around on his bandaged leg. Everybody loved him. Even Smoky didn't seem bothered by his presence and often snuggled up next to him in his basket.

Beth got up the following morning to go to school as usual, seemingly quite recovered from her dizzy spell the night before but three days later, she asked Daisy if she could have a private word.

Daisy showed her to the cupboard in the bathroom where they kept all the sanitary wear and instructed her to change regularly and keep herself clean.

Beth breezed in to the kitchen and announced, "I'm a young lady now, Aunty Grace." She wasn't at all embarrassed by any of it.

Grace realised they were all young adults now, except for little Jenny who was now going to school. The other children in her class weren't very friendly to her at first, calling her a "vaccie", but she told them she hadn't been evacuated, announcing she'd been born at Blythe Wood and that although she'd never met her daddy, he was away fighting in the war and hadn't come home yet. After that little announcement, they seemed to be friendlier towards her and she started to enjoy herself.

Grace made sure Daisy got some time alone with her daughter every day. It was important for the bonding process she decided and sent her to do the shopping or, if it was nice, for a walk in the park with Howard.

"You're home early, Howard," said Grace, surprised to see him at three o'clock in the afternoon, when he was usually on his post round.

"Peter's home from the war. He's claimed his old job back. Evelyn's delighted."

"I'll bet she is too," murmured Grace under her breath. "Don't you worry about it, lad. You've done your bit for the war. You've earnt your rest and you can now concentrate on your writing."

That evening at supper, Iris announced the factory was to close for a limited period, after which it would eventually reopen. She wasn't sure what the new factory would be making; there being no need for parachutes now. All she knew was she would have to reapply for the jobs as they became available.

Megan also came home with a long face stating Harry was closing the shop, having despatched the last batch of books.

Grace, Dorothea and Daisy had spent a full day trying to sort out the allotment, which was in a sorry state due to all the rain, with many plots being waterlogged. A lot of the vegetables were rotten and not fit to be eaten so they were thrown away. They barely had enough food to put on the table and with very little money coming in, things were worse than they'd anticipated.

"I'll speak to Ivy," Grace offered. "She might be able to let us have some eggs. Butter and milk."

"That would be a great help, Gracie. We could make some pancakes, otherwise we'll have nothing for our Christmas dinner," said Dorothea, suddenly brightening.

Word spread around the village like wildfire. The men were slowly returning from the war and claiming back the jobs the womenfolk had been doing for nearly six years. Dorothea wondered how long it would be before she was laid off at the bus depot.

Josh arrived home at four o'clock, carrying a huge bundle.

"What have you got there, lad?" Grace asked.

"Three sets of old curtains. Edna gave them to me. One set is from the back bedroom, which used to be Dolly's. The other two sets are from a lady at the WRVS. I thought they would do nicely for our sewing room. I'm sure we could make something out of them." He spread them out on the table top for everyone to examine.

"What beautiful material," said Daisy and Beth, rifling through the folds of cloth.

"I had to run all the way as Edna said not to let anyone see me with them, or there might be trouble."

"Well done, Josh," smiled Dorothea, ruffling his hair. "Now, put them away and we'll have a good look at them tomorrow. It'll give us all a project for tomorrow, seeing as nobody has any work to go to."

"Except you, Dotty," Iris said mournfully, feeling guilty at not being able to contribute to the household finances now she'd been laid off at the factory.

"Probably not for much longer, Iris. We'll have to plant some more fruit and vegetables somehow. You can help me, girls." She turned to face Iris and Meg and added, "We might have to do a bit of begging to cadge some more provisions from somewhere, otherwise we'll all starve to death."

Chapter Thirty-Two

Stuart padlocked his bicycle and made his way into the kitchen. He lit the stove to warm the place up a bit then ran upstairs to change out of his uniform. As he put on his slacks and jumper, he immediately thought of the dances at the church hall and the happy hours he'd spent in Iris' company. They were the happiest hours he'd ever known, but his head was overruling his heart and he realised he was wasting his time pursuing any kind of relationship with her. She was married to Bob and very much in love. She wasn't his to have.

An overwhelming feeling of disappointment enveloped him as he put the kettle on for a cup of tea. It was only since he'd met Iris and spent time in her company that he realised what was missing in his life. He was becoming staid and predictable and set in his ways.

Tomorrow was Christmas Eve and he was off duty for five days. His boss had given him a bottle of whisky, which he never drank, so he despatched it to his friend Graham at the London station, promising to make time to visit him in the New Year. An invitation to have Christmas dinner with Earnest and Kathleen had been accepted and not wanting to arrive empty handed, he rifled through his cupboards to see if he could find anything to take by way of a gift.

He cobbled some leftovers together for his tea and suddenly thought of his mother's home cooking and baking. How he used to look forward to her shepherd's pie and apple crumble. The cosy evenings they'd spent around the fire listening to the radio becoming clear in his mind. His father lighting his pipe and the sweet smell of tobacco permeating the air. There was some sort of jumble sale thing going on at the church on Christmas Eve, no doubt to boost funds and rather than sit in the house on his own, he thought he might look in for half an hour.

It was nearly lunchtime by the time Stuart arrived at the church hall. He made his way to the back where the WI ladies were serving cups of tea and cakes. Choosing a slice of Victoria sponge, he glanced across the room for someone to talk to. The vicar was smoking a cigar and nursing a glass of something alcoholic and judging by the look of him, it wasn't his first. This was strange in itself as Cyril didn't drink as a rule.

Accepting a cup of tea, he turned in order to find a seat somewhere, when a voice hissed in his ear.

"He's drunk." It was Ruth, Dr Mattison's wife.

"Hello Ruth. Nice to see you. I am a little surprised at Cyril, but it is Christmas after all and we've all had a terrible war. Let him enjoy himself."

"No doubt he needs a drink, especially with that flighty piece he's married to." Her words sounded harsh but Stuart knew there was no malice in them. Ruth was a gentle soul at heart, for all her bravado.

"I must admit, word got around the village about her exploits with the soldiers." Stuart spotted two vacant seats and made a dive for them. "I've always liked Mary."

"Oh yes, me too. Although I don't approve of the way she's behaving. It's disrespectful."

"This war has done strange things to people. They're grabbing everything life has to offer," Stuart mused.

"Well, if some young Jock took a shine to me, I'd feel insulted, quite honestly," said Ruth.

Stuart laughed and bit into his sponge, which was going hard and didn't taste anything like as good as it looked. He glanced around the hall hoping to catch sight of Iris but he couldn't see any of her lot. His heart gave a lurch in a downwards direction before giving himself a good talking to.

"Penny for them?" smiled Ruth chirpily.

"What? Oh, I was just thinking it's strange not to see Dorothea and the children here. They normally attend these sorts of events."

"They've taken the dog to the vets. The plaster comes off his leg today. He was abandoned, you know. Poor mite."

"Yes, I heard about it. They want their ears boxing. Treating a defenceless animal like that."

"They've all been laid off at the factory, you know," said Ruth, changing the subject.

"Have they?"

"Yes, its closing. It will reopen sometime in the New Year. Kath will be all right, but Iris will have to reapply for a job, as and when they become available. Meg's book shop has closed and Howard's lost his post round to Peter, who's returned, so they're all out of work, except for Dotty."

"Goodness me, they'll be struggling. It's bad enough for me and I've only got myself to feed."

"I've spoken to Ivy. She's going to try to help but don't mention it to anyone else. You know what folk are like around here. If they think someone's getting preferential treatment, world war three will break out." They both laughed at this, knowing it to be true.

"Did you notice Cyril smoking cigars, Dad?" asked Kath.

"Yes." Earnest was putting his warm coat on. He was meeting Alf and Aubrey in the pub.

"I've never seen him smoking before."

"They're only human, you know, like the rest of us. Vicar or no," he chuckled.

"He'd had a drink or two, that's for sure." Kath folded up the tea towel and contemplated another lonely night in the back room listening to the radio.

"Yes, I know. I hope he's in a fit state to conduct the evening service."

They laughed, although Kath was a little concerned as it seemed out of character for the vicar she knew and loved. If it wasn't for the cold weather, she'd a mind to attend the service just to see what kind of a hash he made of it.

"What was going on with you and Edna?" asked Kath. "I heard raised voices."

"It wasn't me. I was just trying to break it up. Honestly, that woman takes the biscuit sometimes. It was over a painting, donated from that exhibition at the library. Edna wanted it for her lounge but another lady said she had hold of it first. Edna wouldn't let go of it. Silly woman. But I must admit it was a lovely picture. Samuel painted it. St Michael's Mount, in oils."

"Oh yes, I saw it. I remember it now. So, who got it in the end?"

"Who do you think?" said Earnest. "Edna, of course. The other lady wasn't amused and threatened to stuff her head in the bran tub."

"Good for her," laughed Kath. "Don't be too late tonight, will you, Dad?"

"Now don't you go fretting, lass. I can manage."

She secretly looked forward to him coming home with all the gossip. She would warm his slippers by the fire and have the cocoa ready.

Dorothea had been determined to make Christmas Day enjoyable for all the family. Thanks to Ivy and Alf, they had managed to put a meal on the table. Ivy had called on Christmas Eve wheeling a pram, which she'd borrowed from a neighbour. Underneath the blankets lay a hidden treasure trove of goodies, which Grace had spirited away into the kitchen cupboards. It saved the day. Ivy didn't want anyone to see her carting goods across from the farm because they'd all want something. It was the only way she could think of to get the goods across to them.

They all sat in the kitchen drinking tea and had a good laugh about the jumble sale at the church, which descended into chaos with everyone grabbing things at random off the tables then throwing them back. Mary had tried wading in, shouting "ladies, ladies, please!" Everyone ignored her and carried on as though she wasn't there. Ivy said she couldn't understand what all the furore was about as she'd never seen so much rubbish in all her life.

"Did you go to the evening service, Ivy?" asked Meg.

"Yes, I did. Cyril tripped and knocked the lectern flying, much to the hilarity of the congregation, but he took it all in good spirit. Do you know, I don't think that man's got a bad bone in his body. Mary doesn't know how lucky she is. He seemed to keep losing his place when he was conducting the sermon and ended up repeating himself several times, but nobody minded. There was mulled wine and mince pies afterwards, which went down well. Although the pastry was rock hard and there wasn't much mincemeat in them. It was a nice thought though."

On Christmas morning, they all attended the church service then they returned to the house to change into their outdoor clothes for a walk in the fresh air. It was a dry, crisp day and they meandered across the golf course, ending up around the duck pond in the park.

Arriving home mid-afternoon, Dorothea insisted on making the dinner, with the help of Iris and Meg. Daisy and Grace kept the children amused in the library, playing games. After their meal, Dorothea kept them all entertained with a Christmas quiz which she'd compiled herself. After the children had gone to bed, Dorothea produced a bottle of sherry and they all pondered on what the coming year would bring and how they were going to survive with so little money and provisions.

"Sam! Sam. It's your father. He's coming up the driveway with another man in uniform," shouted Beth.

Meg rushed over to the window, hoping it would be Eddie, but her heart sank when she saw who it was.

"Iris, it's Bob," she yelled.

They all clambered into the hallway in order to greet their visitors. Sam raced through the door but stopped in his tracks when he saw his father was ill. Bob was practically holding him upright.

"Hello young man," smiled Bob and offered him his hand. "This gentleman's extremely unwell. You must be Samuel. Your father needs his bed."

"Come inside, everyone, quickly or we'll all catch our death," ordered Dorothea. "Bob, it's so good to see you."

Iris clambered down the stairs, having aborted her attempt to have a bath and flew into his arms with complete abandon, her face a picture of pure delight. Meg felt a twinge of jealousy creep over her but she quickly squashed it. Of course, she was happy for Iris. Bob had come home in one piece and was fit and well.

"Sam, get your father upstairs and into his bed, while I run across to Doctor Mattison," announced Dorothea, starting to panic.

"It's all right, I don't need a doctor. It's a chest infection. I've got my medication," said Bhutan, gasping for breath.

An hour later, he was tucked up in bed with a mug of Grace's excellent cocoa. Sam sat on the bed with a worried look on his face.

"Don't worry, son. I'll be all right in a few days. I just need to rest," he reassured him.

"Father, you look terrible. You've been overdoing things. You need to slow down. The war is over now. You've done your bit."

"You're right. I am exhausted mentally and physically. I've seen things no man should ever see in his lifetime. Things that will haunt me for the rest of my days. I've still not found Selina and your mother. Her sister is blaming me. She said if I'd been a proper husband, I'd have made sure that she was all right and taken proper care of her before taking off like that."

"Don't torture yourself, Dad. You did what you thought was right. Your skills were greatly needed."

They talked for another half hour before Sam turned off the bedside lamp and made his way downstairs.

Beth ran towards him. "How is he, Sam?"

"He's not good. I've never seen him so ill."

"Has he found your mum and sister yet?" asked Grace.

"No. That's another thing that's bothering him. My aunt's blaming him for not taking proper care of her. My mother's English is not good. I think she panicked when Dad left for active service."

"That's understandable. What about Selina?"

"Her English is excellent. She's a bright girl."

"Well, we must keep a close eye on him," said Dorothea, for want of something to say that would put his mind at rest. She was secretly worried about how they were going to manage with two extra mouths to feed. Iris and Bob had taken root in the lounge at Dorothea's insistence, to give them some space. The rest of the family were gathered in the kitchen, where it was warm. There was a tap at the back door and Grace opened it to find Stuart on the doorstep.

"Hello Stuart. Come in, we're just having our cocoa. Would you like a cup?"

"Thank you, Grace. That would be champion."

"There's nothing wrong I hope, is there?" asked Dorothea, mindful of his last visit to impart news of Howard's mother. They weren't used to seeing the local police at this hour of the night.

"I'm afraid there is, Dorothea," said Stuart, settling himself down at the table. All eyes were upon him as he removed his coat and hung it on the back of the chair. "There has been a severe bout of food poisoning throughout the village."

"Oh?"

"Yes. They've traced it to the mince pies served at the jumble sale at the church on Christmas Eve."

"We didn't attend, but Ivy did. Was she all right?"

"No. She spent all night throwing up and Dolly was very nearly a goner. She ended up in the hospital."

"Goodness me. Where on earth did the mincemeat come from? Presumably Mary made the pies herself?"

"So it would seem, but she said she couldn't remember where she bought it. It was old stock that she was just using up. We fished the empty jars out of the dustbin and sent them off to our laboratory for testing. So I take it that nobody in this house has been ill then?"

"Luckily, no."

"Ivy said the pies didn't taste too good but she seemed all right when she called on us later in the afternoon."

"She took ill in the early evening, according to Alf. The boss asked me to find out exactly how many people were affected."

"You get all the good jobs, Stuart," mused Dorothea.

"Don't I just."

"It must be serious if the whole village is affected."

"There were a lot of children involved and some very angry mothers. Complaints have been filed."

"It's not usually a police matter, is it?" asked Grace.

"No, it's usually Environmental Health that get involved if it's anything serious but seeing as how complaints have been made, we're obliged to be seen to be doing something."

Stuart was hoping for a glimpse of Iris and a friendly chat but on hearing the news of her husband's return, he realised he'd wasted enough time hoping for the impossible. Iris would never be his and he had to get on with his life.

As he cycled back up the lane, he glimpsed across to the pub and saw Alf, Earnest and Aubrey enjoying a pint by the open fire and wondered if Kath would fancy enjoying a meal with him at the cottage instead of sitting in the house on her own on Friday evenings. Not that his cooking skills were up to much but he could keep it simple. Hoping for the best, he decided to take a chance and ask her.

The morning post brought two letters: one for Meg and one for Dorothea. Meg's letter was from Harry asking her if she would consider coming back to the shop as he'd decided to rent the premises and open it up as a second-hand book store. She was delighted and rushed off a reply straight away. She didn't mention anything to the family, in case it all fell through.

Dorothea's letter was from Celia informing her that the move to Scotland was off. John's daughter was expecting another baby and although not exactly planned, it did alter things slightly as she wanted to stay in the house she loved where there were good neighbours who'd been friends for years. She knew their help would be invaluable when the baby arrived.

John was in bed with flu and was so bad that she called the doctor, who assured her there was every chance he'd be as right as rain in a day or two with complete bed rest and plenty of fluids. She moved in temporarily, sleeping downstairs on the couch. If anything should happen to him, she wanted to be there for him. Her feelings ran a lot deeper than she realised and she couldn't imagine life without him now.

There were several enclosed letters, all bills, which Dorothea had no idea if there were enough funds in the bank to pay. Putting them to one side, she determined to think about it later. Right now, she was too exhausted. It had been a long war and she felt demoralised and dispirited. The thought of losing the children weighed heavily on her mind. She knew they weren't hers to keep but she'd begun to think of them all as hers. They were like a real family and she wondered what she'd be left with once they went back to their respective families.

Now Bob was home, she wondered if Iris would be keen to get back to London, to resume her old life. As regards to Megan, she supposed it was possible she would move to Canada to be with Eddie. Part of her wanted to ask her if they'd discussed it but she didn't want to put ideas into her head either, so she decided against it.

Later that evening, Sam informed her Mrs Kloot had received a letter from her husband Charles, who had been released due to his health and was now on his way home. He was still on medication and needed regular check-ups.

Dorothea decided to get a second opinion regarding Sam's father, who was coughing all night. She summoned Dr Mattison who gave strict instructions that Bhutan was to remain in bed, otherwise he'd end up with pneumonia.

Bob was proving very useful around the house as he liked to keep busy, spending hours on the allotment planting new seeds and generally sorting out the garden. He had also decorated two of the bedrooms and put up some extra shelving in the kitchen and pantry.

On Mondays, he helped Daisy with the washing, working the mangle and hanging the sheets out on the line. On Wednesdays, he made the evening meal as it was Grace's day off, who usually spent it in the company of Ivy down on the farm. The first Wednesday, he made some patties out of sausage meat and served them in a toasted bun with chips. He said it was what the Americans ate, which went down well with the children, who loved them. In the evenings, he regaled them with tales of his travels on the ship, keeping them entertained with anecdotes about the countries he'd visited, the food he'd eaten and the people he'd met. There was much poring over maps and looking at flags and currency.

Dorothea had to admit to herself it was good to have a man about the house and like Iris, Bob had slotted straight into the family with ease and seemed quite happy to go along with anything. He often sat with Bhutan, talking for hours and she could hear laughter, so she assumed Bhutan was getting better.

Meg had moved into Dorothea's bedroom in order to make room for Bob. That evening, as they sat up in bed sipping their cocoa, Dorothea asked Meg if she'd heard from Eddie lately. Meg shook her head and continued to stare into space, lost in her thoughts.

"When he called at the house that time, did you discuss the future?"

"I told him I couldn't live in Canada. Couldn't… wouldn't leave my family. I adore living in Blythe Wood, Dotty. With the children and Iris and Grace and Daisy. It's the happiest I've ever been in my life, even though there's a war on."

"How did he react to that?"

"I think he understood, but I'm not sure if I'll ever see him again," she said mournfully.

"Would he consider settling here, do you think?"

"He said he would. He likes it here and the English people. We could always visit his family in Canada. It would be a nice holiday for us."

"Rosine's due tomorrow. I'm going to ask her about Raif. If her husband's been released, he might know what's happening with regards to… well, I can only hope. Like you, I'm not sure he'll be heading home here, even if he does get discharged." Dorothea sighed and turned out the light, the two of them snuggling up together under the blankets.

Sleep, however, eluded her as her mind was too active. Although the war was supposed to be at an end, things didn't seem to be getting back to normal anytime soon. She couldn't see a way forward, but she supposed most people were feeling the same and it was a case of hoping for the best.

Closing her eyes, she focused her mind on the happy times she'd had with Raif when they were first married: the holidays they'd taken, the romantic dinners in little bijou restaurants, the long walks in Hyde Park and evenings at the theatre watching plays or the touring opera companies. Thinking back to their working life at the laboratory, she recalled how she used to write up his notes and reports because he didn't like doing it. No wonder she hadn't had any letters from him. He never did like putting pen to paper.

Josh clipped Max's lead onto his collar and bounded down the lane towards Rebecca's house. They'd taken to walking the dogs every morning before school. Rebecca's dog was a border terrier and although a lot older than Max, he was still lively and eager for his walk. They did two laps around the park, then headed for home.

Josh noticed Rebecca was more quiet than usual this particular morning and wondered if everything was all right, when she suddenly sat down on one of the benches. Josh settled down next to her without saying anything.

"Josh, promise me that if you do have to go back home to London, that you'll take me with you."

"I'm not going back," he reassured her. "Ever. I'm staying here."

"I cannot imagine my life without you now. I want to stay with you."

"Don't worry. I'm not going anywhere and I can't imagine my life without you either, or the family for that matter."

"But what if your father sends for you? Dorothea made you write home, didn't she?"

"I never wrote a letter."

"Oh," smiled Rebecca, "Come on, we'd better get going or we'll be late for school."

Sam, Howard and Josh were just leaving school, having finished for the day, when Rebecca came running towards them.

"Josh, wait!"

"What's the matter?" shouted Josh, on seeing the look of horror on her face.

"It's Beth. She had another one of her dizzy spells and she fainted. Mrs Bray's taken her to the infirmary. You'd better let Dotty know straight away."

Josh was too stunned to speak and didn't know what to do first.

"I'll run to the bus depot," said Sam. "She'll just be finishing her shift any time now. You run home and let Grace and Daisy know what's happening." He shot off in the direction of the depot before anyone could object.

"Come on, Josh, quickly," said Howard, "We'd better hurry."

Sam arrived home at six o'clock, having left Dorothea at the hospital. She wouldn't come home without Beth she said and sent Sam home for his tea. When he came in the back door, the others were eager for news.

"She's having tests," said Sam. "They think there's something not quite right. Doctor Mattison was there as well. He said she had all the symptoms of a growth on the brain. A meningioma."

"Oh, dear Lord!" gasped Grace and sat down with a thud.

"Doctor Mattison said he'd known cases like this before and it is possible to operate, depending on where it is, of course. He also said her symptoms would be a lot worse if the growth was larger, so he thinks it's only small and with surgery she should be all right."

There was a stony silence whilst everyone digested the information.

"We can only pray and hope for the best," said Daisy. "Doctor Mattison is an excellent doctor and very experienced in these matters, so there's no reason to suspect the worst. Poor Beth."

Nobody spoke for a full ten minutes, after which Bob said, "Right, let's get the meal over with, then I'll drive to the hospital and find out what's happening."

"I'll come too, if I may?" said Grace.

Iris was just about to object, but seeing the concerned look on Grace's face, decided to stay silent. The poor woman had gone deathly pale and was clearly distraught.

"I'll clear the dishes and clean up," offered Meg who was also feeling anxious for she was very fond of Beth and thought of her as her own daughter, although she knew that not to be true.

Sam went up to his father's room with the tray and repeated all the news to him.

"What do you think, Dad?" he asked, hoping for confirmation that Dr Mattison's diagnosis was indeed correct.

"Has she had these dizzy spells before?" he asked.

"Yes, a couple of times, but she quickly recovered. This is the first time she's actually passed out."

"From what you've told me, I would have to agree with Doctor Mattison but it's impossible to say without seeing the x-rays."

"Will she be all right, Father? I'm so very fond of Beth. We all are."

"There's every reason to believe so. I'll ring the hospital in the morning and get a full report."

Sam was about to object and insist he do it straight away as he couldn't wait until the morning, but knowing how ill he'd been, it would be unfair to argue. He knew he wouldn't get any sleep that night. If anything happened to his darling Beth, he'd never get over it.

That night as the boys were all clambering into their beds, Josh suddenly asked, "Howard, have you ever been inside a hospital? I haven't."

"Only once and I don't care to dwell on it. It was too awful for words," said Howard, recalling vividly in his memory the unhappy past he'd long ago left behind, the images coming back occasionally to haunt him as though they'd only happened yesterday.

"What happened? Were you very ill?" asked Sam, who was concerned.

"No, I wasn't ill."

"What then?" Josh wasn't going to let it go until he'd heard the full details.

"I hadn't eaten for five days and I collapsed in the school playground. They couldn't bring me round, so they called for an ambulance. I came to in the ward. I was wired up to a drip and a lady from the welfare came to speak to me."

"Not eaten for five days?" Josh was credulous. "I can't go one day without food, never mind five."

"It was all very embarrassing. My mother was sent for and they took her into the office. When she came out, she was crying. I thought perhaps they'd given her bad news and that I was going to die. It turned out that they had given her a stern talking to and threatened to have me taken into care if she didn't buck her ideas up. I was desperately sorry for her. She was sick, you see. It wasn't her fault. We had no money. Some weeks, she couldn't even pay the rent. There was never any food in the larder."

"When you say 'she was sick', what exactly was wrong with her?" asked Josh.

"She was an alcoholic. That's where all her money went. Not that she had much to start with. She wasn't a bad woman but when my father died, she changed. She couldn't cope very well on her own. She relied on my dad for everything, you see."

"So, did things improve for you after that?" Sam asked.

"Not really, but I did get a good feed at the hospital. They kept me in for two days, so I felt good by the time I got home."

Daisy entered, carrying a tray with three mugs of cocoa. "Sorry it's so late, boys. I had to nip to the post office to use the telephone.

Beth's parents were both out. Her brother answered and said he'd make his way up here tomorrow."

"Are Bob and Grace back yet?" asked Sam, eager for news.

"Not yet. Meg, Iris and myself will wait up for them. Drink up, then it's lights out. You've got school tomorrow."

"Can't we have a day off?" asked Josh, hopefully.

"No. Now, don't you worry. She's in good hands."

Dr Mattison's original diagnosis proved to be correct. It was a small growth which was removed successfully. Beth had to remain fully awake during the operation and Dorothea said she couldn't have been more proud of her. She wouldn't leave her bedside and fully intended to camp out in the ward until Beth was discharged.

Three days later, Beth was back home in her own bed enjoying all the home comforts of family life in the house she loved so much.

Sam spent all his free time at her bedside, updating her with events at the school and in the village.

"And how is our little cherub today?" asked a voice form the doorway. It was Bhutan.

"Hi Dad. Come in and sit down here," he said, vacating the only spare chair in the room. "Should you be out of bed yet?"

"Well, Doctor Mattison has given me some stronger antibiotics."

He was wearing Raif's dressing gown, Beth noticed. Sam plonked himself down on the end of the bed.

An hour later, they were still laughing and joking when Daisy came in with the tea tray.

"I've made some biscuits. Grace has gone to see Ivy. It's her day off. They're not as good as hers."

"Do you want a hand preparing the meal, Daisy?" asked Sam, suddenly feeling guilty at wasting so much time doing nothing.

"No, Bob's got it all organised. He managed to get some sausages from the butcher. He's done a casserole. I'll bring it up when it's ready."

Beth's brother Alan arrived later that evening just as they were all settling down in the library. He apologised for his delay in arriving as there had been an altercation at home he said, without going into too much detail. Daisy offered to fix him some supper, which he declined, having called in at the pub first. Dorothea showed him up to Beth's room and with Daisy's help, made up the bed in one of the spare bedrooms.

"If anyone else turns up, we'll have to double up," said Dorothea, for although the house had ten bedrooms in total, some of them were being used for storage.

Just as they were about to retire, there was another knock at the door. It was Mary, the vicar's wife.

"We're trying to raise funds for the church as the boiler won't last much longer. We thought another dance would be the best thing as the last jumble sale was a bit of a disaster," she said handing over a sheet of paper with all the details. "I hope you'll all come. I must dash or Cyril will wonder where I've got to. I've been delivering these for over three hours." And with that, she was halfway down the driveway, without waiting for an answer.

Dorothea wasn't in the mood for another dance but she felt it her duty to attend as the church was a central hub for the whole village, which would be a sorry place without it.

Chapter Thirty-Three

Meg wrote another letter to Eddie explaining about the book shop. Having no other news for him, she was finding it more and more difficult to make her letters sound interesting. The cinemas and the theatres hadn't yet reopened so there was nothing jolly to report. Life was rattling along in the same fashion as it had been doing for the last five years except for the fact there were no more flying bombs.

She marvelled at how the children always managed to find something to laugh about and so did Bhutan, who was a very jolly character and kept them all entertained with his anecdotes. Life was never dull with them around and Meg realised just how much she valued their company and would be lost without them.

A week after posting the letter, she received a letter postmarked Wilmington, Devon and assumed it must be from Eddie, except it wasn't from Eddie but a fellow officer in the same regiment, Michael Lloyd-White. He was writing to notify her that Eddie was on a training exercise with four other officers when their aircraft suddenly began to lose height with alarming speed and with no time to bail out, they hit the ground. There were no survivors. All five of them were killed. One of the crew was only eighteen years old and undergoing his first training session.

He went on to say that he was meant to be in the aircraft instead of Eddie but he was called away at the last minute to run another assignment. Eddie volunteered to take his place. He said it was something which would be etched on his memory for the rest of his days, but if this war had taught him anything, it was that life was for the living and he intended to get on with it and advised her to do the same. She suddenly felt the world slipping away from her, as though she was on the outside looking in. She couldn't seem to get her senses in order. Numbness took over her mind and body.

Stuart took the chicken out of the oven, having stuffed it with fresh lemon, thyme and garlic. The aroma was permeating the kitchen and it looked golden and succulent. He just hoped it tasted as good as it looked. He couldn't quite get the stuffing right and, adding a huge knob of butter to the dish, he stuck it back in the oven with the roast potatoes, which were almost done.

Kath should have arrived half an hour ago and he wondered if she'd changed her mind. He poured himself a glass of wine and turned up the fire in the lounge to warm the place up a bit. Looking around the room, he realised he should have tidied up a bit. Lighting the small table lamp, he put out the main light in the hope of creating more of an atmosphere.

It was the church hall dance tomorrow night but he knew Iris would be dancing with Bob and he found himself lacking the enthusiasm to attend. Still, it was either that or spend another night at the cottage, so he supposed he could do his usual trick of people watching from the side-lines, which was always good for a laugh. A light tapping noise woke him from his reverie.

"Kath, thank goodness you've come. I thought you'd changed your mind," he said enthusiastically, ushering her through the front door.

"Sorry I'm late. It was Dad. He drives me mad sometimes," she laughed.

"What's he been up to then?"

"Oh, something smells good." She followed him through into the kitchen and saw the chicken resting amongst a bed of vegetables.

"I'll just make the gravy," said Stuart. "Would you like a glass of wine whilst you're waiting?"

"I'll do the gravy, if you like?" she offered, hanging her coat up in the hall. She washed her hands at the sink and pushed up her sleeves ready to pitch in.

"Thanks. It might be a bit lumpy if I do it," he laughed. He poured her a glass of wine and topped up his own glass then got out the carving knife.

"So, what was Earnest up to then? Is he all right? He's not ill, is he?"

"Oh, you just wouldn't believe the state he came home in today. He went into Minehead to get himself a new tie for tomorrow night's dance at the church. Don't ask me what's wrong with his old ones, but he said they were all fraying. Anyway, when he got off the bus, he got talking to two ladies who were sat on the wall enjoying the sea view. They asked him if he'd take a photograph of them. You know what he's like, always ready to oblige. He said it was a very old camera and he was busy trying to work the thing when a huge wave came over the sea wall. The two ladies were saturated and the force of the water hit Dad full on and he fell backwards. He ended up flat on his back with his legs in the air. The water washed right over him."

"Good grief. Was he all right?"

"Oh yes. The two ladies wanted to take him back to their hotel room to dry out, but he refused. Luckily, when he got to the bus stop who do you think was driving the bus? Dotty. When she saw the sorry state he was in, she drove him right to the door. The neighbours were all wondering what on earth the bus was doing coming down our street."

Stuart laughed. "Didn't he notice the wave? It must have been huge."

"That's what I said, but he said he didn't. He was fiddling with the camera. Anyway, I ran him a hot bath and pressed him a clean shirt. He'll have something to tell the lads in the pub tonight."

"I'm not really in the mood for this, Dotty. My heart's not in it. I think I'd rather be at home with Meg. The poor girl hasn't eaten a thing since she got that letter about Eddie. I'm a bit worried about her," said Grace.

"Yes. I might not stay long. The children don't seem as keen either."

Alan had offered to sit with Beth and Bhutan as dancing wasn't one of his favourite things to do and neither of them were yet fit enough to leave the house. Megan said she wanted to be alone with her thoughts and refused to attend.

They linked arms as they all trudged up the pathway to the church; their feet crunching on the gravel. Edna and Dolly were on the door collecting the money as they went in. They were each given a raffle ticket for the prize draw. Daisy asked what the prize was but they weren't sure as Mary had organised it all. She linked Howard's arm as they made their way into the hall. As usual, it was freezing cold and most of the seats were taken. They all headed towards the table at the back where the drinks were being dished out.

"I wish they'd sort the heating out in here," grumbled Grace.

"That's probably why they're trying to raise funds," mused Dorothea. "They need a new boiler, according to Cyril."

"I can't see them getting it just yet. The war's only just finished. It'll be a long time before—"

"Hello Grace," shouted Ivy from across the room. "I've saved us some seats." She waved to them and instructed Alf to get the drinks in.

Dorothea was relieved. Ivy was always good company.

They'd been there for over two hours when Cyril called everyone to attention to do the raffle. There were three prizes. The third prize was a ladies' silk scarf. Dorothea assumed it was one of Mary's cast offs but it was still in its box so it obviously hadn't been used. The second prize was a gentleman's toiletry set.

"One of Cyril's unwanted Christmas presents, I expect," whispered Ruth. "It looks expensive though."

The first prize was a food hamper, beautifully presented in a wicker basket.

"Aunty Dot, can we go home yet?" asked Josh who didn't seem himself tonight and was very quiet.

"Yes, let's get our coats. I've had enough. I'll ask the others if they want to stay."

Bob and Iris were eager to get back home as Iris was feeling a bit under the weather. The only ones who seemed to be enjoying themselves were Daisy and Howard. Grace only had one dance with Earnest as his back was hurting after his fall a couple of days ago.

"Come on, Kath, let's get your dad back home to his bed," ordered Stuart, hoping she wouldn't be offended.

"Will you come in for a nightcap?" Kath offered. They were getting on a lot better than Stuart ever imagined they would.

"You bet," he replied with a big grin. He had thoroughly enjoyed their evening together at the cottage and hoped Kath had too. She was proving to be good company and they laughed all night, the conversation flowing easily between them with no awkward gaps. She had helped him wash up and then he took her home, arriving just as Earnest was coming back from the pub.

"What's up with Josh tonight?" asked Dotty.

Sam looked over his shoulder to make sure nobody was listening then replied, "It's Rebecca. She danced all night with another boy from her class. She totally ignored him."

"How odd," said Grace. "You must ask him for all the details later and let us know. Poor lad. No wonder he's upset."

"So, Alan," asked Dorothea, "Is your mother coming to see Beth? She would be most welcome."

"To be honest, that's what the row was about. I haven't said anything to Beth, just that she's very busy. Dad's away in Scotland playing golf with his chums. Mum's launching herself into this new business venture she's hell bent on pursuing."

"Oh, that sounds interesting. Tell us about it."

"Well, it's a sort of events organiser thing. Weddings, birthdays, anniversaries, that sort of thing. She organises the whole thing, the venue, catering, flowers. She said she's waited years for this and nothing and nobody is going to stand in her way. I said 'Mother, your daughter's just had brain surgery.' She literally hit the roof, shouting and getting very angry. I told her she was being selfish but she wouldn't back down, arguing that it was too important and she deserved a life too. There was some big event on at the golf club that she was organising and she was determined to see it through. It wasn't convenient to just go swanning off like that she said. In the end, she told me to pack my bags and get out as she'd 'had enough'. So, you see, I can't really go back."

Dorothea was so shocked she didn't know how to answer. Eventually, she asked, "How old are you, Alan?"

"I'll be eighteen soon. I'll have to find work of some sort. I did think about joining the Navy."

"Don't rush into anything. You can stay here with us for now. We'll think of something."

"Thank you so much, Dorothea. I would like to spend some time with Beth."

"What's the hold-up?" whispered Howard. "I'm starving."

Daisy smiled at him and told him he'd have to wait as Meg and Alan hadn't returned yet, but it was all ready.

"Where have they gone?"

"Meg went out for a walk after lunch. She's been gone for over five hours. Grace is a bit worried. Meg's not been herself since she got the letter about Eddie. She's hardly eaten a thing, poor girl."

"Life can be very cruel at times. Can't it, Daisy?"

Daisy nodded and went back to her duties. She knew if her relationship with Howard was to continue, she'd have to tell him about Jenny's father, but she was at a loss as to how much to tell him or indeed if it was better to just tell him the truth. A nagging feeling at the back of her mind was urging her to be careful as Howard might not want her if he knew what had happened. She was a fallen woman after all. Her attacker said she had asked for it and got what she deserved. All because she had refused to dance with him. What kind of man behaved like that just because a girl refused him a dance? She could understand him being disappointed or slightly embarrassed but she'd declined as politely as she could, saying she was feeling a little off colour and therefore about to head for home but she thanked him all the same. After which, she headed for the cloakroom to fetch her hat and coat.

Alan breezed in the back door and headed straight over to Grace who was at the stove stirring the casserole. He planted a kiss on her cheek and gave her a hug.

"What's that for, lad?" she joked, but was secretly pleased as she'd quite taken to the boy.

"Your little plan worked a treat, Grace. I've got a job."

"A job? Where?"

"I went to see Ivy and Alf. They've given me a job on the farm helping out. I start in the morning."

"Oh Alan, I'm so pleased for you. It'll be hard work, mind."

"Alf said he's feeling the strain now that age is creeping up on him but to give up the farm would break his heart. Ivy was thrilled. She's given me a basket of fruit." He handed the basket to Grace who was beaming from ear to ear. She ladled out two portions of stew and handed the trays to Sam and Josh.

"Take these upstairs, boys, for Beth and Bhutan. I'm not sure about dessert yet but we'll think about that later. Then wash your hands and we can eat."

"I can't see Meg," said Daisy, who was at the kitchen window glancing up the lane. "Shall I put my coat on and go and look for her, do you think?"

"No, we'll hang on a bit longer," said Dorothea, who was now getting more than a little concerned about her sister's welfare.

They heard the front door bang and Meg wandered into the kitchen looking windswept but happy.

"Sorry, everyone. I went into Minehead about a job." She quickly told them about Harry reopening the book shop. They were all ears and it provided much lively conversation around the table.

They'd just finished their meal when two figures appeared in the doorway, sporting dressing gowns and eager expressions.

"What's going on?" asked Beth. "We can hear you all. What's happened?"

Dorothea jumped up and ushered them around the table. "Boys, fetch some more chairs from the library."

"The shop next door has just become vacant as well," continued Meg, after she'd repeated the whole story for their benefit. "Harry's thinking he might rent that as well and turn it into a little cafe. He could knock through the joining wall. He'll have to get planning permission, of course."

Alan then told Beth about his job on the farm with Ivy and Alf.

Beth couldn't hide her joy and shot off her chair, running straight into his arms. "My clever, clever brother. I'm so proud of you both." She ran over to Meg to hug her too.

Meg felt her heart melt a little. Perhaps, just perhaps, life was worth living after all and she might just survive. It was the first time she'd felt anything since that letter arrived and she was amazed at herself by actually wanting to help Harry run the shop.

"I could help out at the cafe," offered Bhutan, who was joining in the conversation as always. "I love cooking. Magda and her sisters ran a transport cafe in the early years of our marriage whilst I was still a student at medical school. I helped out when I could. I loved it."

"Aren't you going back to the hospital then, Father?" asked Sam, who was shocked at this sudden declaration.

"I'm not sure I want that kind of life anymore, son. I've had enough. I'm not young, you know, and this war and this health scare has made me think and see things very differently."

They all decamped to the library where Dorothea told them of her conversation with the bank manager regarding a bank loan to start their tailoring business. "He wants me to draw up a business plan. Whatever that is."

"What's a business plan, Aunty Dot?" Josh was thrilled his own project was being given consideration and therefore still on track. Not that he wasn't pleased for the others but he was more determined than ever now to work hard and achieve his dreams.

Rebecca's behaviour at the dance had taught him a lesson he wouldn't forget. He knew what had happened, of course. It took him a while to work it out but now, he was sure. He'd beaten George Blair in the spelling test at school. George Blair, who nobody could touch, who always came top in everything, who always got "star pupil" every month. It didn't sit well with him when Josh outshone him and the whole class clapped and cheered.

Later, in the playground he'd crept up behind him and sneered in his ear, "You'll be sorry. I'll make you pay for this." So, that was his revenge. He'd made a play for Rebecca. No doubt encouraged by her mother who was eager for her daughter to get on in life and only wanted the very best for her. George was from a very wealthy family and could offer her the sort of lifestyle he could only dream about. Her mother would have pointed this out to her, he was sure of that. Even so, he was disappointed that she hadn't put up more resistance. After all, it was only a few days previously that she'd told him she couldn't imagine living without him. How fickle life was.

It left him feeling confused and more than a little annoyed and angry with George Blair, but he'd decided to let it go and chalk it down to experience. After all, he still had the family up at the house. He still had Howard, Sam, Beth, Aunty Dot, Aunty Meg, Aunty Iris, Uncle Bob, Aunty Grace and Daisy and Jenny, and more importantly, the beautiful house itself, Blythe Wood. Ever since he'd first set eyes on it, he knew instinctively that there was something very special about it. There really was nowhere on Earth like it and he couldn't ever imagine living anywhere else.

"I'm not sure, Josh, but I'll go up to the warehouse tomorrow morning and have a word with the manager there. Gerry's a friend of Raif's and I'm sure he'll know what to do."

Samuel was feeling a little lost. He wasn't sure where he was going in life or what he was going to do to earn his living. Josh and Beth were both keen to pursue their clothing business and, with Aunty Dot's help, he was in no doubt they would succeed.

Howard was now writing plays for the radio. His two children's books had been a success and the sales figures were moderate, even for a new writer like himself.

Dorothea had asked Sam what he liked doing and he told her he loved painting and would love to go to art college.

"But Aunty Dot, I have to earn my living. How can I do that and go to art school at the same time?"

"Well, if you are good, and I truly think you are, you can sell your paintings or artwork. Lots of other people do. You have to believe you can succeed, Sam, and you will. Have faith in your abilities. Believe in yourself."

Her words turned over and over in his mind so much that he wanted to discuss it with his father but he'd been too ill and to burden him with it would be selfish.

Before the war, his parents had talked of himself and his sister Selina going to university. Would they be disappointed if he chose a different path in life? Of course, all of that was before the war had come along and thrown everyone's lives into turmoil.

Every night when he climbed into bed, he wondered if his mother and sister were still alive. Writing to his aunt requesting to be informed the minute they were found had produced no response. He hoped and prayed that wherever they were, they were together, for he felt sure Selina would survive. She was bright and street-wise and spoke very good English. He had no doubt his mother would be quite safe under her guidance. Of course, being clever wouldn't necessarily stop them getting hit by a flying bomb.

"Penny for your thoughts, Sam?"

He turned around to see Beth staring at him from the doorway.

"Hey, no dressing gown?" he laughed.

"Doctor Mattison said I can get up now but I've to take things easy for a bit. You seem a bit sad, it's not like you."

"Oh, I was just thinking of my mother and Selina, wondering if they are still alive."

"No news from your aunt yet then?"

"No. I just need to know that they're safe, wherever they are. Is that too much to ask?"

Beth sat down beside him and lay her head on his shoulder. She was secretly disappointed her own mother hadn't come to see her. Having undergone major surgery which could have easily resulted in her losing her life, it was the least she'd expected but neither of her parents had put in an appearance. Her mother was tied up in her new business venture, but what about Dad? Why hadn't he come? His golfing holiday must be over by now, surely? She knew Dorothea had written to them with all the details of her operation and her recovery. Most of the tumour had been removed but there was a very small bit left which, due to its location, they couldn't get at. Confident that with luck, she would live a normal life, they'd discharged her. As long as she could stay within the walls of the beautiful Blythe Wood, she knew she'd be safe.

Swinging the jeep into the warehouse car park, Dorothea was amazed to see it practically empty. Normally, she would have trouble finding a space. Something was wrong here. Making her way into the building, she was pleased to see Tim, the concierge, sat at his desk reading a newspaper.

"Hello Tim. Where is everyone?" she asked jauntily.

Tim looked up from his paper and stood up to greet her. "Hello Dotty. You're lucky you've caught us here. We're closing down after this week. All the staff have been given notice. Half of them haven't even bothered to turn in and work their notice. Gerry's very upset about it."

"Goodness, what's happened then, Tim?"

"He'll tell you himself. Go on up. I'll buzz him and let him know you're on your way."

She headed for the lifts and felt her heart sinking to her boots. If Gerry couldn't make a go of things with all his expertise and experience, what chance had the rest of them got? She knocked tentatively on his office door before popping her head around. He was knee-deep in files and folders, having emptied out one of his filing cabinets. His secretary Pat was making a separate pile by the waste bin.

"So, what's news, Gerry?" she shouted across from the doorway.

"Oh, hello Dotty. Come in. Pat is helping me sort through this dross that's accumulated in my cabinets over the years."

"I'll pop the kettle on, shall I?" Pat smiled at Dorothea and heaved her bulky frame across to the back of the room. She looked less like a secretary than anyone she'd ever seen. Her curly hair was a tangled mess and her skirt was stretching at the seams. A thick woolly jumper was hiding rolls of fat and she was sporting flat lace-up brogues. Dorothea liked her instantly. *She's my kind of right-hand woman*, she thought. Looking at it in a more practical light, she supposed if you worked in a warehouse such as this you didn't want to be ruining your best clothes humping boxes around.

Gerry ushered Dorothea into a chair opposite his desk and cleared a space amongst all the paperwork. "Sorry about all this mess. Things aren't normally as bad as this, believe me. I'm just trying to declutter. Bigger job than I thought."

"Is it right that you're closing down?" Dorothea couldn't help but feel sorry for him. The warehouse had been his life for as long as she'd known him, certainly for as long as she and Raif had been married.

"Well, it's been on the cards for a while but with the war and everything, things have been gradually grinding to a halt. I couldn't delay the inevitable any longer. I've just got one last large order to despatch, then we're done. The trouble is most of the staff have done a runner, so I don't even know if or when this order will get completed."

"Good grief, Gerry. After all these years, it's come down to this. What will you do?"

"Ask me another."

Pat placed a tray on his desk containing two mugs of tea, a milk jug, sugar bowl and a plate of digestive biscuits. "I'll just nip downstairs and see how things are going on the shop floor whilst you two have a chat," she said, heading towards the lifts.

"I'm so sorry, Gerry," said Dorothea. "I suppose a lot of businesses have gone the same way. Not that that's any consolation."

"No, well, we're still alive. That's the main thing."

"If the receivers are coming in, I'd spirit away some of your stock."

"Don't worry, I've already thought of that. So, what can I do for you?"

"Gosh, I feel guilty even asking now. It doesn't seem appropriate now you've got all this on your plate. How is Hilary, by the way?"

"Oh, she's fine. The dogs take up most of her time. When she's not trekking across the common in muddy boots, she's mostly in her studio. We converted one of the outbuildings."

"Does she still paint then?"

"Yes, very much so. She used to teach at the art college until just before the war."

Dorothea quickly told him about Samuel and found herself gushing effusively about all the children. She couldn't help it as she was so proud of them all.

"I'll have a word with her," he said. "Write your address down for me and I'll be in touch. She may be able to help him but I don't want to push it, just in case."

Mentioning the possibility of acquiring the contract to make the club blazers, she asked him for advice.

"I'm not sure that I'm the right person to be asking considering the mess I've made of things here, but you'll certainly need additional orders besides the club blazers. Once each club member has been kitted out, it'll just be a case of supplying new members. You'll need to diversify. Did you say the kids had made dresses too?"

"Yes, out of some old curtains. Two cocktail dresses, a three-quarter length jacket and a ladies' trouser suit."

"Let me have a think about all this, Dotty. I can certainly draw up a business plan for you. I had to do it when I started up here. Bank managers need to know where their money's going. How about meeting up again next week?"

She thanked him and tried to reassure him that something would turn up. "Don't give up hope, Gerry. You've been in this business for too long to just throw it all away. Even if it means starting all over again on a new project, you can do it, you know you can."

"Hmm," was his only response, scratching his head.

Chapter Thirty-Four

Dr Mattison snapped his bag shut and advised Bhutan to get as much fresh air into his lungs as possible. He wasn't to overexert himself and he didn't advise returning to work just yet. Although he was now out of the danger zone, he was by no means fighting fit and needed to take more care of himself. He wouldn't sign Beth off either and advised her to have a further two weeks at home before returning to school.

"Mummy, look," said Jenny, handing Daisy a black and white photograph of a cart horse pulling a gypsy caravan.

"Where did you get that, darling?" Daisy studied the photograph with interest.

"Alan got it off Ivy. Can we go please, Mummy?"

"Go where, darling?"

"Not sure where. Can we go?"

Bob peered over Daisy's shoulder. "I'll go and ask him about it," he laughed, ruffling Jenny's hair.

Daisy thought no more about it and returned to her duties. Samuel arrived home earlier than usual and seemed forlorn.

"You're early today, Sam."

"Yes. They've dispensed with my services at the library, unfortunately."

"Oh Sam, no. Why?" Daisy sat down with him at the kitchen table, ironing forgotten temporarily.

"Well, it was Mr Potts, the manager. He said it was his duty to repatriate the soldiers who fought in the war. It was important he assured me. He's given Charles the job."

"Ah." Daisy couldn't think of anything to say that would make him feel any better.

"I don't begrudge him taking my place. He did fight for his country after all, but I will miss it."

"It does seem cruel but yes, you're right. The soldiers have to find work somewhere. Dear me, Sam, what's to become of us all? What's happening to us?"

"The world is changing, Daisy. That's what."

During dinner, the subject of the black and white photograph came up again. It belonged to Ivy's brother who ran a farm in Ireland. Alan explained that people hired the horse and caravan, for a fee of course, and they travelled all over the countryside. Her brother made quite a lot of money from it.

"Let me see that," said Dorothea, suddenly getting ideas.

"I really fancy having a go at it," said Alan, looking around the table to see if there were any other takers.

"So do I," said Bob, looking at Iris.

"I'm game if you are," she laughed.

"Me too," shouted Jenny, "And Mummy."

"We could all do with a holiday," Dorothea said forcefully. "The fresh air would do us good. We've been cooped up indoors for too long. Alan, can you find out from Ivy how much it would cost?"

"Of course. I'll ask her in the morning."

"There's a lot of us. We'd need about three caravans."

"Right. Bhutan, are you up for it?"

"Yes, please. It would be an adventure for me and Sam. We've never done anything like this before and it will give us a chance to talk and be together. I've been separated from him for far too long," he said, looking guiltily across at his son, who seemed to have lost his spirit lately.

"Grace? Meg? Daisy?" asked Bob hopefully.

"Where on earth would we get the money?" asked Grace who had neither the money nor the clothes for holidays. The practicalities of this trip didn't seem feasible to her.

"Let's find out what it would cost first, then we'll cobble something together," Dorothea's voice had taken on a "no-nonsense" tone and she would brook no argument. "Either we all go or not at all."

The children couldn't hide their joy.

"What about Smokey and Max?" asked Josh, looking worried. He didn't like the thought of leaving them behind, even if it was only for a week.

"They're part of the family, so they'll be coming with us," said Dorothea. "We won't need fancy clothes. It's not that sort of holiday. We'll slum it for once. It'll be good for us. We'll be free and easy to enjoy ourselves. You can't do that if you're worried about messing up your attire. We'll take our swimwear for the beach, a toothbrush and our pyjamas. We'll manage."

Jumping into bed next to Dorothea, Meg placed two mugs of cocoa on the bedside table. "Sorry it's so late. I had to help Daisy with Jenny."

"What's the matter with Jenny?" asked Dorothea, feeling the hot liquid warming her through.

"An upset stomach. She thinks it's the apples."

"Oh yes, she mentioned it once before. It might be an allergy or something."

"Rosine was very vague the other night when you asked about Raif, wasn't she?" said Meg, changing the subject.

"Yes. I went into the library last week to see if I could speak directly with Charles but he kept disappearing. I'm sure he was avoiding me. And Rosine hot-footed it into Norman's office."

"She isn't doing our French lesson anymore either, is she?"

"No, she said she wants to devote all her free time to Charles, now that he's home. She's not convinced he's one hundred percent fit and he won't talk about his war experiences other than what we already know. Raif was instrumental in saving his life and hailed him an absolute hero."

"Bob said it was Raif that kept Charles afloat when their aircraft came down. They'd been in the water for hours before Bob's ship picked them up. He said it was a miracle they survived."

"Bob doesn't seem to be too badly affected by his war experiences, does he?"

"Iris says he rarely talks about it, which infuriates her. She's convinced he doesn't want to worry her. Same old Bob. Keeping himself busy the way he does is probably his way of dealing with it."

Dorothea sighed into the silence. "It's been a terrible business, this war. I hope that I never have to live through another one in my lifetime. I don't think I could stand it."

"No, neither could I," said Meg, thinking of Eddie.

"What happened to that girl at the factory? The Irish girl who had a 'liaison' with Douglas? Has she had the baby yet, do you know?"

"Iris didn't know when I mentioned it but she talked of being honest with her husband when he returned and just telling him the truth. There's not much else she can do really."

"I wonder how many other girls are in the same boat?"

"Me included. I could have been nursing an infant myself."

"Oh Meg, don't."

"I'm sorry I lost the baby. Just nature's way. Looking back now, it was probably for the best." Meg wondered what had happened in Daisy's case. Where was Jenny's father? Dorothea never mentioned the circumstances surrounding her situation and she didn't feel as though it was her place to ask. Grace hadn't mentioned it either. Daisy was so young to have a child, but she proved to be a wonderful mother all the same. Jenny told her friends at school her daddy was away fighting in the war, but Meg wasn't convinced that was true. Dotty wasn't convinced Raif would return either. Thank goodness, they all had each other. Having survived the worst of it, surely the rest would be easy now, wouldn't it? Life had to get better now that the war was officially over, didn't it?

"When is Harry opening the shop?" asked Dorothea.

"He's got to get permission to knock the wall through first, then he can set about getting a coat of paint on the walls. When things get going, he'll be in touch. That's providing he doesn't hit any problems."

"It's something to look forward to then."

"What about you, Dotty? What does the future hold for you?"

"I can't bear to even contemplate it. Not without Raif."

"Why don't you have a word with Earnest? See what he can find out for you from the Home Office? You need to know if and when Raif will be discharged at the very least."

"Yes, I might do." There was a long silence before she added, "I'm almost afraid to discover the truth. What if he's already been demobbed and living elsewhere?"

"Surely not?"

"Rosine and Charles have been avoiding me. There's got to be a reason for that. Something's up."

"Not necessarily," soothed Meg, suddenly feeling a bit panicky. What if her sister was right? What if they all had to get out of the house and look for somewhere else to live? This lovely house that she had come to love so much. The very thought of leaving Blythe Wood filled her with dread. "I can't see Raif walking out on you just because you had a silly row all those years ago. Lots of couples argue. It doesn't mean anything."

"According to Gerry, if Raif had invested money in that business venture that he was hell bent on getting involved in, he would have lost everything."

"How does he know that?"

"Well, there was a fire at the depot and he lost all his stock. He wasn't insured. He had to declare himself bankrupt, as will Gerry shortly."

"Thank goodness you had the sense to talk him out of it."

"I'm not sure he saw it that way at the time."

"You've got more business acumen and insight than he'll ever have. He should be grateful, not resentful."

"Why thank you, dear sister," she laughed.

* * *

It had been quite an eventful week. Dorothea completed her last shift at the bus depot. She was given two weeks wages in lieu and finished on the spot. She knew what had happened, of course, and although expected, she was sad to go. There were new faces everywhere. Soldiers were returning to their homeland to pick up where they had left off.

When Dorothea arrived home, there seemed to be a discussion under way. Josh had received a letter from his step-mother informing him his father had passed away two weeks ago after a short illness. He was buried alongside his wife, Josh's mother. There was an apology for the lateness of the letter but due to the speed that everything had happened, she was still in a state of extreme shock and hadn't yet come to terms with it. She had decided to pack up everything and go to her brother's house in Norfolk for the foreseeable future as there was now nothing to keep her in London. His father hadn't made a will. Not that he possessed anything of any value. The house was owned by the council and there was only enough savings to cover the cost of the funeral. Sadly, he owned very little in the way of personal possessions. Even his watch no longer worked.

She promised to send him the money from the sale of the furniture and hoped he would be happy staying with the nice lady Dorothea. Promising to write to him in the near future, she didn't elaborate as to how often or indeed what he was to do if he wasn't happy with the arrangement or if Dorothea could no longer extend his stay. Enclosed was a copy of the death certificate which listed TB as the cause of death. Being a heavy smoker for most of his life, he always had a chest which rattled like an express train.

"Well," snapped Grace. "I don't know what to make of all this. You should have been informed and at least been able to attend the funeral. Heck, lad, I'm so very sorry."

Josh's face turned white and Dorothea threw her arms round him and hugged him so tightly she nearly knocked the breath out of him. "What a thing to happen."

She took the letter from him and read it through out loud for everyone to hear.

"Right, well, that's settled then. This is your home now, Josh my lad. That goes for all of you," she said softly, looking across at Beth, Sam and Howard.

"Thank you, Aunty Dot. I'd like to stay please, if that's all right." Josh's voice was barely above a whisper.

"It's more than all right. It's a given."

The result of Dorothea being finished at the depot meant no one in the household was earning any money. The only income was the rent money from Celia who was still at the townhouse in London.

Fortunately, Alan was loving his job on the farm and came home with eggs, butter and milk most days. He offered up all his wages but Dorothea refused to take the money. She didn't think it would be fair. Ivy had written to her brother in Ireland telling him all about the family and asked if he could accommodate them all. Alan could hardly contain his excitement and enthusiasm. Dorothea made up her mind to get the family over there somehow. They all needed a change of scene. She was determined to speak to Ivy in person to get more details.

It was Grace's day off and she hot-footed it over to Ivy's. Dorothea had taken Howard to London for a meeting regarding the play he'd written for the radio, based on his children's book. Daisy was disappointed not to have her usual walk in the park with Howard, but she was so pleased his writing seemed to be attracting attention in all the right places with the right people who could help him. Bob had taken Bhutan out in the jeep to purchase more seeds to plant in the allotment. Meg had gone to meet Harry regarding plans for the shop, so Daisy had the house to herself.

As much as she loved the house, she much preferred it when the children were around. The meagre rations she'd managed to purchase didn't seem nearly enough to keep them all going. The butcher had given her four extra sausages but she knew they wouldn't be much use in feeding a family of twelve, as they were now. She glanced down into her basket and wished she had more persuasive powers like Iris, who always did quite well in obtaining extra bits and pieces to pad out the meals.

As she made her way up the driveway towards the house, she could hear voices.

"This can't be the right house. There's nobody here."

"It is the right house, Mother. I can assure you."

Two ladies in land army uniforms appeared from around the side of the house.

"Oh hello," said Daisy. She knew immediately who they were as the resemblance to Samuel was unmistakable. "You must be Magda and Selina."

Putting down her basket, she ran towards them, hugging each of them in turn. "I'm so pleased to meet you both. Come into the house and I'll make some tea."

Daisy filled the kettle and placed it on the range. "So, you joined the land army then?"

"Yes. It was very tiring. Very hard work," said Selina. "It was my idea. I've been in Mum's bad books ever since."

Daisy heard Bob's voice and ran out to meet them. "Come in the kitchen a minute."

"Why, what's wrong?" asked Bob who was eager to get planting the seeds before it got dark.

Bhutan nearly collapsed with shock. "My prayers have been answered. At long last. Both my precious girls home safe."

There were more hugs then tears as Daisy busied herself with the tea and biscuits.

"I'll help you plant the seeds, Bob," she said, pulling off her apron and heading for the door. "Bhutan, you stay and catch up with your family."

The trip to Ireland proved to be a roaring success. Ivy's brother and his wife welcomed them with open arms and made them very welcome. They saddled up three horses for them and with the help of maps and guides they trotted all around the coastal paths, heading in a different direction each day.

Max was in his element, riding pillion on the horse's back, enjoying the fresh air whilst Smoky seemed quite content to stay in the caravan. They breakfasted on porridge made with cream topped with fruit, unlike their own version back home which was always made with water. They ate nothing during the day as they had no money to buy anything. Bhutan and Dorothea split the cost of their stay between them and no one complained of feeling hungry as they were happy to be out and about. They returned each evening to a meal at the farmhouse, which was all fresh, home-cooked produce. The children played outside, enjoying games of tennis or cricket or just kicking a ball around whilst the adults sat indoors around the log fire sampling the local beer and stout.

The biggest surprise had been the arrival of Raif two days before they were due to depart for their holiday. He let himself into the house with his own key and stood in the hallway with his kit bag when Josh came out of the library to see who it was.

"You must be Uncle Raif," he gasped. "Very pleased to meet you, sir. I'm Joshua." He offered his hand and then shouted through the library doorway. "It's Uncle Raif!"

An avalanche of people came tumbling out to greet him with Josh doing all the introductions.

"Goodness, you're injured," said Grace on seeing him limping and leaning heavily on his stick.

They ushered him into the library and the children told him of their holiday plans, hoping desperately they wouldn't have to cancel all the arrangements, but he seemed eager to join in the excursion as he too needed a change of scenery and new horizons.

For the last two days of their stay, they left the horses and caravans at the farmhouse and headed off to the beach, where they lazed about in the sun and swam in the sea. Dorothea and Raif wandered along the beach arm in arm and sat on the rocks watching the waves crashing and rolling in and out. Raif spoke only briefly of his war work, stating he'd spent most of it on the German borders and how he'd cheated death on three or four occasions. After which he never referred to it again but he was eager to learn all about the children, where they'd come from and who their families were. Dorothea and Raif were the only ones who never swam in the sea, preferring to remain in the shade on the beach deep in conversation.

Grace noticed Dorothea was quieter than usual, and didn't seem quite her normal self despite the fact Raif had made it home safe. All too soon their stay in Ireland was at an end and they headed to the port to catch the boat back to England. Dorothea just made it through the front door before collapsing in the hallway. She hadn't felt well for the duration of the holiday but didn't want to spoil it for the children by complaining, so she had borne up as best as she could.

Jenny screamed. "I knew she was ill. I knew it," she said on seeing Dotty sprawled out on the hall carpet drenched in sweat.

Bob and Raif parked the jeep and entered the kitchen to see Meg sitting, nursing a mug of tea. She leapt to her feet and got two mugs from the cupboard, then poured the tea, nervously awaiting their news.

"Nothing doing at the shop, Meg," said Bob. "It was all locked up. We looked through the window and there was a set of step ladders and a tin of paint on the floor, but it didn't look as though much had been done."

Meg was disappointed and hoped with all her heart Harry hadn't encountered problems with his plans for the shop. "I'll write a letter and take it to the post," she said. "Perhaps there's a delay of some sort. He was keen to get going on it, I know that much."

"How's Dotty?" asked Raif, sipping the hot tea.

"She's asleep. Bhutan's gone across to Doctor Mattison to have a word."

"Has she eaten any breakfast?"

"No, but she drank her tea and took two aspirin, then fell asleep."

"She looked like death last night. She's had these bouts of rheumatic fever before but she's never collapsed like that."

"The holiday doesn't seem to have done her much good, does it? It's been a bad war and she pushed herself too hard. She's not strong and she hasn't eaten much these last few months."

"Iris said she thought Dotty had overdone things. She kept telling her to rest but you know what she's like," said Bob.

"Well, she'll rest now, all right. I shall insist upon it. We need to get some proper meals sorted out. Hearty soups and stews. How's the allotment looking, Bob?" asked Raif, draining the last of his tea and placing the mug in the sink.

Bob followed suit and made for the back door. "The vegetable patch is back on track and looking good. Come and see."

Meg watched them make their way into the garden just as Grace came down the stairs.

"Was that Raif?" Grace asked.

"Yes, they're checking the allotment."

Grace poured herself some tea from the pot on the range. "Any news of the shop?"

"No. It was all shut up and not much has been done from what they could see. I'm going to write a letter and see what's happening. Did you enjoy the holiday, Grace?"

"Yes, I did. The evenings more so than the days. Especially the ale," she laughed.

"The children had a grand time, didn't they?"

"I've never seen them so excited. Where are they all, by the way?"

"They've gone into town with Magda and Selina. They needed some personal items and such. The children offered to show them around so they'd know where to find everything. Daisy's taken Jenny for a walk in the park with Howard."

"I thought it was quiet. Poor Jenny cried for over half an hour last night. The poor little mite."

"What did Ivy have to say when you took her the package her brother sent?"

"Oh, she was upset about Dotty and promised us some provisions once she's had a word with Alf. I don't know what was in the parcel. She didn't open it whilst I was there. We'll talk better next week. I was eager to get back. I don't like leaving Dotty when she's ill."

"Dad had rheumatic fever," said Meg mournfully. "It weakened his heart in the end. He died at an early age, he was only fifty. She's inherited it from him."

"Don't mention the word death, Meg. I couldn't stand it if anything happened to her."

"No, I shouldn't have mentioned that. Sorry."

Bhutan returned from his visit to Dr Mattison carrying a bottle of tonic for Dorothea. He'd been offered a partnership in the practice, working the morning surgery and needed to discuss this with his wife Magda before making any decisions.

The hospital in London was eager for his return but he'd been so happy in this house, happier than he'd ever been in his life and he was reluctant to leave. Working alongside Dr Mattison would provide him with the perfect excuse to stay, but he needed to be sure Magda was happy too. He knew Selina would thrive wherever she was. She was just that sort of girl.

He wondered how Samuel was getting on this morning as he'd gone to meet Gerry's wife who was an artist and had her own studio. He hoped things would work out for him. He'd done a lot of drawing and sketching during their stay in Ireland. There was no doubting his talent but as to earning a living at it... well, he just wasn't sure.

He was amazed at the change in Magda. During the holiday, she really came out of her shell and was eager to join in all the conversations. Although she still made silly mistakes with her English, she had improved considerably and her vocabulary was actually quite good. She had impressed Ivy's brother and sister-in-law with her knowledge of Irish history, talking animatedly about the potato famine, which the children were very interested in and they asked lots of questions.

He took the tonic up to Dorothea and found Grace sat by her bedside applying a cold compress.

"She's literally boiling up. The sweat's just rolling off her. I'm a bit worried."

"It will pass, I can assure you," said Bhutan, tipping some of the tonic into a small glass. "I'll cook the meal tonight. Bob's helping me. You stay here with Dotty."

"That's kind of you. Yes, I'd like to stay by her side whilst she's like this," Grace whispered.

"Make sure she sips this when she wakes up," he said, handing her the glass.

Chapter Thirty-Five

Raif ordered two pints at the bar and carried them over to the table in the corner. "So, Gerry, what's been happening?"

"One of my ex-employees, in an act of revenge for sacking him, decided to set up his own company and undercut me in all bids for the contracts I'd had for twenty-five years."

"Why did you sack him?"

"I had to. He was a troublemaker from the very beginning of his employment with me. I gave him lots of leeway and overlooked a lot of his behaviour in the hope that he would settle down eventually, but he never did. Things came to a head when I caught him on the phone to one of my best customers. Without going into too much detail, he was trying to poach customers so that he could set up on his own. Within six months of him leaving my employment, I hadn't a single customer left. He must have been delving into my files and copying supplier lists and client base information. It's my own fault. I should have been more careful about access to personal data. If I'd had the proper checks in place, he wouldn't have been able to access the information. To be honest, I don't know how he's managing it. I kept my profit margins as low as I possibly could. I couldn't have dropped my prices any lower or I'd have been working for nothing."

The waitress appeared with two plates of hotpot and placed them on the table with a basket of crusty bread and a dish of pickled cabbage.

"Lunch is on me. Tuck in," said Raif, picking up his knife and fork.

"Thanks, I appreciate this. How's Dotty, by the way?"

"Still bad. Grace is keeping vigil by her bedside. Whilst we were in Ireland, she mentioned coming to see you regarding a business plan. We've no idea how to go about it but we're keen to get going."

"I've drawn up a basic draft. We'll get our heads together and make up some figures. Have you got any premises?"

"Not yet." Raif briefed him regarding Harry and the second-hand book shop and cafe. "We were hoping to use the upstairs space but when we called last week, there was no sign of Harry. Meg's written to him but he hasn't replied yet."

There was silence for a little while as they both tucked into their meal. Taking a big swig of his beer, Raif asked, "What's the name of this ex-employee of yours?"

Gerry's face registered a look of surprise before answering. "Iain Boothroyd. Do you know him by any chance?"

"I know his father. Tom Boothroyd. He's not the sort of man you'd want to do business with to be honest."

"Like father, like son, eh? The awful thing is, I can't get this last order finished as he's taken all my staff."

"How difficult is the sewing? I mean, if it's reasonably straight-forward, not too complex, I could ask the girls to pitch in. I'm sure they'd be glad to help."

"That would be marvellous. Pat's still with me. She could show them the ropes."

"Leave it with me. I'll mention it at supper tonight."

Daisy was just putting the ration books back into her bag when it happened. Once again the meagre rations in her basket didn't seem anywhere near adequate to feed the family. Glancing at the contents in the basket, she was momentarily distracted when she heard a familiar voice at the counter asking for cigarettes. Surely it couldn't be who she thought it was.

A quick look over her shoulder confirmed her suspicions. It was definitely him. Iain Boothroyd. The man who had forced himself upon her in an alleyway more than six years ago. She felt her whole body recoil in shock and just managed to stop herself from shouting out before hot-footing it through the door onto the pavement outside the shop.

The roots of her hair and scalp were tingling and she was breaking out in a sweat. Fighting for her breath, she almost ran over the bridge which took her back to the house. What on earth was he doing here? Why had he left London? Had he found out about Jenny? Was he intent on abducting her? Her thoughts were in a muddle. Surely Celia wouldn't have told him about her granddaughter. What if he waited for her outside the school gate? The child was so eager to meet her daddy, she wouldn't take much persuading.

By the time she reached the house, her face was as white as a sheet. Dumping her shopping bags on the kitchen floor, she sank into the nearest chair before her legs gave way.

The children all walked home from school together. Beth would always wait for Jenny. Beth was a sensible girl. She wouldn't let Jenny go off with a strange man, but what if he was to declare who he was? Would Beth invite him back to the house? A feeling of nausea swept over her just as Grace entered the kitchen, carrying a tray.

"She's eaten all the soup but not touched the bread. Still, it's an improvement. We're getting there slowly." Grace made her way over to the sink to deposit the dishes and took the bread back into the larder as they couldn't afford to waste anything. "Goodness, Daisy, are you all right? You look as though you've seen a ghost."

Meg pressed the bell twice before deciding Harry must be out. His bungalow looked immaculate and the front garden was a mass of colour. She turned to make her way back to the bus stop when she heard a voice.

"He won't open the door, dear. Is there anything I can help you with?" It was the next-door neighbour. A grey-haired lady put down her shears and made her way over to the hedge, carefully stepping over a pile of clippings at her feet.

Meg explained who she was and told her about the shop. "I thought perhaps his wife might be ill or something. It's not like Harry to ignore my letters. I just wondered if I could help in any way."

"Oh dear. You'd better come inside a moment. Let's have a cup of tea and I'll explain."

Her name was Geraldine. She had five grandchildren and her husband was a market gardener. She'd just celebrated her seventieth birthday and the house was littered with cards and flowers. Meg was glad to sit down as it had been a long walk from the bus stop.

"I'm afraid his wife passed away. He's taken it very badly. He's not left the house since the funeral."

"I'm so sorry," said Meg, placing her tea cup back on the saucer. "It must have been very sudden then. She was all right before I went to Ireland."

"Not really. She'd been ill for quite some time. Her immune system was weak, you see. She caught some sort of virus and it finished her off."

"Poor Harry. No wonder he can't face the world."

"It's the shock. I think he's given up on himself."

"I suppose that's natural when you've spent your whole life with someone."

"I'm the only one he'll speak to at the moment. I'll let him know you've called, dear."

Meg took that last comment as her cue to leave. She didn't want to outstay her welcome. Draining the last of her tea, she stood up to button her coat. "I'll write him another letter. Thank you for the tea, Geraldine. It was nice to meet you. Thank goodness he's got someone like you to look out for him."

Geraldine was thinking much the same thing as she watched Meg make her way back down the lane. If her instincts were serving her correctly, that young lady could be exactly what Harry needed right now to take him out of himself. She would be a very welcome distraction indeed.

Dorothea glanced at the clock on her bedside table. It was two o'clock in the afternoon. She'd been in bed for a month and was feeling annoyed with herself for collapsing like that in front of the children. If only she could have made it up to her bed, then it wouldn't have happened. She was fed up with being ill all the time but she knew she wasn't yet ready to join the land of the living.

She could hear Iris' laughter and the children chattering. Meg had promised to sit with her this afternoon after her visit to see Harry. It was Grace's day off and as usual she'd gone to see Ivy at the farm. Daisy didn't seem her usual self and she wondered if she was happy living in this house. She was still a young girl after all. It couldn't be much fun cooking and cleaning and running around after other people all day. She wouldn't blame her if she was tired of it. *I'll speak to Grace about it later*, she thought.

The door opened and Meg and Daisy entered with the tea tray.

"The others have all gone up to the warehouse with Raif," said Meg. "Gerry needs help completing an order, so it's just us."

"Oh. How did you get on? Did you speak to Harry?" Dorothea asked, propping herself up on her pillows. Daisy had piled a plate up with homemade biscuits and busied herself pouring out the tea.

"Are you all right, Daisy?" asked Dorothea. "You seem a bit peaky, if you don't mind me mentioning it. You will tell me there's anything wrong, won't you?"

Daisy's face flushed red and she seemed nervous. Yes, there was definitely something wrong, Dorothea now knew.

"I'll tell you later," said Daisy. "Let Meg tell you about Harry first." She handed out the tea and put the biscuits on the bed.

Meg and Daisy both kicked off their shoes and jumped on the bed.

"Well, there was no reply when I knocked," began Meg. "Then his next-door neighbour shouted over the hedge that he wouldn't answer. She invited me in for a cup of tea and explained that his wife had passed away. He's taken it very badly and can't bring himself to leave the house."

"Oh Meg. How awful. Poor man," said Daisy.

"What happened exactly?" Dorothea was enjoying the company of the two girls. "What exactly did she die of?"

"She had lupus and was confined to a wheelchair for quite some time. Geraldine thinks, that's his neighbour, that she caught some sort of a virus and her system just couldn't fight it. She was too weak."

"Write to him again, Meg. He needs to know he's got friends. Raif and Bob will help with decorating the shop and getting everything ready."

"I've drafted a letter. I'll post it tomorrow."

There was silence as they drank their tea, before Dorothea said, "So, Daisy, what's been happening? Has something occurred?"

"Yes, you could say that. I've had a bit of a shock that's all and I'm more than a little concerned."

"Why? What on earth happened?" asked Meg.

"Jenny's father was in the supermarket the other day, buying cigarettes."

"Here in Minehead?"

"Yes."

"Are you sure it was definitely him?"

"Oh yes. Quite sure."

"What's he doing here?"

"I don't know. That's what's worrying me. Do you think Celia's mentioned…"

"No, I'm sure Celia hasn't said anything," said Dorothea. "She wouldn't."

"If he sees me out and about with Jenny, he might cause trouble. I'm worried about him carting her off."

"Over my dead body," snapped Dorothea.

Meg sat silently sipping her tea, waiting patiently for someone to explain the situation regarding Jenny's father. Whatever had occurred in the past between Daisy and Jenny's father had obviously ended acrimoniously. She wondered if they were married. Daisy didn't seem the type of girl to be an unmarried mother, but, of course, with the onset of the war and everything, they were living in strange times.

"I've tried so hard to put all that behind me. Coming here was the start of a new life. I've no desire to even speak to him. I certainly don't want him turning up here at the house. You do hear of children being abducted. What if he lingers at the school gate? I don't know what to do about this. Jenny's so keen to meet her father, she'll go to any lengths to meet him. But I don't ever want her to know about how she was conceived. At some time in the not-too-distant future, I'm going to have to sit down and have a frank talk with her and try to explain that her father and I never had a relationship in the normal sense. She's too young yet, she wouldn't understand, but perhaps when she's older…"

"Yes, I agree," said Dorothea. "We don't want the whole world knowing all our business. This needs to be kept to ourselves. We'll deal with it our own way. Don't worry, we'll think of something."

The house was deathly quiet and Dorothea assumed everyone was still at the factory helping Gerry with his last order. The deadline was lunchtime today and they'd all gone to help out. She was sick of lying in bed and decided to run herself a hot bath.

After soaking in the hot suds for half an hour, she dressed and made her way down to the kitchen. There was no sign of anyone. She rummaged in the larder to assess what provisions they had, but all she could find was some sausage meat and heaps of vegetables. She peeled all the vegetables and prepared the casserole for the evening meal and she was just rolling out the pastry to make some pasties for lunch when the back door opened. It was Alan, looking pale and worried.

"Alan? Gosh, you're home early. Are you all right? Not ill or anything, are you? You do look pale."

"No, I'm all right really. Just reeling from events that transpired at the farm. There was an almighty rumpus."

"At the farm? Why? What's happened?"

"Ivy and Alf's son came home. He was in the army, as you know. Well, when he found out about me, he took exception to my being there and kicked up a fuss."

"I don't see why."

"Well," said Alan, settling himself down at the table. "He said it was his place to work on the farm with his father as it was to be his inheritance. I explained that I was only helping out as Alf was getting older and finding it a struggle. He told me to 'sling my hook'. So, I went to speak to Alf. He wasn't best pleased as he said his son was lazy and didn't like working on the farm anyway and never pulled his weight. Getting him out of bed in the mornings was an ordeal in itself, he said. Ivy protested that being in the army will have changed him and he deserved to be given a chance to prove himself. So she suggested it might be better all round if I left."

Dorothea sank into the chair beside him. She knew the lad loved working on the farm and would be devastated at this turn of events. Patting his hand and smiling she said, "Well, lad, not to worry. We've other fish to fry. Help me finish these pasties and we can get them into the oven. Then we'll have a nice cup of tea and take them round to the factory."

"I thought it was quiet. Is that where they've all gone?"

"I'm assuming so. There's no note lying around or anything."

"Are you sure you're up to it, Aunty Dot? Should you even be out of bed yet?"

"I can't stay in bed any longer, lad. I'll go mad."

"Aunty Dot? What should I do now? I'm scared."

"We fill these pastry squares with the sausage meat mixture, then seal the edges. We'll brush the tops with milk and then get them in the oven. It's not hard."

"No," he laughed, "I mean, what do I do now I've no job? I can't ask you to keep me, it wouldn't be fair. You've a houseful already."

"That's enough of that. You're family now. We stick together. We'll manage somehow. We've got to. We're all looking for work. Let Raif decide what's best for us. He's good at that sort of thing." This was said with more compunction than she felt, adding quickly, "Now, get your sleeves rolled up and wash your hands."

He smiled and threw his arms around her shoulders. "You're all right, you are. You're my saviour, Aunty Dot. What on earth would we all do without you?"

"So, where's Earnest going?" asked Stuart as he parked himself on the kitchen stool next to the stove to get warm. He'd been on his bike all day and he was chilled to the marrow.

"With the lads, up to Plymouth," said Kath. "They're staying overnight and making a weekend of it. There's a meeting with the other club members. I've warned him about his drinking. You know what it's like when they all get together."

Stuart laughed. "Aw, let him be. Let him have a bit of fun whilst he still can."

There was silence whilst Kath brewed the tea. Stuart got two mugs out of the cupboard and set them down on the table.

"I say, Kath. How do you fancy coming up to London? I've had an invitation from my pal Graham. We could stay over and make a night of it. We might not get another chance, with your dad going away like. I know you don't like leaving him on his own. What do you say?" Stuart was holding his breath. He didn't want to jeopardise their relationship by being too bold but he was disappointed when she didn't reply straight away.

"It's a lovely idea, Stuart, but I couldn't afford to stay in a hotel. I've virtually no money, what with finishing at the factory and everything." She handed him his tea and suddenly realised how much she wanted to go, but there was no way in which she could raise the money as she hadn't anything to sell or pawn. Her heart fell to her boots.

"I'm paying. It'll be my treat. I haven't spent my Christmas bonus yet, so we'll use that."

"Oh Stuart, are you sure?"

"Of course, I'm sure. I wouldn't have mentioned it otherwise. We'll catch the train and Graham can meet us at the station."

Kath felt her heart skip with excitement. She'd never been away with a man before and knew she wouldn't get a moment's sleep thinking about it.

* * *

It was eleven thirty by the time Dorothea and Alan arrived at the factory with the pasties. Alan carried the tray through the reception area, which was deserted, so they continued along the corridor to the workshop. There were boxes and boxes piled up everywhere. Raif and Gerry were ticking them off on a list attached to a clipboard.

"That's the lot. We're done," shouted Gerry. "Well done, everyone."

There was a round of applause from all the children. Grace, Daisy, Meg and Iris were clearing up the work benches and Magda was cleaning all the surfaces with a cloth.

"Lunch is served," shouted Dorothea from the doorway.

They all cheered when they saw Alan with the tray of pasties making his way towards them.

"Congratulations, Gerry. You've done it I see," said Dorothea.

"Not me. These wonderful people have. Gosh, they smell good. Pat, put the kettle on for tea."

Raif hobbled over to Dorothea and kissed her. "What a welcome sight," he said, eyeing the pasties. "We're starving. Tuck in, everyone."

"Alan, why aren't you at the farm?" asked Beth, shaking little Jenny awake, who was curled up asleep in the chair.

"I got the bullet," he said flatly.

"Why?"

"Sit down and I'll tell you about it."

"Oh Alan, this is Susan. Susan, this is my brother Alan," said Beth, pointing to a young lady sat next to her.

Alan smiled and offered his hand. "Pleased to meet you, Susan. I hope you like pasties. They're fresh out of the oven half an hour ago."

"Lovely to meet you too, Alan. I love pasties." She gave him her best smile and added, "Beth's been telling me all about you."

"Oh dear," he laughed.

"No, no. All good I assure you." Susan was the only member of Gerry's staff who'd refused to follow the others to go and work for Iain Boothroyd. She liked working with Gerry. Besides which, her mother was a good friend of Pat's, so she wouldn't hear of her daughter leaving under a cloud like that. Susan thought Alan was very handsome and was glad now that she'd stayed as she wouldn't have met him. She'd no idea what she was going to do after today, but she'd think about that later.

Howard took two pasties off the pile and handed one each to Daisy and Jenny.

"Selina?" said Jenny, clutching her warm pasty in both hands, "What was it like working on the farm?"

"Very hard work. At first, we struggled to cope. We went to bed every night with aching muscles, sore feet and our hands were red raw. But after a while, we got to like working outside in the fresh air and then, of course, we fell in love with all the animals."

"What sort of animals?" Jenny was eager to know.

"There were two dogs, three cats, goats, cows, horses, a few sheep and pigs."

"Golly. I'd like to work with animals. Howard's shown me pictures of lots of animals. Giraffes and tigers, monkeys and gorillas. They live in Africa and such like." She bit into her pasty, then added, "Did you manage to milk the cows?"

"Yes, every day. It was a little tricky at first, but we soon got the hang of it."

Alan thought Susan was the loveliest girl he'd ever met and hoped with all his heart that she didn't have a sweetheart. She wasn't beautiful in the usual way of things, but she had blue green eyes that sparkled when she laughed and her long fair hair was swept up into a top knot on the top of her head. She was easy to talk to and good fun.

Beth liked her too and was glad to make a friend at long last, having not made any real friends at the village school. She reckoned Rebecca had something to do with that. Having dumped Josh so callously, she wasted no time in dropping Beth from her circle of friends.

Bhutan handed a pasty to his wife and took one for himself. He was so immensely proud of Magda, who'd chatted all night with the others whilst she sewed. Her English had improved beyond anything he thought her capable of. Although still making errors, these were fewer and less frequent. Having settled into life in Somerset with such ease, his admiration for her increased.

"Home to bed when we've had this," he said, sitting himself beside her.

"That sounds good to me," she laughed.

Grace was annoyed with Ivy for giving Alan his marching orders like that and she'd have something to say to her next week. She supposed it was a mother's love for her son and she immediately thought of Gordon, her own son. She had an urgent longing to see him and to meet this new lady that had won his heart. Had they set a date for their wedding yet? Where would they live? What was this new venture that he'd mentioned? The questions tumbled around in her head, making her restless and eager for answers. Having made up her mind to write him a letter as soon as she got home, she wondered if Daisy would accompany her.

"So, how are the painting sessions going with Gerry's wife?" Selina asked her brother. "What's her studio like?"

"It's fabulous. I'm so jealous," said Sam. "I took my portfolio for her to look through. I was so nervous but she soon put me at ease. You'd like her, she's so nice. I've learnt loads from her already."

"That's great, Sam. Will you go to art college?"

"I don't know. I'll need to speak to Dad. I've not dared to mention it as he's been so ill and I didn't want to worry him. What about you? What do you want to do?" Sam was concerned for his sister, who'd clearly lost a lot of weight, which she put down to all the hard work on the farm.

"I'd like to study fashion with Beth and Josh," she smiled and added, "We're so lucky, aren't we? Finding Aunty Dot and Uncle Raif?"

"So, Gerry, what's next after today?" asked Dorothea, pouring herself a cup of tea. She couldn't face a pasty but Pat was refilling the teapot every time it emptied.

"Pat, Susan and myself are coming in on Monday morning to clear up here. There's still quite a lot to do."

"Gerry, I'm a bit concerned about these young girls that have gone to work for this Iain Boothroyd. Raif told me he was the one who'd opened this new factory."

"Don't mention that arrogant little jobs-worth to me, Dotty. I'd still be in business if it wasn't for him."

"I know and I'm sorry. Truly I am. It's just that…" she hesitated, not knowing how to tell him about what had happened to Daisy, but she knew she would never forgive herself if one of those girls suffered the same experience. "He's not to be trusted around young girls. If he can't get his own way, he becomes aggressive."

"Oh?" Gerry put down his pasty and looked concerned. "What are you trying to say?"

"Look over there at Jenny."

Gerry glanced over to where Jenny was sat, tucking into her lunch with Beth and the boys.

"What do you see?" asked Dorothea.

"She's a beautiful child."

"Iain's her father and the conception wasn't consensual."

"Oh Lord. You don't mean—"

"Yes, I do. That's why I'm so concerned for those girls. If anything happened to one of them, I'd never forgive myself, knowing what I do and what he's like."

"I knew he was aggressive but I'd never have suspected him capable of anything like that."

"He's a big lad for his age. No girl would stand a chance against him. If we confronted him, he'd only deny everything."

"You're right, he would," agreed Gerry. "We need advice. Would it be any use having a chat with Stuart?"

"We need to do something. Daisy's concerned that Jenny will be abducted. She's afraid he'll wait for her outside the school gates and cart her off somewhere. She's worried sick. Jenny's so eager to meet her daddy, she wouldn't take much persuading. Luckily, Beth always waits for her and they walk home together."

"Does Iain know about Jenny?"

"No, but if he sees her out and about with Daisy, he might become suspicious. The resemblance is unmistakable. I'll speak to Raif about it tonight when we're alone." Lost in thought as she sipped her tea, Dorothea waited for Gerry to reply.

"Sorry, Dotty, I'm so worried about the business and everything, I can hardly think straight at the moment."

"We're not faring much better. Meg lost her job at the newsagents, then Iris got finished at the factory and Howard lost his job on the post round. Poor Sam had to leave the library and I got finished at the bus depot. Now poor Alan's been given his marching orders. He loved it on the farm, but I suppose family comes first and, of course, we have to honour those brave men who've fought for their country."

"Yes, you're right. At least we're still alive and kicking. That's a blessing in itself."

Chapter Thirty-Six

Monica lay in bed reflecting on the events of the previous evening. She felt an overwhelming sense of disappointment at how things had turned out and she only had herself to blame. Realising how stupid she'd been, her heart was broken and her spirit crushed.

Mr Boothroyd had indicated she was in line for a promotion and he wanted to discuss it over a drink after work. He said he wanted someone he could rely on and she fitted the bill perfectly.

Over the course of the next week, he'd waited until all the other girls had gone home before asking her out for their usual soiree at the pub. She enjoyed all the attention and began to feel special. After all, he'd singled her out from all the others.

Last night, as she was putting on her coat to go home, he asked her if she would like a bite to eat at this little place he knew. How she wished now she had refused and gone straight home. But she didn't. Her ego got in the way. She began to imagine being a shop floor supervisor, then his personal secretary and then who knew what else – his wife perhaps.

Realising too late how stupid she'd been, she pulled the covers over her head to drown out her mother's voice asking if she was getting up as her breakfast was ready.

She didn't like the restaurant he had taken her to. It was dark and shabby. After a twenty-minute drive down country lanes, she had no idea where she was and began to get nervous. He ordered the food for both of them, which she felt was very strange. How on earth did he know what she liked? When the meal arrived, it was spicy and greasy and after two mouthfuls, she knew she'd never manage the rest of it, so she sipped her wine instead. Not being used to drinking, she began to feel lightheaded and disorientated.

Before she knew what was happening, she was being steered forcefully towards the lifts. He had a firm hold on her arm like a vice. She wished now that she'd had the courage to shout out or scream or slap his face. Why didn't she ask him what on earth he thought he was doing?

The next minute, she was being thrust through a doorway onto a bed. He threw himself on top of her, nearly knocking her unconscious. She began to protest but he seemed not to hear her and continued to maul her and pull at her clothing. It never seemed to happen like this in the movies, she told herself, where the heroine was wined and dined before being made love to by a suitor who was gentle and kind and declared his undying love for his lady. The rough way he thrust himself into her both shocked and appalled her. She never imagined lovemaking to be like this.

The rest of the evening remained a blur and before long, she was putting her key in the door. Fortunately, her parents were both in bed and she was able to creep upstairs and get into her bed without explanations.

"Monica. What's wrong? Are you ill?" It was her mother. Wiping her hands on her apron, she stood over the bed with a cup of tea which she placed on the bedside table. "We didn't hear you come in last night. It must have been late."

"Sorry, Mum. Mr Boothroyd took me out for supper but I couldn't eat it."

"Took you out to supper? Watch yourself there, Monica. He's after something. Mark my words."

Too late for that advice, thought Monica, sipping her tea. "I'll be up as soon as I've had this."

"Graham's good company, isn't he?" said Kathleen, settling herself into a seat next to the window. She heard the whistle blow and then the train chugged its way out of the station.

"He's been a good friend actually," said Stuart. "We trained together when we first joined the force. He hasn't changed. Same old Graham."

Kath smiled to herself. She couldn't remember a happier time than the weekend she'd just had. Stuart had been everything she expected and more besides. He was gentle and kind and paid for everything. Graham took them to a good restaurant and introduced them to his wife Jeanette. After the meal, they went back to the hotel where they all had mugs of cocoa by a roaring fire in the lounge. Kath knew she'd cherish these memories forever.

"I wonder how your dad's weekend went?" mused Stuart.

"Oh, I hope he's had a good time. I'm so pleased he's found three good friends at last. When Mum died, he didn't leave the house for three months. Now I can't keep him in," she laughed.

Stuart wondered if Kath would ever consider moving into the cottage with him. Her father would have to be accommodated too and he was prepared for that but he wasn't sure if they'd ever get him to leave the house he'd been so happy in throughout his marriage. He wasn't sure how to broach the subject without causing offence. The weekend had gone better than he ever could have hoped for and knew he wanted to spend the rest of his life with her. Not wanting to spoil things, he decided to tread carefully, despite his friend Graham's advice to "get on with it".

Dorothea was in the kitchen kneading the bread dough when she heard a tapping noise at the back door. The others were all in bed except for Alan who was in the garden working on the allotment. She couldn't believe how hard they'd worked all through the night to get Gerry's order out on time.

Little Jenny screamed blue murder at being left behind and insisted on being included. Fortunately, she had fallen asleep on the chair at ten o'clock, unable to keep her eyes open any longer, which pleased Daisy as she wouldn't have the bother of having to keep an eye on her.

"Oh Ivy. Come in," said Dorothea. "The others are all in bed."

She quickly told her about the factory and filled the kettle for tea. "I'll just get this bread in the oven then we can enjoy our tea."

"It's nice to see you up and about again, Dotty," said Ivy. "How are you feeling?"

"Not too bad. I'm a bit weak and wobbly but that's to be expected. I can't stay in bed any longer or I'll go mad."

"You're like me. I like to keep busy. I can't stand having nothing to do. Not that there's much chance of that on the farm. I wanted to speak to Grace, to explain why… well, you know the situation. The trouble is, things aren't working out too well. Robert's so lazy and doesn't like farming anyway. Alf and I had a terrible row about it but what could I do? He's my son."

"Why was he so against Alan helping out? You'd think he'd be grateful of the extra help. Less pressure on himself," said Dorothea, closing the oven door.

"Jealousy, I think. Alan was a good worker. A hard worker. Alf was so pleased with him. He would have shown Robert up for what he is: bone idle!"

Dorothea could feel herself becoming irritated, but fought against it and decided to hold her tongue. She busied herself pouring the tea and fiddling with the cups.

"Anyway, on a lighter note, I come with some good news. I've had a letter from my brother in Ireland. They want you to spend next August with them. They're going to make sure everything's ready for you by keeping the whole month free. They so enjoyed having you all."

"Oh, that is kind, Ivy. The children will be delighted."

That's if they're still here, Dorothea thought. She hoped with all her heart they would still be with her, for she couldn't contemplate giving them up now. It would be too painful.

"There are rumours flying around town about that Iain Boothroyd," said Ivy, sipping her tea.

"Oh?" Dorothea wondered what on earth Ivy was going to say.

"The girls on the shop floor have noticed the way he speaks to people. He's had run-ins with a few of the suppliers. They're refusing to deal with him. The girls have also heard him arguing with that partner of his, so things don't seem too rosy."

"How do you know all this?"

"From the women at the WI. Their girls arrive home full of it. They're not too happy either by all accounts. He's making them work extra hours, which hasn't gone down well. You know what these youngsters are like. All they're interested in is going to the pictures and such like."

Dorothea smiled as she recalled her own youth. "I was never allowed that sort of luxury. I went from school to university, then on to working at the laboratory. I never stopped working."

"If you had your time again, would you do things differently?"

"No, not really. I wouldn't have met Raif. It's all been worth it. I just wish that Mum and Dad could have been proud of me. They weren't good at dishing out praise," said Dorothea, solemnly.

"I wouldn't lose any sleep over that, Dotty, to be honest. Just live your life."

Monica had been plagued by flashbacks all weekend. The way he'd put his hand over her mouth when she tried to scream. The pain was excruciating and she was still sore. He hadn't bothered to use a johnny either, which added to her anxiety. What if she was now with child? She felt sure her parents would disown her. Why had she allowed it to happen? She couldn't understand it.

Having only taken a few sips of her drink before she began to feel peculiar, made her think he'd put something in her glass. The girls at the factory had mentioned the trick that men had of spiking their drinks. She felt sure now he'd put something in hers. That would account for her inability to react. What on earth was she going to do on Monday morning? She couldn't face going back. She just couldn't.

"Monica. You've been moping about all day. You're in a dream world. Wake up, girl."

"Sorry, Mum. I'm not feeling too good. It's my monthlies," she lied, knowing full well this wasn't true. The bleed she was having was as a result of the rough treatment she'd been subjected to. "Mum?"

"Yes, what is it?" said her mother, putting the plates in the oven.

"You know when Dad offered me that job at his office? Well, I wish now that I'd taken it. He gave me good advice and I didn't take it. I'm sorry for it now. Do you think the placement is still available? Has he forgiven me?"

"Well, you've changed your tune, girl. What's brought all this on?"

"I don't think things will work out at the factory."

"What makes you say that?"

"He's already increased our hours and he's talking about pay cuts if we don't get the orders out on time. All the girls are looking for other jobs." The thought of working for her father filled Monica with horror but she could see no alternative.

"You'll have to speak to him yourself. He'll be home at one o'clock."

"Will you help me to persuade him, Mum?"

"He won't take any notice of me or listen to anything I've got to say, Monica. You know that."

"Please, Mum. You're my best friend." She gave her mother a hug and hoped with all her heart she wasn't about to let both her parents down.

Chapter Thirty-Seven

"Gerry? Thank goodness, you're still there. It's me, Reg."

"Hello Reg. Yes, we're just clearing up. We'll be here for a few days yet."

"Look. I know it's a bit late in the day but I'm not happy about this new kid on the block."

"I presume you're referring to Mr Boothroyd?"

"The very one. He's arrogant. I don't like his tactics. What's more, I don't like the way he speaks to me or my staff. He had my secretary in tears last week."

Gerry was tempted to say "sorry about that", but decided against it. If things had gone pear-shaped for Reg, then he was glad. He'd brought it all on himself by being eager to jump ship after all the years they'd done business together. Where was the loyalty?

"I'd rather do business with you. I've got a meeting with the board tomorrow. Think it over and let me know. It would be good to tell them you and I are back in business."

Well, well, thought Gerry. He knew the offer had come too late to save things, but he was pleased things weren't all sweetness and light in the Boothroyd camp.

Over the course of the next week, he had a dozen similar calls from other suppliers, all spouting tales of woe and wanting to reinstate their business. Pat and Susan stayed loyal to him throughout, even though he'd no money to pay them. They turned up every day offering their help and making endless cups of tea and sandwiches.

"Are you all right, Gerry?" asked Pat, placing a mug of hot tea on his desk.

"I've got the most terrible headache, Pat. I feel a bit sick."

"I'll get you some aspirin. I'm not surprised with all this going on. It's enough to make anyone ill."

"I heard a rumour that Mr Boothroyd's partner has walked out after a huge row," said Susan, seating herself on the opposite side of Gerry's desk.

"Serves him right," said Pat, crisply.

"I met some of the girls for lunch at the weekend," said Susan. "They're all looking for jobs elsewhere. He's making them work extra hours and docking their pay if the orders aren't out on time."

An hour later, Gerry was bright green and had to go home to his bed, leaving Pat to lock up.

Pat and Susan were just settling down to eat their sandwiches when Alan appeared, carrying a bag of homemade biscuits which, with Dorothea's help, he'd made himself. He was desperate to see Susan again, fearing the closure of the factory would remove her from his life forever. Dorothea had told him to take a chance and get himself to the factory before it was too late. Seeing the delighted look on Susan's face gave him hope and he hot-footed it across the factory floor with a spring in his step and a smile on his face.

Dorothea took the bread out of the oven and put the casserole in for their evening meal. Alan had gone to the factory to see Susan and the others were all still fast asleep after their night shift. She got out her sketching pad and pastels and settled herself at the kitchen table. She'd taken to drawing and sketching during her stay in bed, to help pass the time and to stop herself getting bored. The designs were of waistcoats, ties and cravats, bow-ties, three-quarter length smoking jackets and ladies' dance dresses. She was working on shirts with matching ties for boys and dancewear for girls, when there was a knock at the door. It was Edna.

"Hello Edna, come in." Dorothea couldn't remember Edna ever

visiting them before and hoped it wasn't bad news. "Have you walked all the way from the village?"

"Yes. I come bearing a message for Megan," she said between puffs of breath.

"Here, sit down a minute. I'll pop the kettle on." Dorothea was glad of the company, although she wasn't a big fan of Edna, who could be forthright in her opinions.

Edna seated herself at the table and started mopping her brow with a handkerchief. "I'm not as fit as I used to be. I used to be able to walk miles. Now I can hardly make it to the end of the street without getting out of breath."

Dorothea poured the tea and sat down. She hoped Edna had some gossip to impart as life was terribly dull at present. Food was still rationed and if it wasn't for the allotment, they would have all starved. They had no money and the outlook was grim.

"A lady came into the newsagents. Never seen her before. She was asking Evelyn about Megan. I just happened to be in the shop and I overheard them. Evelyn wasn't being very helpful, so I offered to deliver a message if she cared to write a note. So, here it is." She retrieved a folded piece of paper out of her handbag and handed it to Dorothea.

"I won't read it. It might be personal," she said and placed it in the drawer. "I'll see that she gets it when she wakes up."

"It's very quiet, Dotty. Where are they all?"

"In bed." She explained about the factory, but didn't mention the fact Gerry had gone bankrupt as, knowing Edna as she did, she'd have plenty to say on the matter.

"Do you see much of Dolly these days?" Dorothea quickly asked, in order to change the subject before Edna could ask too many questions. The situation surrounding Iain Boothroyd still bothered her and she was wary of speaking out of turn.

"I've not seen her since she got married," chipped Edna banging her mug down on the table in defiance.

"Didn't you get an invite at Christmas?"

"She was ill with that food poisoning episode. They couldn't find anything wrong with the mincemeat when they tested it. Stuart reckons it must have been a virus or something."

"I wonder if someone spiked the mulled wine?" laughed Dorothea.

"That's what I thought," mused Edna, starting to laugh, bad mood momentarily forgotten.

"Didn't you and Dolly go to the Maitland's for Christmas lunch one year? The year before Dolly got married?"

"Oh yes, we did. It was a disaster."

"Oh? Why?"

"Mary's not known for her skills in the kitchen, as you know. She served up some sort of small salad for the starter and there was a suspicious-looking bit of greenery on the top of mine. She said it was a parsley garnish, but it certainly wasn't. I think it was something that fell off the Christmas tree. When the dinner arrived… well, dear me, you've never seen anything like it. The roast potatoes were burnt and the vegetables weren't cooked. You couldn't get your fork through them and I've never seen gravy the way she makes it. Gelatinous wasn't the word. The whole thing was stone cold. 'It would have helped, Mary,' I said, 'If you'd stayed sober, but no, you've been on the sauce since you got up this morning.'

"She said 'aw, shaddup… shaddup,' and then she passed out, face-down in the cheese board, smashing all the crackers. I stood up and put my coat on. Then Dolly said, 'Do you think we should offer to wash up?' I said 'I'm not washing up, I'm a guest! She can do it herself in the morning, when she's sobered up!' I marched out after that leaving poor Cyril in the doorway, red faced and mumbling apologies. He'd had quite a bit to drink as well. Him a vicar too."

Dorothea couldn't help but laugh. "Poor Cyril. Were there any other guests besides you and Dolly?"

"Just the old lady from number six. She normally goes to her sister's in Exeter but she was recovering from a bad bout of flu and didn't feel up to making the journey. She's ninety-two now."

"Did Dolly follow you home then?"

"No. The two of them wrapped all the food and placed it in the fridge, then they cleared the table and washed up. It was gone six o'clock when she eventually got home."

"Would you like some shortbread? Alan made them this morning." Dorothea was beginning to enjoy herself. "Have you seen or heard anything of the young girl from the factory? The Irish lass who was seeing Douglas?"

"Oh, her. Yes," said Edna biting into her biscuit. "Goodness, these are good. What flavour are they? Strawberry? Well, I saw her pushing a pram. It was a little boy. Bonnie little thing. Can't remember what she's named him. Her husband was furious at first but he's calmed down now. They're still together. She said it hasn't been easy but they talked and talked and well… they're moving back to Ireland. Her mother has a place in County Mayo. Oh, that reminds me. Mrs Kloot is going back to France."

"That doesn't surprise me," said Dorothea. "Charles never settled here like Rosine did."

"According to Norman Potts, they've had a few rows about it. Rose has made a lot of friends here and doesn't want to leave. Charles threatened to go without her."

"I feel heartily sorry for her then."

"Men are a blithering nuisance," said Edna, standing to button up her coat.

"You're right," laughed Dorothea, "But where would we be without them?"

Megan hoped she hadn't misunderstood the note about coming to tea. She placed her hand tentatively on the knocker and gave it two short raps. Geraldine opened the door after what seemed like an inordinately long time.

"Oh, I'm so glad the note reached you. I wasn't sure, you see. The lady in the post office wasn't very forthcoming."

No, she wouldn't be, thought Meg.

"Harry will be joining us," added Geraldine. "It was my husband's idea. Hopefully, it will get him back into the land of the living. Come on through. I've set the table. Everything's ready. I'll just fill the kettle for tea. Go through to the conservatory."

Meg could hear voices as she made her way to the back of the bungalow.

"If I've had this haircut for nothing…"

She could hear laughter as she stood in the doorway. The table was beautifully set out with a lace tablecloth and china cups and saucers. There were sandwiches and cakes and a trifle. She'd never seen such a feast. Harry came towards her and gave her a warm hug.

"Meg, this is Derek. Derek, this is Megan. She's going to be helping me in the shop."

Derek shook her hand and showed her to the table. Apart from appearing a little thinner, Harry didn't look too bad. She began to wonder if Geraldine had been exaggerating when she said he was in a bad way.

"I'll just see if Geraldine needs a hand," she said, slipping off her jacket. Her nerves were beginning to settle down a bit as she went back into the kitchen.

"He's cheered up considerably since he knew you were coming," Geraldine whispered.

"I'm so sorry to hear the sad news about your wife," said Meg on returning to the conservatory, teapot in hand. Harry's face clouded over and Meg saw the pain for herself.

"It's hit me hard but I think I've finally turned a corner. I didn't want to go on living at first. It just didn't seem worth the effort. This last year has been particularly difficult. It was a cruel disease, with no known cure. The last few months before her death, she became very demanding and bad tempered. Not at all like the woman I married."

"I've always said to Derek that our health is the most precious gift we possess," said Geraldine. "Without it, you have nothing. All the money in the world wouldn't make any difference. Now, let's eat. Tuck in, everyone."

Meg poured out the tea and seated herself next to Harry. "It's good that you can talk about it, Harry," she said, handing out the cups. Further study of his features made her realise how much weight he'd lost. He had a rather gaunt, haunted look about him. *Well, I'll soon change that*, she thought. *I shall feed him up.*

She explained about Gerry having to close the factory and the plans to get the new clothing business off the ground by renting the premises above the shop. Raif, Bob and Alan would help with getting the place decorated and updated and she was delighted when Harry accepted her reassurances as a welcome relief.

"I don't feel up to tackling it on my own somehow," he added.

"Well, you won't have to. Raif and Gerry have lots of contacts in the trade. We'll be all right," she reassured him.

"We can help out too, can't we, dear?" said Derek, looking across at Geraldine.

"Be glad to for the cafe. We're market gardeners so that'll come in very handy."

Geraldine handed out the sandwiches and for the first time in her life, Meg began to feel optimistic about the future.

Grace was just about to start preparing the lunch when the kitchen door burst open. A very out of breath Joshua stood in the doorway, his face as white as a sheet. Grace glanced at the clock. It was only eleven o'clock and she knew something must be wrong.

"Where's Uncle Raif and Aunty Dot?" he asked, gasping for breath as he'd run all the way from school as fast as his legs would carry him.

"She's in the library with Bhutan. Raif, Bob and Alan have gone to get more seeds for the allotment. What on earth's the matter, lad?" She followed him into the library where they were looking at Dorothea's designs.

"Aunty Dot. There's been a bit of a rumpus up at the school. I'm very sorry. You have to come at once. The headmaster has requested your attendance straight away."

Dorothea saw the stricken look on his face. He looked afraid.

"What's happened, Josh? Sit down and tell us all about it," she soothed.

"We were all in the gym doing PE when Rebecca threw the medicine ball at Beth and it hit her on the head and knocked her over. Sam flew across the hall and grabbed Rebecca by the shoulders and pinned her up against the wall.

"'You stupid idiot!' he yelled. 'Don't you realise Beth's recently had brain surgery to remove a tumour! You could have killed her!' That's when I waded in with my two pence. I told her she'd become very cocky since she took up with that new boyfriend of hers. I'm so sorry, Aunty Dot, but I couldn't just stand there and see Beth being bullied like that. She threw that ball on purpose, the whole class saw her."

"What happened then, Josh? Is Beth all right? Where is she?"

"They're all in the headmaster's office. Rebecca's parents have been summoned as well."

"My boy is in trouble?" asked Bhutan. "I'd better come with you, Dotty. A blow to the head with a heavy ball like that can potentially have very serious consequences. I'll fetch my medical bag."

There wasn't much petrol in Raif's car, but Dorothea hoped there would be enough to get them to the school.

"So, Josh, tell me again. What on earth did Rebecca think she was doing?"

"She said it was an accident, but it wasn't, Aunty Dot. She did it on purpose. Mary spoke up and said 'No, it wasn't I saw you. You were supposed to be throwing the ball to me but you suddenly turned around and aimed the ball at Beth.' Then Peter said 'Yes, I saw you as well. It was no accident.' That's when the gym mistress sent for the headmaster."

"What do you think, Bhutan? Will Beth be all right? I'm very concerned about all this," said Dorothea.

"She will need a thorough checking over. Of all the stupid things to do. I shall certainly give that girl a good talking to."

By the time they got to the school and parked the car, Raif was hot on their heels in the jeep. He tooted the horn to alert them and Dorothea heaved a sigh of relief at not having to tackle this alone. She knew Raif wouldn't stand for any nonsense.

"Grace told me what happened," he said, limping along beside them.

Joshua was terrified that he'd not only have to leave the school but also the lovely home life he'd enjoyed for the past five years. The fear of being sent away filled him with horror. He could feel bile rising in his throat and had to swallow hard to hold it down.

Monica lay in bed counting her blessings. After a bit of persuasion and with her mother's help, they managed to get her father to take her on at his office. The position originally offered to her had been given to someone else so she had to report to the personnel office to see if there were any other vacancies. Wanting to present herself well, she'd put on her best suit and sensible shoes and brushed her hair into a neat French roll.

"How do I look, Mum?" she asked nervously.

"You'll do," said her mother.

There wasn't a vacancy but as she was the daughter of one of the directors, they placed her in the archive department. It involved lifting a lot of heavy boxes of files, but she didn't mind. There were only two others in the office besides herself: a man in his forties who still lived at home with his mother and a middle-aged lady who was also unmarried and lived alone. She liked them both immediately and got on very well with them. After a week, she began to feel like the luckiest girl in the world, especially as her period arrived bang on time as usual. Yes, she had been a very lucky girl indeed.

"The idea was, we'd knock this wall through so that customers in the shop can get themselves a snack in the cafe," said Raif, showing Gerry the new premises. "Then upstairs, we'll set up the office and a small workshop. What do you think?" Raif hoped Gerry wouldn't point out too many pitfalls.

"Let's take a look upstairs," said Gerry, making no comment.

After a thorough inspection of the premises, upstairs and down, Gerry still hadn't made any comment.

Raif added, "The estate agent has spoken to the owner about the work involved. We're just waiting for feedback. If he refuses, we'll just have to work with it as it stands."

"Have you had any quotes for the work involved?"

"Yes, we have two quotes. Both similar actually."

"It might work," said Gerry. "It would be a huge gamble, but as things stand in the world at the moment, what have you got to lose?"

"It all hinges on the bank loan. I've got another meeting with them next week, but I'm not holding my breath."

"What will you do if they refuse?"

"We'll have to think again."

"It's a tough business. I'm beginning to think that perhaps if I'd been a bit stricter and adopted some of Iain Boothroyd's tactics, I'd still be in business. He's obviously got it right, which is more than I can say for myself."

"I wouldn't be too sure about that. According to Dotty, his partner has upped sticks and gone."

"Some of the suppliers aren't happy either."

"Fancy a pint in the pub?" asked Raif.

"That's the best offer I've had this week," Gerry laughed.

"Howard, come into the parlour a minute. I've got something to show you," said Dorothea.

Howard couldn't believe his eyes. On following Aunty Dot into their "best" sitting room, there, sitting on the writing bureau, was a typewriter.

"I'll teach you and Daisy to type on it. You can then present your scripts professionally. Daisy can help you. What do you think?"

"Oh, Aunty Dot, it's marvellous. Thank you."

"Next time Raif goes into town, I'll get him to purchase some reams of paper. With regular practice, you and Daisy will pick up speed and be able to knock out scripts easily. Now, about next week. Celia will meet us at the station. We haven't enough petrol in the car or the jeep to do a long journey, so we'll have to make do. It will be an early start as your interview at the radio station is at two o'clock. We'll dine at John's then the following morning we'll meet with the publisher. Belinda will be there as well to go through the illustrations."

"I'll make sure I have everything ready. Can I show Daisy the typewriter?"

"Of course, off you go. Dinner's nearly ready," Dorothea said before making her way back into the kitchen where Grace was just setting the table.

"Round everyone up, Dotty. It's all ready." Grace couldn't wait to hear what went on at the school. Raif, Bhutan, Sam, Josh and Beth had been in the library for over an hour, with the door shut. She hoped everything was all right, but couldn't help worrying. The sight of Joshua's stricken face was still haunting her.

"Is everything all right now?" Grace asked nervously, realising Raif might not want to discuss things at the dinner table. Not wanting to miss out on all the details, she decided to take a chance.

"Yes, Grace. Raif and Bhutan soon sorted things out. Bhutan gave Beth a thorough examination then gave Rebecca a lecture about her behaviour and the potential dangers of blows to the head of that nature. Medicine balls are extremely heavy. Raif informed the headmaster that he'd be contacting the appropriate authorities if he didn't tackle the bullying in his school. He soon changed his tune after that. Rebecca's parents were there too."

"What did they have to say on the matter?"

"Well, the mother didn't open her mouth but her father seemed a very nice man. He said things had obviously become very slack since he'd been away in the army and he openly admitted that Rebecca had changed. She wasn't the daughter he knew before he left to take up his duties. There was a lot of 'back-chat' and voicing of opinions. Opinions which he knew weren't her own. He said he intended to put a stop to it before it got out of hand. Rebecca was to be grounded and absolutely forbidden to see this boyfriend of hers. He gave his assurances to everyone that it wouldn't happen again and that he personally would make sure she knuckled down and did her homework."

"Good for him. She's lucky she wasn't expelled."

"She was so close, Grace. I tell you."

"It wouldn't benefit the girl, would it? Being expelled? It could set her off on the path to rack and ruin. I've seen it happen before. They're at an impressionable age. They've only got to get in with the wrong crowd and then it's downhill all the way."

"I agree. I hope her father can knock some sense into her. She seems a very headstrong girl and her mother obviously wasn't handling the situation."

"I do hope Beth will be all right, Dotty."

"So do I. Only time will tell. Now, come on. Let's eat before it gets cold."

Chapter Thirty-Eight

Iris ordered a pot of tea at the counter and selected two slices of fruit cake before sitting down at the table next to Kathleen.

"Tell me again, how was the trip to London?" Iris could see by Kath's face things had gone well and couldn't wait to hear all the details.

"Oh Iris, it was super. We had a lovely time. Graham and Jeanette are such good company. Stuart's asked me to marry him."

"No! What did you say?" Iris' eyes were as big as saucers and there was a big grin on her face.

"I said yes, of course. But there is the problem of Dad. We've not told him yet. Stuart wants us to move into The Honeypot, but we're not sure if Dad will want that, so we'll have to tread carefully."

"The Honeypot?"

"It's Stuart's cottage. It's round like a honeypot, with a thatched roof."

"Sounds idyllic, but I see what you mean about your dad. You wouldn't want to go upsetting him. Old people hang on to their memories and such like."

The waitress arrived with their tea and Iris busied herself filling the cups whilst Kath told her about her stay in London. They ate their cake in silence, neither commenting on the poor quality but the tea was good and hot.

"Will there be any jobs going when the business is up and running?" asked Kath, sipping her tea.

"Do you fancy it? We'll need help in the cafe for sure. Oh Kath, it will be so good to work together again. No word from the factory yet then?"

"Not a thing. It's still closed. I can't get to know what's going on."

"We're hoping to get things ready by the end of the year, with a view to opening on the second of January. If you can hang on until then?"

"I haven't got much choice, but I need to find something soon even if it's just to tide me over. I don't like taking money off Dad. He's only got his pension."

"How's his cold? Is he still in bed?"

"Yes. He was pretty bad when he got back from his trip, but he's a bit better now. He ate his porridge this morning. He said he only had one drink, if you can believe that," she laughed. "He blamed it on the hotel as they had no central heating on and the hot water was only lukewarm."

"Central heating costs money and we've not long since come out of a war," said Iris, thinking of their own situation at Blythe Wood, where they all sat in their dressing gowns to keep warm.

"What was Edna doing at your house the other day?" Kath was curious, as Edna wasn't known for her social visits.

"Word's spread around about the business and all the women at the WI have been collecting together their old curtains and such. She borrowed Alf's wheelbarrow and covered it up with a bit of tarpaulin. There was a huge pile of it. Beth and Josh were thrilled to bits. The WI ladies are very fond of Josh. He's such a nice natured boy."

"Good for her. How's Beth doing? Has she been all right since the accident at the school?"

"Thankfully, yes."

"There was a terrible row at Rebecca's house after the meeting with the headmaster."

"Oh? How do you know?"

"One of the neighbours told me. The shouting could be heard all over the estate. It went on for over three hours. It seems Rebecca wasn't happy about being tied to the house and in an act of revenge, told her father about her mother seeing Douglas whilst he was away."

"Oh dear. Silly girl."

"She said nobody was going to stop her seeing her boyfriend, but rumour has it that he's dumped her for someone else anyway. Typical of a man, first sign of trouble and they're off."

Iris laughed. "The traumas of youth. I'm glad that I'm over that stage of my life."

"She's far too young to have a serious relationship like that. I don't know what her mother was thinking about, allowing it in the first place."

"It'll blow over. Things usually do," said Iris philosophically.

Dorothea was just posting a letter to Celia when she spotted Mrs Kloot coming out of the bank.

"Rosine," she shouted and waved, crossing the road towards her before she had a chance to escape. She'd been avoiding her ever since her husband Charles had returned and she was curious to know why.

"Oh Dotty, so nice to see you. I must speak to you. You have time for a cup of tea, yes?"

"I'm always ready for a cup of tea, Rose, you know that," she said, smiling. They linked arms and strolled up the road together like good friends.

"Come back to the library with me. Norman and Charles aren't in this afternoon so we can have the place to ourselves. We'll go into the office."

"It's nice and warm in here, Rose," said Dorothea, removing her coat and scarf as they entered the library.

"It's too warm sometimes. I'll just fill the kettle."

"So, how are things with Charles?"

"He is very… how do you say? Unsettled?"

"Why?"

"He wants to return to his homeland. He thinks things will be exactly the same as they were when we left it all those years ago, but I tell him this will not be so. There has been a war and the country must rebuild, same as here."

"Does he like working in the library?"

"No. That is the problem also."

"What was his profession before the war?"

"He was a teacher."

"Well, can't he go back to that? Surely there will be openings he can apply for."

"He wants a change."

"To do what?"

"This is the difficulty. He does not know. He is bored and restless. He cannot settle his mind to anything. He says he will return to France without me if I do not agree."

"Oh goodness me, Rose. I'm so sorry. What will you do?"

"I like it here. I have many friends but Charles does not. It's hard for him."

"Yes, but surely we can find something to get his social life going again. What does he like doing?"

"Cycling, playing cricket, playing chess. I wanted to say how sorry I was at having to let Samuel go. Norman insisted that we give the job to Charles. I thought perhaps it would settle him but it hasn't. It's too boring for him."

"Doesn't he like books?"

"He never read a book in his life," she laughed as she poured out the tea.

"Well, he's not in the right job then. Isn't there a cycling club around here that he could join?"

"There are a few actually but he has no bicycle at the moment."

"I'll ask around. If I come up with anything, I'll let you know."

"How are the children? I heard about Beth. Is she all right?"

"Yes, thankfully. News travels fast in this village."

"I miss our Thursday evenings. Are they still practising their French?"

"I'm afraid not. Sam's having art lessons, so he's concentrating on that. Howard's writing all the time now and doing well. He's a bright boy."

"As soon as I sort Charles out, we can resume again?"

"If you like," said Dorothea nonchalantly. "I must get back or the others will wonder where I am." As she came out of the office, Dorothea spotted Rebecca sat at a desk, writing. "What's she doing here?" she whispered.

"She's been in every day this week. Her father's laid down the law and insisted that she concentrate on her studies. I think she'd rather be in here than at home at the moment. She comes every afternoon after school and stays until closing time at four o'clock."

"No sign of the boyfriend then?"

"He's been seen about town with another girl, but she's not from the school. I haven't seen her before. She looks older than him and dresses very smartly. Smells of money if you ask me, judging by her jewellery and such."

"Fancy," said Dorothea, tiptoeing towards the doorway.

Howard couldn't understand why Daisy was reluctant to go for their usual walk in the park. Every time he suggested it, she made some excuse that she was too busy or wasn't feeling up to it. He wondered if perhaps she'd gone off him and the thought filled him with sadness. Jenny too had become confused as to why they weren't going out as much as usual and handed Howard her piggy bank.

"Take the money out of here," she whispered to him one Sunday afternoon.

"No, Jenny, that's your money. You must keep it safe. You never know when you'll need it. Girls need to have their own money. I'll speak to your mum, don't worry."

So, without further ado, he waited until Daisy was alone in the back garden pegging out the washing before approaching her and gently asking her if he'd done something to offend her. He knew instinctively something wasn't right and there was a distancing between them that wasn't there until a few weeks ago. To begin with she looked startled, then went pale.

Touching his hand, she said, "Oh Howard, you could never upset me. You mean more to me than anyone else in the world, besides Jenny. But you're right, we need to talk."

"Has something happened?" he asked, at a loss as to what could have occurred.

"Yes, in a way. Let's sit down over here." She led him to the bench overlooking the rose bushes. "I was reluctant to tell you because you may not want to know me once you've learnt the truth."

"Whatever can you mean, Daisy? Why would I do that?"

"Have you heard the name Iain Boothroyd being talked about lately?"

"Yes, he's the one who stole all Gerry's staff."

"Well, he's Jenny's father."

Howard frowned, clearly not understanding how that could possibly be. Surely Daisy couldn't have been married to him, could she? Of course, he now realised she could have been in a relationship when she was younger, before he knew her.

"Were you married to him then?"

"No. He wasn't my boyfriend either."

She spent the next half hour explaining to him exactly what had happened that night during the bomb raid, right up to the moment she met Grace in the church, having lost her mother, her home and her virginity, all on the same night.

Howard knew full well men of Iain Boothroyd's type existed. He'd seen if often enough in the back streets of London when his mother was in the grip of her alcoholism. Left to his own devices most evenings, he'd wander the streets and parks just for something to do and to escape from their lodgings, which were cold and damp with no food available. He preferred the outdoors.

"Does he know about Jenny then?"

"No, but I've seen him out and about. If he sees me with her, he'll know for sure that she's his child. She's so like him in looks. I'm terrified he'll abduct her."

"I can't see that happening somehow. He doesn't seem the type to take on the responsibility of bringing up a child, but I suppose there's an outside chance he could cause trouble. We need to speak to Uncle Raif about this. He'll know what to do."

"He already knows. So does Stuart. They're keeping a careful watch over him. Stuart says that's all they can do."

"We must make sure that Jenny always has someone with her." Howard was silent for a few moments, collecting his thoughts. "It's a cruel world sometimes, Daisy. I saw a lot of poverty and violence when I lived in London. Funnily enough, I was never afraid, even as the bombs began to fall. I suppose I was too young to process it then. But looking back now, I realise how awful my own life was."

"Oh Howard…" said Daisy, putting her arm around him.

"Let's not think about any of it now. We've got each other and we've got this wonderful family and beautiful house to live in. I couldn't ask for anything more and I'm doing what I love best: writing."

Snapping his bag shut, Dr Mattison announced, "You've got a touch of pneumonia, Mr Glass. You must stay in bed until I order you to get out of it. Is that understood? Or you'll certainly end up in the infirmary with TB."

"I'll see he does as he's told, doctor," said Kath, straightening the bed covers.

"I'll write you a prescription out. Stronger medication is needed. I'll call again next week."

"Thank you. I'll see you out." Kath made her way down the stairs and opened the front door to see Josh and Selina coming up the path.

"Hello Doctor Mattison," said Josh.

"Hello young man, and who's this young lady?"

"Oh, this is Selina, Bhutan's daughter. Selina, this is Doctor Mattison, the village doctor."

"Bhutan's daughter, eh?" he said, lifting his hat. "Pleased to meet you, my dear." He turned to Kath and whispered, "What a beauty."

"Oh Josh, I'm so glad you've come. Dad's driving me mad. He's always pleased to see you. It'll cheer him up a bit. You go on up and I'll fetch some drinks and cake."

The four of them spent the next two hours crowded around the bed, laughing and joking. It didn't take long for Josh to dispel the gloom after hearing about the lumpy mattress, the cold, draughty room, no news worth reading in the newspapers and no decent programmes on the radio. Josh wanted to know all about the meeting with Mr Glass' fellow club members, then very cleverly steered the conversation towards the subjects he knew he liked best, with the help of Selina, who was quick witted and knowledgeable and made him laugh despite himself. Josh was amazed at Selina's knowledge of history and geography. She certainly knew far more than he did and was interested in anything and everything.

After they'd gone, Kath was about to go downstairs to start the evening meal. "Do you want mash or chips with your chop, Dad?"

"Oh, mash please. I'm not up to chips. She'll go far that young lady, you mark my words. Very smart lass that."

"Yes, I agree, Dad. Attractive too. Stunning in fact. I wish I looked like that."

"There's nothing wrong with your looks, lass. You're fine and dandy just as you are."

"Thanks, Dad." She smiled to herself as she made her way downstairs.

Samuel noticed a change in the classroom since the incident with the medicine ball in the gym. Rebecca was no longer as popular as she was and lost her influence over some of her fellow classmates. Mary and Peter were seen as heroes for daring to speak up and Sam too noticed people being more friendly towards him, even those that had previously shunned him because of the colour of his skin.

The headmaster addressed the whole school on the serious nature of bullying and gave a warning that pupils would be dealt with severely if they were caught. There was to be a new bullying policy which all teachers were now aware of and Rebecca was forced to compile a written apology to Beth.

Beth focused on the headmaster's words "*if* they were caught" and wondered if things would change or if indeed all this was just a paper exercise. Only time would tell, but she was in her last year at this school now and was happily contemplating a career in dressmaking along with Josh and Selina.

Howard had already applied for a place at university studying English and Sam, after a discussion with his parents, had applied for a place studying art and history. Raif was gathering information regarding the best course for the girls and Josh. Beth felt truly excited and inspired at the way her life was developing and nothing could cloud her joy.

Raif and Dorothea advised them all to study hard during this last year at school as their exam marks could be the deciding factor in gaining a place at their chosen location. Selina was a year older than Sam and already had four A Levels but she was constantly studying the history and geography books in Raif's library. She was also able to help Beth with her homework, which was a great advantage. Beth, in turn, was able to get together with Josh to make sure they were both up to speed in all subjects. He was better at mathematics, she was better at English and they were both a bit weak at history, but their geography was excellent, thanks to all the hard work Dorothea had put in over the years during their cosy evenings together in the library.

Samuel didn't appear to be struggling at all and breezed through his school work with ease. He was undoubtedly the brightest boy in the class, if not the whole school. The children had been with Dorothea for six years now and a delighted Mrs Bray told Raif and Dorothea they were a credit to the school.

"I have to take my hat off to you, Mrs Swift," she said. "You've done a marvellous job with these children. When I think back to how they were when they first arrived… well, dear me. But look at them now. You should be very proud."

This left Dorothea glowing with pride. Raif merely smiled and nodded as if to say, "well, what did you expect?"

Rebecca had also done exceptionally well, much to the delight of both her parents. The firm hand her father had shown was obviously paying off, for Rebecca was now looking for a place at university. The atmosphere at home had been frosty after the incident in the gym with her mother not speaking to anyone, but Rebecca wasn't concerned about this for she spent all her afternoons in the library and only went home at tea time. She was enjoying the solitude and time for reflection. Of course, it meant she was very hungry by the time she got home, having not eaten since breakfast but Mrs Kloot was kind to her and made her a cup of tea and if she was lucky, she'd get a biscuit as well.

Over time, she began to feel a certain amount of sympathy for her mother, who was stuck at home all day on her own. It must be very monotonous at times for her. Other than knitting and a bit of gardening, she didn't appear to have any hobbies either so when Douglas came along and lavished attention on her, Rebecca could see how her mother had become drawn in by it all. Eventually, the atmosphere at home had thawed and things reverted back to relative normality, but Rebecca wasn't about to give up her afternoons at the library, for she treasured this time alone more than anything.

Stuart had just arrived at the station and was pumping up the tyres on his bike when the desk sergeant called him back inside.

"Stuart, there's a lady here asking to speak to you. A Mrs Durran."

"Did she say what it was about?"

"She wouldn't say. Says it's confidential and she'll only speak to you."

"Right. Tell her I'll be in shortly."

"I'll place her in the interview room and make her a cup of tea."

"Do I get one as well?"

"If you're a good boy and do my diary for next year."

"Don't I always?" Stuart always marked his shifts for the whole year into his new diary and had taken to doing Charlie's as well for he was only a year off retirement and found the chore tedious, often arriving for work on the wrong shift.

"Sorry to keep you waiting, Mrs Durran. How can I help you?"

asked Stuart, sitting himself opposite a very smartly dressed lady. A lady of considerable means, judging by her clothing.

"It's about a Mr Boothroyd. I want to lodge an official complaint. My daughter is in his employ… or was, until yesterday."

"What occurred, Mrs Durran?"

"The man's a monster. Preying on young girls the way he does." She removed her coat and scarf to reveal a very expensive looking two-piece suit. The scarf looked like pure silk and the coat pure wool, Stuart observed.

"My Lavinia was lucky to escape with her dignity intact last night. She came home in a right state. She's a shop floor supervisor and responsible for making sure all the girls are wearing the correct protective clothing, overalls and such. One of the girls accidently tore her overalls whilst moving some boxes into the delivery van."

"Don't they have men to do that heavy lifting?" asked Stuart.

"Mr Gerry did, but not this tyke. Anyway, Lavinia went to the stockroom to get this girl another set of overalls before Mr Boothroyd saw it, otherwise he'd dock her wages. All of a sudden, the door slammed shut and there he was, looming over her with a lecherous grin on his face. Started pawing at her clothing and slobbering all over her. Kept saying, 'come on, you know you want it as much as I do' and 'come on, you know you want it.' She wasn't strong enough to fight him off and came home with marks all over her neck and wrists where he'd tried to restrain her. She thought he was going to strangle her and started to scream. Fortunately, one of the girls was passing the door on her way back from paying a visit to the lavatory, when she heard the scream. She flung open the door and switched the light on."

"Then what?" Stuart demanded, feeling himself getting more and more annoyed as the story unfolded.

"He said it was all a joke and he was only 'teasing'. Teasing, my foot. He had his hands around her neck. She's got the marks to prove it and her wrists as well. Lavinia's too frightened to go out now. She's only seventeen, officer. The other girl has been sacked. Ordered off the premises, just like that. Well, it's good riddance. She's not going back there. My husband's furious and he's not a violent man, but there's no reasoning with Mr Boothroyd's sort, is there? He'll always bluff his way out of trouble." She took her handkerchief out of her bag and paused briefly to blow her nose before adding, "I'm not the flaky sort who'll just brush this incident under the carpet, officer. My daughter was too frightened to accompany me here today. She thinks he'll come after her and cause trouble, but I want this lodging in your police records. I'll sign the paperwork myself if you draft up a report."

"Can you give me the name and address of Lavinia's colleague who was sacked?" asked Stuart, getting out his pad and pen.

"Yes, I have it here." She rummaged around in her bag, producing a very expensive looking leather-bound diary and flicked through the pages. "Here we are. Joyce Manford. She lives in a cottage just the other side of the railway. You can see her back garden from the railway track."

"What have you got there?" asked Dorothea, eyeing the huge box Raif had dumped on the kitchen table. She was going over her designs with Magda, who had some good ideas of her own.

"This, my dear wife, is the start of our new enterprise," he said, looking very pleased with himself. They waited until he unpacked it to reveal a sewing machine, complete with a built-in overlocker.

"Oh Raif!" exclaimed Dorothea. "This is magnificent. Where on earth did you get it?"

"Gerry purchased this machine with his own money when he first set up the factory, so he's claimed it back. Unofficially, of course. He's siphoned off two others as well and hidden them away. The rest have been handed over to the debt collectors, I'm afraid."

Dorothea and Magda didn't care where it had come from as they were both eager to get going on it and spent the next two hours learning how to thread the needle and work the overlocker, practising on scraps of material until they got the stitch tension just right. Raif produced a bottle of machine oil, which Gerry had given him and he proceeded to service it.

"You have to keep them well oiled," he advised. "It helps them to run better."

By midnight, they'd cut out and sewn one of the waistcoat designs. Deliberately choosing a heavy cloth for the front and a matching silk for the back, the end result was exquisite. Over the course of the next two days, they made up two more in different colours and a smoking jacket too, which was finished in a heavy brocade and lined with silk. Bhutan tried them all on and looked incredibly smart in them.

"They're good quality," he remarked. "I've never seen anything quite like them before. They're well-made and beautifully finished."

"I'll take them to London with me next week," said Dorothea. "We'll show them to Belinda. She might be able to photograph them and make up a promotional booklet or something."

Chapter Thirty-Nine

Beth crept into Grace's bedroom with two mugs of tea in her hands. "Are you awake, Aunty Grace?" she whispered.

Grace turned over and switched on the bedside lamp. "Come in, Beth," she said, propping herself up on her pillows.

"How are you feeling? Any better?" asked Beth, plumping up her pillows. "I've brought you some tea."

"A little bit better. Thank you, darling. Did you go to the jumble sale at the church?"

"Yes, but I didn't stay long. I helped Edna dish out the teas and cake, then left."

"Was Ivy there?"

"Yes, she asked why you didn't go to the WI meeting yesterday. I told her you were off colour. She's going to call round later." Just as she spoke the doorbell went. "Oh, that might be her now, I'll let her in."

Beth opened the door to a very fed up looking Ivy. "Hi Ivy, go up. I'll fetch you a cup of tea."

"I missed you yesterday at the meeting, Grace," said Ivy, seating herself on the end of the bed.

"Sorry, Ivy. I just felt too ill to leave the house. I've been in bed for two days. How are things at the farm?"

Ivy grimaced and sat collecting her thoughts for a minute or two before speaking. "It's not working out, to be honest. I hate to say it but that son of mine is bone idle."

"Wouldn't he be better off doing something he enjoys?" offered

Grace, who had no time for the lad but didn't want to upset Ivy unnecessarily.

Ivy shrugged. "He doesn't get out of bed before eleven o'clock most days. Alf's nearly done a day's work by then."

Beth handed Ivy her tea then left them alone to talk.

An hour later, she heard footsteps on the stairs.

"Thanks for the tea, Beth," Ivy shouted and made her way back up the path. Beth returned to the bedroom to find Grace looking pale and uncomfortable.

"Can I get you anything?" asked Beth.

"No, I'll be all right as long as I can stay in my bed. It'll pass. I've never seen Ivy looking so down."

"She had a bit of a run-in with that lady at the post office."

"Evelyn?"

"Yes. She was showing off, saying she'd had her hair done by some Italian stylist. Paid a fortune for it. Well, you know Ivy, she doesn't hold back with her opinions. She said no haircut was worth paying that amount of money for and frankly, she'd seen better hair round a coconut. Then Edna had a go. Evelyn was taking that long to eat her cake that Edna asked her if her false teeth were loose. She stormed off in a huff, after which Edna said, 'Well, she obviously can't chew her food properly.'"

Grace couldn't feel any sympathy for the woman, not after the way she'd sacked Meg.

"Aunty Grace, can I ask you something?"

"Of course. What is it?"

"I want you to be honest with me. Am I ugly?"

"Ugly? Heavens, child, what's brought this on? Don't be ridiculous. Take it from me, you are not ugly. Why do you ask?"

"It was something Rebecca said, that no man would ever want to marry me."

"Oh? And how would she know? She's an expert on the matter, is she? Looks are not everything, Beth, take it from me. I wasn't a looker but it didn't matter to my George."

"What was he like, your George?"

"Kind, loyal, generous to a fault. He'd give me his last halfpenny, not that we ever had much mind, and he thought the world of me."

"If I don't get married, can I stay here with you, Aunty Grace?"

"Aye, you can that. We'll be all right."

Beth smiled and curled up on the bed, resting her head on Grace's shoulder. Grace was glowing with pride, just to know that this young lass couldn't bear to be parted from her.

Daisy was alone in the back garden, weeding the flowerbed. The roses were looking magnificent, which always filled her heart with joy. It was her half-day off, but Howard hadn't mentioned going for a walk like he usually did and he'd been less chatty with her since their little talk the other day.

She knew he'd soon be off to university in London. The plan was for all the children to stay at the townhouse where Celia would keep house for them. Her mind wandered aimlessly, wondering if he still felt the same way about her or if indeed he still wanted her, after all he was five years younger. *I've got to let him live his life*, she thought. *If he's decided to move on and forget about me then I'll have to accept it.* But she couldn't bear to think about it. He'd make new friends at university, be mixing with young people his own age and she sobbed into her apron.

In readiness for Dr Mattison's visit, Dorothea was tidying up the bedroom. Bhutan had expressed his concerns regarding Grace and wanted a second opinion.

"He'll be here in a minute, Grace. I'll nip downstairs and wait for him."

The house was deathly quiet as everyone was out and about and Dorothea supposed she'd have to get used to the solitude as the children ventured out into the world to start their adult lives. Would they be the same children when they returned from university? If they returned at all. Would they want to stay in London with their new friends? She hoped with all heart they wouldn't forget about her and that one day they would return to the home she'd offered them all those years ago when she had taken them in and smothered them with love and care the best way she knew how. She promised herself she wasn't going to cry but the pains in her chest had returned. When Raif returned home from active service, the chest pains had dissipated but now they were back with a vengeance and she was struggling to breathe.

"Yes, I agree with Doctor Ansard. Mrs McGuire, you've had a mild heart attack. We need to get you to the infirmary."

"Oh no, doctor! Can't I stay here?" Grace protested.

"Don't worry, it will only be for a few days whilst they assess you and get you on medication, then you can come back to your own bed."

"I'll come with you, Grace," said Dorothea. "I'll just run down-stairs and speak to Daisy."

Megan was waiting at the bus stop. She was meeting Harry, who had some news to impart regarding the shop. She hoped it wasn't bad news as the whole family was relying on it being a viable enterprise. They were all hoping to make a success of it and were eager to get started.

Lost in her thoughts, she heard a voice behind her, "Excuse me, please."

Turning around to see a young woman pushing a pram, she said, "Oh, I'm so sorry."

She moved to one side to let the lady pass and realised her face seemed vaguely familiar.

"You're Lucy, aren't you? You worked with my sister Iris at the factory."

"Yes, that's right," she smiled.

"I'm Meg. It's a little boy, isn't it?"

"Yes. Declan."

"Can I see?" Meg put her head into the hood of the pram to get a closer look at him. Seeing a crown of downy hair and tiny fingers, she was suddenly reminded of her own baby loss and of Eddie. Her eyes filled with tears as she said, "He's so beautiful, Lucy."

"Well, he is when he's asleep like this," she laughed. "He has a healthy pair of lungs on him, I can tell you. He lets you know when he's hungry."

Meg mopped her eyes with a tissue. "I lost a baby myself a few years ago. Brings it all back."

"Dear me, how sad. Sorry to hear that, Meg. Jonathan and I never thought we'd have children. We had all the tests, you see. I'm all right but the problem was on his side."

"Oh. Well, it's a blessing then. How are things at home? I mean between the two of you, if you don't mind me asking?"

"Well, the whole village knew about me and Douglas, so there was no point in hiding it, was there? It wasn't easy, believe me. I promised him that Douglas would never be mentioned ever again and that he'll be the only dad Declan will ever know. He'll be his daddy in every sense of the word. It's what we always wanted really. I was stupid. I made a mistake. I was lonely and bored but that doesn't excuse my reckless behaviour. I can't think what came over me. I acted without thinking of the consequences."

"Don't we all?" sympathised Meg.

"Anyway, he wants us to move back to Ireland. Start a new life. I'd rather stay here to be honest but if it means we can stay together as a family, then I'm okay with it."

"Here's my bus. It's been nice talking to you, Lucy. Good luck, I hope everything works out for you."

Harry was waiting for her when she got off the bus. "There's a coffee shop just at the back of the market, we'll go there. It's only small but we'll be away from the crowds." He tucked her hand under his arm as they made their way through the throng of people queuing at the stalls.

"They're Polish people that run this little place," said Harry guiding her to a table. "I always come in here. Best coffee in town. Would you like a cup or do you prefer tea?"

"I'll try a coffee please, Harry. I'm a bit sick of tea."

He was right. The coffee was hot and strong and although

small, the place was spotlessly clean and the cups and saucers were bone china.

"They've been given notice on the place. They've got to move out," said Harry, stirring two sugars into his cup.

"Given notice? By whom?"

"The council. They're building a new road or something. It's going to be a one-way system. It's to ease the traffic."

"It is very congested here," said Meg. "Cars everywhere. What will they do? How many people run this place exactly?"

"Just the two of them now. That's Chris in the blue dress and Povinder's her husband. Chris' father owned it actually, but he died last year and she and Pov took it over. They've been offered a good price."

"What if they refuse to accept?"

"They can't really. The whole row's being demolished. They've already started at the far end."

"Yes, I noticed."

"It's a shame because they're such good people. Friendly, obliging and hard workers."

"What will they do?"

"Jury's out on that one, Meg. Anyway, the good news is that I heard from the owner of the shop and he's agreed to putting a door in. A wide one. He says the cost of demolishing the whole wall is too expensive, but the door will be wider than a standard door, so we can wedge it open. People can wander in and out between the shop and the cafe. Raif's already got a quote for the work and it's been agreed. He's gone to the bank manager today to see about a loan."

"Yes, I know, but he didn't seem very optimistic."

"It's the after-effect of the war. Left us in a sorry state all round, Meg."

"Do you think Chris and Pov…"

"Povinder."

"Povinder. Do you think they'd be interested in investing in the cafe?"

"I never thought about it. I could mention it to Raif, see what he thinks."

"It might be our only option if the bank lets us down."

Stuart leant his bicycle against the gatepost of Rose Cottage and before he had a chance to ring the bell, the door opened.

"Come in, officer. The kettle's just boiled."

"That's music to my ears, Mrs Manford."

"It's miss, actually. Call me Joyce. Come on through." She led him into a nicely furnished lounge. There wasn't a speck of dust anywhere, which made him ashamed of his own cottage. He could write his name in the dust lying in wait at The Honeypot.

Joyce was of average height, slightly thick set, with a clear complexion and short dark hair, which was thick and lustrous. He noticed her beautifully manicured fingernails, sporting bright red polish and two sapphire rings, one on each hand.

"I suppose this is about the incident at the factory?" Joyce said, handing Stuart a hand-thrown pottery mug.

"Yes, it is. We've had a complaint from Mrs Durran, Lavinia's mother."

"How is Lavinia?"

"She won't leave the house, according to her mother. Could you tell me exactly what happened, Joyce? In your own words."

She spent the next twenty minutes giving him all the details of what she saw when she heard the scream and barged in, switching on the light.

"In your opinion, could his behaviour be described as 'playful' or 'teasing'?"

"Playful? Hardly. He was trying to strangle her."

"Did he ever make advances to you?"

"Not exactly."

"Meaning?"

"Well, we all knew what he was like. None of the girls would take him his coffee. They were all too scared. But he doesn't scare me."

"So, he didn't try anything on then?"

"No, but on the third morning, I placed a cup on his desk and made for the door when he said, 'Are you happily married, Joyce?' David and I have been together for fourteen years now, but he's reluctant to marry me. It's common knowledge at the factory. I just ignored him and shut the door on my way out. It did get me thinking actually. I've had an offer of a job and I've decided to take it. I can hold my own with the fellas as much as the next girl, but Iain Boothroyd is a big lad. You've only got to look at the size of his hands. They're massive. I'll call and see Lavinia, just to make sure she's all right."

"She feels guilty about you getting the sack, all because of her. Could you call in at the station tomorrow to sign the statement?"

"Of course."

"Get that fella of yours to do the decent thing and make an honest woman of you," he said as he mounted his bike.

"We're like a married couple already, except for that piece of paper."

As Stuart cycled up the lane, he couldn't help thinking that some blokes didn't know when they were well off.

Monica was just putting on her hat and coat when one of the cleaners popped her head around the door.

"Your father's waiting for you downstairs, Monica. He'll run you home."

"Really? He doesn't usually finish this early."

"It's cold out. It'll save you standing at that bus stop, freezing to death."

Her heart gave a little flutter at what was to come. Had she performed well? Had she outstayed her welcome here? She wasn't aware of having made any mistakes and she'd certainly worked hard. Surely he wouldn't sack her, would he?

"Thanks, Dad," she said, jumping into the passenger seat. "You're early tonight. Is it your pub night?"

"No, it was last night. That's what I want to talk to you about. Something of a very serious nature has occurred."

Monica's head was thudding hard at this point and she started to feel decidedly uncomfortable. Her father wasn't known for his pep talks and his "no-nonsense" approach to solving problems usually meant she was in for a telling off. What on earth was he talking about? What could possibly have happened in the pub last night that involved her?

He drove in silence for a few minutes before turning into a quiet lane opposite the common. Switching off the engine, he turned to face her and said, "Now, I want you to be honest with me, Monica. What occurred that Saturday evening when you came home late? Why were you so insistent on not going back to the factory?"

"Have I done something wrong, Dad? Has someone complained?"

"Does the name Lavinia Durran mean anything to you?"

"Lavinia? Yes, we worked together at the factory. Why do you ask?"

"I met her father in the pub last night. He gave me all the lurid details about what happened to his daughter, at the hands of Iain Boothroyd."

Monica sat in silence. So, Lavinia had suffered too. If she'd been brave and reported him when he had attacked her, that wouldn't have happened. She could feel her cheeks burning.

"Oh Lord," she whispered, not daring to look her father in the face.

Stuart finished typing up his latest report. Monica and her father arrived early in the morning and they spent most of it going over every detail of her ordeal. Her father did the initial introduction then sat back and let his daughter tell the story. His face remained passive throughout and he made no attempt to comment or pass judgement, showing no inclination to interrupt or interfere.

"Right," said Stuart, "I'll order some coffees, if you could read through everything and make sure it's correct and accurate. Then if you're happy, sign it. If you think of anything else we've missed out, we can deal with that."

He pressed the intercom button on his telephone and issued instructions to the young desk clerk, who was to be his new assistant in the New Year when he took up his promotion to sergeant. He was a likeable lad and Stuart was looking forward to having someone with him when doing his rounds. His old bike had been relegated to the police yard and he was to have a patrol vehicle. Thank goodness he'd had the sense to learn to drive when he was younger.

He left them alone for a few minutes whilst Monica read through the report. He now had three complaints against Iain Boothroyd, although one was unofficial. He knew he'd have to pay a visit to Daisy and try to get her to sign a report. A visit to Mr Boothroyd was also on the cards. He decided he would take young Mike with him; it would be a good learning experience for him.

It was two o'clock in the afternoon before Monica and her father arrived back at the office, having stopped off at the pub for a sandwich first.

"Now, Monica, your mother doesn't need to know about any of this. It would only upset her. We'll keep it between ourselves."

Monica's eyes filled with tears. She didn't think she had ever loved her father more than she did at this moment. "Thanks, Dad. I blame myself for what happened. I should have been more guarded. I genuinely thought I was in line for a promotion. I was naive and stupid and I'm so sorry."

"That may be, my dear, but the fact remains that he drugged you and that's illegal."

Dorothea awoke early, glancing over at Raif who was awake and staring at the ceiling.

"What time is it?" she asked sleepily.

"Seven o'clock. Are you going to the hospital to see Grace?"

"Yes. Can you drop me off?"

"Of course. I'm seeing Gerry later. The builder's coming tomorrow to fit the door, then we can get cracking with the decorating. Alan, Bob and Bhutan are going to pitch in, so we should soon get organised."

Dorothea smiled and snuggled up to him. For the first time this week, the pains in her chest seemed to have disappeared.

"It was nice of Gerry to give us the rucksacks for the children, wasn't it?" she said.

They had been given one each, which Dorothea proceeded to fill, for when they went off to London in September to start their new lives at university. The house would be strangely empty without them she knew, but they would be home for Christmas and they could at least be a family for the festive season. She looked forward to giving them a Christmas to remember.

"Is Gerry now officially bankrupt?" she asked.

"It's not turned out too badly for him. In the cold light of day, he's managed to pay off most of his debts. The business has gone to the wall unfortunately, but he's still got a lot of contacts in the trade which might come in handy for us if we can get up and running."

"What will happen to Pat and Susan?"

"He's hoping to keep them on. They're willing to join us if we can make a go of it. Who knows? It's all a bit of a gamble. The bank manager won't lend us any money, so we'll have to do it the hard way. Gerry will help us. We're all in this together."

Chapter Forty

Two Years Later

Mike hung up his raincoat in his locker before going into the interview room where a lady and a young girl were waiting to talk to him. The sergeant had emphasised the urgency of the matter and he'd cycled back as fast as he could. The rain was hurtling down in stair rods and he was soaked to the skin. Sitting himself down behind the desk, he eased off his squelching shoes in order to let his socks dry out. He introduced himself and asked them how he could help.

"There's been an abduction. This is Jenny. Now, tell the gentleman exactly what you told me, dear," she said, turning to the child. "I found her crouching behind my hedge in the garden, officer," said the lady, whose name was Bessie. "She's had the most terrifying ordeal. Someone threw a coat over her head and then chucked her into the back of a small van."

"Who did, madam?"

"That's just it, we don't know," said Bessie.

"I know who it was," Jenny piped up, speaking for the first time. "His name is Mr Boothroyd."

At least she doesn't seem too traumatised by the ordeal, thought Mike.

"And where were you when this happened, Jenny?" he asked.

"I was just coming out of the school gates when all of a sudden, everything went black and then someone lifted me up and threw me into the back of a van." She paused for a few moments before adding, "Goodness, what's happened to your socks, sir? They're full of holes and soaking wet. They're all wrinkled. My mummy irons mine. She'd do yours too if you lived at our house."

"Jenny," said Bessie, trying her best not to laugh.

Mike glanced down at his feet to see his big toe poking through the holes and there were more holes starting at the heels.

"Hazard of the job. It's all the walking about," he offered by way of an apology, feeling acutely embarrassed. "So, how did you manage to escape and where did he take you? Did you travel far? How long were you in the van?" He realised he was rolling out the questions a little too fast for a young child, but a confident one at that.

"I live on Park Road South. It's only about half a mile from the school, so they can't have gone far," Bessie interjected.

"I realised what had happened straight away because my mother had warned me about him," continued Jenny. "Normally, I'd walk home with my half-sister Beth but she's away at university in London, so for the past two years my mother comes for me, but she must have been late yesterday as I couldn't see her as I came out of the gate."

"How old are you, Jenny?" asked Mike, gently.

"I'm seven, sir. I'll be eight in August."

Mike knew the past history of this man Boothroyd as Stuart had been over the whole scenario with him and he'd read all the reports on file. He also knew Iain Boothroyd was this little girl's father, although he wasn't sure if the child knew it, so he'd have to be careful not to let anything slip.

The court case last year hadn't been a success with Boothroyd wriggling off the hook, due to the evidence against him being circumstantial. The judge ruled that without evidence the allegations were unsustainable and wholly without foundation. Stuart suspected Iain's father, who was known to be "not short of a bob or two" had greased a few palms to get his son exonerated. Consequently, he'd walked out of court with his head held high and his dignity intact.

The locals weren't fooled though and word got around about his unsavoury behaviour. Everywhere he went, he was met with black looks and indifference. He'd had to stop going into the local pub as there'd been a few skirmishes with the locals, some of them threatening to rearrange his features. He was beginning to feel distinctly uncomfortable and he wasn't sure what his next move should be. The factory was losing money at an alarming rate and the debts were mounting. The staff came and went, resulting in the orders rarely being finished on time. A mass walk-out a couple of weeks ago had cost him an arm and a leg to get things back on track.

Well, he's not going to get away with it this time, thought Mike. Abduction was a very serious matter and he intended to see that justice was done. Luckily, the child was unharmed, but things could have been a lot worse.

"The man's a monster," shouted Bessie.

"He's got no moral compass," said Jenny calmly and confidently. "Uncle Raif said so."

"So, what happened when you realised you'd been abducted, Jenny?"

"Well, I'd hurt my hands when he threw me in the van."

"I've sorted them out, officer. She's got plasters on them. I had to clean her up a bit," said Bessie, putting a protective arm around the child's shoulders.

"I tried the handle on the back door, but it was locked," said Jenny, continuing her story. "Then I noticed a brick in the corner. It was on top of a white sheet, so I grabbed it and hurled it through the glass. It smashed and I was able to crawl out, falling onto the ground. That's when I grazed my knees. I dashed into the nearest garden and hid behind a bush. I heard the van screech to a halt. He opened the doors and must have realised that I'd escaped. I saw him come into the garden and look around but luckily, he didn't see me. He then went into the other gardens and had a good look around before driving off. That's when the nice lady here spotted me and came out to get me."

Mike rang the front doorbell of the impressive-looking house. Bessie and Jenny were beside him and the three of them stood waiting in the rain, which hadn't stopped all day. When the door finally opened, they were greeted by the whole household, who had all assembled in the hallway. Max the dog and Smoky the cat jumped into Jenny's arms the moment they set eyes on her. She sank to her knees, embracing them both in her arms and then she burst into tears.

"She's been incredibly brave," offered Bessie.

"Constable Gould," said Mike, offering Raif his hand. "And this is Bessie, the lady who took such good care of Jenny."

Daisy's eyes were red and swollen from all the crying, but on seeing her child returned to her unharmed was all she needed to pull herself together. "We're so grateful to you, Bessie," she said, giving her a hug, then turning her attention to her child.

"Let's all go into the lounge. We'll organise some refreshments," said Dorothea, breathing a huge sigh of relief at seeing the child unharmed.

"So, who's your little friend?" asked Mike, tickling Max affectionately behind his ears.

"This is Max. Josh asked me to look after him whilst he's away at university. I walk him round the garden twice a day, then I give him a good brush. He has four dog biscuits with milk for his breakfast. Aunty Dot's quite strict with his food because the vet said he's slightly overweight, so he's sort of on a diet. He eats tomatoes off the tomato plants in the allotment which makes her cross. They make him fart, so he gives himself away. But he's a good boy really. He can't help that he's hungry, poor chap. I know what it's like to be hungry, as our food was rationed during the war."

Mike laughed, in spite of himself. Oh, how he loved this adorable child. If only she was ten years older, he'd marry her.

"My Samson's just the same. Always looking for food."

"Samson? That's a nice name."

"I called him that because he's a coward. If he sees so much as a spider, he jumps up on a chair."

"What type of dog is he?"

"He's a poodle and very affectionate. I wouldn't be without him.

He's my best friend and good company. On cold, lonely nights, we curl up on the settee together."

It was only when he was on his way home that Mike realised how lonely he really was. It was about time he found himself a girlfriend. He'd have to do something about it otherwise it would be more of the same. The lonely nights stretching out before him, eating supper on his own, going to the cinema on his own. All his colleagues at the station seemed to be married or courting and even his two best friends from school were now with regular girlfriends.

Stuart turned into the factory yard and parked the car at the front entrance where a crowd of women were all gathered.

"Hello, what's all this then?"

"Looks as though they're locked out, sir," said Mike.

"Either that or he's done a runner."

"That's a distinct possibility."

"Good morning ladies. What's the situation here then?" asked Stuart.

"That's what we'd like to know," shouted one of the ladies who was in the middle of lighting herself a cigarette. "Place is all locked up."

They all started to talk at once.

"He might at least have paid us this week's wages. We've worked the whole week for nothing."

"My old man'll go spare. The rent's due tomorrow."

"I reckon he's hopped it."

"He might just be late. Perhaps he's been delayed for some reason."

"No chance, Eileen. Look at the place, it's all in darkness."

Stuart turned to Mike and said, "Let's take a look around."

Slowly, they toured the whole building. All doors and windows were locked and there was no sign of life inside.

"We'll organise a search warrant and take a look inside," said Stuart. "Not that it'll do us much good mind."

They made their way back to the front of the building where the ladies were starting to disperse.

"I'm not standing here any longer," one of the ladies was saying.

"No point in you all hanging around here, ladies," said Stuart. "We'll try and find out what's happening. Is there a shop floor supervisor? Do they have a set of keys, by any chance?" he asked the loud mouthed one who'd been the first to speak.

"We did have. He sacked her. And we all know why."

"Probably wouldn't drop her knickers," one of the other ladies muttered as they made their way out of the gate amongst titters of laughter.

"Gosh, I feel sorry for them," said Mike. "They're hard-working girls. They don't deserve to be treated like this. What a rat, just abandoning them all."

"Only to be expected really, the mess he was in. I don't think he's paid any bills since the day he arrived."

Howard lay on his bed enjoying a rare moment of peace and quiet. The others had all gone to the cinema, which was their usual Saturday night haunt. He feigned a headache and made for his bed. He wanted to be alone with his thoughts.

Although he was enjoying his studies, his heart was still back at Blythe Wood and he couldn't wait to get back to it, and, of course, he was missing Daisy and Jenny. He couldn't wait for the day when his exams were over and he could return to the house he knew and loved so much. There was something magical about that house, or perhaps it was the people that inhabited it, but he felt secure and safe within its walls. There really was nowhere like it. He wondered if Josh and Beth were feeling the same.

The interview with the radio station hadn't gone well and they'd declined to take his plays, a series of six in total. He wasn't altogether surprised but he was disappointed nonetheless. By a stroke of luck, he'd happened upon an American magazine who were interested. They offered him, what seemed to Howard, a ridiculous amount of money for the six plays. Of course, he didn't know what to do for the best and in the end, he consulted Raif, who advised him to grab the offer with both hands.

"You don't get that kind of offer every day, my lad," he had advised. "Take it."

So, he did. Raif invested the money for him into a separate bank account. Truthfully, he was not wealthy but the sales from his books, five now in total, were steadily breaking into the open market and appearing on bookshelves around the country. Now he was in his last year, he decided to do a course in play writing once his English degree was completed. It was what he enjoyed doing the most. He knew without a doubt it would be hard to get established but he also knew he had the ability to make a go of it, if he worked hard. He was going to do it anyway.

Drifting off to sleep, he dreamt of the big kitchen at Blythe Wood, the allotment and the rose garden.

Joshua wasn't enjoying the film they'd gone to see and wished he'd stayed at home with Howard. He was finding his coursework very hard going and he knew that if it wasn't for Selina helping him, he'd have no chance of getting through his exams. He loved the practical work but not being academic hindered his progress in the written stuff. He'd be lucky to pass his final exams if truth be told. The thought of wasting three years of study and not getting his degree at the end of it weighed heavily on his mind.

Uncle Raif and Aunty Dot had given him so much, he felt he owed it to them to do well. It was a chance in a lifetime and he knew he wouldn't have had this opportunity if he'd remained at home with his father and step-mother. Blythe Wood was pulling at his heartstrings and he'd felt homesick since the day he'd left it. He couldn't wait for his university life to be over so he could get back to Somerset.

Selina was confidently breezing through all her coursework with ease. Beth not so much. Like himself, help was required with the written work. All three of them enjoyed making garments for the fashion shows, which were an end of term regular feature. He wondered how Beth was feeling. She certainly got on well with Selina and the two of them were like sisters in every way. Listening to their friendly badinage made him smile.

He waited until they were all in bed that evening before asking Sam if he felt homesick.

"Homesick?" said Sam, with an element of surprise. "Let me put it this way, I can't wait to get back to my old life in Somerset. My daily art lessons with Hilary were the happiest times I'd ever known. This last year can't go quick enough for me."

"Good," said Josh, pleased he wasn't the only one missing home. "Me too. What will you do, Sam, when you're qualified?"

"I spoke to Hilary before I started my course and she said that once I'm qualified, she can help me get placed in teaching. She's hoping to set up her own academy in her studio."

"Wow!" Josh sat bolt upright in his bed. "That sounds amazing."

Howard also turned over and sat up in his bed. "Sounds good, Sam. I hope it all works out. I'm sure it will."

"You two are lucky," said Josh, miserably. "You both know where you're going. I'm not sure what I'm going to be doing or if I'll even pass my exams. It'll be three years wasted if I don't."

"Don't think like that, Josh. You'll pass. Think positively," said Sam.

"I am, I mean, I do try but…"

"Are you going to continue writing, Howard?" asked Sam.

"You bet. The sooner I get back to Somerset, the happier I'll be. I can hear voices in the hall. Who can that be at this time of night?"

"I'll go and see," said Josh, shooting out of bed to peer over the banister, just as Celia was coming up the stairs.

"It's Beth's mother," she whispered and knocked on the girls' bedroom door.

Beth followed her downstairs tying her dressing gown around her. "What a strange time to visit," said Beth. "I hope nothing's wrong."

"She seems in good spirits," said Celia. "So, don't worry."

"Celia," said Beth, placing her hand on Celia's arm. "Will you stay with me, please? Don't leave me alone with her, no matter what she says, please."

"Of course, dear."

Selina, Howard, Josh and Sam all congregated at the top of the stairs, not sure whether to venture downstairs or not. After twenty minutes, they heard raised voices and it seemed as though they were arguing. After another twenty minutes, Beth came charging out of the lounge and stormed up the stairs, slamming the bedroom door. The boys weren't allowed in the girls' bedroom so they all looked at Selina.

"What should I do?" she asked them.

"Leave it for a few minutes," whispered Sam. "Someone's coming. Quick, into our room, everyone."

"It's Beth's mother," whispered Josh.

They heard her knock on the bedroom door, then try the handle, but the door was locked.

"Beth, darling. Now don't be silly. We need to be sensible about this. Come down and let's discuss it."

"There's nothing to discuss! I've given you my answer and also given you the reasons why, so just leave me alone. I'm not going to change my mind. You're being selfish and unfair, as usual. I've nothing more to say to you."

The bedroom light went off, then they heard her crying. Beth's mother sat on the top stair for a good half hour, waiting for Beth to come out, but she didn't. Celia came up to meet her and asked her to come back down to the lounge where John the next-door neighbour was waiting.

After another half hour, they heard voices in the hall, then the front door open and shut. They all charged downstairs, eager to find out what had happened.

"She wants Beth to give up everything here and go back home," said Celia.

"Why?" asked Josh.

"She's set up her own catering business or something. All sounds a bit precarious to me. She organises parties, gatherings, weddings and special occasions. She does the whole lot, table decorations, flowers, drinks. Her idea was for Beth to help her out."

"To go and work for her?" asked Sam, suddenly realising he might lose his beloved Beth.

"That was the general idea," said Celia. "Now, off back to bed all of you."

Two days later, Beth's father arrived at the door demanding to speak to his daughter.

"It's no use, Dad. If she's sent you to make me change my mind, I won't. Why can't she employ some other young girl to train up? There must be plenty of young ladies willing to take up the offer."

"She'd have to pay them a wage. That would cost money and there isn't any."

"Surely she wasn't expecting me to work for nothing?"

"That was the general idea. She'd probably treat you to the odd gift now and again. A new pair of shoes or some perfume."

"Dad, really? Charming."

"Those are her words, darling, not mine. I'm on your side."

"What would be in it for me then? I spent a lot of time as a child, sitting in the house all alone, night after night whilst you and Mum enjoyed yourselves. You with your golfing pals, her with her wine chums. Well, I'm not going back to all that, Dad. I've built a good life for myself here and I'm finishing my degree whether you and Mum like it or not. Please try and see it from my point of view. Believe me when I say that I love you very much, Dad, but I must be allowed to live my own life."

He took hold of her hand between his own and pressed it to his lips. "I've told her all this, Beth, but you know what she's like."

"Yes. Selfish. I haven't seen or heard from either of you for six years and now this."

"Guilty as charged. We've both been preoccupied.. The row with

Alan should never have happened. If I'd been at home that day, I'd have prevented him from leaving. It's all wrong."

Two days later, Beth received a letter from her mother saying how disappointed she was in her and how she expected more from her own daughter, for whom she'd sacrificed so much. She accused her of being ungrateful and spoilt. Beth showed the letter to Samuel, then threw it on the fire. There were tears, of course, but she resolved to put it behind her and concentrate on her studies. She knew that whatever she did, there would be no pleasing her mother.

Raif was pouring himself a second cup of tea, which was unusual for him as he only ever had one cup.

"There's another rather disturbing letter here from Celia," said Dorothea. "You'd better read it." She handed him the thick wad of paper containing all the details of the situation regarding the visit from Beth's parents. "I've been dreading something like this happening. Poor Beth. Do you think we ought to go and see her parents?" she added hastily as he finally reached the end of the letter and placed it down in front of him.

"No. I say we leave well alone. John seems to have the situation in hand. I'll draft him a letter before I leave this morning, then I can get it in the post." He then proceeded to sip his tea, deep in thought. He didn't share his thoughts with Dorothea however and she picked up the letter and read it through again.

"How on earth did they get away with leaving the poor child on her own in the evenings like that? It's a wonder they weren't reported to the authorities. Beth could have been taken into care," he said finally.

"It crossed my mind too. They must have good neighbours."

"Unless they were all at it," he said resignedly.

"Some people don't deserve to be the guardians of children," she sighed. "I won't rest until they're all back home. Celia and John are doing a marvellous job and it's working out well but still…"

"We owe Celia and John a great debt of gratitude. One more year and then they'll all be home. Meanwhile, we need to think about the business. We broke even the first year, which according to Gerry is a good sign. This last year's looking a bit grim, to be honest. We need an injection of cash to keep us going otherwise we'll sink."

"The cafe's picking up a bit, especially since the tea shop near the bus station closed. Povinder and Chris are making a real success of the evening supper club."

"Yes, and the book shop sales are ticking over nicely. Gerry's seeing some of his contacts next week regarding getting us a contract to supply some of the big stores in London with men's waistcoats and jackets. If we get it, we're on our way, Dotty."

She smiled at him but didn't share his conviction. It was the only thing keeping Raif going. If the business failed, it would be catastrophic in every sense.

Mike was cycling through the village at some pace as he was twenty minutes late, having overslept, when he heard someone calling out from behind him.

"Excuse me, officer," yelled Belinda. She had been touring around the village for some time but couldn't get her bearings.

Mike applied the brakes and turned around to face a young lady waving at him. "Can I help you, madam?"

"Oh, I do hope so. I'm sorry to disturb you. I can see that you're in a hurry but I'm terribly lost. Can you direct me to the book shop and cafe on The Parade?"

"Yes, it's just behind you. If you go down this little alleyway here, to the end, then it's just on the left."

"Oh, thank you." She smiled at him and picked up her bags which she'd abandoned on the pavement.

"You're new around here, aren't you?" said Mike.

"Yes, it's my first visit. I couldn't make any sense of the map Dorothea drew for me."

"Would that be Dorothea Swift?"

"Yes, do you know her?"

"Why, yes, of course. I'll walk you round. Follow me," he offered, beginning to enjoy himself.

By the time they reached the shop, he'd learnt her name was Belinda and she was a designer and book illustrator who worked for a large publishing house in London. She was staying for three nights to discuss matters with Dorothea, Raif and Gerry. Not wanting to miss out on an opportunity, he quickly introduced himself and asked her where she was staying. She had a room booked at the pub, she told him. He quickly asked her if she would join him for a meal the following evening. Fully expecting her to refuse, he was overjoyed when she accepted. He watched her cross the street towards the book shop.

On arrival at the police station, Stuart was just finishing a telephone call.

"Any news on the Iain Boothroyd case?" Mike asked.

"Graham from the London office has just called. He paid a visit to his father's work place but he wasn't available. He's on a trip to New York. They seem to think he may have taken his son with him."

"Lord, that's all we need. New York's a big place."

"Where've you been anyway? You're forty minutes late."

"I had to help a young lady who was terribly lost. Sorry. I felt sorry for her. She looked a bit careworn," he said lamely, expecting a rebuke. "Do you want a coffee, boss?" he offered, in the hope of getting into his good books.

"Thanks."

"I was talking to the vicar yesterday. He got another plumber to look at the boiler in the church. He's fixed it, apparently. Just needed a new part fitting. He was livid, as old Bambridge told him he needed a whole new system."

"How many years has he been saving up for that?" laughed Stuart.

"Bainbridge has retired now anyway. Probably just as well. Doesn't sound as though he's on top of his game anymore."

"Well, happens to us all eventually, unfortunately."

"So, what's on the agenda today?"

"We need to get down to the factory. Someone torched it in the early hours."

"Well, it can't be Boothroyd, he's not in the country."

"No, but he could have organised it before or after he left."

"You mean he might have paid someone to do it?"

"It's been done before. It's a tax fiddle. A sure way of destroying all paper records."

"He won't be the first or the last person to try that one."

At the factory, they were met at the scene by the senior fire officer. "There's nothing left of the main building. The whole lot's gone," he advised them. "Just a small annexe at the side, which seems unaffected."

"What's in there?" asked Stuart.

"It appears to be empty. Just a table and a few chairs. Might have been a rest room or something."

"Is it safe to take a look inside?"

"Not yet, sir."

Stuart glanced around him and wandered back onto the road. There was just a small row of five terraced houses opposite, with nothing but wasteland on the other sides.

"We'd better get knocking on a few doors," ordered Stuart. "See if anyone saw or heard anything during the night. You start at the far end and we'll meet in the middle."

"Right, boss." Mike hot-footed it up the road with a spring in his step.

He seems very chirpy this morning, thought Stuart.

Chapter Forty-One

Celia was getting concerned about Beth, who'd been very quiet since her parents' visit and she wasn't eating much either. The weight loss was considerable. Choosing her moment carefully, she waited until the others were out of the house before having a quiet word with her. Beth was a little behind with her studies and had opted to stay home to try to catch up.

"Is everything all right, Beth? I know it's been difficult for you but do try to put it behind you," Celia offered, for want of anything better to say.

"I'm all right, Celia, honestly. I need to get myself up to speed with this last project, otherwise I'll never make it."

"What bad timing, your mother turning up when she did. If it had been after your final exams, it wouldn't have mattered so much."

"Oh, it's not her fault. She's just trying to do what I'm trying to do and that's to build a life for herself. She's had a terrible marriage to be truthful. I mean, don't get me wrong, I love my dad to bits, but he's been the most terrible husband."

"Really? Why do you say that?" Celia was astonished.

"He's had affairs all over the place. There were some terrible rows. She's had a lot to put up with. If she's making a break for freedom now, I can't blame her."

"She has friends though, doesn't she?"

"Yes. Lots. She was always out in the evenings. Bridge parties, whist drives, that sort of thing."

"Sounds like they were living separate lives."

"They were. Absolutely. It's a marriage of convenience."

"Will they stay together, do you think?"

"I expect so. They've both got the freedom to do what they like now that Alan and I are out of the way."

"Dear me, Beth, what a way to live," Celia said. She was reminded of her own marriage.

"It suits them both, believe me. As long as they can come and go as they please, they're happy."

Celia was lost in thought, wondering if there would be another visit from them.

"I'm over eighteen now, so she can't force me to do anything," said Beth defiantly.

"That's true. We'll be all right, darling."

"So, what are you working on at the moment?" asked Mike.

Belinda said she was meant to be on a diet but loved chicken so she'd opted for chicken and chips. Mike was delighted as he couldn't stand girls that didn't eat or picked at their food. He liked a woman with a good appetite.

The pub was three-quarters full but they'd managed to find a table on the mezzanine, near the window. He offered her a glass of wine but she opted for a glass of beer, having never acquired a taste for wines. She loved beer and lager, which was another plus in Mike's book.

"We're trying to put together a colour brochure. Like a promotional catalogue. Raif and Gerry are going to show it to prospective buyers in the trade, hopefully to help secure new business."

"They've got one or two items on display in the cafe and shop windows, haven't they?"

"That's right. It's bringing in a steady stream of orders."

The evening went by in a flash with Belinda talking about her projects at art college and Mike regaling her with stories of his training as a young cadet. They laughed a lot and ended the evening with an exchange of contact details. They made a further date to share a meal on her last evening before she returned to London.

* * *

"Morning all," breezed Mike on entering the station to start his shift.

Stuart was just getting himself a coffee in the kitchen. He pulled a face after taking a sip. "I think this milk's gone off," he grumbled.

"Any news yet on Boothroyd?" asked Mike, sniffing the milk. "You're quite right, it's off." He tipped the rest of the milk down the sink and rinsed the bottle under the tap.

"No, but we've found the white van complete with broken back window and white sheet. Whatever was under there has obviously been moved."

"Jenny did look under it, didn't she? She thought there were sewing machines."

"What's the betting he's sold them, before making a dash for freedom?"

"I don't suppose there was anything else worth selling, other than rolls of cloth."

"We'll never know now, seeing as the place has been obliterated."

"Any news from across the pond?" asked Mike.

"They've been in touch with his father at the offices. His son was nowhere to be found. He said he hasn't seen his son for quite some time."

"Do you believe him?"

"No. I'm sure they must have travelled together but since then he's done a disappearing act."

"How convenient. Shall I nip out for some fresh milk?"

"No. We'll get some on the way. We've a few calls to make."

In the car, Stuart brought Mike up to date on developments. A stallholder on the market was spotted selling two sewing machines. When questioned, he was vague and evasive, but eventually confessed to purchasing them from what he understood to be a wholesaler, who happened to be a burly chap with red hair. The next bit was even more interesting. He said he watched him go into a travel agent across the road. The young man in there distinctly remembered dealing with Boothroyd as his manner was aggressive and demanding. He purchased a single ticket, travelling from New York to Chicago.

"He found the money from somewhere then," said Mike.

"All provided by his father, no doubt, who's known in the trade to be a first-class rake," replied Stuart.

"There's a letter for you, Josh," said Celia, handing him an envelope. "It looks like Dorothea's writing."

"Oh, thank you." He eagerly ripped it open to find a short note from Aunty Dot and two envelopes. One contained a letter from his step-mother informing him she would be in London the following weekend and would call to see him on Sunday morning. She could only spare an hour as she had other calls to make. There were no address details on the letter, so he had no way of getting in touch with her, should the arrangements not be convenient.

She had posted the letter to Blythe Wood in Somerset and Dorothea had informed her he was studying in London. He wished with all his heart she hadn't done this. It wasn't that he particularly disliked her, just that he never felt at ease in her company and couldn't think why on earth she would want to see him after all this time. Josh could only assume there was another sheet to the letter with contact details on, or Aunty Dot wouldn't have been able to tell her his whereabouts.

The other letter was from Jenny and it was several pages long. He noted how very neat her handwriting was. He read it out loud so the others could all hear.

Dear Josh,

So much has happened in the past two months, for there have been big changes here. Firstly, sadly, poor Max passed away. Aunty Dot noticed a large lump on the side of his body and so we took him to the vet, who told us it was a tumour and there was nothing he could do. He advised us to do the kind thing and let him go, so he had the injection and we all cried. Three weeks later, we found Smoky stiff in his basket.

I've never cried so much. Mummy was very worried about me. The good news is that we now have two new kittens, Bella and Willow. They really are beautiful. Willow spends most of the day curled up on his special cushion but Bella's a bit more adventurous and likes to wander around, to see what's going on.

The house is very quiet without you all as there's only Aunty Dot and Uncle Raif, me and Mummy. Aunty Grace has gone to Plymouth for her son Gordon's wedding and she's taken Mr Glass with her for company. Aunty Dot and Magda made her a lovely new outfit with a matching hat. Mummy has been spending a lot of time on the typewriter. She can type like the wind now, as can Aunty Grace, who used to be a typist in an office before she married. Between the two of them, they've been rattling through all Howard's scripts and written notes.

Now, the other big news is, and you won't believe this – well, you will because I'm going to tell you. Aunty Meg and Harry got married and have gone away for a few days on their honeymoon. Harry sold his bungalow as he said it held too many memories of his poor wife. An American gentleman gave him a good price for it and he and Meg moved into the flat above the book shop. Aunty Iris and Uncle Bob have moved into the flat above the cafe. It's better for them as they open very early in the morning.

Bhutan is now taking the morning surgery for Dr Mattison. All the locals love him, Uncle Raif says. In the afternoons, he goes into the cafe and helps out as it's now quite busy. He's taken Magda to the Isle of Wight on the ferry for a few days as it's their wedding anniversary. It's some-where that Magda wanted to go, so he surprised her with the tickets.

Aunty Kath married Stuart. The local church was packed to the rafters. I think the whole village attended. They finally managed to get Mr Glass to move into The Honeypot cottage after two bouts of flu over the winter which he blamed on the house being cold and damp. Stuart very cleverly turned up the heating and gave him the bedroom which leads into the conservatory at the back of the house. It overlooks the hills and he uses it to entertain all his friends who drop in every day for morning coffee and tea and scones in the afternoon. Stuart's renamed it The Kardomah Cafe as he's always got a full house. Edna and Jimmy, Alf and Ivy, Dolly and Aubrey are all regular visitors. Aunty Kath says she's never seen him so happy.

Beth's brother got engaged to Susan who works in the factory with Aunty Dot and Uncle Raif. They're going to live with Susan's mother, who is a widow. Susan doesn't want to leave her mother on her own. I'm not sure what's happening with the business but they have moved into new premises as Gerry got contracts to supply some of the big stores in London.

There is another matter that Mummy says I must not mention in this letter, so I will tell you when you come home. I had to give a statement to the police and I was mentioned in the Gazette, not to mention being the talk of the whole school.

I can't wait for you all to be home for good so that we can be a proper family again. Mummy checked this letter for spelling mistakes. I had to rewrite it three times, which took me a whole week. I hope you can make sense of it.

Love

Jenny

"Aunty Meg married?" exclaimed Beth. "The house won't be the same without her, or Iris and Bob. I hope Aunty Grace doesn't come back married to Mr Glass."

"Why ever not?" asked Sam.

"I'm not ready to part with her yet. I couldn't stand it. It's bad enough that Aunty Meg and Aunty Iris have gone."

"You'll still see them. We'll call in at the shop every day. It'll be fine, you'll see," he said.

Celia waited until they were all safely in bed before reading Jenny's letter again for herself. It was the bit about the police that concerned her and she couldn't help wondering if it had anything to do with her son Iain. She hadn't heard from him since parting from his father, so there was no knowing what he'd been up to in the intervening years. She showed the letter to John and asked his advice.

"There's only one way to find out," he said. "I'll write a note to Raif telling him that we're concerned."

Celia wasn't at all sure she wanted to know the truth, not that she would be able to help the police in any way, for she knew very little about her husband or son's business affairs. Iain was her only son after all and she couldn't in her heart shop him to the police even if she was privy to the information. She hoped it would turn out to be something completely unrelated and that she was worrying for nothing.

Something instinctively told her this wasn't the case though and it was with a heavy heart that she tucked herself in bed that night, knowing she wouldn't get a moment of rest until she knew the truth.

The following morning, just after the children had all left to catch the bus into the city centre, there was a knock at the front door.

"Mrs Boothroyd?"

"Yes, I'm Mrs Boothroyd," said Celia eyeing up the police constable stood in front of her.

"I'm Constable Walker, Metropolitan Police," said Graham, showing her his ID card. "We'd just like to ask you a few questions in regards to the whereabouts of your son."

Celia's heart fell to her boots. "Oh, I see." Her face clouded over. She'd been dreading something like this happening. "You'd better come in."

* * *

"Graham, good to hear from you. Any news for us from America?" Stuart was always glad to hear from his friend at the London branch.

"Yes, that's why I'm calling. Tom Boothroyd died of a heart attack earlier today. He collapsed at his offices in New York. He was still alive when they got him into the ambulance but he later passed away in the hospital."

"I see." Stuart sat gathering his thoughts for a few minutes before speaking. "His wife Celia will have to be informed, of course."

"Yes, I'm just on my way now. No news yet of the son, I'm afraid. He's nowhere to be found."

Mike appeared with two cups of coffee just as Stuart put the phone down.

"Bad news?" he asked, placing the cups on the desk and sitting on a pile of box files in the corner.

"Iain Boothroyd's father had a heart attack earlier today. Died in the hospital in New York."

"Really? No sign of the son yet then?"

"No."

"I can't see this bringing him out of his hidey-hole. Nobody knows where he is for a start."

"It's what he's up to that concerns me. Graham got no information out of Celia when he called on her. They've been separated for years. She reckons she hasn't seen her son since the day she walked out on his father."

"Do you believe her?"

"I'm not sure. She knew her husband often travelled abroad for his job but it was usually Denmark, Italy, Germany and occasionally Japan. She said he never went to the States as far as she was aware."

"She's not likely to shop her own son. Blood's thicker than water in that respect." Mike drained his coffee and stood looking out of the window.

He wondered when he would see Belinda again. There were no visits to Dorothea planned and she was very busy with new projects, so she wasn't sure when she'd be free, which filled him with an overwhelming sense of disappointment. He'd have to snap out of it, as he had work to do himself. Stuart had already pulled him up twice for day-dreaming.

"Another letter from Jenny," announced Beth. They were all seated at the table about to have their lunch prior to Josh's step-mother calling.

"What's news?"

"They've got a baby rabbit called Thomas. Uncle Raif found him amongst the cabbages in the allotment. Nobody knows how he got there or where he came from, so they've kept him. He's latched on to Willow and they sit together on the cushion. They're inseparable." Beth paused whilst she read the next sentence. "She's learning to type on the typewriter and Aunty Dot's teaching her to crochet. She's working on a scarf for the next jumble sale at the church."

"She sounds like a busy little bee," said Celia. "Now, eat up, everyone. Josh's mother will be arriving shortly, that's if she's still coming. She was supposed to be her earlier this morning."

Josh secretly hoped something had cropped up and she wouldn't now be coming.

It was ten minutes to four before they heard a knock at the door. Celia opened it to find Beth's mother standing on the step.

"Oh!" said Celia, somewhat bewildered.

"Hello Celia. Have I called at a bad time?" She sailed past her into the hallway leaving a trail of perfume behind.

"Er, no. Not at all. It's just that we're expecting Josh's mother any minute. Do come in." Celia felt a bit flustered as she knew Beth had only just recovered from her mother's last visit. She didn't want her upset again. Normally, she would get John to help her out but he'd gone into town this afternoon and wouldn't be back until this evening. *I'll have to be firm with her*, she thought. *I can't have Beth upset again, not with her final exams so near.*

"Beth, it's your mother," Celia announced, just as there was another knock at the door. "That'll be Josh's mother. Go on through to the lounge, they're all waiting."

Celia watched Beth's mother march up the hallway with an air of confidence she'd only ever seen on screen at the cinema. She was wearing an emerald green two-piece suit which fitted her slim figure perfectly. Her dark hair was coiffured into soft waves which framed her face. Her black high-heeled shoes clip-clopped on the linoleum. It reminded Celia of herself in her earlier life.

A wave of nostalgia briefly washed over her but she quickly dismissed it. She wouldn't trade in her life now for anything, especially since she'd met John. He was a perfect gentleman and quite the best man she'd ever known.

In contrast, Josh's step-mother was casually dressed in a wool coat, hat and scarf. Her feet were clad in boots which had seen better days but her face was nicely made up, Celia noticed.

"You must be Celia." She extended her hand. "I'm Miriam. I meant to get here earlier but I got delayed."

"That's quite all right." Celia led her into the lounge and made the introductions.

"I'll make the tea," said Beth, jumping up and disappearing into the kitchen.

"I'll give you a hand," said Selina, eager to escape. She wasn't going to let Beth out of her sight, not after what happened the last time. If Beth's mother started on her again, she'd be ready for her.

By the time they re-entered the lounge with the tea trolley, the two visitors were getting on famously. They sat together on the settee laughing and chatting; the children being largely ignored, which infuriated Celia. Poor Josh was staring down at his shoes. So it was with a great sigh of relief all round when the two ladies jumped up and announced it was time to leave. Miriam fished in her handbag and produced an envelope which she handed to Josh.

"It's from the sale of your dad's furniture. It's not much, I'm afraid, as I had to pay a man to take the items I couldn't sell. I'm so glad you're doing well. Your dad would have been proud. As I am." With that, she kissed him on the cheek and proceeded to the hall to collect her coat. "Thank you for the lovely tea and cake, Celia. It's been a flying visit, I know, but I've got other calls to make before I return to my brother's tomorrow and it's been a juggling act fitting it all in."

"Hang on, Miriam," shouted Beth's mother. "I'd like a quick word before you go." She threw on her coat and turned to Beth with a big smile. "Beth, darling, I'm so sorry for the way I behaved. Shouting and getting worked up like that. It was inexcusable. Will you ever forgive me? Look after yourself, darling." She gave her a warm hug and ran through the door to catch up with her new best friend without a backwards glance.

Celia closed the door on them and stood in the hallway collecting her thoughts. *What an ignorant pair*, she thought. Neither of them showed the slightest interest in what their children were doing and hadn't even asked about the courses they were studying. She felt near to tears and wished John was here to comfort her. She forced a smile onto her face before returning to the lounge, determined not to let the children know how upset she was.

Josh was in the process of ripping open his envelope. He counted the notes out onto the coffee table. "It's a hundred pounds," he gasped.

"Well, you put that away for a rainy day, Josh," ordered Celia. "I'll start the meal. Are you all going to the cinema?"

"No, we're having a night in. We've seen the film that's showing this week anyway," said Howard.

Secretly relishing the thought that she'd have their company this evening, Celia collected up the cups and saucers and wheeled the trolley back into the kitchen. The house was going to be very strange without them when they all returned to Somerset and she wasn't looking forward to parting with them.

Yes, they were noisy and messy and they had their petty squabbles but any spats were quickly forgotten, often ending in laughter. Above all, they were well mannered and respectful. Something her own son could do with a dose of. *Dorothea's parenting skills are obviously superior to my own*, she thought.

* * *

Dorothea made her way into the kitchen to find Daisy writing in a diary.

"Good morning Daisy. What have you got there?"

"Oh, good morning Dotty. It's for Jenny. She's got that much going on it's getting a bit out of hand."

Dorothea picked up the sheet of paper Daisy was copying from and read aloud. "Thursday, ballroom dancing. Friday, bell ringing. Saturday morning, choir practice. Sunday afternoon, pottery. I see what you mean, Daisy. What's this bell ringing?"

"Not church bells, hand bells. Most of the girls in the choir are doing it and you know Jenny, she won't be left out of anything. It's only a small group but they travel up and down the country, giving performances and such like."

"Does she enjoy it?"

"I think so. That's why I'm trying to put it all down in this diary, so I can keep track of everything. Raif gave it to me. It's come in handy."

"Any news from Howard?" asked Dorothea.

"Yes, I had a letter yesterday. His final exams are next week, as are Sam's. The others have two weeks to wait yet. They're all on edge. None of them are confident they'll pass, except for Selina."

"She's a bright girl. Sam is a clever boy too. I'm sure they'll all do well."

"Will Raif be angry if any of them fail?"

"Angry? No, Raif's not the type to get worked up about things like that. We both want them all to do well but at the end of the day, they can only do their best. That's good enough for us."

"They all think they'd be letting you and Raif down."

"I felt the same when I was at university. My parents were very strict. They wouldn't have tolerated failure. I knew I had to pass or face their wrath. It wasn't a nice feeling, I can tell you."

"Did Raif reply to John's letter? Celia must be worried, wouldn't you say?"

"Yes, he did. I don't know what he told him. He assured me that he'd dealt with it and that I wasn't to worry."

"I dread Iain coming back here," said Daisy. "Jenny's in so many things, it's impossible for me to keep my eye on her all the time."

"Yes, you're right. Fortunately, the school are aware of the situation as are half the village. I can't see him showing his face around here again. Surely he wouldn't have the nerve."

"That's what worries me. I think he would have the nerve. He doesn't seem to have a conscience about anything at all. I've never known a more arrogant person."

"He certainly seems good at wriggling off the hook. According to Stuart, he's walked out of court on two previous occasions. Even if they do arrest him, there's no hard evidence. No proof. He'd just deny everything. It would be his word against Jenny's. He'd make out the child was fantasising or something. As regards to his business, he's left debts behind and he owes the tax man a fair bit. I can't see how he can avoid arrest on that score."

"I'd feel a lot happier if he was locked up," said Daisy, closing the diary. "I'd better start the porridge."

"I'll give you a hand. The others will be up soon."

Chapter Forty-Two

"There's a Dolly Lambert waiting to see you, sir," said the desk sergeant. "Wants a quick word with you about Iain Boothroyd."

Stuart stopped in his tracks momentarily. "Really?"

"She reckons she spotted him yesterday, lurking in the bushes at the church. It was the day of the jumble sale. Mike's just making her a cup of tea. Interview room one."

So, the lone ranger returns, thought Stuart. *Come to collect his inheritance from his father's will, no doubt.*

Dolly seemed a little flustered and was dabbing at her neck with a lace handkerchief when Stuart entered the room. "Good morning Mrs Lambert."

"Oh, call me Dolly, please."

"Dolly. Thank you for taking the trouble to come and see us. What occurred exactly?"

Mike placed three cups of tea on the desk then sat down with his notebook and pen.

"It was yesterday at the church," Dolly said. "I was helping Edna with the organising of the tables. It turns into a bit of a free-for-all if you're not careful, so we allocate the space as best we can."

Stuart was well aware of what went on at these jumble sales. He'd had to step in once or twice as things almost descended into hooliganism. They were a militant lot once they got going.

"Anyway, it was about ten minutes past three when Edna asked me to take a bag of rubbish out to the bins."

"Why couldn't she do that herself?" Stuart knew Edna was inclined to boss her sister around and he didn't like it.

"Well, she was just about to start the teas. I was glad of the fresh air, to be honest. Now that the heating has been fixed, it's too hot in there for me. Aubrey and I don't like it too hot. We hardly ever use our heating at home.

"I made my way around the back of the church, that's where the bins are kept. I dumped the bag in the bin and clanged the lid shut. That's when I spotted him. It was the red hair, you see. He was wearing a black cap, but it was definitely him. Edna said I'd imagined it and we had an argument about it. She said I was being ridiculous as he wasn't even in the country and that he'd gone to America with his father. But I mean honestly, why would I lie about such a thing?"

"Can you tell me exactly where he was?"

"In between some bushes. He was looking initially at the entrance, as though he was waiting for someone."

"And what was he wearing?"

"A black jumper, black trousers and no coat."

"Did he see you?" asked Stuart.

"No, I don't think so. I went back inside and told Edna. She came outside with me to have a look, but, of course, he'd disappeared by then. That's when she started arguing."

"Right. Well, thank you once again for taking the trouble to inform us, Dolly. You've been most helpful."

"How are we doing with the new samples, ladies?" asked Gerry. He'd secured two new contracts on the strength of the new designs, particularly the silk ties, cravats and waistcoats.

"Nearly finished. Should be completed by the end of the week. Belinda's coming the following week to prepare for the photo shoots."

"Good." Gerry couldn't believe his luck at dropping straight into this partnership with Raif and his family. Managing to pay off most of his debts meant the bankruptcy hadn't materialised, so he'd come out of what appeared to be a catastrophic situation better than he ever could have dreamt. The new business was going from strength to strength and slowly, they were building up a good name in the trade with more and more enquiries coming in a steady stream.

"How's Hilary doing with her new studio?" asked Dorothea.

"All the walls have now been replastered and she's got some new work benches which are currently in storage. We sanded them down and gave them a coat of paint. Once the plaster's dry, we'll give the walls and ceiling a coat of paint to freshen everywhere up. She should be ready to go then. She's got most of her other materials."

"It sounds wonderful. Can I come to see it when it's finished?"

"Of course. We're having a launch party when Sam gets home. His final exams are next week, I believe."

Dorothea smiled and nodded. Every time anyone mentioned the children, her heart gave a little flutter. She'd missed them all much more than words could say and she wondered if Raif felt the same. The house was so quiet and the walls seemed to cry out for their chatter and laughter. The rooms in the house had never looked so tidy. The children seemed to leave their clutter in every room in the house and on every available surface.

These days, Daisy did the dusting in no time at all. Once cleaned, it stayed clean. With Bob's help, Raif had redecorated every room in the house, except the kitchen, and they were planning to tackle the outside in the summer. The rose garden at the side of the house was the only patch they'd retained as a flower bed, the rest being used to grow vegetables, fruit and herbs. Magda, Dorothea and Daisy tackled the rose garden between them. With their hard work, it was now looking glorious.

Daisy was sat at the kitchen table studying Gordon's wedding photographs. It was a small group of twenty people, made up of mainly work colleagues and close friends.

"You look lovely, Grace. Did Mr Glass enjoy himself?"

"Oh well, you know Earnest. You could stick him on the moon and he'd find someone to talk to. By the end of the night, he could give me chapter and verse on everyone in the group. Where they lived, what they did for a living, who their friends were, what their hobbies were, where they spent their free time, where they went for their holidays, what food they ate…"

Daisy laughed. "Anyone would think he'd been locked up for years and was enjoying his first day of freedom."

"He's jolly good company, I'll say that for him. Mind you, he can sink the ale. I had to keep my eye on him. He reminds me of my George in lots of ways."

"Would you ever get married again, Grace?"

"No, lass. George was the only man for me. If I can live out my days here, in this beautiful house, in comfort, that'll do for me."

"I know how you feel. I wouldn't want to leave Blythe Wood either. It really is beautiful and I'm so happy here. When our house in London got bombed, I had no idea where I'd end up. This is more than I ever could have hoped for and it's all down to you, Gracie. If I hadn't met you…"

"I don't dwell on that scenario too much. It's best forgotten. We survived, that's all that counts. There are lots that didn't. Poor souls."

"I'd better peel the vegetables, then I'll start the soup. What did you say Gordon was going to be doing? Did you mention that he'd be working for himself?"

"They're starting their own business. Running a cookery school. They've rented some premises. All sounds a bit precarious to me, but he's old enough to look after himself."

"What's his wife like?"

"She's quite a bit younger than him, only twenty-eight, but she seems a decent sort. Friendly and chatty. No airs and graces, very down to earth. They seem well matched. I'm happy for him. I don't need to worry about him as much now. She'll look after him, I've no doubts about that."

"Is she a trained cook then?"

"Oh yes. She trained in France then taught in the schools for years. She started when she was very young."

"I'll prepare the cheeseboard after this. It's funny, isn't it? When the children were here, they always looked forward to a pudding or dessert. Now we never have one. Dorothea and Raif prefer cheese with grapes and celery."

"I'm getting to like it myself. Not lost any weight mind. I'm still bursting out of my pinny."

They laughed heartily as they bustled about the kitchen, happy in their work.

"Where's Stuart tonight?" asked Earnest, stabbing his steak pie with his fork.

"He's working late. He wants to get up to date with his reports. He'll be home about ten," said Kath, placing her husband's plate back in the oven.

"That Boothroyd's been spotted all over the village, you know."

"Yes, I know. They've had him in for questioning. They couldn't pin anything on him. He reckons he knew nothing about the fire at the factory, only learning about it when he arrived back in England. He also denied knowing anything about abducting little Jenny. He claimed he didn't even know he had a daughter, making it quite clear that the last thing he'd want is to saddle himself with looking after a child. He was a free agent he said, and intended to stay that way. He said someone must have stolen the van whilst he was in America."

"That's not true and he knows it," exploded Earnest. "He only cleared off to America after it happened."

"Proof, Dad. There isn't any. None of the neighbours who live in the cottages near the factory saw or heard anything. Nobody saw him bundle Jenny into the back of the van either. It could have been anyone."

"Well, his father's no longer around to bail him out of his troubles. He'll have to watch his step. The tax man's after him, I know that much."

"That may well turn out to be the undoing of him, Dad. They don't muck about at the tax office. You either pay up or end up in court. I don't see how he can wriggle out of that one."

"I assume he'll inherit his father's estate, being the only son."

"According to Dorothea, there was no divorce, so technically Celia has a claim on his estate, I would have thought. Not that I know much about these things. They've been separated for years but I can't see her wanting anything of her husband's anyway. She's rebuilt her life without him and is very happy according to the letters Dotty gets."

"Good for her. According to Raif, Tom Boothroyd didn't have a good name in the trade either. He was a tyrant. Like father, like son. You can see where he gets his arrogance from."

"I feel sorry for all those girls at the factory. They were happy working for Gerry. Most of them are still out of work. They haven't managed to find jobs."

"More fool them for being so easily persuaded."

"It's not easy, Dad, especially when you've a family and mouths to feed. He offered them more money initially, then docked their wages when they didn't deliver on time. Dangled the carrot, then snatched it away. Dirty trick."

"That's what business is all about, I'm afraid," said Earnest. "It's cutthroat. Ruthless. There's many a successful businessman resorted to tricks like that. It's how they make their money. You don't get to be successful by being nice and letting people walk all over you."

"No but still…"

"This pie's good, Kath."

"Oh. Thanks, Dad."

"On a lighter note, young Josh should be home in another month. Eh, I've missed that lad."

"You'll have a lot to catch up on. It'll be good to see them all home again. It'll be like old times."

Edna stood admiring the immaculate garden before entering through the gate. *If only I could get my garden to look this good*, she thought.

A magnificent cloudburst of colour stood before her. She eyed the neatly trimmed borders and bushes strategically placed for magnificent effect. There was a small patio at the side sporting a table and chairs with chintzy cushions. A trellis with sweet peas decorated one wall with hanging baskets and majestic crown imperials. She was just about to enter through the gate when Aubrey appeared, pushing a wheelbarrow.

"Hello Aubrey," she shouted. "I was just admiring your garden. It's a glorious sight. There's a lot of hard work gone into this. I'm so jealous."

"Thank you kindly, ma'am," he laughed. "We've worked all summer long on it. Come on inside, we'll make some refreshments."

Dolly was sat in the lounge unpicking her knitting, having dropped a stitch several rows down. She jumped up on seeing her sister. "Edna. What a surprise. Nothing wrong, is there?"

"No, no. Everything's fine." She sat herself down and kicked off her shoes.

"I'll put the kettle on for tea," shouted Aubrey from the kitchen.

"Oh, that's better. My feet are killing me. Dolly, I owe you an apology."

"What about?"

"For jumping to conclusions. Wrongly, as it happens. You were right, that Boothroyd chap is around. He's been seen all around the village. He's got a nerve showing his face around here after what he's done."

"Oh that," said Dolly, smiling to herself. She'd never known Edna to apologise before.

"I keep saying that I'll stop doing this, but I can't seem to help myself. I get so worked up about things. If something annoys me, I blow a fuse. I wish I could be more like you, Dolly. You never get angry about anything."

"I wouldn't say that. Aubrey and I have our moments, you know," Dolly said, putting her knitting to one side. "I've dropped a stitch three rows down, I'm just trying to sort it out."

"Give it to me, I'll soon sort that," said Edna, grabbing the needles, melancholy forgotten temporarily.

Aubrey entered with a tray of cups and saucers and a fruit cake.

They chatted away merrily for an hour. Edna had forgotten what good fun Aubrey was and she'd missed her sister too. The lonely days and nights stretched out before her. *You don't realise what you've got until it's gone*, she thought.

"I want to ask your advice," Edna suddenly blurted out.

Dolly and Aubrey both looked at her, intrigued as to what she could possibly need to consult them about. This wasn't like the Edna they knew. She never took advice from anybody as a rule. She just wasn't that sort of person.

"Jim wants me to marry him." Her words hung in the air, neither of them knowing what to say in response. "What do you think? I'm not young anymore and neither is he. I've been so lonely since you left, Dolly. Sometimes I think I'll go mad with boredom. It would be so nice to have company, especially during the dark winter evenings."

The pair of them sat glassy-eyed, saying nothing.

"Well, say something," Edna urged, massaging her bunions.

Aubrey was the first to break the silence. His hearty laugh filled the room. "I say go for it then, girl. What have you got to lose? If that damn war's taught me anything, it's that life is for living. Just get on with it. We could all be dead tomorrow."

"I agree," said Dolly, smiling at her sister. "Jim's a lovely bloke. You'll not go far wrong with him." She knew full well Jim could be a grumpy curmudgeon at times, but then again so could her sister Edna, so they would be a good match for each other.

"I'll not get another opportunity at my age, will I? Right-ho. That's settled then." She put her shoes in her handbag and stood up.

"What on earth are you doing with those?" asked Aubrey.

"Oh, I can't put them back on, my feet are killing me. I'll walk to the bus stop in my bare feet. It's not raining. I'll be all right."

"You daft woman," laughed Aubrey. "You'll do no such thing. I'll run you back in the car. Get your coat, Dolly. We'll call on young Jim whilst we're at it and break the news to him. I can't wait to see his face. He owes me a pint anyway."

* * *

"Stuart? It's Graham."

"Graham, what's news?" said Stuart stirring his coffee.

"We've had a call from Tom Boothroyd's employers. It seems that Iain has been making a bit of a nuisance of himself."

"In what way exactly?"

"Barged into the boardroom and demanded to speak to the directors. He wants to step into his father's shoes. He got very aggressive and they couldn't get him off the premises. They've made an official complaint against him. I'll give you more information when I've had a chance to speak to them."

"Right, keep me posted. Good luck."

Mike appeared at his desk with a mug of tea and two bacon sandwiches.

"Breakfast is served," he grinned, placing the plates on the only available space amongst the mess.

"What? On a Friday? What's come over you, lad?"

"Belinda's coming down next week."

"Ah-ha. So, that's what's put you in such a good mood." He brought him up to date on the phone call from Graham.

"What a cheek he's got. Demanding his father's job like that. Who does he think he is?"

"He was very rude to the receptionist. He barged straight past her when she said he needed an appointment. She ended up in tears."

"That doesn't surprise me. Arrogance is his middle name. What's made him like that, do you think? His upbringing? Faulty parenting or what?"

"It's all beyond me. Takes all sorts," said Stuart, taking a bite of his sandwich.

"There's a Constable Walker here to see you, Mr Marsden," announced the secretary.

"Good. Send him in. Two cups of tea please, Audrey, when you've a minute."

Audrey showed Graham into the office.

"I'm Harold Marsden, one of the directors here. Thank you for coming to see us. Please take a seat," he motioned to a leather armchair opposite a large mahogany desk.

"What line of business are you in here?" asked Graham, relishing the chance to enjoy a sit down and a nice cup of tea.

"We're architects, primarily. We specialise in building design and refit. Tom, that's Mr Boothroyd senior, was good at getting the contracts and he was only six months away from retirement when he died. There's five of us left and we're all nearing that age when we have to make a decision as to whether to continue or call it a day."

"So, in effect you would probably sell the practice?"

"We're in discussions about it at the moment. I wouldn't normally bother you with things like this but I'm afraid Iain assaulted one of our security officers on entering the building. We had to take him to the infirmary as he sustained a nasty gash on the side of the head. He needed stitches. No permanent damage, thankfully."

Graham got out his notebook. "We'll need to take the guard's name and have a word with him."

"He threatened my secretary too. She's a bit nervous about travelling alone now. She gets her husband to collect her and drop her off in the mornings, which isn't exactly convenient for him, as he works some distance away. She was still here at six thirty last night. The cleaners were waiting to lock up."

"I'll need to speak to her as well before I go."

"I'd like to be able to say that it was all hot air on his part, but I don't know him well enough to make that sort of assessment and I have to protect my staff."

"Quite."

"And there's more. On his way out, he had an altercation with our accounts lady. Swiped his hand across her desk and knocked a pile of papers all over the floor, together with a cup of coffee. She had to redo a whole day's work. I know it all sounds very petty, Constable Walker, but I have a suspicion that we haven't seen the last of him.

What's wrong with ringing up and making an appointment with us, like any normal person would? The board would have been more than willing to explain the situation to him."

"People like Iain don't operate like that, I'm afraid. He's used to getting what he wants by threats and intimidation."

"Not in this company. We pride ourselves in maintaining the very highest standards, or used to. Tom Boothroyd had his moments. We had to deal with a few complaints over the years, but he was a good salesman. Now, I have an urgent meeting to attend with our accountant, but feel free to use the boardroom next door to interview staff."

Chapter Forty-Three

"I'll wait here for you," said John, squeezing Celia's hand. "Try not to worry too much and don't let that son of yours bully you."

"I'll be glad when this is all over and I can start a new life." She stood up and left the cafe without a backwards glance.

Crossing the road to the solicitor's office, she took a deep breath before pushing open the door. Looking around for signs of her son, she approached the reception desk and gave her name. She was already starting to lose her nerve and wished now she'd asked John to accompany her. The receptionist asked her to take a seat whilst she rang through.

Ten minutes passed before she was summoned, by which time her head was throbbing and she felt hot and flustered.

"Please take a seat, Mrs Boothroyd." A gentleman of senior years stood up and motioned to the vacant chair opposite his desk. Celia looked around the room for signs of Iain, but he was nowhere to be seen.

"Has my son not arrived yet?" she asked, nervously.

"He sent his apologies. He's tied up on another matter and has asked us to reschedule his meeting until tomorrow."

"Oh. Would you like me to come back tomorrow then?"

"No, that won't be necessary. I assume you have a copy of your husband's will? Please accept my condolences for your loss, Mrs Boothroyd."

"Thank you. We've been separated for several years actually. I don't want anything. Please give everything to my son."

"Well, there doesn't appear to be any liquid cash, just the house. There should be enough to settle his debts, which are considerable, once the estate is sold."

Celia wondered why Tom didn't have any savings or investments. He was always lecturing her about such things during their marriage, but not being a conventional marriage, she realised she knew very little about what he earnt or indeed what he did with his money. All she knew was he always seemed to have plenty.

"You are, of course, entitled to his estate as technically you are still his next of kin. I take it you were never divorced?"

"No. He wouldn't grant me one, but as I said, I don't want anything. I've built a new life for myself now and please forgive me when I say this, but I'd rather not divulge to my son where I'm living. Don't get me wrong, Mr Royce, I love my son and I'd never do anything to hurt him, but I'm afraid he's beyond redemption. Believe me when I tell you that I have tried. Really, I have. But he won't listen to anything I say to him. He's very much like his father. He idolised his father and copied his behaviour but I have to take some of the blame because I wasn't strict enough with him when he was young."

"I see, yes. Well, we will need something in writing."

"Yes, of course. If you type it up, I'll sign it."

"We can draft something up now if you're free to wait. I'll get my secretary on to it now."

"That would be perfect. Thank you."

It was over an hour later when she was able to re-join John in the cafe.

"I'm sorry it took so long. I had to wait whilst the secretary typed up the documentation for me to sign. Have you eaten?" She threw her coat onto the back of her chair and quickly sat down.

"Yes, I've eaten but I'll order you something and we can have a pot of tea."

"Just a slice of cake for me, John. My head's thumping."

"Was it very bad?"

"No. Iain didn't turn up."

"Didn't turn up? Where on earth is he then?"

"He said he was tied up and asked for his appointment to be rescheduled until tomorrow. Mr Royce was a lovely man, a perfect gentleman."

"So, everything is sorted out to your satisfaction?"

"Yes," she whispered.

"I'll just order the tea and cakes then we can talk."

There was such a mixture of feelings flooding through her mind that she couldn't relax. Guilt at the way Iain had turned out, regret of her own foolish behaviour when she was young, allowing herself to get pregnant when she had no ring on her finger, bringing shame on her parents. Then the ridiculous sham of a marriage to Tom, which was really no marriage at all. Why on earth had she sold herself short and allowed herself to be used like that? The shame at letting a man treat her so badly. Where was her self-respect? All those wasted years when she could have been building a career and making something of herself.

"Penny for them?" said John.

"Sorry. I was miles away."

"Don't be sad. Let's just live for today. Forget the past. It's over and done with. It's the here and now that matters."

"I was just thinking that I haven't achieved much in my life."

"Don't waste energy on regrets. Look, here's the cake and tea. We can enjoy that at least."

"I'm ashamed of the way Iain's turned out, John. When I married Tom, I was young and naive. Tom had money and a large house in the best part of London. Marrying him gave me a false sense of having done rather well for myself. It gave me confidence and I'm afraid I acted as though the world was my oyster. Looking back now, I realise my behaviour was arrogant and overbearing. Is it any wonder Iain turned out the way he did?"

"We can't erase the past, Celia. We can only learn from our mistakes and move on. Perhaps we become better people because of it."

"I suppose so. I'm not the woman I used to be and it's only since I met you that I realised what was missing from my life. You're a good man. A gentleman. There aren't many left in the world as it stands today, or maybe I've just been mixing in all the wrong social circles," she laughed.

"Headache gone?"

"It's easing. Shall we have a bottle of wine with our meal this evening?"

"What are we having?"

"I've got something special. It's a surprise, but you can help me to prepare it."

Dorothea carried two mugs of cocoa into the library and found Raif studying a letter.

"Grace and Daisy have gone to bed early. Jenny's got a sore throat so she's tucked up already. What are you reading?" she asked, placing the two mugs down on the table.

"It's a letter from Howard. His final exams are next week. The radio's keen to interview him regarding putting his plays on air. A series of six, no less."

"Oh Raif. That's marvellous news. Does he want us to go up to London? I went with him last time but it didn't end well on that occasion."

"I'll write back to Celia and ask her to keep us posted. Gerry and I were discussing earlier today about having telephone lines put in. It'll make things a lot easier now that the business is picking up."

Dorothea sipped her cocoa, lost in her thoughts. After a while, she said, "Raif, are you happy with the way things have turned out? Not just with the business, but with the children too?"

"It's the best thing that's happened to me in years, Dotty. I couldn't go back to working in that laboratory. I'd come to despise it. If the war hadn't come along… well, there would have been big changes. As for the children, to be honest, I just couldn't imagine our life without them now."

"They'll all be home soon."

"Yes. We'll sit down with them and discuss what they want to do. They might have ideas of their own about what direction their careers are to go in, but it's our duty as their guardians to guide them and help them."

"Do you think Josh, Beth and Selina will want to join us in the business?"

"I'm hoping so. Selina and Magda are very close. I think it'll work well. Gerry's networking like mad to get us more contracts. That reminds me, Belinda's due tomorrow. Are the samples ready?"

"Almost. Just a bit of finishing off to do. Magda and I are going in tomorrow morning for a few hours. We should be finished by lunchtime."

Raif sipped his cocoa and seemed to be deep in thought before saying, "You know, Dotty, when I was in the ocean, our plane having taken a hit, I made a pact with myself that if I managed to survive the war, I was going to make the most of every available opportunity that came my way. I cheated death on several occasions but miraculously I survived somehow. We were floating about in the ocean for hours before I spotted Bob's ship. When you've been through something like that, it makes you appreciate things more. A lot of my comrades never made it home, you know. They were wiped out in the fields."

"Don't feel guilty about that, Raif. You did your bit. More than your bit actually. You're my hero and you came home. That means the world to me."

"Right. I'm off now, Grace," said Daisy. "I've peeled all the vegetables, so everything's ready. I won't be long, half an hour at the most."

"Where's Jenny today?" asked Grace, sitting up in bed after her afternoon nap. Dorothea had insisted upon her doing this since her mild heart attack. She didn't always feel like it at first, but she'd become used to it now and actually felt better for it. She picked up her mug of tea which Daisy had placed on her bedside table.

"She's at her pottery class. According to her teacher, Jenny's got a real talent for it. They make the pots, fire them in the kiln, then paint a glaze on them. She loves it."

"Well, off you go then. I'll get up as soon as I've drunk this. I'll see if we've enough ingredients to make a Victoria sponge. I just feel like a bit of cake. It'll help pass the time until you and Jenny get back."

Belinda stepped off the train and made her way out of the station. She tried to retrace her steps exactly the way she remembered the route from her last visit, but once again she seemed to lose her bearings. It all looked so simple on the map and Mike had been over it with her several times but she was completely lost. She didn't recognise any of the buildings or landmarks and could have sworn she was in the wrong town.

Sitting herself down on a bench, she rummaged in her bag for the map. After five minutes of turning it this way and that, she gave up and folded it up, tossing it back into her bag. *I'll have to ask someone*, she thought, which was all very well but there didn't seem to be anyone around.

Spotting a building across the road which had a light showing, she thought that would be her best option. Glancing through the window, she discovered it was a pottery class. Immediately her eyes were drawn to a little girl with red hair who she recognised as Daisy's daughter, Jenny. *Thank goodness*, she thought, deciding to wait until the class finished so they could walk home together.

Daisy realised she should have changed her shoes before setting off. *I'll have blisters by the time I get home*, she thought. Stopping momentarily to loosen the laces on her sturdy brogues, she suddenly felt someone grab hold of her left elbow. Swinging around, she found herself face to face with Iain Boothroyd. A sharp intake of breath stopped her in her tracks.

"What on earth do you want?" she spat.

"So, it is you. I thought so. Is that any way to greet an old friend?"

"Friend? Let go of my arm this minute or I'll scream."

"Go ahead, there's nobody about. Who'll hear you?"

Raif swung the jeep into the garage. It was six o'clock and they were all exhausted after a long day. Dorothea, Magda, Bhutan and Alan climbed out and headed towards the kitchen door.

"I'll just top her up with oil and water," said Raif.

Grace stood by the range looking anxious. "Oh Dotty. Thank goodness, you're home," she blurted out.

"What's wrong, Grace?"

"It's Daisy. She hasn't come home yet. She left at three o'clock this afternoon to collect Jenny from her pottery class. Jenny came home with Belinda. They waited nearly an hour for Daisy but she didn't show up. I'm very worried. I've just got a bad feeling that something terrible has happened to her, especially since that Iain Boothroyd is back in town."

Dorothea sank into the nearest chair with a thud as though someone had punched her in the stomach.

There was silence for a few minutes before Alan said, "Where are Jenny and Belinda now?"

"Belinda's got a date with Mike. They're eating at the pub. She got lost again when she came out of the train station and just happened to pass the building where the pottery class was being held. She glanced through the window and spotted Jenny, so she decided to wait. Poor Jenny's very upset. She knows that her mother wouldn't just abandon her like that unless there's a good reason."

"Right, wait here. I'll go and speak to Raif. We'll conduct a search," said Alan making for the door.

"I'll come too, Alan. Let me fetch my medical bag first," said Bhutan, running upstairs to his room.

"If anything has happened to that girl, I'll swing for that reprobate, I swear I will. I'll never get over it," cried Grace, mopping her eyes on the end of her apron.

"Let's not jump to conclusions. We don't know anything yet. Belinda will speak to Mike about it, I'm sure of that."

"Will Mike be able to use his radio to inform Stuart?" asked Magda, looking very concerned at both ladies.

Jenny came out of the lounge holding the two cats. "Mummy will be all right, won't she, Aunty Dot?"

"Uncle Raif and the boys have gone to look for her, darling," soothed Dorothea putting her arms around the child, not knowing what to think or say.

"I will make us all a hot drink whilst we wait," offered Magda, filling the kettle.

Raif had just reached the end of the road when he spotted Kath running towards them, waving frantically.

"Raif, Daisy's in the hospital. They think someone tried to strangle her. Stuart and Mike have gone there now to speak to her," gasped Kath, fighting for her breath and gulping mouthfuls of air with every sentence.

"Jump in, Kath," said Alan opening the door.

"No, I'll sit with the girls, if that's all right. Stuart will come for me later."

Chapter Forty-Four

Stuart took a mouthful of the milky lukewarm tea that the nurse had given him and winced. "Now, tell me again Mr…"

"Moseley. Charles Moseley."

"Mr Moseley. Where were you when you spotted Daisy lying on the pavement?"

"She wasn't on the pavement, officer. She was slumped in a doorway. It's a regular occurrence around here, especially on a Saturday evening after the pubs close."

"Quite."

"But it was only three thirty in the afternoon so I was curious. It's unusual for the ladies to drink so much at lunchtime as a rule, if you know what I mean. I went over and asked her if she was all right. That's when I realised, she was unconscious. I ran back into the pub and asked the landlord, that's Clifford, nice chap, to telephone for an ambulance.

"When I went back outside, I took a good look at her and that's when I noticed the red marks around her neck. By that time, several other people had come out of the pub to take a look. You know how nosey they are around here. Well, big Ada blurted out, 'Someone's strangled her. You need to contact the police.' Ada is Clifford's wife, the local big mouth. You don't mess with her, she's six feet tall and Clifford's six feet four. So, I said, 'Right, wait here with her, Ada, whilst I run back into the pub.'"

"Did you notice anyone else apart from the people from the pub? Anyone running away from the scene or acting suspiciously?"

"No, there was no one about. I could tell by looking at her that she was a decent sort, if you get my drift. Nicely dressed young lady and all that, not at all the usual type that you see around here."

Mike flicked over to a new page in his already bulging notebook and started collecting names and addresses.

"You've been very helpful, Mr Moseley. If it hadn't been for your swift action, we may now have had a corpse on our hands and be dealing with a murder case. The constable here will take your details. We may need to speak to you again." Stuart got up and made his way towards the nurses' station in the centre of the ward.

"I'd like to speak to Miss Daisy Roberts if it's possible," he ventured, not wanting to sound too forceful.

"The doctor is still with her at the moment. I'll let you know the situation when he's finished his examination."

"Thank you, sister. Is she going to be all right?" he added, holding his breath for fear of a negative answer.

"We've every reason to hope so, officer. She was conscious when they brought her in. They gave her oxygen in the ambulance."

"Thank goodness."

It was ten o'clock before Raif, Bhutan and Alan returned to the house. Grace was beside herself with worry and had obviously been weeping. No one had moved from the kitchen and the stew remained in the oven, uneaten.

"It's all right. She's okay," Bhutan reassured them.

"Where is she? What's happened to her?" asked Magda, who was the first to speak.

"She's in the infirmary. They're keeping her in overnight for observation. We've to go back tomorrow lunchtime to collect her. The doctor will have done his rounds by then and hopefully she'll be discharged."

"Oh, dear God. I just knew it," wailed Grace.

"Don't panic, Grace. She's all right," said Bhutan. "I took a good look at her. She should make a full recovery."

They all sat around the table whilst Raif gave them all the details, as he understood them.

* * *

"Your lift's here, Kath. Leave the pots, I'll swill them," said Earnest. "I'll peel the vegetables later for our tea."

"Thanks, Dad." Kath grabbed her coat and ran down the path.

Ten minutes later, there was a knock at the back door.

"Oh, it's you, Grace," said Earnest. "Come in. I'll just finish washing these pots. Sit yourself down and I'll make us a drink. You look fed up. What's—oh, it's this situation regarding that young lass Daisy I expect. A bad business that."

"I'm worried about her, Earnest. She's threatening to up sticks and leave, taking Jenny with her. She said she can't live around here any longer, not with that Boothroyd fella on the prowl. She's terrified to even leave the house."

"Oh no. She doesn't want to be doing anything rash like that. Where would she go anyway? Has she got any relatives? Has she any savings? Who'd mind Jenny whilst she's at work?"

"I've told her all this, Earnest. She's got a good home here, the likes of which she'll never see again. I'm so worried."

"Well, hang on. He's due in court next week on tax evasion charges. Wait and see what happens."

"She'll not rest until he's locked up. I can't say that I blame her. The law's an arse at times. The number of occasions he's appeared in court and walked free. It's not right."

"I suspect that his father may have had something to do with that, from what I've heard. His father isn't around any longer to bail him out, so who knows what will transpire nowadays. The tax people won't let him wriggle off the hook."

"He'd need a good excuse. What if he declares himself bankrupt?"

"I don't know about all that, Grace. It's beyond me. Let's have a nice cup of tea and a biscuit. We'll think of something. Young Howard is due home soon, isn't he? Surely she won't leave without speaking to him first, will she?"

"There's a letter for you, Raif. It came in Celia's envelope this morning," said Dorothea. "Howard has completed all his exams. Celia says he wouldn't comment on how everything went. That's so typical of Howard. He has an interview at the radio station on Friday regarding the recording of his plays. Celia's going with him.

"Beth's getting very stressed about her final exams. Oh, I do wish I could be there with them all. Selina's starting with a heavy cold and a sore throat. Celia and John are throwing a party this weekend for all their university friends. Josh has a whole notebook of names and addresses. Isn't that just like him? Sam's painting every minute of the day but doesn't seem at all stressed like the others." Dorothea smiled to herself as she handed the letter over to Grace and Magda.

Grace was still in a state about Daisy and she hoped the letter containing news of Howard might distract her a little. Raif opened his letter and frowned.

"What's wrong, darling?" asked Dorothea.

"Strange. It's a solicitor's letter. Mildred's passed away."

"Oh Raif. I didn't even know that she was ill. We should have been informed. We could have gone down to see her. Poor girl."

"It seems to have happened very suddenly. A brain haemorrhage. She collapsed whilst out shopping and died instantly. I shall have to go down. Will you come with me, Dotty? We can stay overnight."

Yes, I think that would be best but I want to make sure that Daisy is all right first. Will you be all right, girls?" she asked, looking at Grace and Magda.

"For one night? I should think so. I know I'm upset about Daisy but I haven't lost my senses. I'll make a sherry trifle, it's Daisy's favourite. I'm sorry about Mildred though, Raif. Were you very close?"

"No, unfortunately. She never married, you know, which immediately makes me feel guilty. As the elder, I should have made more of an effort to go and see her, make sure that she was all right."

"She had a good career at the school, didn't she?" said Magda.

"Oh yes. She was on every education committee going and she did have a lot of friends. Well, when I say 'friends' it makes me think, were they friends or just acquaintances. Dad left everything to her, seeing as she was unmarried with no man in her life, but I've no idea what's in her own will. We'll find out, no doubt."

Ivy was feeding the pigs in the yard, having had yet another row with her bone idle son who never stirred out of his bed before eleven o'clock most mornings. She loved her son as any mother would but to say she was disappointed in his behaviour would be an understatement. Robert was past the age of being a sulky teenager but they hardly got two words out of him these days. He was constantly asking for money. What he did with it all was a mystery. Alf was generous with him to begin with but of late he'd started to question what he was spending all his money on, which had fuelled more rows. She felt near to tears.

Suddenly, she heard someone calling her name.

"Good morning Ivy."

She turned to see big Ada and her husband Clifford walking across the yard towards her.

"Hello Ada, what brings you here so early in the morning?"

Ada worked at the pub washing up and wiping tables, usually well into the small hours.

"We've come to ask a favour, actually," said Clifford stepping in front of his wife. "Do you possess a pitch fork?"

"A pitchfork?" Ivy's antenna went up. What on earth would Clifford and Ada be wanting with a pitchfork? She decided it was probably best not to ask. "Yes, I think we do have just the one. It's in the barn. Follow me."

She led them around the side of the barn and unhooked the fork off the wall and handed it to Clifford.

"Can we borrow it for a couple of hours? We'll bring it straight back."

"Of course."

She watched them march back across the yard before running to find Alf.

"Ask no questions, Ivy," he said. "If the police come round, deny everything. You haven't seen them and they didn't borrow anything."

Ivy got the distinct impression Alf knew more than he was letting on but knew he was protecting her and there would be a good reason for it, although she couldn't for the life of her think what it could be. To frighten somebody perhaps? Or heaven forbid, to kill someone. Surely not? She wouldn't like that on her conscience.

"They're not going to kill someone with it, are they? I'm too old to do porridge at my age, Alf."

"I sincerely hope not, Ivy. Is that lazy son of ours up yet? Let's make a brew, we've earnt a break. It's about time we had a long talk with that errant son of ours."

"Why have I been frog-marched in here?" barked Iain Boothroyd.

"We need to speak to you regarding complaints of assault on two of your former employees, namely Lavinia Durran and Monica Braydon. Also an arson attack on your factory and recently, the attempted murder of Daisy Roberts."

There was a momentary silence which was broken by his cackling laugh. "Are you serious? You can't pin any of that on me, you've no proof," he yelled and stood up to leave.

"Your bully-boy tactics won't wash in here, my lad, so I suggest that you do the sensible thing by sitting down and answering some questions. Alternatively, you can spend the night in one of our cells. Which is it to be?" said Stuart.

Mike was standing with his back to the door, blocking the escape route.

"Look, son, your mother and I, all we've ever wanted is for you to be happy," said Alf, handing his son a mug of tea and a plate of hot buttered toast. "When you went into the army, we were both so proud of you, but since you've come home, you don't seem happy and that concerns us. If you don't like farming, and I admit it's not to everyone's taste, then we must find you a job that's better suited for you."

Ivy was gulping her tea down, trying not to let it show how upset she was. "You have to tell us what you want to do. We're here to help, you know that," she said hopefully, not at all confident they were going to get anything out of him.

There followed an interminable silence, whilst Robert digested their words, then with a resigned sigh he said, "All right. It's cards on the table time. Actually, I'm at my wits end. I've been incredibly stupid and I'm sorry I got involved in the first place."

Ivy frowned and looked at Alf.

"Tell us about it, we're listening," said Alf. If Alf was slowly losing his patience and his temper, he certainly wasn't letting it show. "Has this got anything to do with that Boothroyd chap?"

With eyes as big as saucers, he said, "How did you know?"

"I thought as much. All that money. Has he been blackmailing you?"

"Yes. I've just about had enough but he won't leave me alone."

"Then you must go to the police."

"I can't."

"Why ever not? Extorting money out of people is an offence," said Ivy.

"Start from the beginning," said Alf. "How on earth did you get involved with the likes of him in the first place?"

"I met him in the pub one night shortly after I was demobbed," said Robert. "There were a few of us all celebrating and he came over to us at the bar and started chatting. I was the last to leave and he took me to one side and asked me if I'd like to make a bit of money. I asked him how much and he said 'a lot'. He told me he was planning to burn down his factory and claim the insurance money. He offered to split it with me if I'd do the deed."

"You burnt down the factory?" stormed Alf. "Good God, what on earth possessed you?"

"I was drunk, Dad. It's no excuse, I know, but after what I'd been through in that war, I saw it as a way of making a decent sum of money. He made it sound so easy. Of course, he never paid me and now he's threatening to report me to the police if I don't give in to his demands. I'm in a lot of trouble. I've let you both down and I'm sorry. Is it best if I just give myself up?" He looked so dejected and forlorn it was hard to feel anything but pity for the lad.

"I say not," shouted Ivy. "What do you say, Alf?"

"Absolutely. You did a terrible thing, that's without doubt. Your own conscience should have prevented you from doing such a thing like that and we've failed as parents if—"

"No. No, don't say that. I wasn't thinking straight. It was an act of madness. One I'll never forgive myself for, but I can't go on like this. Tell me what to do. Please."

"Go to Ireland. They'll have you on the ranch there. They could do with an extra pair of hands. Pack your bags and just go. I'll go to the post office and use the telephone this afternoon," said Ivy.

"I'm not too happy about letting him go," said Mike. "You never know what he's going to do next. I don't trust him."

"Neither do I, Mike, but we couldn't detain him any longer. Like he so rightly repeatedly reminded us, we have no evidence and no proof of anything."

"I've got a bad feeling about all this. Assaulting young girls, child abduction, arson attacks, attempted murder. What next? The man has no conscience whatsoever. I've never met anyone so arrogant."

"It's all bravado, Mike, believe me. I've seen it all before. Underneath it all, there's one weak individual who isn't coping with life. He's looking for ways to make big money without having to work for it. His father taught him that life owed him as much. It's learned behaviour. If things don't go his way, he uses the only methods he knows, his fists, bullying, intimidation, coercion, corruption."

"It's gone on long enough in my opinion. There must be something we can nail him for."

"We'll keep trying. He'll make a mistake sooner or later. He might think he's been very clever, but he'll come unstuck and when he does, we'll be ready for him."

* * *

"Listen, you scumbag. We don't want your sort in this town, terrorising and assaulting our women, burning down that factory and throwing all our women out of work, abducting a child, strangling that lovely lass Daisy Roberts and leaving her for dead. So, you just cleat off out of this town, otherwise you'll get this pitchfork rammed up your arse!" roared Clifford.

His wife Ada was behind him with half the men of the neighbourhood, all lined up with pick axes, shovels, spades, rakes and cast-iron frying pans.

"If the law won't do for you, then we will," they bellowed in unison.

Chapter Forty-Five

Celia and Howard arrived home to find Selina pacing the hallway looking anxious. The interview at the radio station had gone extremely well and Howard was more hopeful this time as the new producer was keen and making all the right noises, so it was with elated spirits he and Celia entered the house laughing and joking.

"Celia, thank goodness, you've come," wailed Selina, sneezing into her handkerchief.

"Darling, you look dreadful. That cold of yours isn't getting any better. You ought to be in bed. How did it all go?"

"It went well, I think. Beth's convinced that she's failed. She's upstairs packing her bag. She says that she's leaving tonight as she wants to get back to Blythe Wood. She won't wait until tomorrow. She's been sobbing non-stop since we got home."

"But the train tickets are for tomorrow, not today," said Howard.

"I know but she said she'll get it changed at the station. There's a train at six o'clock that gets in Somerset around eleven."

"Goodness me, that's far too late to be hanging around at that time of night," protested Celia who was now getting more than a little vexed, not to say concerned.

"I'll go up and speak to her," offered Howard. "Celia, you look after Selina, she's not at all well. I'm all packed up and ready so I could go with Beth if need be. She certainly can't go on her own." He scrambled up the stairs, pausing halfway, he shouted over the banister, "Send Sam up as soon as he gets home. She'll listen to him.

He's just gone to the art shop for some more paints as he's run out. He'll be here in about twenty minutes."

Ivy was disinfecting the prongs of the pitchfork when Alf appeared.

"I don't want any fingerprints left on here," she said, scrubbing the prongs with vigour.

"They'll have worn gloves anyway, I expect," said Alf, knowing full well they probably hadn't but he didn't want Ivy getting any more upset than she already was.

"I'm not taking any chances. We need to hide it. If the police come sniffing around, we can say someone pinched it off the hook in the barn."

"We won't be needing it for a while yet anyway. Give it to me. I'll find somewhere for it." He took the fork off of her and disappeared across the yard with it.

She was just clearing away the breakfast pots at the sink in the kitchen when she spotted a familiar face at the window. She knew immediately why he'd come and what he was after.

"That son of yours around?" Iain roared, banging his fist on the back door.

"Why? Who wants to know?"

"I do. He owes me money."

"Don't know anything about that, I'm afraid."

"Where is he?" he demanded.

"No idea." Ivy kept her head down and continued with the washing up without making eye contact with him. She hoped Alf would appear soon or she would be in trouble. Where on earth could he have gone with that pitchfork?

"Mike? It's Belinda. I've just seen that Iain Boothroyd making his way up the track to the farm. I don't trust that man. If Ivy's there on her own..."

"Leave it to me," he shouted, banging down the receiver and grabbing his jacket from the hook in the corridor. He dashed into Stuart's office.

* * *

"How's Daisy been today?" asked Dorothea, dumping her bag and kicking off her shoes. It had been a tedious day at the factory and she was glad to be home.

"A bit better," said Grace. "She ate her porridge this morning but she's still very quiet. Not at all her normal self. She's having flashbacks. She wakes up screaming in the night."

"It's going to take a while. Poor girl. She doesn't deserve any of it. At least he didn't sexually assault her this time. Not that that's any consolation but hopefully over time…"

"I'm not so sure, Dotty. She's still talking about moving away with Jenny."

"We can't let that happen, Grace. She's nowhere to go and she has no money. What on earth would she do? Where would she go?"

"I don't think she cares as long as she's away from that beast. I've brewed some tea. Do you want a cup?"

"When do I ever not want a cup of tea?" Dorothea laughed.

"I've made up all the beds in the children's rooms. Clean sheets on them all. I'll have to stop calling them children now, won't I? They're all young adults," mused Grace, pouring the tea into Dotty's favourite mug.

"I'm so looking forward to them all coming home and to hearing all their news. The house will be a proper home again. It's been like a morgue here without them."

"Did Raif telephone the solicitor regarding Mildred's funeral?" Grace ventured tentatively, for technically speaking it was none of her business.

"Yes. There's a delay whilst they complete the post mortem. He's going to send a copy of the will in the post. There's a gentleman… well, I say gentleman, an acquaintance I suppose, come forward laying claim to a stake of the estate. He reckons he's her common law husband."

"Really?" gasped Grace, sitting herself down and beginning to enjoy herself, for she loved gossip of this sort.

"Well, the ladies from the school all say he was nothing of the sort and he's just trying to 'cash in' or whatever they call it. Not that she had much mind, from what Raif says."

"Well, well. Isn't that just typical. What does Raif think?"

"He said it's highly unlikely that Mildred had a partner. She just wasn't the type. She was married to her job. A career girl. She never found the time for romance, which is a shame."

"What was she like? You met her at your father-in-law's funeral, didn't you?"

"Yes. She was terribly nice, actually. A bit prim and proper, if you know what I mean. A typical school ma'am, but very pleasant. She'd have made an excellent wife for some nice man. Her brain was razor sharp."

"Men don't always go for brains. Nobody likes a clever clogs. I know my George didn't. He couldn't stand clever women."

They both laughed as they sipped their tea.

"He was quite a character, your George."

"Yes, especially when he'd had a drink inside him. He could charm the birds out of the trees."

"How is your Gordon doing? Have you heard from him lately?"

"Oh yes, he writes every week, or she does. They're loving it. Everything seems to be going well for them."

"How about if you visit him and take Daisy with you? It would be a nice little break for you both. Maybe that's what she needs just now. A change of scenery."

"Yes, you could be right, Dotty. I'll mention it to them in my next letter."

"Fancy another pint, Gerry?"

"We've worked hard today, so why not?"

Raif made his way to the bar. There was quite a crowd at the far end and there seemed to be a discussion going on which they all found amusing. Raif couldn't help overhearing some of the banter.

"It was that pitchfork that did it."

Laughter.

"He wasn't scared until you shoved the prongs up his nostrils. He took note then all right."

More laughter.

"Penny for them?" said Raif, placing the drinks on the table.

"Oh, I was just thinking," said Gerry. "It's funny, isn't it? Food's still rationed, money's still tight for most people… well, the people we know anyway. There are men still looking for work, yet all that doesn't seem to affect the gentry. They just carry on as normal."

"Thankfully for us, most of our goods are being bought by the upper echelons of society. Who would have thought it? Two years in business and we've broken even. We don't owe anybody anything. We're solvent. The first year is always the hardest, so they say."

"It certainly is, Raif, believe me," said Gerry, taking a swig of his pint. "If we can break even in the first two years, then the prospects for this next year are looking good, I reckon. Especially now that we've got the contract for the club blazers, ties and badges."

"Here's to us," said Raif, raising his glass.

"Josh, where on earth have you been?" asked Celia. "There's uproar here. Beth's determined to leave for Somerset tonight. The others are all upstairs packing. I'm trying to help Selina. She's not well."

"Why tonight?" Josh was puzzled. "It's all arranged for us to leave tomorrow morning."

"Beth's been crying since she came home. I think she's on the verge of a breakdown. She's not been herself since that visit from her mother. The damage that woman's done."

Josh was silent for a few minutes before speaking. "I know what's caused this. It's that nasty piece of work: Trudie. She's had it in for Beth ever since the incident at the fashion show last year."

"What happened?"

"Oh, it's a long story. But basically, Beth outshone her and she didn't like it. As far as she was concerned, she was top dog and nothing or no one was going to rain on her parade. The great Gertrude Blackwell.

There were some very big names in the fashion world at that show, Celia, and Beth caused quite a stir with her designs. She was mentioned in some of the top fashion magazines as a name to watch. Trudie didn't like it one bit. Selina was also mentioned as a fresh young talent worth watching.

"As I came out of college today, one of the girls in our class stopped me and told me about the 'set to' which had gone on between Beth and this Trudie. She told Beth she'd never amount to anything and if she thought for one minute that she was going to make a name for herself in the fashion world then she was pipe dreaming. She told her to quit now whilst she was ahead. In truth, it's her that needs to give it up, if you ask me. Some of her designs were diabolical."

"That sounds like childish jealously to me. Unfortunately, you have to be able to take criticism in business today otherwise you won't survive. It's tough. I'll nip next door and ask John to run us all to the station. You'd better start getting your things together, lad. Put a move on."

Alf opened the back door to find Stuart and Mike standing on the doorstep.

"Oh. Hello lads. You've just missed him. Come in, I'll make some tea. Ivy, it's Stuart and Mike," he shouted up the stairs in the hallway. "She's a bit shaken up but I sent him packing. He needn't think he can keep coming round here threatening us like that. I'm not standing for it."

"What exactly was he after?" asked Stuart, sitting himself down at the table.

"Money."

"Money?" asked Mike. "For what?"

"The good Lord only knows. To live on, presumably." Alf wasn't about to say anything that would incriminate his son, even though he did torch the factory. They'd soon hunt him down even though he'd gone to Ireland.

Ivy appeared and immediately set about brewing the tea. They'd both agreed not to mention their son. He'd made a stupid mistake but thankfully nobody had been hurt or killed.

"So, he just turned up and demanded money?" asked Stuart, becoming suspicious. There had to be more to it than that. There was something they were not telling him. Of that, he was certain.

Alf dished out the tea and sat down next to his wife. "Well, he reckons some lads from the village threatened him with a pitchfork. Shoved the prongs in his face and seeing as we're the only folk around here in possession of one, he reckons it could only have come from here. He threatened to report us to the police if we didn't pay him what he was asking for."

"How much did he want?" asked Mike, scribbling away in his notebook.

"We didn't get that far. I ordered him off the premises. Once you start that sort of thing… well, he'll just keep coming back for more, won't he? There'd be no end to it. Besides, if someone's pinched our fork, it's news to us. The first thing I did when he'd gone was to go to the barn to check if it's still there. And it is, hanging on the wall where it always is. So, if someone 'borrowed' it, they must have put it back."

"And what did he hope to gain by going to the police?" asked Mike.

"Your guess is as good as mine, Mike. Supplying someone with a dangerous weapon perhaps, but I tell you now if someone threatened him with that fork, it was nothing to do with us. It's the first we've heard about it. If the lads in the village had a pop at him then quite frankly, I'm glad. Arrogant little brat. Who does he think he is terrifying half the village with his attitude? Well, he's picked the wrong village this time because the people of this village are made of strong stuff. They won't stand for it."

Stuart noticed Ivy hadn't spoken a word, but sat sipping her tea, not making eye contact with anyone. It wasn't like her at all. She was a very chatty sociable woman. She did indeed look upset, Stuart noticed.

As he and Mike made their way to leave, he noticed their son was nowhere to be seen and he wondered if Iain Boothroyd's visit had anything to do with him.

"Your son not around?" asked Stuart as casually as he could.

"That's another bone of contention," whispered Alf, following them both out into the yard. "He wasn't pulling his weight on the farm so Ivy and I decided to have a word with him. I don't think that he's cut out for farming, to be honest. To cut a long story short, he's upped sticks and left."

"Really. Where to?"

"That's just it. We're not sure where he's headed. He packed up his rucksack and said he was going travelling and he'd contact us when he got settled. Ivy's upset about it all, but you know I can't blame the lad really. He's only young and farming's a hard life. You either like it or you hate it. It's not everyone's cup of tea."

During the drive back to the station, Mike said, "I can't help thinking that Iain Boothroyd's visit had something to do with the son. Funny that he should go travelling then Boy Wonder appears demanding money."

"Yes, there's more to it than what they're letting on. We'll get to the bottom of it eventually."

"They're obviously protecting him for some reason. I wonder what he's been up to."

"Exactly."

"Do you miss the house and the children, Meg?" asked Iris as she dished out the shepherd's pie. They'd taken to having all their evening meals together as it was cheaper to share the costs.

"Just lately I've been missing them more and more," said Meg. "Especially Beth. I do hope she finds time to come into the shop and see me occasionally. I can't bear the thought of not being part of all their lives. How about you?"

"I miss them all too and especially Dotty, Grace and Daisy. Besides, Pov and Chris have started dropping hints about wanting to turn the cafe into a restaurant. I think it would suit them if Bob and I moved on. It's the evening supper club that's done it. It's doing quite well and they think they can increase the turnover by providing proper meals during the day, like fine dining."

"I'm not sure about any of that, Iris. The people around here haven't got that sort of money. There's a big difference in tea and scones and fillet steak and fancy chips."

"Not chips, Meg. Dauphinois potatoes," Iris laughed.

"I heard Bob arguing with Pov about it yesterday. Where are the boys, by the way?"

"They'll be back in a minute. Harry needed help fixing one of the shelves. Oh, here they are. Everything all right, boys?"

"Yes. All sorted," said Harry sitting himself down next to Meg. "This looks good."

Bob kissed the top of Iris' head and sat down before saying, "Have we any wine? I could do with a drink."

"No, but we can go to the pub after this if you like," offered Iris.

"Good idea. We need to discuss what's going on in the cafe. I can't stand much more of this atmosphere. It's funny, isn't it? At first, we thought we were doing them a favour letting them take over the cafe in the evenings for their supper club. Now, they want to take over during the day as well. Where did we go wrong?"

"They're young and ambitious, Bob," said Harry. "They just want to make the most of their opportunities. It's the war that's done that."

"We all got on so well in the beginning," said Meg. "I think it's Povinder that's pushing it. Chris told me she was happy as she was but I suppose she has to be seen to support her husband in his ambitions."

Later in the pub, Harry and Bob went to the bar to get the drinks whilst the girls looked for a table.

"Let's try for a table over by the window on the mezzanine," said Meg, "It's quieter there."

They just got sat down at a table when Iris spotted some familiar faces. "Look. it's Raif and Gerry. Hi there. You two doing the same as us? Drowning your sorrows?" she shouted and waved. "Mind if we join you?"

An hour later, they were all sharing a huge plate of chips and Raif had just bought another round of drinks in when he said, "How are things at the cafe and shop then, girls?"

"Well, to be honest," said Bob taking a huge gulp of his pint, "Things are getting a bit heated in the cafe. Pov and Chris are after taking over and turning it into a proper restaurant. I can't blame them for wanting to run things as they see fit. They're both young and full of energy. I'm beginning to feel as though Iris and I are in the way."

"Hmmm," said Raif. "They were turfed out of their old place, weren't they? You kept the wolf from the door by taking them on in the first place. I'm not convinced about their plans though. Don't forget the pub is just around the corner. They serve meals all day."

"Well, that was over a year ago, Raif. A lot of water has gone under the bridge since then, but I agree with you. Clifford told me only last year that he had to change the menu several times before getting one that worked."

"Actually, we could do with some extra help at the factory now that we have more contracts," said Gerry. "If you fancy a change, just say the word. Now would be a good time to join us as we're just about to start on the production of the new range. We have to hire more staff or we'll not meet the orders."

"Bob and I would have to vacate the flat," said Iris sheepishly. "Bhutan will be disappointed as he loves cooking."

"Don't worry about that, Iris. He's doing far too much anyway. He needs to slow down. That morning surgery is very busy. He should be resting in the afternoons, but he can always come to the factory and help us out. There are spare bedrooms at Blythe Wood for you all, you know that," Raif reassured them, looking directly at Meg and Harry. "Dotty and I would love to have you all back, so would Grace and Daisy. The children will be home soon too, so the extra help will be appreciated. It's not been the same without you all. The house seems strangely empty and forlorn."

Harry glanced across at Meg and saw the tears in her eyes. "What would we be doing exactly?" he asked Gerry.

"Well, Belinda's putting together a promotional catalogue, featuring all our lines. We'll need someone to distribute them to all prospective buyers. As an ex-salesman, Harry, you'd be the ideal person to do that. Alan's doing most of the collections and deliveries single-handedly so you could help him there, Bob. Iris and Meg would help Pat and Susan. They do the sewing and all the admin alongside Dotty and Magda. There's a good variety, you'll not be bored. We'll take Kathleen on too. She's a good machinist. What do you say? If you need time to think about it, that's fine, but don't take too long about it because we desperately need help. Sooner rather than later."

Iris noticed Bob seemed to have brightened up considerably. She wasn't sure if that was down to the beer or the prospect of a more suitable job. Being out and about in the van all day with Alan would suit Bob down to the ground. She knew that without a doubt.

Bob wouldn't take much persuading but Harry might not want to give up the book shop and he hadn't been married to Meg for very long. They might have secret plans of their own.

"Can we talk it over and let you know tomorrow morning?" Iris asked, looking at Gerry then at Raif. "Meg, you and Harry come to ours tonight and we'll discuss it over our cocoa."

Iris poured out the cocoa and went to the cupboard to find some biscuits.

Harry took hold of Meg's hand and said, "I'm sorry, my dear, that I haven't got much to offer you. It's a poor start to married life. It's not much of a job, flogging second-hand books. I had hoped for better things but I didn't make as much as I expected on the sale of the bungalow. It was the war, of course. We're hardly making enough to live on with the book sales we're getting at the moment. We're only really busy at the weekends. The rest of the week, it's pretty dismal and that landlord of ours has increased our rent for the third time this year. We can't survive like this for much longer."

"Don't talk like that, Harry, for goodness' sake," laughed Bob. "Iris and I hadn't a shilling between us when we married and we still haven't. It doesn't matter to us as long as we're together. We survived the war and we're alive and living. That's something to celebrate."

"Yes, but still…" said Harry, sipping his cocoa.

"Would you be happy working for Raif and Gerry?" Meg asked her husband in earnest, hoping with all her heart he'd say yes.

"I'd prefer it actually. The shop was a nice stop-gap but I think we've outgrown it somehow."

"What about you, Bob?"

"I'm in. What do you say, Iris?"

"Anything to get out of that cafe and from under Pov's feet. I'll go to Kath's tomorrow and let her know. Bob, you let Gerry know that we're all for it. That's settled then."

They clinked mugs, talking and laughing well into the small hours.

Chapter Forty-Six

"Now, girls and boys, you won't forget about Celia and I up here in London, will you? You'll come and see us from time to time. We love you all very much. The house is going to be so quiet without you all," said John, heaving all the rucksacks out of the boot of the car.

Celia was weeping into her handkerchief. She'd never felt so miserable in all her life. This was the moment she had been dreading, the day she had to say goodbye to them all.

"Yes, John's right. Think of this as your second home all of you," she managed, hugging everyone in turn. "Sam, get Selina settled in the carriage and wrap her up in the blanket. She's not at all well. I'm worried about her."

"Don't worry, Aunt Celia, I'll look after her," said Josh, cheerily. He picked up her rucksack as well as his own.

Beth was already racing up the platform towards the train. There didn't appear to be any staff around to check their tickets and the ticket office was closed, so they boarded the train and sat down in a carriage all to themselves.

Howard stuck his head out of the window and shouted up the platform as the train was departing, "I'll write to you next week when we're settled."

The others all popped their heads out of the window and waved until they were out of sight. Howard only hoped there would be no guard on board checking the tickets, otherwise they'd be in big trouble. The others didn't seem even remotely bothered, so he settled down to his diary and started writing.

Josh sat himself in the corner with Selina, who looked pale and distinctly unwell. Sam sat opposite Beth, who hadn't spoken since tea time. She'd sat with her hat and coat on in the hallway amongst all the rucksacks whilst the others sat at the table to eat their meal. Celia got a bit cross and made her sit at the table with the others.

"You're not going anywhere, young lady, until you've eaten your meal," Celia had snapped.

"Are you all right now, Beth?" asked Sam, taking hold of both her hands in his.

"I'm so sorry, everyone," she whispered. "I don't know what's the matter with me. I just want to go home to Blythe Wood." Then she burst into tears. Great bellowing sobs which lasted a full five minutes.

"Let's see what's in the tuck box," said Howard by means of a diversion. "I think Celia's packed some cake. That'll cheer us up."

"Dorothea, there's a telephone message for you. It's Belinda," said Pat handing her the receiver.

"Thank you, Pat." Dorothea flung off her coat and sat at her desk, throwing her handbag at her feet. "Hello Belinda. Everything all right?"

"No actually, Dorothea. That's why I'm calling. I've been thrown out of my lodgings. The landlord's selling up. We're all out on the street. The others have all got friends or relatives to go to but I'm a bit stuck. I've not been in London for very long and I don't really know anyone. What shall I do?" She was on the verge of tears and was struggling to control the quiver in her voice. She'd never been homeless before and she was scared.

"Well, I'm sure he's breaking the law by not giving you proper notice. Go and see Celia, she'll take you in at the townhouse. Tell her you've spoken to me and we'll sort the rent out when I've spoken to Raif." Dorothea felt sorry for the girl. She was so very young and she'd become fond of her. "Don't worry, everything will be all right. We're getting a telephone installed this week, so I'll ring you when it's all sorted. You'll stay here with us anyway when you next come down."

They said their goodbyes and Dorothea put down the receiver.

"Poor lass. She's been turned out of her lodgings," she said to Pat, who'd just placed a steaming hot mug of tea on the corner of her desk. "She's out on the streets. It's not right. These landlords are a law unto themselves. They shouldn't be allowed to do this."

"I agree. If he wants his tenants out, he should give them proper notification," said Pat.

"Quite. The pig."

"She could always stay with me when she comes up, next time. I've got a spare room."

"That's very kind of you, Pat. I'll bear that in mind, in case we run out of space. Meg and Iris are moving back in." She quickly related the story about the problems at the cafe and book shop and told her to expect five extra staff, including Kathleen.

"Thank goodness. We're getting swamped," said Pat, sifting through a pile of invoices. "These are all last month's. I've not even started on this month's yet. We're getting further and further behind."

"Don't worry, we'll soon catch up and get everything up to date," assured Dorothea, with more confidence than she felt. The accounts were in a bit of a mess but she had every faith in Pat, who seemed utterly reliable.

Belinda made her way through the black wrought iron gate. The house was very grand and she couldn't believe she was going to be living in such splendour.

John was waiting for her and made his way to greet her. "Hello Belinda. I got Celia's message. You've been made homeless, I believe."

"Yes. I've just got back from Somerset so it was a bit of a shock. All the other residents had three weeks' notice but I came back to an eviction order. It didn't leave me much time to find somewhere else. I'm a bit shaken up, to be honest."

"I'm not surprised. I'll let you in and we'll have a cup of tea. Celia's usually home any time after six o'clock. We eat together so

I usually have the meal started so we can just finish it off. I'll show you around, then you can make yourself at home."

After a cup of tea and several biscuits, Belinda was feeling more like her old self.

"I'll let Celia sort out which bedroom she wants you in, but we can take a look around."

He showed her the bathroom and one of the spare rooms which was full of all the garments from the fashion show.

"These are all the clothes they made for their end of term fashion show. There was too much of it for them to take on the train. I suppose they'll collect them all sometime in the future."

"Wow, these are amazing, John," said Belinda, looking through all the dresses and jackets. "Such beautiful material and so well made. The finishing is top class," she said, inspecting the seams and zips. "We should put all these in the brochure. I'll ring Dorothea tomorrow. I've got a good feeling about all this, John. They're so unusual, Cosmopolitan, I think you'd call them."

"Selina was quite determined to produce clothes that could be worn by all age groups. If that's possible. I'd better start the meal," said John, making his way downstairs.

Belinda wasn't sure if she'd be included in these meals, so she ventured, "Could I possible join you tonight, John, just until I can get myself organised?"

"Of course, my dear. You will be eating with us every night. Do you want to give me a hand?"

"That's kind of you. Thank you." She wasn't sure how much the rent was going to be or if indeed she'd be able to afford to stay here. She wasn't used to such luxury and was sure it was all going to be beyond her pocket. She started to feel a little uneasy but decided to put it out of her mind for the time being. She'd deal with that when she had to.

Raif opened his mail to discover another letter from his sister Mildred's solicitor informing him that a gentleman was contesting the will and there was to be an enquiry. Meanwhile, the body had been released. The coroner's report confirmed her death by a brain haemorrhage and according to instructions in her will, a cremation had been arranged for Thursday week at the crematorium close to the school.

He showed the letter to Dotty, adding, "We'll have to go down on Wednesday evening as it's arranged for the Thursday."

"Will the telephone be installed by then?" she asked.

"Yes, fortunately. They're coming here on Monday. Celia's is booked for Tuesday. I'll write and let her know we're coming, just to be sure."

"The children are due back tomorrow. Oh dear, I must stop calling them children now. Bad habit. They're all adults. I can't wait to see them all again."

"Yes, I'll be glad when they're all back with us. We've been incredibly lucky, haven't we? I never thought we'd have a family of our own, but look at us now."

Dorothea smiled to herself and rested her head on Raif's shoulder. She thought of her sisters Meg and Iris, neither of whom had been blessed with any children and she wondered if they would ever have any now. Harry and Bob would make wonderful fathers, of that she was certain. As for the girls… well, Meg and Iris both possessed strong maternal instincts, having witnessed it for herself after the children arrived on her doorstep. There were times when she knew she wouldn't have coped half as well had it not been for their help, together with Grace and Daisy.

Jenny burst through the doorway carrying Bella and Willow.

"The cocoa is ready," she said, settling herself into the chair next to Raif. Grace and Daisy followed her carrying the tray.

"Sorry about the delay," said Grace. "We made two cakes at the last minute, just in case the children are hungry when they get home tomorrow. They're in the oven now. Two chocolate sponges. I've got a tin of black cherries and fresh cream to go in the middle."

"Bhutan and Magda are making some Indian cakes as well, with spices," said Jenny. "They smell delicious. They'll be in soon. The mixture has to stand for an hour before baking."

"I couldn't figure out what they were doing, so I just left them to it," laughed Grace, handing out the mugs.

"Are you all right, Mummy?" asked Jenny, for she knew her mother hadn't been herself since she came out of hospital and seemed unusually quiet.

"Yes, darling. I'm all right," she said softly, patting her daughter's hand.

"Howard's home tomorrow, Mummy. We'll be able to go to the park like we used to, won't we?" she gushed. "I can't wait to show them all our new members of the family. Bella and Willow will wonder what's happened when all these faces suddenly appear, but they'll soon get used to it."

Daisy didn't reply to her daughter's request about the walks in the park for she didn't feel safe leaving the house, not with the likes of Iain Boothroyd on the loose. Raif and Dorothea had both spoken to Stuart about him but to no avail. She wondered if she'd feel happy ever again.

Iain was desperate for a drink but after the fiasco in the pub the other night, he knew he couldn't show his face in there ever again. Everywhere he went, he was met with black looks and animosity. It was beginning to get on his nerves. He'd had it with this town and all the people in it.

The business had collapsed, he owed the tax man a huge amount of money which he'd no way of paying, his father's house had been re-mortgaged, leaving only just enough money to cover the funeral costs and little else. What's more, there was no liquid cash anywhere, either in his father's bank account or his own. There was only one thing for it, he'd have to declare himself bankrupt and somehow start again. But what to do?

He'd no interest in office work and couldn't stand taking orders from other people. The only option was to work for himself, but he'd tried that and failed. Having no idea where his mother was living was frustrating. The solicitor wouldn't divulge any details but confirmed her instructions that she didn't want anything from his father's estate, which was just as well because the house would have to be sold to meet all the debts.

He was just coming out of the off licence with four cans of beer in a carrier bag when he heard a voice behind him, "One of those in there for me, is there?"

He turned to see a familiar face from his recent trip to Chicago. "Ruby? What are you doing here?" He was shocked that she'd succeeded in finding him. His past was slowly catching up with him.

"That's a nice way to greet an old friend. Aren't you glad to see me? I seem to remember we have some unfinished business to attend to." She smiled at him, placing her overnight bag on the pavement. She was wearing a very expensive coat and her perfume overpowered him.

"Sorry, Ruby. It's just… well, it's a bad time for me at the moment. Everything has gone wrong. I'm in a terrible mess. Do you want to come back to the flat and we can talk? We can't talk here. There are eyes and ears everywhere."

He escorted her back to his car and an hour later, they were seated around his small kitchen table eating a curry. He opened the beers and handed her a glass.

She took off her coat to reveal a V-necked wool dress and knee length boots. An expensive silk scarf was draped loosely around her shoulders, concealing an expensive-looking gold necklace.

How on earth had she managed to track him down? He left no forwarding address or telephone contact details when he left her. That was the way he liked it and he wondered why she'd come all this way from Chicago. Was it to claim the money he owed her? If so, she wasn't going to be fobbed off easily, he knew that for a fact. He had no intentions of tying himself down to any woman. He was a free agent and he wasn't going to let her get in his way, but how to get rid of her?

"You look very elegant, Ruby, as always," he said smiling at her. "I'm sorry that I haven't anything better to offer you but since our last meeting, well… everything you… well, it's not going to happen now."

They ate their curries whilst he laid all his cards on the table, telling her about the factory being burnt down whilst he was in the States, to his father dying and leaving huge debts and about the court case the following week regarding his tax liabilities.

"So, you see, Ruby, I'm bankrupt. What's more, I've no way of paying the tax man what I owe. I could end up in prison."

"Wasn't the factory insured?" she asked, not being entirely sure she believed his story.

"Yes, it was insured. That's another bone of contention. They won't pay up. They said the fire was started deliberately and they think that I was behind it."

"And were you?" she asked, eyeing him directly for signs of deceit.

"Of course not. How could I have been? I was in Chicago at the time on business with my father. Oh Ruby, I don't know what to do for the best. I'll declare myself bankrupt, of course, but I'll still have to appear in court next week. So, you see, I have nothing to offer you. All my good intentions turned to dust. I tried to get a job with my father's employers but they wouldn't have me."

Ruby wondered why that was, but didn't voice her suspicions. She suspected he was embroidering the truth but she didn't care. Having issues of her own to deal with, she needed a man in her life and Iain fitted the bill perfectly and she was determined to have him.

"How about coming back to the States with me, after the court case? I'll settle your tax bill and we can start over again. I have enough money for both of us, for now at least." She didn't elaborate on how she had acquired her wealth and he never asked her. She'd seen off seven husbands and wrung each one of them dry of every penny they possessed but suddenly she was tired of running. She just wanted to lie low for a while. After that, well, who knew?

Bhutan had just finished clearing up in the kitchen and was making his way upstairs to bed when he saw headlights on the driveway. Who on earth could this be at this hour of the night? He opened the door to see a taxi approaching the house.

Sam jumped out and ran up the path to greet his father.

"Hello Father," he shouted, throwing his arms around him.

"Sam? Goodness, we were expecting you all tomorrow."

"Change of plan," he said evasively.

"Are all the others with you?" he asked, making his way out of the house to greet them all.

"Yes. We need to get Selina up to her bed. She's got influenza."

Suddenly, Magda appeared at the door. "Who is it, Bhutan? Oh, Sam. Let me look at you. I'm sure you're a foot taller than when I last saw you," she laughed, embracing her boy.

Raif and Dorothea appeared, tying their dressing gowns around themselves.

"They're back," shouted Raif. "I thought you said they were coming tomorrow, Dotty."

"I'm sure it was meant to be tomorrow. Not that it matters."

The next half hour was all hugs and laughter. Grace, Daisy and Jenny descended to the kitchen, lighting the range for warmth and making mugs of cocoa. They all sat around the big table listening to tales of university life, the friends they'd made and how the coursework had panned out. Selina and Beth had been tucked up in their beds, following Bhutan's orders. He'd given them both a mild sleeping tablet.

"I'm worried about Beth," said Grace. "How long has she been like this, Sam?"

"It all started with a visit from her mother. It seemed to unsettle her, but Selina's convinced they've both done well. She'll buck up when the exam results arrive, I'm sure."

"It's a wonder that Selina made the journey," said Dorothea. "The poor girl looked about to drop any minute."

"My girl is strong. She will be all right. I will make her well again," said Magda.

"We must feed them up. Get some good food inside them," said Dotty. "We'll go to the butchers tomorrow, Magda, and get some hearty casseroles in the oven. The garden's ripe with vegetables and fruit, which is lucky for us because Iris and Meg are moving back in on Sunday afternoon. They're all having lunch in the pub first, so they'll be with us by tea time."

"What happened to the cafe and book shop then?" asked Howard, who was losing track of everything.

"A long story that. We'll let them tell you in their own words when they arrive. Basically, it didn't work out quite as planned."

Howard noticed Daisy had hardly spoken and looked sad and dejected. He wondered if she still felt the same affection for him. His own feelings hadn't changed but if she felt differently, then he knew he'd have to let her go.

"We've got a lot to tell you, Howard," Jenny whispered to him. The others were all laughing and joking, so she had his full attention. "Something terrible happened to me and Mummy. It was really awful. We'll talk tomorrow." She jumped off her stool and made her way over to the corner where the cats' basket was nestled.

"Come and look, Josh," she shouted. "These are our cats, Bella and Willow."

Josh made his way over to her and knelt by the side of the basket. The two cats were curled up in little balls, fast asleep. Bella was white with grey flecks and Willow was black with white tips on his two front paws.

"Aren't they beautiful?" She lowered her voice to a whisper so as not to wake them.

"They certainly are," said Josh.

"They're no trouble," she added. "Well, not much anyway. They're good most of the time."

"Come on, everyone, we'd best get to our beds. We'll talk in the morning. Your room is all ready for you, lads, with clean pyjamas on your pillows," ordered Raif.

Daisy started collecting the mugs to wash up when Dorothea stopped her.

"Leave those, Daisy. I'll do them in the morning. You get Jenny back to bed. You too, Grace. That's an order," she laughed.

Howard lay in bed that night wondering what the terrible

news was that Jenny had mentioned. What on earth could have happened? Did Daisy have a secret past that he knew nothing about? He wondered if it had anything to do with Jenny's father. Daisy certainly didn't seem like the happy girl he'd left behind when he departed for London. He drifted off into a troubled sleep, vowing to get to the bottom of it all tomorrow.

Chapter Forty-Seven

Grace and Daisy strolled along the sea front licking their ice creams. They had one more night left with Grace's son Gordon before boarding the train home tomorrow. Gordon and his wife had been very good company and their cooking skills were surprisingly good.

He takes after his mother, thought Daisy. She was enjoying all the fresh air and the shops, not that she could afford to buy anything, but Grace had been very generous to her. She was able to take home a few treats for Jenny, which was all she wanted.

She reflected on how lucky she'd been on meeting Grace that day in the church hall after the bomb fell on their street. That day would be forever etched in her memory, having lost her mother, her home and her virginity all on the same night. She marvelled at the fact she was still alive and had somehow survived it all, thanks largely to Grace and Dorothea, whose kindness and compassion was something she would be forever grateful for.

During their long preambles in the fresh air, Grace and Daisy had become closer than ever. At night, they snuggled up together in the double bed in Gordon's spare room. Having plenty of time to reflect, especially after recent events which had left her for dead in a doorway, Daisy realised she couldn't let what happened to her dictate the rest of her life. She had to be strong for Jenny's sake and get on with living. She wanted to live the full life she was born to live and hoped with all her heart Howard still loved her, for she knew without a doubt she still loved him.

His face had turned black when she had told him about Jenny's abduction and when she related all the details leading up to her attack, he hadn't spoken for a full five minutes, after which he changed the subject. She resolved to remember him in her prayers tonight and ask God for his help.

Chapter Forty-Eight

"Who was that dolly bird you were speaking to last night?" asked Clifford. "Bit upmarket for you."

"Cheeky sod," laughed Bert. "No, she was American. Ruby her name was. She just came up to me asking about that Boothroyd chap. Did I know him like? So, I put her straight on that score. I said, 'Aye, are you one of them reporter people? Which newspaper do you work for?' I didn't go into details, but I left her in no doubt that he wasn't popular around here. She asked me why, so I told her about him abducting that kiddie and strangling that young lass from Blythe Wood. She wanted to know who that was so I told her she was a maid that worked for a very respectable family. Told her the young kiddie belonged to her. Her husband was killed during the war. Nice lass. I wasn't going to give her any more details like, but I said she could get a good story for her paper if she was prepared to pay up. Well, why should she get it for nothing?"

"I assume you'd had a few pints when all this took place?" laughed Clifford.

"Aye, I had that. A few more than usual actually. I must have gone out like a light. Woke up at four o'clock this afternoon on the settee. The wife gave me a right ear bashing. 'Do you realise that whilst you've been sleeping, I've completed a full shift of work. Not to mention barging around the supermarket, then queuing up at the bus stop getting wet through in the pouring rain. You'd better buck your ideas up, lad!' she barked."

"Still got your tea though, I'll bet."

"I did. Steak and kidney pie, mash and gravy. She's a good lass is our Joan. Her bark's worse than her bite."

"You don't deserve her."

"I'll have you know I was considered a good catch in my younger days."

"Aye. Well, no doubt she's realised the error of her ways. The poor deluded soul."

"Morning Eric, what's news?"

"Good morning, young Michael. Stuart's left a report on your desk. He wants you to read it. It came through late last night form the Chicago police."

"Chicago? It's got to be connected to a certain Mr Boothroyd, I take it?"

"You've got it in one. Stuart will be back in an hour, so I'd get cracking if I were you."

Mike got himself a coffee from the kitchen and sat down at his desk. He read through the report then threw the papers down. Drugs. *That would explain his aggressive behaviour*, he thought. He'd heard rumours from Raif Swift about Iain's father Tom being an occasional drug user. Recreational drugs they called it. That's probably why he'd become involved. Mike ran his fingers through his hair and took a sip of his coffee just as Stuart appeared.

"Morning boss. Anything further on this?" he asked, waving the report.

"I've just been on the phone to them. It seems he was involved in a consignment of drugs with a market price of £200,000 sterling."

Mike waited for more information.

"They've got one man in custody," Stuart continued. "He's refusing to name the ringleader but Iain's name was mentioned together with a woman called Ruby. They think she may have come here looking for him. He made off with her share of the money."

"He certainly runs true to form. That's just the sort of thing you'd expect from the likes of him."

"We'll get asking around. See if anyone's seen this American woman."

"The pub would be a good place to start," offered Mike.

"Is that a hint that you want a free lunch?" laughed Stuart.

"Who? Me? Whatever gave you that idea? But now that you mention it…" he chuckled.

"So, she was in here last night then?" Stuart leant on the bar watching Clifford pull his pint.

"Yes. Bert spoke to her. He thought she was a newspaper reporter."

"What made him think that?"

"I'm not sure. He'd had a few, by all accounts. More than a few actually, but he made his way home all right."

"Right," said Stuart, "We need to speak to Bert straight away."

"If you hang on a bit, he'll be in here soon. I've never known him miss his lunchtime pint," said Clifford. "She was a very well-dressed lady from what I could see. Nice coat, boots, smart handbag, silk scarf, expensive necklace. Someone not short of a bob or two, I'd say."

"Did Bert say what she was after?" asked Mike.

"He said she was asking about Iain Boothroyd. Wanted to know, did anyone around here know him? That sort of thing. Bert told her he wasn't popular but didn't go into details. Fancied making himself a bob or two if she wanted a good story for her paper. That was the beer talking, of course. She wasn't having any of that." Clifford didn't want to incriminate one of his best customers. He didn't know what sort of trouble this American lady was in or why they were looking for her. It could mean trouble.

He couldn't believe Iain Boothroyd would be romantically involved with her; she just wasn't his type. She was considerably older than him for a start. He then realised he didn't know what Iain's type of woman would be and couldn't imagine any woman tolerating being treated the way he treated women, but maybe he was wrong about that. Some women like to be dominated. *Takes all sorts*, he thought.

"Stuart, it's the station on the phone for you," shouted big Ada from the other side of the bar.

"Thanks, Ada." He took the call then ran back for his jacket. "Get your coat, Mike. Something urgent has occurred."

Five minutes later, they were speeding down the lane towards the edge of the town centre.

"We'll need to conduct a thorough search of the premises, Mrs Lewisham. Routine procedure," said Mike.

"Will he survive, do you think?" she asked, biting her bottom lip. "He owes me two months' rent. That's why I came knocking on his door. I knew he was still in there because I always hear him thumping down the stairs when he goes out."

"And you let yourself in with the master key?" asked Stuart.

"Yes. There was no response, so I wasn't going to let him get away with not paying any longer."

"And you found him slumped in the chair?" asked Mike, scribbling away in his notebook.

"Yes, I thought he was dead. I panicked and called an ambulance. When they came, they said he was unconscious but still alive."

"Was there anyone else in the flat at the time?" Stuart asked.

"Certainly not. I don't allow that sort of thing. I run a very respectable house here, officer," she snapped, pulling her cardigan around herself and folding her arms in indignation. "I don't want no trouble or I won't be able to re-let the room. People are funny about that sort of thing."

"Did he, by any chance, have any visitors yesterday? In particular, an American lady?"

"I didn't see anyone. Unless he sneaked her in later on. I see there's two empty cartons of what smells like curry on the kitchen drainer, together with four empty beer cans."

"Right. That will be all for now, Mrs Lewisham. We'll start the search."

* * *

"I'm putting the dinner out. Round everyone up, Raif. Where's Josh?" said Dorothea.

"He's gone to see Mr Glass. We'll put his in the oven. He might be late. They've a lot to catch up on."

"Oh, I'll be glad when Grace and Daisy get back. This cooking lark's driving me mad," said Dotty, mashing the potatoes. "This gravy's gone lumpy again, I'm afraid."

"Give it to me, I'll stir it. I can hear someone coming up the path now. It might be him."

"Sorry, I'm late," breezed Josh, washing his hands in the sink. "Big news," he declared.

"What is it?" said Raif and Dotty in unison.

"Iain Boothroyd's in hospital. He's been poisoned. Cyanide. He's had a stomach pump or something. He's survived somehow but he's very weak. There's talk of him being transferred to some sort of a hospice to recuperate."

"Cyanide?" gasped Dorothea. "Goodness. Do they know who's responsible?"

"No, but there was an American woman asking about him in the pub yesterday. They're trying to trace her."

"American, you say?" said Raif, stirring vigorously to try to rescue the gravy. "His father died during a business trip to America, didn't he? It was rumoured that Iain might have gone with him. I wonder what occurred. He's been up to no good, I'll bet. If that woman has come all the way over here looking for him…"

"Stuart wouldn't divulge any more details but I think you're right, Uncle Raif. He was up to something. It's like something out of a murder mystery film, isn't it? Are we having sausages? Goody! My favourite."

"Celia, there's a police constable in the lounge to see you," said John. "I'll make some tea. I think he's got some news about Iain."

"Oh dear. What's he been up to now?" groaned Celia, putting down her shopping bag on the kitchen table. Her heart was thumping when she entered the sitting room. "Sorry to keep you waiting, officer. Is everything all right?"

"I'm afraid I've some bad news, Mrs Boothroyd. Your son Iain has been poisoned. They seem to think it was cyanide. He's in hospital. He's pulled through the worst of it and they think he'll be all right eventually after plenty of rest. They're transferring him to a convalescent home. Here's the address." He handed her a sheet of paper.

John entered with the tea tray and started to pour it whilst Celia studied the address.

"Cyanide, did you say?" asked John, handing the constable his tea.

"That's right."

"What on earth happened? Do they know who tried to poison him? I presume he didn't take it of his own accord. It wasn't a suicide attempt, was it?"

"We're not sure of anything as yet, but it wasn't a suicide attempt according to Iain. He's not saying much but we're trying to trace an American lady that was seen in the area asking about him."

He might well keep quiet, thought John, but didn't say so. He'd been up to no good again, he would bet his life on it. For Celia's sake, he didn't make any comment.

"I think we should go and see him," said Celia, folding the sheet of paper and placing it behind the clock on the mantelpiece. "I haven't spoken to my son for quite some time, officer. We had a bit of a falling out you see when his father and I parted company."

"I think that would be a good idea, my dear," said John patting her hand. "We need a long talk with him. See if we can heal the rift in some way. He's obviously a very angry young man with a lot of old scores to settle. We need to get to the bottom of it."

"Believe me, I've tried all that in the past, John. He's so headstrong. Takes after his father. He idolised his father."

"Pardon me for asking, Mrs Boothroyd, but did your son ever take drugs?" asked the policeman.

"His father did occasionally, although never in front of me. It's only the rumours that got back to me via the grapevine. You know how it is when you mix in certain circles. He used to go away a lot on business. I wasn't always invited to go with him, but I never suspected Iain for a single moment. It wouldn't surprise me if his father introduced him to them. Thinking back, they're both aggressive. I often wondered why they were like that. Is my son in trouble then?"

"We're not clear on anything at the moment. We're still conducting enquiries."

After the policeman had left, Celia sat staring at the hearth, lost in thought. John came back in after seeing the constable out.

"I'm not standing for any nonsense from him," she said, decidedly. "He either straightens himself out and starts behaving like a decent human being or I'll not have anything more to do with him. And I'm definitely not giving him any money."

"Let's see what he has to say for himself first. Perhaps this will be the wake-up call that he needs." John put a reassuring hand on her shoulder.

Somehow Celia doubted it, but didn't voice her thoughts out loud.

Howard was in the kitchen helping Bhutan and Magda get the evening meal ready. Raif and Dorothea had gone to the train station in the jeep to collect Grace and Daisy. His heart was as light as a feather at the thought of seeing Daisy again. She'd only been away for a few days but he'd missed her terribly.

Iris and Meg were setting the table in the dining room. Josh was at the kitchen table studying the compass Aubrey had given to Howard. It was eighteenth century and quite rare. Sotheby's in London had offered Howard a hundred pounds for it but he refused to part with it. He wanted to pass it on to his own son, if he was ever lucky enough to have one.

Mr Glass had given Josh his own Royal Nautical Marine compass, which he reassured him was still fully functional. He looked up suddenly and blurted out, "Gosh! I forgot, there's to be a wedding next Friday. Edna and James are getting married. We're all to be at the church for two thirty, then there's tea and cakes in the vestry.

They're not having a reception. Edna's just inviting a few close friends. We, being the lucky ones, are all invited. Here's the invitation," he said, pulling a crumpled envelope out of his pocket.

"Good grief, Josh. Look at the state of this. Never mind," laughed Howard taking it from him. "I'll let Aunty Dot open it when she gets back. It should make for some lively discussion around the dinner table." He stared at the envelope and was lost temporarily in the moment. If only it was himself and Daisy getting married.

Chapter Forty-Nine

Celia and John sat in the reception area of the solicitor's office. She'd promised Mrs Lewisham she would try to get her the rent money that Iain owed her. She also wanted to know what the situation was regarding her late husband's estate and what exactly was going on with her errant son.

"Mr Royce will see you now, Mrs Boothroyd," announced the secretary.

"Good morning, Mrs Boothroyd, take a seat. Sorry to keep you waiting like that. I took an urgent call and couldn't get away."

"That's quite all right. We're not in any hurry." She introduced John, then they sat down in the comfortable leather wing chairs. "I'd like to know the situation regarding my late husband's estate. The last time I was here you mentioned he left a lot of debts. What exactly is the situation?" She tried to sound firm and forthright, keeping her voice steady and measured. "My son is ill at the moment, you see, and I know he was due in court this week. He owes the tax people a lot of money but I'm afraid he won't be fit enough to attend. Can we get the date adjourned until he's in a more fit state to attend?"

"Ah, yes. He came to see me quite recently about all that. We had a long chat, as a matter of fact. I'll try to explain the situation as clearly as I can. Firstly, your husband's estate has finally been settled. The sale of the house brought in sufficient funds to settle his debts and pay our fees. Now, the balance of his estate won't be enough to pay your son's entire tax bill, I'm afraid. However, we can make a part-payment which Iain has instructed us to do."

"He has?" gasped Celia in surprise.

"Yes. He was quite adamant that he intended to pay everything he owes. He realises he'll have to declare himself bankrupt, of course. The tax people have been informed and the court case has been adjourned. He's convinced that he can start again and earn enough money to stay solvent this time. He blamed his business failing on the war. A bad time for us all, I'm afraid."

"Indeed," said Celia who was still finding it difficult to come to terms with this change in her son. Perhaps she didn't know him as well as she thought she did. "He owes a couple of months' rent at his lodgings. Can we get something done about that? I'd hate for him to be homeless."

"That would be for a Mrs Edith Lewisham, I take it? We've already dealt with that, there's something in the post for her. She should receive it in a day or two and may I offer my regards as to your son making a full recovery. Everyone deserves a fresh start in my opinion. We all make mistakes, especially when we're young. Lack of judgement. I know my two boys did in their younger days. They're all right now though, thank goodness. Would you like some tea?" He smiled kindly at them and asked his secretary to bring refreshments.

Celia thought back to her own lack of judgement in marrying Tom and wondered how different her life would have been had she chosen a different path, but no, she wouldn't have met John. He was the best thing that had ever happened to her.

Jenny had insisted on coming in the car with Raif and Dorothea to collect Grace and her mother. She was on the verge of tears and felt totally lost without her mother at her side. Just knowing she wasn't there shook her confidence. She felt sad and lonely, even though there was a house full of people. If it wasn't for Bella and Willow, she would have broken down completely. She'd counted off the days on her calendar and had woken up with renewed energy this morning, knowing today was the day everything would be back to normal.

Uncle Raif had instructed them to wait in the car until the train arrived at the platform as it was raining quite heavily. Jenny pressed her face up to the car window, her little heart beating like a drum.

Dotty knew there would be tears at any moment. "She'll be here soon, darling," she soothed, ruffling her hair. "We've checked, there's no delay. The train's on time."

"It's here!" shouted Raif, jumping out of the car. "You two stay here whilst I get the bags. No sense in us all getting wet through." He headed towards the platform, disappearing from sight momentarily.

Three minutes later, he was back, carrying two small cases, followed by Grace and Daisy in floral summer dresses and no coats.

"It was sunny when we left," laughed Grace, making a dash for the car.

Jenny jumped into her mother's arms and hugged her so tightly she could hardly breathe.

"Get back in the car, child, you'll be soaked," said Grace.

"Anything so far?" asked Mike, checking the floorboards under a rug. He pressed and prodded the wood for any signs of looseness. *It's not unknown for people to hide money beneath the floorboards*, he thought.

"Nothing. If he was doing drugs, there's no trace of any here. I'll check the bathroom," said Stuart, switching on the light.

He checked the bathroom cabinet above the wash basin then turned to the wooden panelling which housed the hot water tank. He unscrewed the front panel and shone his torch inside. There was an empty plastic bag wedged at the back of the tank. *Had this been the bag that contained the money*, he wondered, *and had Ruby done a search after she administered the poison?* If so, she could have made off with the money. Half of which was technically hers anyway. Or had the landlady herself done a search, found the money and decided to keep it? There were endless possibilities, all of which had no answers right now. Iain was obviously good at covering his tracks but had certainly met his match in Ruby – if that was indeed her real name, which he doubted. The chances of tracking her down were slim. She could be anywhere.

* * *

Bert was starting to get nervous. Stuart and Mike were firing questions at him, most of which he couldn't answer as he'd been drunk at the time. He did give them a description of what she looked like and what she was wearing. He never forgot a face, especially of an attractive woman.

"Another pint?" asked Mike.

"I'll not say no," said Bert, wishing he'd kept his mouth shut about revealing so much information regarding Iain Boothroyd. Was he responsible for the lad now languishing in hospital, fighting for his life? He started to sweat and was feeling distinctly uncomfortable. "I assume that foul play is surrounding your enquiries?"

"I can't reveal too much, but yes, you're right. Foul play is certainly involved. The pair of them are up to no good. It's evidence and proof that we're after, without which we can't manifest a conviction."

"I see. Hence all these questions. Heck, Stuart. Had I known all that I'd have kept my mouth shut. I'd had a few at the time, I don't mind admitting."

"Don't make yourself uncomfortable," said Stuart. "If it hadn't been you, she'd have got the information from somebody else."

Mike arrived with the drinks and set them down on the table. "Did Ruby say where she was going when she left the pub?" he asked.

"No. She thanked me and smiled sweetly, saying I'd been most helpful. She didn't take me up on my offer of a story, thank goodness. What a twit I'd have looked if she had."

"She's not a reporter. Not that we know of anyway."

"I don't know what made me jump to that conclusion. Must have been the beer."

"What time was it when she left?"

"Just after ten o'clock. About ten minutes past. I watched her as she went through the door out into the street. She turned right towards the train station. Not that there'd be any trains at that time of night, mind."

"We'll check," said Mike, scribbling away in his notepad.

* * *

"Looks like this one's dead in the water," said Mike as they climbed into the car to head towards the railway station.

"We'll make our way over to the hospital again. Iain wasn't very talkative last time, but he's had a chance to recover and might feel more like talking."

Mike looked at Stuart and said, "You're determined to make me smile, boss," he laughed. "When has Iain Boothroyd ever been talkative?"

"We can hope. He might slip up. They all do eventually."

"Not him."

"This looks a nice place, Celia," said John, swinging the car into the car park. The grounds were extensive with bushes and trees surrounding a well-kept lawn with a border of rose bushes. They made their way towards the main entrance and climbed the stone steps towards the reception area.

"Yes, it certainly is very nice. Too nice for the likes of him."

"Now, now. Don't go in with that attitude. We don't know what state he's in. We'll play it by ear."

"But honestly, John… well, I mean just look at the way he's behaved. I'm ashamed to say he's my son. I admit I've failed miserably as a mother. Abducting his own child, attempting to strangle Daisy and leaving her for dead in a doorway. What kind of monster does things like that?"

"It could have been the drugs he was taking. They do terrible things to people. They alter the structure of your mind and emotions."

"We don't know if he was on drugs though, do we?"

"He might benefit from seeing some form of counsellor."

"You mean a psychiatrist?"

"I suppose so. It couldn't do any harm. We could talk to the staff in here and see what they think. They might be able to help."

"To be perfectly honest with you, John, I think he's beyond help. Before I left Tom, I tried very hard to get through to Iain about the way he was behaving, but it all fell on deaf ears. The blueprint had been set in stone."

"He'll have to learn to re-programme himself then, either that or he'll spend the rest of his days in prison. If he carries on the way he has been doing, that's where he'll end up, Celia. Rest assured, they'll catch up with him eventually. The chickens will come home to roost."

"The problem with Iain is, he gets bored very easily. Normal life is too mundane for him. It's not exciting enough. He likes to live his life on a knife edge."

"Then there's no hope for him, I'm afraid," said John.

Chapter Fifty

"There are more letters here for you, Josh. You must have been very popular in London," mused Grace, handing him his post.

"I didn't do too badly, Grace. Aunty Dot says I can invite a few of them down for the weekend occasionally. Some of Sam's art friends are coming next week. Hilary's art studio opens on Monday. Sam's really excited."

"Yes, we're all going to the opening. I'm looking forward to seeing all Sam's work."

"I've seen most of the paintings and drawings. You won't believe how good they are. He's definitely got 'the eye', as they say."

"There's a letter here for Howard. I think it might be his exam results. Look at the postmark," she handed him the envelope to examine.

"It is! I'll take it up to him now." Josh shot upstairs with the letter and shook Howard awake. "Howard, wake up. Your exam results have arrived!"

A few seconds later, Beth and Selina appeared in the doorway with eager faces. Sam sat bolt upright and switched on his bedside lamp. Howard groaned and turned over, then grappled in his bedside drawer for his spectacles and put them on. Taking the envelope from Josh, he slowly opened it and spent several minutes studying the contents.

"Well?" asked Selina who was practically holding her breath.

He looked up and muttered, "Well…"

"Come on, Howard, tell us," shouted Sam impatiently. "Don't keep us in suspense."

"I've got a first. An honours degree. Would you just believe it?"

"Oh Howard," shrieked Selina and Beth in unison. They rushed towards him, hugging him in turn.

"Congratulations, brother. You so deserve this. You never stopped working and it's paid off," said Josh, feeling immensely proud and stressed in equal measures, for he now felt under even more pressure to pass his own exam. *Trust Howard to outshine the lot of us*, he thought.

"Well done, Howard. We're all so proud of you. I'll go and tell the others," said Sam, shooting down the stairs two at a time.

Grace and Daisy were at the range stirring the porridge and brewing the tea when he broke the news to them.

"Dotty, this calls for a celebration. We'll roast a chicken and make a trifle," said Raif, making his way upstairs to shake Howard's hand. "We're very proud of you, Howard. Well done."

"All those nights in the library with Aunty Dot paid off," laughed Josh sitting on the end of the bed. They were all in their dressing gowns, including Jenny, Meg and Iris.

"What's going on?" asked Harry, appearing in the doorway.

"It's Howard's exam results," said Meg, smiling at him. "He's passed. He's now the proud owner of a first class honours degree in English."

"Well done, son," beamed Harry. He was loving his new family and felt like a different man since moving into Blythe Wood. The new catalogue had arrived yesterday and he was looking forward to being on the road next week distributing them to prospective buyers and fashion houses. He just hoped his car, which wasn't new, would stand up to all the extra mileage.

Belinda had worked hard on the production of the new catalogue, including some of the items Beth, Selina and Josh had produced for their coursework. She had washed and ironed them all and got a model from an agency in London to model them. The results were very impressive, giving it a fresh modern look.

"Come on, everyone. Breakfast is ready. Let's get the day started," ushered Raif, herding everyone out.

Daisy remained standing in the doorway, smiling fit to burst. Jenny was bouncing on Howard's bed.

"What's a first?" she asked. "Is that good?"

"Good?" said Daisy. "It's only the highest possible rating, darling. You are looking at a genius."

"I'm not a genius, Daisy, but I did work hard. When I think back to all those nights in the library with Aunty Dot, poring over the history and geography books, some of it must have gone in," he laughed. Pausing for a few moments, he turned to Daisy and asked, "Do you and Jenny fancy a turn around the park? You know, like we used to?" His heart was beating faster than usual in case she refused.

"Oh yes, please," shouted Jenny. "What do you say, Mummy?"

"I say that would be lovely, Howard. Thank you. You'd better get dressed first though," she laughed.

Iain arrived back at his lodgings around lunchtime. He was still feeling weak but the doctor in charge gave him the all clear and discharged him. Deciding to spend a week in bed to get his strength back would also give him time to think about what to do with his life.

He made his way up the stairs and locked his door behind him and wedged a table behind the door just in case his landlady decided to use her own key. He didn't want her snooping around.

Dumping his things on the bed, he made his way over to the bathroom window and hitched up the curtain. Using a screwdriver, he levered the loose brick in the corner and slowly pulled it away from the wall. Inserting his hand into the gap, he felt for the package containing the money and counted it carefully. It was all there. Placing the package back into the cavity, he replaced the brick and lowered the curtain.

He soaked in a hot bath and put on clean pyjamas. There was hardly any food in the fridge but he found some ham, cheese and pickle which he put on a tray with some crackers. He filled the kettle and made himself a mug of tea and took it into the bedroom.

Sitting on the bed, he contemplated his next move. He knew he couldn't stay in Somerset. The locals wouldn't stand for it. But where to go? What to do? His mother had read him the riot act when she visited him at the nursing home. Most of it was perfectly justified as he knew he hadn't been a model son. Lying in the hospice had given him time for reflection. He'd made a complete mess of everything, of that he was certainly guilty.

Having made a solemn promise to his mother not to touch drugs anymore, he realised he'd wasted far too much money on them over the years anyway. There was no doubt in his mind that the poisoning was down to Ruby. Having refused to comply with her wishes to join her in the States, she'd extracted her revenge. He wasn't going to be beholden to anyone, least of all to a woman years older than himself who held the purse strings. His life wouldn't be his own. She was also one of his father's cast-offs and he should never have entertained her in the first place, but she was easy prey and good fun – for a short while. They'd had fun together in Chicago and he felt guilty about cheating her out of her half of the money but he knew if he was ever going to make a fresh start in life, he'd need the whole amount.

The insurance company had let him down over the fire at the factory and his father had left a mountain of debts which ate away most of his estate. The shocking truth of his father having no liquid cash shocked him and he realised he must have been living way beyond his means for years.

He sipped his tea and buttered some crackers. The cheese and pickle tasted surprisingly good with the ham. Making his mother proud was not on his list of priorities. He didn't feel he owed her anything, not after the way she'd upped sticks and walked out like that.

Letting his mind wander, he pictured himself working on a sheep farm in the Australian outback, far away from civilisation, enjoying the sunshine and the outdoor life, answerable to no one. *Yes, that would suit me very well indeed,* he thought.

Raif was in the kitchen carving the chickens, having roasted three, as they were now a family of seventeen. Luckily, they had ten bedrooms and several bathrooms, so there was room for everyone. Blythe Wood stood in quite a considerable amount of land which these days was mainly used to grow fruit and vegetables. There was a small rose garden which ran the full length of the house at one side. It was where all the family spent most of their time when they were at leisure, weather permitting. There was a general air of jollity about the place since the children had returned. The house was once more filled with noise, laughter and friendly banter, not to mention the clutter which now rested on nearly every available surface.

Selina had fully recovered from her influenza but Beth still wasn't her usual self. She'd taken to sitting alone in the lounge staring at the portrait of Raif's grandmother which took pride of place above the large open fireplace. It was where Dorothea found her.

"The meal's nearly ready, Beth. Are you all right, darling?" she soothed, sitting herself down on the sofa and plumping the large squishy cushions. She knew the only thing that would set the lass right would be the exam results telling her she'd passed.

"I understand how you feel, really I do," Dorothea continued. "My parents were very strict with me. Not so much with Meg and Iris but I was the eldest so I was expected to set a good example by doing well. Failing my degree wasn't an option, you see. A lot was resting on it and believe me when I say that I felt the pressure. They were a pompous pair, I'm sorry to say."

"Did you get on with them?" Beth asked, suddenly snapping out of her reverie.

"No, not particularly," she laughed. "Especially my mother. We never agreed on anything. My father was better in a sense. He was a bit more worldly, although they were both blinkered in some respects. Oh, I don't blame them really. It wasn't their fault. It was the way in which they were brought up. I did love them both dearly but I always felt that I'd let them down in some way. No matter what I did, it was never good enough. There was no pleasing them."

"But why? Why on earth should they think you'd let them down? I don't understand."

"That's what I'm trying to make you realise, Beth. You must live your own life, irrespective of the fact that it doesn't meet with your parents' approval. It's your life. Live it to the full, as you see fit."

Beth remained pensive for a while, staring at the portrait above the mantelpiece before asking, "Did you see much of Raif's grandparents?"

"I only met his grandmother once. She didn't approve of me. I think they had grand things planned for Raif, being the only boy in the family, but his sister Mildred said it wouldn't have made any difference who Raif brought home, they wouldn't have measured up to their expectations. The queen herself excepting. I got on a little better with his father, but he too expected big things of his son. My parents were the same with me, so I understood. I tried my best to win them round but after a while I realised that I was wasting my time. There were some long faces at our wedding, I can tell you, Beth."

"Didn't it bother you?"

"A little. I thought it would get better with time, but it never did. During the wedding reception, one of Raif's aunts came to speak to me and said she was glad Raif had chosen me for his wife. She thought we were so well suited and were a perfect match. I agreed with her, of course," she laughed.

"Aunty Dot, can I ask you something?"

"Of course."

"If I don't choose to get married… I mean, if nobody asks me, can I stay here?"

"Why, Beth darling, of course you can. This is your home now. There will always be a place for you here, no matter what happens, although I don't think you'll be waiting long for someone to come along. You're prettier than I ever was. Now, no more of this melancholy. Come along, dinner's ready."

The following Saturday, Beth came down to breakfast to discover the postman had just been. There were three brown envelopes. One for herself, one for Selina and one for Josh, all postmarked London.

"Our results," shrieked Selina, shooting out of her chair and pouncing on her envelope. She handed Beth and Josh theirs and then without hesitation, tore open the envelope. Everyone stopped eating and waited with baited breath. Beth's face turned bright red and she ran from the room without opening hers.

"Well?" asked Josh, whose eyes were fixed on Selina's face for signs. He was nervous about opening his own envelope so he could sympathise with Beth. He knew exactly how she felt and could feel all his confidence draining away. If Selina had failed, he knew Beth and himself would have no chance.

John hadn't spoken for over half an hour and just concentrated on manoeuvring the car through all the traffic. It was only when they stopped for lunch that Celia broke the silence.

"So, what do you think, John? Tell me honestly," she said, pouring out the tea into two china cups. "This is a lovely little cafe," she added, looking around her at the chintzy decor.

John helped himself to sugar and stirred his tea before saying, "Well, I don't think he was even listening to a word you said. That's the impression I got."

"It's like I said, the die is cast. I had hoped that being so ill might make him less aggressive somehow, but I was wrong. All that time for reflection, not a glimmer of remorse. Oh John, I'm so ashamed, not to mention annoyed. My head's thumping."

"Thankfully he's old enough to take care of himself now. Whatever mess he's got himself into, he'll have to seek advice and get himself sorted out."

"That's where I feel so guilty. Should I be doing more for him?"

"The only thing he needs help with is an endless supply of money to fund his extravagant lifestyle."

"I've got a feeling I'll never see him again after today. Don't ask me why, it's just a gut feeling I've got. If only he'd shown an ounce of regret for all that he's done, I could have forgiven him, but he wasn't sorry. Not one little bit." She began to weep silently into her napkin for a good few minutes before dabbing her eyes and apologising.

"I thought it best to let you cry. Get it out of your system."

"I didn't leave him any forwarding address for him to contact me. Should I have done?"

"He knows the solicitor handling Tom's estate will contact you on his behalf if he needs to. Let him do that if he gets desperate."

"What will he get up to next, John? I'm so worried about him."

The waitress arrived with their sandwiches, which they ate in silence before walking back to the car for the journey home.

Chapter Fifty-One

The first person to arrive at the art studio was Mrs Bray, alongside the headmaster Lionel. Hilary and Gerry met them at the door and handed them both a glass of cider. Next to arrive were Edna and Jim, followed closely by Mr Glass and Kathleen. Within half an hour, the place was simply rocking. They ran out of glasses and plates twice.

Dorothea and Raif arrived in the jeep with Grace, Daisy and Jerry whilst Bob, Iris Meg and Harry jumped into the car. The others all piled into the back of the van which Alan drove, having picked up Susan and her mother along the way.

"It's all very impressive, Hilary," gushed Mrs Bray. "It's beautifully kitted out. You must be so proud."

"Thank you. We've worked very hard on it."

"Sam's artwork is incredible. What a talented young man he is. I never realised. I have to take my hat off to Dorothea for the way she's guided those children. When I think of the sorry state they were in when they first arrived. Dear me. But look at them all now."

"Yes, I agree. They all passed their degrees, you know. Howard got a first."

"So I heard. I couldn't be more proud. What a testament to our school, don't you think, Lionel?" she said turning towards the headmaster who was on his third glass of cider and looking very pleased with himself.

"What a turnout, Hilary. The entire village must be here. Even Cyril and Mary are here. Cyril cancelled the afternoon service at the church so they could attend. They both said they wouldn't have missed this for the world."

Mrs Bray thought it was probably the attraction of the free alcohol more than anything. They both liked a drink and neither of them appeared to have a stop button. She glanced around the room and saw Dr Mattison and his wife Ruth talking to Bhutan and Magda. Behind them, Ivy and Alf were deep in conversation with Stuart and his assistant Mike, who had his arm around a very attractive young lady.

"Who's that young lass with Mike?" she asked.

"That's Belinda, his fiancée. She's a book illustrator from London. She works for Dorothea and Raif and does Howard's book covers and illustrations. Clever girl by all that I've heard. Also, do you see that young man over there?" Hilary said pointing to Alan, who was escorting Susan around the art gallery. "That's Beth's brother. He also works for Gerry and Raif now. The young girl is his fiancée."

"Really?" said Mrs Bray, straining her neck to see over the sea of heads. "There's going to be a lot of weddings. Cyril will have his hands full."

"It's Edna and James' wedding next week. Are you both planning to attend?" said Hilary.

"Oh, I expect so," said Mrs Bray. "How about you, Lionel?"

"I'll be there. I've had my invitation. We've known Edna for a good number of years, haven't we, Elsie?" he said turning towards Mrs Bray, who was quite taken aback as he didn't normally use her Christian name in public.

"Er, yes," she faltered. "It must be getting on for twenty-five years, or thereabouts."

Josh was escorting Selina and Beth to the refreshment table when he spotted Rebecca and her mother at the far end of the studio. *I don't want to speak to her*, he thought, *or her mother for that matter.* He deliberately ushered the girls behind a huge landscape painting so they wouldn't be seen. The three of them had lost sight of the rest of the family and secretly enjoyed a glass of cider each. They were of age now, but they didn't want to be seen consuming alcohol in front of Howard, who never indulged himself, due to the situation regarding his mother's death. The poor woman had ended her days on Earth earlier than she should have done, due to her addiction.

"Grab one of these, girls, before they all disappear," ushered Josh, handing them a plate of hot pastries which Hilary had just taken out of the oven.

"Let's eat them outside in the garden," said Selina. "There's a little gazebo type thing over on the far side."

They headed outside just in time to see Stuart and Mike dashing for their cars.

"Where are they going in such a hurry?" asked Beth. "They've probably had a call from the station. It looks to be important, judging by the speed they were going."

"I'm sorry to interrupt your afternoon, gentlemen," said the superintendent, "But I thought I'd better update you on the latest developments from across the pond. The coroner's report has been dissected with a fine-tooth comb. It seems more likely than not, that Tom Boothroyd didn't die of natural causes, as was first thought."

"He didn't?" Mike was trying to find a spare chair but decided to remain standing with his back to the window.

"No indeed. They think he was murdered."

"Presumably the heart attack was triggered by an excess of something in his bloodstream then?" asked Stuart, helping himself to a biscuit off the plate in front of him.

"You presume correct. Cyanide."

"His son was also poisoned recently with cyanide, but he survived," Mike reminded them.

"You do well to make that comparison. There's more to this than we thought. Tom Boothroyd also had a… whatever you'd call it… a 'liaison' with this Ruby. It went on for several years according to sources in the know. She considered herself his 'common law wife' even though he had a wife in England. No doubt he spun her a tale about the state of his marriage, but he also named her in his will as the sole recipient of his entire estate upon the unlikely death of his son."

"Ah-ha," said Stuart, beginning to get the full picture at last.

"What's the background on this Ruby?" Mike was curious to learn more about her.

"She's got form, having been married and widowed seven times, each husband dying of natural causes according to the death certificates. Ruby isn't her real name of course. She's Italian by birth. Arianna Simonetti."

"Seems too much of a coincidence to me," said Stuart. "Are they sure they all died of natural causes?"

"Exactly my thoughts too. They were all gentlemen of wealth and considerable means, if you get my drift. I want you to get back in touch with the solicitor that handled Tom Boothroyd's estate. She may be unaware that Iain survived. That's assuming she was responsible, of course, but it seems very likely."

"Have we time for a coffee before we head off to London?" asked Mike hopefully, having missed out on his free glass of cider at the art studio.

"I'll get Graham to check that out. He's nearer than us. I don't want to waste all that time travelling only to hit a brick wall. We might be barking up the wrong tree entirely. We'll have that coffee then head back to Iain's lodgings. We need to find out what happened to all that money he made in Chicago. We must have missed something. He wouldn't dare put it in the bank. It's got to be in that flat somewhere."

"Oh, it's you," said Mrs Lewisham. "You'd better come in." She ushered them into the lounge and sat down. "Take a seat, gentlemen. What is it this time?"

Stuart noted that every surface gleamed with a high shine. She was certainly a very clean woman. Without giving too much away, he briefly explained they were still missing vital information to aid their enquiries.

"He won't take kindly to you conducting another search," she said, lighting a cigarette and tossing the match into the fire, which blazed in the grate.

"We do have a search warrant," said Mike, "Is he in?"

"He's not been out of his room since he came back from the hospital. I offered to get him some food shopping, but he said he'd manage." She disappeared into the kitchen and returned with a set of keys, which she placed in her apron pocket.

They followed her up the stairs and waited whilst she knocked on his door. They waited a few minutes before she shouted, "Iain, it's the police. They'd like a word with you."

After a few more minutes, she turned to face them and said, "He might be fast asleep." She knocked again, louder this time and called his name again, "Iain, it's Mrs Lewisham. You've got visitors. They'd like a word. It's important." Still there was no movement from within and the door remained firmly shut.

"Open up if you would be so kind, Mrs Lewisham," ordered Stuart. There was a strange smell on entering the room, which Stuart recognised immediately. It was a smell you never forgot in the police profession. They made their way into the bedroom to find Iain slumped at an awkward angle against his pillows.

Stuart shot forward and tried for a pulse. After a few seconds, he said, "He's dead."

"Oh my God. Are you sure, officer?" said Mrs Lewisham, wringing her hands.

"Don't touch anything. I'll contact the station. We need to get our team out here."

"Use the telephone in my hallway. It's on the left." She sat on the nearest chair; the colour having drained out of her face. "What do you think happened?" she asked Mike, once Stuart made his way downstairs.

"Impossible to say at this stage. He's been dead for quite a while I'd estimate."

"He's so young. What a terrible waste of a life. Not that I

particularly liked him, mind. He could be aggressive in his manner, if you know what I mean. When he first came here, it was three months before he paid me any rent money, you know. I felt sorry for him. He spun me a tale of hardship, like they all do, but I wouldn't have thrown him out. I don't like to see anyone on the streets with nowhere to go, it's not right. I'll go downstairs and make us a cup of tea," she offered.

"That would be a good idea," said Mike, who knew it would be some time before they could get back to the station.

Chapter Fifty-Two

"This porridge has gone lumpy. It's been stood too long. Where is everyone?" said Grace. Breakfast always took place around the big oak table in the kitchen, which everyone preferred because it was warm and cosy.

"Jenny's in the yard spraying the cats. It keeps the fleas at bay. She really looks after those cats. She brushes them and feeds them. I dread anything happening to one of them," laughed Daisy. "Meg and Harry have gone for a walk with Iris and Bob. Bob reckons he's put weight on since he was demobbed."

"I can't see how that's happened. Not with our measly rations," Grace laughed, adding more milk to the porridge. "It's more likely to be lack of exercise, if you ask me."

Daisy thought of all the running around she did on a daily basis, running up and down the stairs with dust pans and brushes and armfuls of bed linen. *No chance of me putting on weight*, she mused. But she didn't mind any of it. It was worth it to be able to live in a beautiful house like Blythe Wood with people she loved. The only break she got was when typing up Howard's scripts and notes, a task which she shared with Grace. It was the only respite they got from the routine housework.

"Good morning ladies," shouted Bhutan from the hallway.

"Ah, at last. Where is everyone?" asked Grace, on the verge of getting vexed. "This porridge won't be any use if it stands much longer."

"I'm having breakfast with Doctor Mattison this morning. He wants to discuss a few things. Magda overslept, she's just dressing."

"Josh has gone to see Mr Glass, as usual," said Daisy. "Sam left half an hour ago. He has his breakfast with Hilary at the gallery most days now. It gives them a chance to plan their day. I've no idea where Howard and the girls are."

They could hear Magda telling the girls to get a move on. Raif came down the stairs just as the post dropped on the mat. There was a letter marked "confidential" which he tore open to discover a solicitor's letter informing him that Mildred's estate had now been settled. He was the sole recipient of her entire estate. He showed the letter to Dorothea.

"Was her little flat rented?" she asked.

"Yes, she didn't own much in the way of possessions, poor girl. Not that she needed much. Dad left everything to her when he died, being a spinster with no man in her life."

"That was thoughtful of him. So, I don't want to… I mean, are we rich?"

Raif laughed heartily before replying, "Hardly, but we can breathe a little easier for a while. The business will take time to get going properly but we're making steady progress. This will cushion us a bit."

"Breakfast," barked Grace, hollering up the stairs.

"Sorry, Gracie," said Dorothea.

"Bad news, is it?" she ventured, on seeing the brown envelope in Raif's hand. In her book, brown envelopes meant trouble. The ones her George got were anyway. Usually because of unpaid utility bills with the threat of being cut off.

"No, just that Mildred's estate has finally been settled."

"Oh, I'm so glad. Nothing became of that gentleman who contested the will then?"

"No. Legally, he hadn't a leg to stand on. One of Mildred's close associates said he was a known opportunist. You have to be so careful these days."

Josh came thundering up the path and burst into the kitchen at full pelt.

"About time you showed up, lad. Where on earth have you been all this time?" said Grace.

"High drama, Aunty Grace. What do you think has happened? You'll never believe it."

"What is it, Josh?" asked Raif.

"Iain Boothroyd's dead," he shouted.

Daisy dropped all the breakfast bowls, which hit the floor with an almighty crash.

"Dead?" said Grace and Dorothea in unison. "Are you sure? How do you know? Who told you?"

"Aunty Kath, Stuart and Mike found him yesterday afternoon. I knew something was up when they dashed out of the art gallery yesterday after taking that phone call from the station."

"I'm so sorry about the bowls, Dotty," said Daisy sheepishly, not knowing whether to be happy or sad at the news. A range of emotions ran through her body. No more fear of being attacked. No more fear at having to look over her shoulder every time she left the house. No more fear of Jenny being abducted outside the school gates.

"What happened to him, Josh? How did he die?" asked Raif. "Did he commit suicide or was he killed?"

"There's to be an inquest but they seem to think he was murdered."

"Oh no," cried Dorothea. "How awful. Who would do such a thing?"

"They're looking for some American lady that was seen in the vicinity a few days ago. Kath didn't know any more."

Daisy could feel her face burning bright red. She busied herself sweeping up the shards of broken crockery. She now realised she'd somehow have to break the news to Jenny that her father was dead. The sound of heavy footsteps descending the stairs broke the silence. Beth, Selina, Magda and Howard stood in the doorway.

"We heard an almighty crash. Is everything all right?" they asked.

It was lunchtime the following day before Mrs Lewisham was able to start cleaning Iain's room. She opened all the windows and stripped the bed. The house had been full of people coming and going all morning but finally she got the all clear from Mike to go in and start cleaning.

"I'll not find it easy to re-let this room after what's happened," she grumbled. "Who's going to want to sleep in a bed that someone was bumped off… When word gets around the village, as it surely will, I'll be all but finished."

"Any plans to retire, Mrs Lewisham?" Mike hoped he didn't sound too impertinent. He wasn't sure how old she was, but by his estimation she wouldn't see seventy again.

"Well, I've thought about it but…"

"Where would you go?"

"I have a sister in Hampshire. She's struggling a bit with her arthritis. Her husband died recently. He was a workaholic. Wouldn't retire, no doubt you know the type."

"What happened to him?" asked Mike, sipping his third cup of tea that morning.

"They were at school together. Courted all through their high school days, eventually married. No children. He started off with a stall on the market selling sheets and pillowcases, that sort of thing. Then he had a little shop selling children's wear. They sold that and he opened a cycle shop. It did very well and they bought a beautiful bungalow. He worked all hours to keep it afloat. One night, he didn't come home for his tea, so she went to the shop and it was locked. Luckily, she had the spare set of keys with her and when she opened up, she found him slumped over the desk with a pen in his hand as though he was doing his books. He'd had a heart attack. Literally worked himself to death. That's what'll happen to me if I'm not careful."

Belinda ordered herself a cup of tea and a toasted teacake and sat in the window. Having finally got the layout of the town sorted out, she could find her way around with ease. The sun was shining through the window, giving the whole cafe a warm glow. She threw off her jacket just as Chris brought her order.

"You look a bit off today, Chris. Is everything all right? You're not unwell, are you? You're normally so cheerful," she laughed.

Chris sat down at the table opposite Belinda with a sigh. "Oh sorry, take no notice of me. I'm just a bit fed up. We all are."

"Why? Has something occurred?"

"It's that landlord of ours. He's increased the rent three times in the past twelve months. It's eating away all our profit. It's hardly worth it."

"Is he allowed to do that?"

"Probably not, but he's already done it. We complained, of course, but he said nobody was going to stop him and he could charge what he liked. He wasn't very polite about it either. He's a rogue."

"There's a lot of it about, Chris. Practically everybody you speak to is on the fiddle these days. Why don't you do something else?"

"Like what? Catering's all we know."

"Mike was saying Mrs Lewisham's thinking of selling up the B&B. She's thinking of retiring and going to her sister's in Hampshire. Why don't you make some enquires? It's easy enough to run from what I gather. You and Pov will manage it easily. It's only bed and breakfast but there's nothing to stop you doing evening meals too. Your mum could help out, couldn't she?"

"Where is this place?"

"Rats," Josh cursed.

"What's up?" said Sam.

"I've no clean pyjamas. They're all in the wash. What are you reading, Howard?"

Howard was sat up in bed with the local rag spread out in front of him. "I'm just reading this scenario surrounding Iain Boothroyd. According to this report, he was wanted for money laundering. They seem to think he was involved with a drugs ring in America. His recent trip to Chicago resulted in a deal worth hundreds of thousands of dollars. This lady, known as Ruby, which is not her real name, was in some way involved. Iain made off with her half of the money, which is why she followed him over here. There's a warrant out for her arrest. They say it's more than likely that she put the poison in a jar of pickles."

"It's Mrs Lewisham I feel sorry for. She's had to sell up, you know," said Josh, jumping into bed in his underwear.

"Why?" Sam asked. "What's Iain's death got to do with her selling up?"

"She didn't think she'd ever be able to re-let the room. She's gone down to her sister's somewhere or other."

"Did they find the money then?"

"Not according to this," said Howard. "They searched every inch of the flat, even took the floorboards up. There was no money in his bank account. But, thinking about it, you wouldn't put the money in the bank anyway, would you? Not if you'd come by it dishonestly. It's the first place the police would look. It all seems a bit curious to me."

"How do you mean?"

"Well, I mean… he comes home with a wad of cash. Hides it somewhere in the flat, presumably. The police failed to find it. It must be somewhere. What's he done with it?"

"I don't suppose they'll ever find out now," said Sam.

"Looking at it logically, the only other person who had access to his flat is this Ruby. I'll bet she took it. Drugged him, then searched the place." Josh was convinced.

"Or Mrs Lewisham could have found it. She had the master key. I wonder if the police searched her flat?" pondered Howard. "Suddenly disappearing like that straight after his death. It seems a bit suspicious, if you ask me."

Sam and Josh both laughed. "You've been reading too many detective stories, Howard."

Chapter Fifty-Three

"Give one of those lamb chops to Hamish, there's one spare." They sat on the patio in the sunshine enjoying their meal with a glass of wine.

"It's not turned out too badly, has it? All things considered?" Mrs Lewisham said, looking out across the bay, watching the fishermen in the harbour tending their boats.

Her mind cast back to the day Bert came knocking on her door.

"I've just been reading the Gazette," Bert had said.

"You'd better come in," she said.

Bert was a gardener and always had a supply of weed killer in his shed. "It weren't cyanide they found in that jar of pickles. It were weed killer. If the police come asking questions…"

"I've thought of that. Look, I'll level with you. Hang on a minute whilst I put the kettle on. We'll discuss it over a pot of tea like civilised humans."

She had busied herself with arranging the cups and saucers on a tray and filling the kettle. It gave her time to think. *I could deny everything*, she thought. *He's no proof that it was me.* But no, she'd known Bert for over forty years, they were good friends. She couldn't lie to him. She placed the tray on the coffee table.

"Sit yourself down," she said. "Gracious, Bert, what's happened to your face? Have you been in a fight?" she gasped on seeing the purple wheal all down one side of his face from brow to jaw. "Your ear's all swollen. Can I get you an aspirin or anything?"

"No thanks, Edie. I'm all right. It's our Nettie, she's been on the war path again. Threw the flippin' iron at me."

"Honestly, Bert, I don't know how you've put up with that woman all these years. One of these days that temper of hers will get her into serious trouble. She'll kill someone."

"Yes, me probably. I hear you're planning on leaving?"

"Yes, I am. I've had an offer on this place, not as much as I'd have liked but it's enough. It's terribly run down. Needs a lot doing to it. It was an opportunity I couldn't afford to turn down. I'm not getting any younger, you know. I can't go on doing this forever. I'll be eighty next year," she said, pouring the tea and offering him a chocolate biscuit.

"I've not seen these for a while," said Bert, helping himself.

"I save them for special guests." She winked. "Look, Bert, you and I go back a long way. I'll not lie to you. It was me that put the weed killer in the pickle jar. I'm not proud of what I did. Believe me when I say it was an act of sheer madness on my part. I found the money, you see."

"What money?" he gasped, not quite believing his ears, but he knew he could be in trouble for supplying her with the weed killer in the first place. It wouldn't take the police long to trace the weed killer back to him.

"Drug money. He'd done a deal in Chicago. Ruby came looking for him. He brought her back here. She put the cyanide in his beer. He did her out of her share of the money. I heard her ransacking the flat before she left."

"That's the American woman that was seen in the pub?"

"Yes, her. When I heard her banging about, I knew the money must be in there somewhere. I waited until they took him to the hospital before conducting a search myself. I found it hidden in the bathroom, by the window."

"How is it the police never found it?"

"There was a loose brick in the wall. It's been there for years. I never got around to fixing it. The money was hidden in the wall cavity. I intended to hang on to it until I could wrap things up here, then retire, but he survived and when I knew he was coming back, I panicked.

I didn't want to give it back, but I had to put it back because I knew he'd check as soon as he got home. He'd have known it was me that took it, you see."

"You could have just handed it over to the police."

"I did think long and hard about that as well but then I thought no, why should I? What would they do with it? It was on my property and I found it. As far as I'm concerned, it's mine. When I think of the life I've had, Bert, all those dreadful years of hardship during the war, my Sid reported missing, presumed dead, having to survive on my own. I tell you, Bert, it's not been easy. When I saw all that money, I knew I'd never get another chance like this. My only chance of happiness. What few years I've got left on this earth, well… I could live in comfort."

"So, you're going to your sister's?"

"No. I haven't got a sister. I made all that up to throw the sergeant off the scent. I didn't want them searching my place, did I?"

"So, where do you intend going?"

"I fancy a little stone cottage, somewhere quiet, where I can go for long walks along the beach. Live the simple life. You're not going to the police, are you? Please say you're not, Bert. It's the only chance of freedom I'll ever get."

"On one condition," he replied, sipping his tea. He noticed her face flushing with anticipation at what he was about to say.

"I'll give you half," she blurted out. "We'll half it."

"No, Edie, that's not what I want at all."

"What then?"

"Take me with you, please."

"What about Nettie?"

"I've had it with her. I should have left years ago. No, she can fend for herself for once. She's very capable."

"What will you tell her?"

"Nowt. I'll sneak out very early in the morning and not come back. She sleeps like the living dead anyway. She'll not wake until nearly lunchtime. The lazy cow."

So, that was how it played out. They had met the following morning at the railway station and took the first train to Exeter. From there, they went to Edinburgh, then on to Oban, eventually settling on the Isle of Mull after boarding the local ferry.

It didn't take them long to find a little cottage to rent. Bert had wanted a dog, so they bought Hamish. He was a lively joyful dog and they both loved him dearly. They sat smiling at him as he ripped into his lamb chop.

"No regrets?" she asked.

"No regrets," he said, smiling fit to burst. "This is the way to live, Edie. Here's to us."

They clinked glasses. "To us," they both chorused in unison.

www.ingramcontent.com/pod-product-compliance
Lightning Source LLC
Chambersburg PA
CBHW051202190726
48288CB00006B/1769